KOENIG'S SPIRIT

by Linda Kuhlmann

Cover Design: Fireside Design Studio

Other Books by
Linda Kuhlmann

The Red Boots

Koenig Triple Crown series
Koenig's Wonder

FOR BARBARO

ACKNOWLEDGMENTS

In writing this sequel to my first novel, *Koenig's Wonder*, I received assistance from so many people that it is impossible to name them all. To everyone, I express my deepest thanks.

In addition, I would like to express my gratitude to the following people for their expertise, help, and encouragement. Although the final responsibility for the accuracy of the text is mine, I could not have completed this novel without these special people: Jack Root at Oakhurst Equine Veterinary; Riley Sanders; Shannon Kaplan of Chehalem Mountain Therapy Riding Center; Lindsey M. Vickers; Brittany Magill at Davidson Surgery Center in Louisville; Mike Passo; Wendell Foltz, Lou Macovsky; Linda Lindow; Tracy Hayes; Carrie Patten; Gabe Fleck; and Judie Braaten.

Finally, a special thank you to my husband for his infinite patience and support.

The derby is a race of aristocratic sleekness
For horses of birth to prove their worth
To run in The Preakness

by Ogden Nash

CHAPTER ONE

April, 1971

She always was predictable, the man thought as he looked at the face on the cover of the horseracing magazine, *until now*. He downed his scotch, angry and tired from the red-eye flight, fortifying himself for what he had to do. The first class section of the plane was quiet, and he was glad the chatty young actor seated across from him was still asleep.

A pretty, blonde stewardess walked by.

"Hey sweetheart," he said, "would you bring me another scotch, neat?"

"We'll be landing in Louisville in a few minutes—"

"Then, make it a quickie." He winked at her.

She smiled and disappeared behind the curtain to the attendant's station.

He laid the magazine on the tray and opened it to the article, as the blonde brought his drink.

"How long is your layover in Louisville?" he asked, looking the slender woman up and down.

"Two days," she said. "Are you here on business?"

"Yes...maybe we can get together sometime later tonight?"

The stewardess smiled and said, "I'll be staying at the Seelbach Hotel." She handed him a slip of paper with her name and telephone number on it. Then, she heard a ding from a call button and walked to the back of the plane.

He took a big swig of his drink and began reading the interview with the owner of Gallano Farm. The photo of the woman standing next to her prize stallion made him sick. Divina Gallano's face smiled back at him as he began to read.

Interviewer: "Your farm has been in Lexington for thirty-two years."

Gallano: "Yes, my family emigrated here from the Philippines in 1939."

Interviewer: "Why did you decide to breed your mare, Charito, to Koenig, Essen Farms' Kentucky Derby winning stallion?"

Gallano: "Essen Farms has produced many winning Thoroughbreds over the years. I thought it was about time we brought our bloodlines together."

The man turned the page and saw Divina and George Mason standing next to each other at the Churchill Downs racetrack. He scowled as he continued to read.

Interviewer: "Your colt, Mr. Divinity, and Mason's, Koenig's Spirit, are from the same sire, but different dams. I think this might be a first in a Kentucky Derby field. Spirit is being touted as this year's Triple Crown winner, what do you say to that?"

Gallano: "I have no doubt his colt will win - unless mine beats him."

Interviewer: "Mr. Divinity seems to be a good contender."

Gallano: "Yes, I like to think so."

Interviewer: "Koenig's Wonder, Mason's last Derby winner in '68 was also sired by Koenig. That colt was stolen the night after he won the race."

Divina: "Yes, Mr. Mason has had a run of bad luck, but I think that may be about to change."

The man chugged down his drink and thought, *George Mason's probably doing more than breeding her mare!* He looked out of the plane's window and saw the large horse farms below. Anger rose inside as he schemed. *Mason's luck IS about to change - it's going to get worse!*

The man looked back at the article in his hand. In the last paragraph, the interviewer had asked Divina about running Gallano Farm alone, and what she was going to do next...

Under his breath, he said, "I know what you're going to do, bitch!"

CHAPTER TWO

KENTUCKY

George was running to the back of the plane, but it felt like his feet were stuck in quicksand and he could hardly move. It was too late. The dark horse reared and his hooves came down heavily on the small man's head. His younger brother screamed as he took his last breath...

He awoke with a start, his pajamas were soaked with sweat and tears ran down his face. "Oh, Franz," he sobbed, covering his eyes with one arm. He could never get the image of that night out of his mind.

Wiping his eyes on his already wet sleeve, George said out loud, "I've got to shake this off." He looked at the clock and saw it was five in the morning. On a Thoroughbred racing farm, the day started early. He shoved the memory back into the corner of his mind, knowing that it would only return again sometime when he least expected it. Throwing back the covers, he placed his feet in his slippers and went to take a shower.

The hot water revived him and he was ready to face the day. Even though he now wore dark-rimmed glasses, he was proud that he was still strong for a man in his late fifties. Life had done it's best to break him, but he survived. Yes, he had regrets about his past mistakes, but he still kept his dream alive. It'd been twenty-two years since the last Triple Crown was won, and George knew it was his turn.

Later, he walked out of his Kentucky home and smelled the misty, early morning spring air. Soft clouds hung low in the trees, creating a hush over the land; and there was an eerie orange glow as the sun rose through the fog bank at Essen Farms. George could see the moon getting close to the western horizon. It made him think of the first men on the moon, something he thought he'd never live to see.

He joined his trainer, Fred Jamison, standing near a white fence as he watched Koenig's Spirit grazing in a nearby pasture. George's new three-year-old colt was more roan than black, with one white sock. Just then, Spirit's head came up as another horse whinnied. The colt sniffed the air and ran to the other side of the pasture as his young, long legs stretched out before him in quick bursts of speed.

"Look at his gait!" George sighed.

"Yes," Fred said, smiling. "Since you and I started working together, we've had a lot of success in horseracing - and we're not finished yet!"

One of George's prize stallions, Koenig's Wonder, raced alongside Spirit in an adjoining pasture. His white-starred forehead nodded in the cool morning air as he ran. For a six-year old, Wonder still had speed. Surprisingly, the younger colt was keeping up, until they reached the fence. The older dark horse leaned over to George and let him scratch his long neck.

George said, "If it hadn't been for Wonder, I may not have met my niece, Emma. I'm just sorry his racing career ended so soon, but he's siring some excellent foals."

"You made a good decision to retire him when we got him back. He'd been out of training for too long after he was taken. If we'd continued racing him, he could've been injured." Fred shuffled his foot in the dirt beside the fence. "Funny how fate put Wonder in Emma's stable in Oregon."

"Fate had nothing to do with it!" George said in a low voice, anger rising inside of him as he remembered that night again. He took a deep breath and looked around the acreage of his farm. "It was greed."

The two men were silent for a few moments. Then, Fred asked, "You know, George, you pretty much have everything you've ever wanted. But, there's one thing missing in your life now."

"What?"

"A girl," Fred said with a grin. "You might want to consider Divina Gallano."

"Oh, I'm just too busy with my business...and the horses."

"What a lame excuse! You've said that since you got this farm from Bob McKenzie."

George knew that someday he would have to make amends from taking the farm away from Bob's only daughter, Karen. But, he had no idea where she was now.

"It's time to get Spirit ready to transport to the track for his morning exercise," he said to change the subject.

"Sure thing." Fred started to walk away, and then stopped. "Have you heard from Emma and Sam yet?"

"No, but I don't expect to, since they're on their honeymoon in Europe!" George turned and started towards one of the barns, with Fred walking beside him.

Fred said, "It was sad that Sam's father had a heart attack and died last year, just after their wedding. That's why they had to postpone their trip until now."

"Yes, but I'm sure they will have a wonderful life together from now on. I know that Emma is excited to go to Piber in Austria to purchase a new Lipizzaner for her breeding farm. I'm pleased that she's following her father's passion for Dressage, which she learned from my elder brother, Hermann."

George thought for a moment, wondering if Emma would uncover the answer to a family mystery while she was in Austria.

****

In one of the grandstand boxes at Churchill Downs, George and Fred watched as Spirit went through his warm-up exercises, galloping around the first turn of the track. Fred held a stop-watch in his hand.

A man dressed in black sat in the top of the grandstand, looking through binoculars.

George nodded towards the track just as Spirit came around the last turn and then raced by the grandstand. Fred pushed the button on his stop watch and grinned. "I told Jesse to urge Spirit on at the last two furlongs to see what his time would be from there." He held out the watch for George to see and the older man nodded and smiled.

"You know young Jesse will soon be moving to eastern Washington, so we will need to start looking for another rider soon."

Fred nodded. Just then, another roan entered the track, almost identical to Spirit, but without the white sock. "That looks like Mr. Divinity, Gallano Farm's horse," Fred said. "He could give Spirit a run for his money."

George looked up. "I'm not worried. Spirit's going to win the Triple Crown for me."

"You said that about Wonder...and his sire, Koenig, before that. What makes you so sure this time?"

"My gut." George smiled.

A flash of red caught George's eye and he watched as Divina Gallano walked towards them. He'd gotten to know Divina three years ago, when they bred Koenig to her mare. Long dark hair fluttered in the gentle breeze, and her petite frame was wrapped in a white shirt, red scarf tied at her throat, and a wide, red skirt that billowed around her slender legs.

"Now there's an exotic woman for you!" Fred whispered to George. "I heard that her family came from a rich Thoroughbred farm in the Philippines."

"I know." George was still leery of Divina - mostly because of the feelings that stirred in him when he was near her. He hadn't allowed himself to feel like that for any woman in many years.

"George, darling, it is so good to see you here," Divina laughed, placing her hand on his arm. "I brought Mr. Divinity for his exercise. Don't you just love the fresh morning air here in the spring?"

"Hello, Divina," George said politely, but kept himself guarded.

"This is so exciting, having our colts exercising together. I can't wait for the Aqueduct race."

"Would you care to join us here in my box? We can watch our horses train together."

"I'd love to!" She sat next to George.

"I read your interview in that magazine," George said with a smile. "I agree with your comment about my luck changing!"

"The reporter was so sweet, I couldn't resist."

"That was a close race at the Florida Derby last week," Fred interjected. "It looked like a tie, until the photo finish showed Koenig's Spirit won by a nose!"

"Yes," Divina smiled demurely. "But, it will be interesting to see what happens at the next race."

George only nodded and wondered to himself if his horse had possibly met his match. Silently, he began to worry about the future races. He made a mental note to talk to Fred about some additional training strategy.

"Well, I'm going down to the track to do my job," Fred said and left the couple alone.

George watched his colt with pride as the two animals jogged around the track together, then their riders kicked them into a slow gallop for a half-mile. He could see Fred was now standing near the track fence, talking with their groom, Johnny Blair. George was a little concerned to see Divina's trainer, Raul Lopez, standing so close to his men. Like all other sports, horseracing was very competitive.

As the two horses came back around the last curve of the track, Jesse, Spirit's rider, breezed him - letting him run full out. Mr. Divinity was keeping up as they passed the grandstand. George saw Fred raise an arm and Jesse pulled his horse up to a slow gallop again, turned and jogged back to his trainer.

Just then, another horse was ridden onto the track for his morning exercise. He was a tall gray, with a white mane and tail. George had seen this horse in the shedrow a few times before. The horse had some real issues, throwing his head back and rearing in an attempt to remove his rider, but the young exerciser held firm and calmed the animal down into a slow jog. As the pair progressed around the track, the horse kicked his hind legs. George was impressed with this rider, keeping his balance on such a high-strung animal.

After their horses had left the track, Divina and George walked down to the backside. They saw that Fred watched as both horses were being hosed down by their grooms. When they approached, George overheard Divina's groom asking the other about their pre-race feeding program. He was glad to see Fred stop their discussion. It was never a good idea to share your training plan with the competition.

As they stood nearby, Divina looked at George. "Would you like to come to my farm for dinner tonight...if you are free?"

George hesitated, he saw Fred wink at him. "I'm not sure...we

Linda Kuhlmann

have lots of work to do—"

"Nonsense," Fred interjected, looking at George sternly. "I can handle everything! You deserve to enjoy yourself once in a while."

Scowling at Fred, George turned back to Divina. "Then, I guess it's decided. I could be there around six o'clock."

"Perfect!" Divina smiled, threw an air kiss George's way, and then turned to leave.

Just then, they heard high-pitched screams from a horse nearby.

"This way," George said, and ran to one of the other barns. The same gray stallion was rearing against his reins, held by a burly man with dyed black hair. He was whipping the horse, causing cuts in the animal's flesh.

Anger rose inside as George thought of prior races, where he'd seen this horse's jockey over-using the riding crop to drive the animal on for the win. "Stop!" he yelled and grabbed the whip, then raised it as if to strike the man. "What the hell do you think you're doing?"

"Mind your own damned business, Mason," Gordon Evers roared, "and give me that thing." He pulled the whip from George's hand. "He's a monster that keeps biting his handlers and won't let his jockey mount him without a fight. Stan could never handle him, so I had to fire him. I've lost more money on this beast."

"I'll take the horse off your hands," George said, his voice calm, but forceful. He quickly glanced at the horse's stall and saw his nameplate was LUCKY STORM.

"He's going to be put down!" Evers said and thrashed the horse again.

"Stop!" Fred yelled. He stepped in and took the horse's reins from Evers and walked the horse around to calm him down. He noticed other scars on the horse that had already healed and pointed them out to George.

"I'm going to report you to the Racing Commission!" Divina yelled at Evers.

The man's face turned red with rage, and then glared at his crew. Two grooms quickly took the horse and led him back to wash him down, keeping a distance between them and the animal.

"I'll make sure you never race in Kentucky again, Evers!" George said as he started to walk away.

Evers threw up his fist and yelled at George and Divina, "I'll get even with you both!"

Later, after Gordon Evers had left the track and everything calmed down in the backside, Fred was leading Spirit into his trailer when George walked up with Stan Gibson, their new jockey.

"That brute is going to kill an animal someday!" Stan said in his southern drawl, shaking his head.

"Did you know Evers was like that when you worked for him?" Fred asked, stepping out of the trailer..

"Why do you think I left? He's told everyone he fired me, but I quit. The stories I could tell of the things he asked me to do to win a race..."

"Why didn't you turn him in?" George asked.

"He threatened me, saying I'd never be able to jockey again. I love riding too much to give that up, so I kept quiet and walked away. I've been working where I can."

"Well, you're with us now. I'll be damned if I ever let anyone hurt an animal on my farm."

"That's what I heard - in spite of your record."

George knew that Stan was referring to when he'd been accused of drugging Koenig before the Kentucky Derby, but he'd been exonerated.

"You're a good man, Stan." George shook hands with the small man. "I'm glad you've come to our side." He was about to walk away, then stopped. "I was watching an exercise boy on Lucky Storm this morning. He seemed to be able to handle that horse better than anyone else today. Would you see if you can find out who that was for me - and if he's interested in working for us?"

"I know him," Stan said with a smile. "Luke Tanner's a good kid, and I always hated how Evers treated him, as well."

"Thank you."

George looked around and saw that Fred was waiting in their truck and got in next to his friend. "I think Stan's going to work out very nicely. He's had quite a few successes and came highly recommended."

"He seems to know what Spirit needs. He was born in Virginia, been riding since he was twelve. He told me he moved to Kentucky to race in the Derby."

"Well, he's going to get his chance this May," George said. He hoped Stan would not be like Carlos Madera, a former jockey, who was involved in stealing Koenig's Wonder. *Not everyone in horse racing is out to win at any cost*, he thought.

As they were pulling away from the backside, George said, "Fred, I want to save that horse from Evers - I don't care what you have to do."

"You got it, boss."

Fred and George drove out of the track gate. "Right now, I don't want you to be late for your date," Fred said with a grin, waving at the guard. "It's about time I get a night to myself!" He laughed, elbowed George, and drove on.

Just then, the man from the grandstand walked into the guard's station.

****

It was dusk when George finally arrived at Gallano Farm. The impressive three-story house was elaborately decorated in a Spanish style of cream-colored stucco, with a red-tiled roof and dark wood doors and window frames. Lights were on outside and in every room of the house. As he stepped out of his car, a recent rain brought out the aroma of the sugary-sweet honeysuckle vine even before he saw the red, tubular flowers. A round three-tiered fountain bubbled near the entrance.

The front door opened and Divina's housekeeper, a small, round woman with dark hair and a sweet smile, greeted him.

"Welcome to Gallano Farm, Mr. Mason." She stepped aside for George to enter, then asked him to follow her. "Ms. Gallano is in the parlor."

When they entered a room with green walls, George stopped in his tracks. Divina was wearing an Oriental-designed, close-fitting silk dress of turquoise with tropical flowers.

"You're late, George!" she exclaimed with a smile, holding a frothy cocktail in a stemmed glass, garnished with a wedge of pineapple and Maraschino cherry. She turned to the small woman standing next to him, placed her arm on her shoulders and said, "Jasmine has been with my family since we came to America. She goes everywhere with me."

George smiled and bowed to the small woman. He realized his throat was dry after seeing Divina.

"Thank you, Jasmine," Divina said to her friend, who smiled, then left the room.

"I apologize," George said, when he found his voice again. "Gordon Evers was at Essen Farms when I got back. I had to threaten to call the police to get rid of him. Before he left, I got him to agree to sell Lucky Storm to me - for an outrageous price, of course. It was worth it, just to get that animal away from him. That man's a mean bastard!" George looked down at the ground, sorry for his language. He looked back up at the beautiful woman standing before him. "Pardon me."

She said, "You're so right - he IS a bastard. I almost sold him one of my mares, until I learned how he treats his animals."

"I'm going to the Commission tomorrow to talk with Simon Day."

"Oh, you're going to have a fight on your hands with Gordon."

She smiled, turned and walked down a long hall. "Follow me into my study and I'll fix you a drink so we can forget all about it."

Colorful paintings by Gauguin hung on the walls leading to the back of the house. George looked around - one wall was lined with bookshelves, filled with leather-bound books. Dark velvet chairs and a settee sat in the center of the room, while a bar, with tall stools, was at one end. A large bank of windows looked out over the immaculate garden, lit now with floodlights.

"What is your pleasure?" Divina asked, raising an empty highball glass with a gold design etched on the side.

"Bourbon, neat." George said, then he watched her pour his favorite alcohol. When he saw the tall, white frothy drink in front of her, he asked, "What are you drinking?"

"A Piña Colada. It reminds me of the Philippine islands, my roots." She looked at George over the rim as she took a sip. "It's made with Tanduay Rum. I add coconut, pineapple juice, Angostura Bitters, and crushed ice, then blend it all together. Would you like a taste?"

"No thanks, I'll stick to bourbon."

Divina walked to the settee and sat down, crossed her legs, then patted the seat next to her. "Let's sit here together."

Reluctantly, George sat down and took a large gulp of his drink.

"Don't you just love my garden? I have a man who comes in every week to maintain it." Divina raised her glass, "A toast to your future success!"

George tapped his glass against hers. "To our success!"

"Mr. Divinity looked strong today during the workout," George began, placing his drink on a coaster on the coffee table.

"Yes, but sadly, he is my last horse to race."

"What do you mean?"

"After this year, Gallano Farm is strictly going to be used for breeding. I'm growing tired of the racing game and the constant competition." Divina thought for a moment, then said, "Since we will be going to New York for the Aqueduct races, maybe we could see some of the city together..."

George was relieved when Jasmine came in. "Dinner is ready, Dayong," she said to Divina and left the room.

"Dayong?" George asked Divina.

"She has called me that since I was a child. It is a term of endearment, sort of like 'darling' in your language. She was my nanny and was named after the Philippines' state flower."

They walked into the dining room and George saw the two place settings at one end of the long table. Crystal and gold-rimmed china gleamed in the soft candlelight. He thought of his mere dinner served at his kitchen table and wondered if Divina always ate like this.

A roasted turkey and bowls of steaming vegetables and potatoes waited, and he realized that he was hungry.

"Where do you come from, George?" Divina asked, serving slices of meat onto his plate. "There is still a bit of accent in your voice."

"Germany... Interestingly, my brothers and I grew up on a warm-blood horse farm near Essen, and we each ended up in different parts of the world with horses."

"Are any of them here in America?"

A shadow fell over George's face. "No." He didn't add that Franz did come to America later...and died because of his greed and pride.

"Oh, I'm so sorry to hear that," Divina said, touching his hand. She paused for a moment, then said, "I don't have any family left...in Kentucky." She stopped for a bit, then added, "Our family came to America from Manila in the late thirties, before the Japanese invaded our islands. She paused, then added, "I love the old blood lines of our horses that Papa brought with him."

"I didn't know they had horseracing there."

"Oh, yes! It's been in the Philippines since the 1800's. But Thoroughbreds were not used until around the mid-thirties. Papa loved the San Lazaro track in Manila. When I was very young, I went there with him to watch the horses." She looked down at her plate, then said, "I was nine years old when we arrived here."

George thought for a moment, surprised that there was such a difference in their ages - she was fourteen years younger than him.

After dinner, they retired to the music room for coffee. Jasmine had set up a tray of beverages on a table near another bank of windows overlooking the garden. A grand piano sat to one side.

"I have some Boracay Rum," she cooed, holding up a bottle with a picture of a palm tree on the front. "It was our island version of Bailey's Irish Cream. It's very tasty in coffee!"

"I take my coffee black," George said, then he noticed a photo of three people on the dark piano.

"That is my wedding photograph," she said, walking up to the picture and caressing the silver frame.

George was crushed, "You're married?"

"No, I am divorced."

"But, your father's name was Gallano—"

"When I married, I decided to keep my family name. My husband hated it...I don't think he ever forgave me."

George looked at the photo again. "Who's the young woman in the photo?"

"That's my sister, Tala. She, uh, left years ago, shortly after my divorce was final. I don't know where she is...or even if she's alive."

George could see the sadness in Divina's face at the mention of her sister's name. He also felt the loss of his own family and decided to change the subject to avoid the pain.

"How did you get your name, Divina?" he asked, walking to sit in one of the chairs. "It's very beautiful."

"It was my grandmother's name. It means Divine One."

Not knowing what else to say, George blurted out, "I have a niece, Emma. She is in Europe on her honeymoon and will be arriving soon..."

"I'd love to meet her."

CHAPTER THREE

PARIS

Emma walked out onto the balcony, smiling as she wrapped the silk robe closer around her in the morning light. The air was cool, but she didn't mind. She looked out at the Eiffel Tower in the distance, then down at the market area below and sighed. She was in love in Paris.

She thought of the adventures they'd already experienced on their honeymoon - the day their ship left New York City, heading east towards the Mediterranean. That was when the world began to open for her. She had no idea what was still in store.

"*Bon Jour*, Mrs. Parker," Sam said as he came up behind her.

Emma smiled and leaned into his arms. "Emma Parker. I like the sound of that."

Sam kissed her gently. "You've had that name now for a while."

"I know, but I don't hear it from you often enough. We got married a year ago—" Emma turned and faced her husband. She saw the glint of sadness in his eyes.

"I'm sorry, Sam, I didn't mean—"

"That's not it. I'm just always going to think of my dad when our anniversary comes around."

"Then, think of the good memories you had with him."

Sam looked out behind her and sighed. "You're right. He was at least able to be at our wedding. I'm just sorry it took us this long to get here."

"You know your mom needed you...and we couldn't leave until she was okay."

She thought of their ceremony at Sam's small chapel. The church was like the one she used to attend when she was young, in her hometown in Indiana. Her newly-found Uncle George had been there and walked her down the aisle. The event was very different from her first wedding. Emma shivered as she remembered Ted Jacobs, then sighed and pushed the images back to their dark place in her mind.

"Are you cold?" Sam asked.

"No, I was just thinking about something else."

Emma turned again and saw the tower. She was glad they'd chosen the hotel on *Rue Cler* in the *Champs de Mars* district. The rising sun glinted across the rooftops of the Parisian neighborhood. "Remember our first day here?"

"What a sight that was from up there," Sam agreed, looking at the famous monument. "The view is amazing. I never knew the streets of the city were laid out like the spokes of a large wheel; but strategically, it makes a lot of sense."

"We could see all the places we'd planned to go while we're here. I just wish we had more time."

"We've already seen more than most people ever get to in a lifetime."

"I know...It's been a whirlwind trip." Emma sighed. "The voyage across the Atlantic on the liner - I felt like Deborah Kerr in that movie, *An Affair to Remember.*"

"The cruise through the Mediterranean and ports along the way..." Sam reminisced.

"Our first stop in Athens, then Naples, the French Riviera, Barcelona," Emma added, sighing softly.

"I still think Italy is my favorite and want to go back there some day."

"Oh, I like Paris best...the *Arc de Triomphe*, walking along the *Champs Élysées*, the *Louvre*...."

"You surprise me," Sam laughed. "Every other woman I know would immediately head for the Paris shops."

"I'm more interested in the art and history than some clothes I can take home."

"My wife - the artist. I thought you'd at least want to take home some painting when we went to the *Montmartre* district yesterday."

"Well, the trip isn't over yet." Emma smiled and laid her head against Sam's chest, listening to his heart beating.

"I'm going downstairs to get a cup of coffee," he said. "Can I get you one?"

"Yes, please."

He kissed her and left the room.

Emma sat down in the chair next to a small desk. She looked at some postcards she'd picked up and thought of the interesting houses of famous painters, such as Monet and Van Gogh. But, the basilica of *Sacré-Coeur* had been the highlight for her. When they were there, Sam had walked around the stunning building's interior, taking photos, while she sat in a pew, fingering the Black Hills Gold locket that hung near her heart. Sam had given it to her years ago on their first date.

Before they were married, Emma had asked Sam about children. He seemed reluctant at first, but then said he would consider it later on. He reminded her that both their mothers lost children at young ages, and he was afraid of that type of pain and loss for them. Emma had told him that they wouldn't be here if their mothers had stopped having children.

The other day, while she'd sat in the basilica, she wondered why she hadn't gotten pregnant yet. After looking at the dome and saying a prayer, she'd heard the voice - *All will be as it should be.* The only person nearby was an old woman in black, kneeling at the far end of her pew. The voice could not have come from her. Emma made a silent wish.

"What are we going to do today?" Sam asked as he entered, pulling her thoughts back into the hotel room. He set her cup on the desk.

"I would like to be a Parisian today. Why don't we go to the market, pick up a few things, and take a bus to the gardens at *Luxembourg* for a picnic brunch."

"Great idea! I'll pack the corkscrew and some glasses from our room for the wine. We still have *Notre Dame* to see," Sam reminded her, then went to get ready.

Vendors in the market were stacking multi-colored fruits and vegetables on their stands. One man painstakingly placed each strawberry next to the other in symmetrical rows, creating ribbons of red in the early light. Emma knew there was a *fromagerie* where they could buy some cheese, and a *boulangerie* for a baguette of bread. She smiled, truly happy for the first time in her life.

****

The gardens near the palace were filled with activity. Students wrote in their notebooks, young couples sat on blankets on the lawn, hugging and kissing. Emma wished she had a palette of paints and canvas so she could capture the moment. She made a few sketches in the pad she'd brought, noting the colors and textures around her. Then, her heart tugged slightly as she watched a small family with a boy and girl playing in the warm sunshine.

"This cheese is fantastic," Sam said as he poured more wine.

"Yes. I think I like the *Cantal* the best. It reminds me of cheddar I've had somewhere." Emma broke off a small chunk of the crusty baguette and handed it to Sam. "The *St. Agur* is tasty, too. Didn't the clerk say it was made with milk from Basque sheep?"

"Mhm," Sam muttered, after he'd taken a bite of a large strawberry.

"I'm glad we came here today. I feel less like a tourist, more Bohemian."

"You look the part in that pretty skirt you're wearing." Sam leaned over and kissed Emma. They held onto each other for a moment, until a small rubber ball rolled into them.

"*Pardon, Madame,*" the young boy said, his little sister bumping into him as she came to a stop. Their golden hair glistened in the bright light. "*Ma balle, s'l vous plaît?*"

"I'm sorry, do you...um...how do you say...*parlez-vous*...English?" Emma asked.

"*Non,*" the boy answered. "*Ma balle? Balle?*"

"I think he wants his ball," Sam said, tossing the ball back to the boy.

"*Merci, Monsieur,*" the boy said. "*Pressé, Sophie.*"

Sam winked at the little girl, who blushed and ran after her brother.

"They're sweet," Emma sighed, remembering her mother,

Sophia, who'd passed away years ago, and her little brother, she never really knew. "Oh, I hope that we have a boy and a girl someday."

A group of young school children walked together in their uniforms, holding hands and laughing. Emma saw a flash of sadness on Sam's face.

"You do want children, right?" She asked.

"I don't know...I'm not sure..."

Concerned, she laid back and eventually felt the warmth of the light on her face, grateful the hotel clerk had insisted they bring a blanket for their picnic. *The Parisians really know how to make time to relax*, she thought. She had been so stressed with her training center and Lipizzaner breeding program in Oregon. And, to add to it all, they were going to Austria soon, so she could go to the Piber Stud Farm. But, for today, she felt her limbs melt as she relaxed under the warm azure sky.

Emma started to tell Sam about the voice she heard at the *Sacré-Coeur*, but stopped. She let her eyes close and decided to keep it her secret for now.

****

While Emma slept with her head in his lap, Sam thought back to his first trip to Paris. It was a time when he'd lost everything - his horse, his plan, his dreams. Memories of years ago flooded his mind - when his mare, Classy Elegance, had been claimed by George Mason in a race at Del Mar. That was when Sam had decided to disappear. If his friend, Jim Barolio, hadn't found him in a bar in New York City, he wouldn't be where he was now. Jim and Sam had been friends since grade school.

Alone, Paris was very different, he thought, looking down at his wife. *Now, life is good!*

Sam smiled as he watched the boats cruise slowly by on the Seine; an old priest walked towards a nearby church, his black cloth whipping in the breeze. When, a woman passed him, pushing a baby carriage, Sam's smile disappeared.

****

Holding on to Gandolf's reins, young Emma raced through the deciduous

forest near her home in Indiana. A small voice in her head told her to slow the
large horse down, but she loved the feeling of her hair flowing in the breeze.
Suddenly, Gandolf stumbled and she fell into darkness.

"Emma, honey."

She heard her name from a distance, then realized she'd fallen
asleep. She rubbed her hands over her face in an attempt to forget
the memory, then sat up and looked around - the Parisian sun was
further down in the west.

"What time is it?" she asked.

"It's time to start walking. You looked so peaceful at first, almost
happy. I hated to wake you, but then you seemed frightened." Sam
brushed a lock of hair that had fallen over Emma's eyes. "Are you
okay?"

"Yes, it's nothing." She brushed at her skirt and smiled.

Sam looked at a map. "We're in the *Saint Germain* district. If we
follow the *Boulevard St. Michel*, we'll eventually come to *Notre Dame* on
the Seine."

They picked up their things and walked hand in hand through
the streets, watching the people pass by. Just then, a couple rode by
on a scooter, the young woman on the back holding on to her lover.

"Oh, that looks like fun," Emma sighed.

"That could be arranged," Sam said with a smile.

Emma spotted an artist selling his paintings along the Left Bank
of the Seine and stopped. The young man was working on a sketch in
charcoal of a tourist's wife who was posing while her husband
watched. Sam walked over to a book vendor nearby.

"That doesn't look anything like her..." the man started. Then, as
the artist's hand moved more quickly, the man began to nod. "Now,
you're getting her."

Looking at the artist's oil paintings, Emma stared at one with the
mosaic inside the *Sacré-Coeur*. Above the large altar, the Risen Christ
was suspended in a brilliance of gold amongst his worshipers with
outstretched arms, the wounds visible in his hands and side. Her
heart skipped a beat.

The woman stood up and looked at her sketch. "I love it! Oh,
my sister will be so jealous." The artist rolled the sketch and wrapped
it in butcher's paper. "John, pay the man," the woman said as she
took the package and walked away.

After they were alone, Emma said to the artist, "This is very good. How much is it?"

"One hundred *Francs*... But, for you, *Madame*, only fifty."

Emma knew the currency conversion and how struggling artists made their living. "I'll take it...for the full price. But, I only want the canvas. I'm traveling, you see. Is that a problem?"

"No, no problem. *Merci*, Madame." The artist smiled as he deftly removed the canvas from the frame, then rolled it gently around a sturdy tube and wrapped it in similar paper he had used before. As he handed it to her, he said, "*Dieu être avec vous.*"

"*Merci*," Emma said and gently laid the treasure in her basket. She knew the artist had said, 'God be with you.' She joined Sam, who was buying an old, leather-bound book.

"I didn't know you liked poetry," Emma said, looking at the title.

"There's a lot about me you still don't know."

Just then, a series of loud chimes were heard. As they turned, they both were shocked by the sight of the large cathedral across the river. The ominous structure was breathtaking as the spires reached towards heaven and the arched buttresses cast shadows against the gray architecture. In contrast, purple plum trees bloomed next to cascading vines that reached down to the Seine below.

"Let's go inside," Emma said in a whisper and led Sam across the bridge to the entrance. "I hope we can hear the organ."

They were disappointed to find that the doors were locked, but they enjoyed walking around the perimeter. Sam captured the warm fading light on the building with his camera, as Emma stood staring up at the Gothic sculptures above the entrance. At the center of the façade, she could see the statue of the Virgin Mary with her child and two angels. Tears came to her eyes as she thought of her wish at the *Sacré-Coeur* earlier.

Just as they turned to walk through the square leading away from the cathedral, Emma looked down and saw a bronze star imbedded into one stone, where *Zero Kilometre* was inscribed.

"What does this mean?" she asked Sam, who was still taking photos.

He looked down and said, "I read somewhere that when Paris was chosen as the capital of France, this point was marked as the center of the country."

They walked towards *Pont Neuf*, the oldest bridge in Paris. Emma had been amazed when she learned that there were thirty-seven bridges in the city, all offering a different view. As they approached, she was in awe of the detail of the 1600's architecture of the numerous masks and turrets that looked like half-moons. In the distance, the Eiffel Tower was illuminated by the colors of the setting sun.

Emma stood in Sam's arms as they watched the sky change colors from a vibrant blue to a glorious gold, and then a final array of wispy clouds of peach. The trees and rooftops were washed with a soft orange just before the sun disappeared over the horizon. Sam bent down and softly kissed Emma, neither of them really seeing the other couples passing by.

"Remember the last time we stood on a bridge and kissed?" she asked softly

"Yes, in Portland. We hadn't seen each other for twelve years."

"You were investigating me for stealing a racehorse."

"Thank you, Koenig's Wonder!" Sam laughed. "If it hadn't been for that horse, I probably would never have found you again."

The street lamps came on along the bridge and a wind stirred the waters. At the same time, the Eiffel Tower was afire with lights, a large searchlight beamed across the city from the tower's top.

"Why don't we go back to our room to freshen up for dinner," Emma said. "I'm starved!"

Sam smiled and hailed a taxi.

****

Like most European rooms, theirs was fairly small and sparsely furnished. Across the room was a large mirror, which gave the illusion of a more spacious area. But, the night view outside their balcony was exquisite.

Emma heard the water of Sam's shower running. Their hotel room in Rome did not have a bath - it was a shared area down the hall. She was glad this one had a bath *en-suite*. She smiled as she slipped out of her dress and stepped in under the water with her husband. As she slowly wrapped her arms around his wet skin and placed her cheek on his strong back, she sighed. *Heaven must be something like this*, she thought. Sam turned and began to soap her shoulders and arms. Emma leaned into him and let the water cascade down her body, rinsing the soap away, as his hands aroused her.

He reached back and turned the water off. Slowly he dried each of them, and carried Emma to the bed. Their bodies entwined, touching and kissing as if for the first time. Slowly, they each reached a climax, fell exhausted against the sheets, and slept in each other's arms.

****

"Where shall we go tonight?" Sam's voice was deep and soft as he came up behind Emma, enclosing her in his strong arms. Emma leaned back and felt his warmth, looking at the two of them in the large mirror. Emma wore a soft lilac dress that set off her dark hair. Sam had chosen a black, linen suit.

She turned slowly and softly kissed him, breathing in his scent. Her hands touched his face, then she ran her fingers through his thick, dark hair, still damp from the shower they'd shared. Her excitement began to rise again - until her stomach growled.

"I think you'd better feed me, Mr. Parker," she laughed softly. "I can't live on love alone."

"Let's find that restaurant we passed earlier - the one near *Notre Dame*."

"Oh, yes, *La Palette*, on the *Rue de Seine*. It's perfect. I want to order a steak and some *pommes frites*."

"What?"

"French Fries, silly!"

Sam kissed her again more deeply. She responded, pressing her body against his, feeling his strength. Even though their lives together had begun on a lie, their love began in Chicago when she'd turned eighteen.

****

Sam looked around the busy Parisian café as waiters bustled through the small tables with trays overhead. The stained glass and dark mahogany wood around the bar glistened in the soft light. He took a deep breath. The air was warm and smoke-filled since everyone was smoking, a phenomenon of Paris he'd forgotten.

He saw one young man sitting alone with a beer in front of him who looked deep in thought. *I used to be that guy*, Sam thought.

22

"This is a wonderful place," Emma said. "I know you were in Paris before, but did you come here?"

"No, this is my first time."

"What was it like then?"

Sam sat back in his chair and fingered the stem of his wine glass. He looked over at the young man again. "Pretty much like that fellow over there."

Emma smiled at the young man.

The man smiled back, then quickly looked away, his smile vanishing.

"I'd just come in from my bush-flying days in Africa...," Sam began, "after I lost everything." He stopped and looked up at Emma. "I'd lost you..." He took a sip of wine, then added, "Alone, Paris is a very different city." He shifted in his chair and smiled, taking Emma's hands in his. "But now, I have you." He leaned over and kissed her across the table.

"*Pardon*, I am *Henri*," the waiter said, then pointed to the menus on the table. "Have you chosen?"

They both looked up and saw a young, dark-haired man in black-rimmed glasses. Emma smiled and said, "*Oui*." They each gave Henri their selections; Sam ordered *Poisson*, the French word for fish, and Emma ordered steak and *frites*.

"*Bon*," Henri said with a bow, then he took the menus and disappeared to the back of the room.

"Oh, Sam, this has been so marvelous," Emma said with excitement. "I loved seeing the *Louvre*, seeing that statue standing at the top of those stairs. Remember when you took me to see the movie, *Funny Face*, in Chicago and Audrey Hepburn ran down those steps in that glorious red gown?"

"I remember," Sam laughed.

"I felt like Audrey standing there. It made it all so real to me. And, the Mona Lisa...I thought she'd be much bigger. We had to wait so long to get up to her because of the crowd of school children. But, once we were face to face with her, her gaze was mesmerizing. I will never forget this as long as I live."

"The *Louvre* is a magnificent collection of the world's art, but it seemed overwhelming to me," Sam said, removing his silverware from the rolled napkin. "It would take a week to see it all. Personally, I preferred the smaller grouping of paintings at the *d'Orsay*."

"When I was studying at the Chicago Art Institute," Emma said, "I'd sit like those students we saw at the museums, copying the work of the masters. To me, it was better than any classroom."

An older couple brushed passed them and walked to an empty table. The volume of voices seemed to rise as a group of young people began laughing. The waiter brought Emma's fries.

"Sam, I'm glad you took the job at the Oregon Racing Commission. I really liked it when I could go with you to other cities in Oregon for your work. I had no idea how amazing Oregon is, with the deserts, mountains, valleys, beaches..."

Sam smiled. "Taking that job at ORC kept me near you. Remember the first time I took you to the ocean? We rode our horses on the beach."

"It was magical for me - I'd never seen the ocean before. I'll never forget my first breath of sea air. When we drove over the Coast Range, and out through those sand dunes, I thought we'd never get there. But then, we came to an opening and there it was - such a beautiful blue, that stretched to forever!"

"I thought Flash was trying to dump me on that dune. Then, I realized all that horse wanted to do was roll around in the sand."

Emma laughed, thinking of how much life they had packed in together since they reconnected three years ago. She took a bite of her fries and asked, "Do you miss Baltimore?"

Sam thought of his prior job at the Thoroughbred Racing Bureau. He'd taken that job after his return from Africa. His life had turned around then.

"Sometimes," he said. "I miss being close to the Jockey Club...and the racing." Sam didn't share his secret dream of getting back into horse racing, instead of investigating their crimes. "I'm just glad Jim was able to stand in for me while I'm here, considering he'd retired from the ORC to give me the job in Oregon."

"Didn't you have a new case that started up before we left?" Emma asked.

Just then, the rest of their food arrived.

"Yes, but I don't want to talk about it over dinner. Let's enjoy!"

During the meal, in between bites of her steak, Emma talked about her plans for her new breeding farm. "I'm so lucky that Shane could help with my horses while we're gone." She took another small bite, chewed quickly, swallowed, then continued. "I'm thinking of revamping my place a little - mostly update my stables, especially if I'm going to attract potential breeders."

She saw Sam look down at his plate. He didn't respond for a few moments.

"Sam?" she asked, placing her hand on his arm. "What do you think?"

"That's a great idea," he lied, smiling at her. It bothered him a little that she kept referring to his new home as 'her' place, but decided to let it go for now. After all, Rising Sun had been hers, until they were married.

"I can't wait to take the train to Vienna in a few days...and then see the Piber Stud Farm. My father–" Emma stopped talking when she saw the look on Sam's face. She wiped her hand across her lips. "What?" she asked. "Do I have something on my face?"

Sam laughed. "I'm just enjoying you devouring that steak like you haven't eaten for a week."

"I don't know why I'm so hungry!"

CHAPTER FOUR

KENTUCKY

Gordon Evers paced in his office at Spring Oaks Farm east of Lexington. He ran through various scenarios in his mind of how he would get his revenge. He already made Mason pay way more for that goddamned horse than it was worth. But Evers wanted more…

"It'll all work out, if you just calm down," Darrell Fisher said, sitting behind the large, walnut desk. "That temper of yours is what's gotten you into trouble."

Evers stopped pacing and yelled, "You've got balls, talking to me like that! How the hell am I going to get even with those two, since they're the poster farms in this area? Essen and Gallano have been here since forever, and I only moved my operation here three years ago."

"In my experience as a guard at these racetracks, I've learned there are many ways to hurt people in the horseracing industry."

"I know that, you idiot, now get the fuck out of my chair!" Evers yelled.

The man smiled as he rose. "You'll think of something. You always do."

AUSTRIA

Emma sat in the train's dining car across from Sam and looked out at the Austrian landscape whisking by in the soft morning light. The striking, snow-capped Alps towered over the green valleys, with occasional small villages of churches and quaint chalets dotting the hillsides. It was picturesque and peaceful. She loved riding on trains and this was her first ride through Western Europe. They left Paris on the night train to Vienna and the sound of the wheels on the rails had helped her to sleep in the tight quarters.

"Would you like a Croissant, my dear?" Sam asked, passing a plate of the sweet, flaky pastry across the table. She smiled as a curl of his hair fell over his forehead.

"*Merci, mon amour.*" She liked using what little French she learned from her small translation book she'd read on the ship. Now, the sweet jam she added to the buttery pastry and her cappuccino was all the food she needed today. She was anticipating visiting the Spanish Riding School in Vienna and then to Piber, where the beautiful Lipizzan horses were bred.

"Is that all you're going to eat?" Sam asked.

"Yes, I'm too excited today. Besides, the porter told me the *Wiener Schnitzel* is worth the wait!"

They looked out the window as the train approached a tall bridge. A stone building came into view that looked like a castle standing on a hill. Then the scenery opened up again with evergreens and green grasses. Emma thought of her father having once lived in Austria when he attended the Spanish Riding School. She knew that he'd loved the school and still wondered what would have caused him to give it all up. While she was here, she was hoping that she would find the answer.

"I'm just sorry we only have a few days in Vienna before going to Piber," she said, finishing the last bite. "But, our flight leaves from London next Tuesday..."

A porter walked up the aisle. "Next stop, Vienna," he said to them in English.

"We'd better get our bags ready." Sam put some coins on the table. "I still haven't gotten used to the money exchanges we have to go through when entering each country here, even though most countries are the size of a state in America."

****

The train arrived at the *Westbahnhof* station in the west side of Vienna. Sam and Emma found a taxi and told the driver they wanted to go to the Hotel Astoria. Luckily, their driver spoke some broken English and he explained a few of the beautiful buildings and monuments they passed along the way. Sam was a little nervous as the driver took his eyes off the busy road to point out various landmarks.

"That is the beautiful *Schönbrunn* Palace – one of the imperial palaces," the driver said. Then he continued on past the Belvedere Place, Art History Museum, Prince Eugene's Monument, and the Imperial Treasury.

After a while, he slowed in front of the Vienna Opera House. When they finally pulled up at their hotel nearby, he added, "Of course, you must see the Hofburg Palace, where the famous Spanish Riding School and Imperial Horse Stables are."

"The school is one of the main reasons I came to Vienna!" Emma said.

Sam thanked the driver and paid him as Emma stepped out and looked around her. The Hotel Astoria was splendid, with a white exterior in the bright sunlight and elegant cupolas on two corners.

They entered the large lobby, with a high ceiling and chandeliers glistening. Two couples sat on large, leather furniture to one side, either waiting for their car or just visiting.

Sam and Emma walked up to the dark wood counter and checked in with the petite young woman. She welcomed them and told them that the Astoria Hotel opened in 1912.

"Is there a concierge we should check with to book a show at the Spanish Riding School?" Emma asked excitedly.

"No, Mrs. Parker, I can help you." The young clerk smiled. "There is a show starting at eleven o'clock today, if you wish. And, there are a few seats left."

Emma looked at Sam and he nodded. "Oh, yes please!"

The clerk made the arrangements and handed Sam their tickets. "In the meantime, there is a guided tour of the Imperial Horse Stables starting in about half an hour. There is no charge for this."

"That would be wonderful!" Emma exclaimed and took the directions from the woman.

Sam smiled, as a bellman came to help them with their luggage.

Their room was spacious with gold brocade drapes hung at the tall windows. A painting of the city of Vienna hung above a desk of mixed woods with small, Bakelite drawer pulls. There was a large wardrobe available with soft, terry bathrobes provided.

"This is so elegant," Emma sighed, hugging Sam. "I love you so much."

Sam kissed Emma and held her close.

"I can't believe we were able to get in to a show so soon," she sighed. "I can hardly wait!"

"I know!"

"Thank you for indulging me in wanting to do all of this here, Sam. It means so much to me."

"I'm also doing this for me," he said with a smile, hugging Emma.

"Why?"

"Because it makes you happy and that's all I want for you."

****

They were stunned by the impressive Imperial Hofburg Palace, as they approached the *Neue Berg* part, which contained the Spanish Riding School. Emma had seen photos from an album her father kept, but she was not prepared for the enormity of it all in real life and the beautiful exterior statuary. A bronze equestrian statue of Archduke Charles stood in the center of the large interior courtyard.

When they came to the Imperial Stable area, Emma caught her breath as she saw a groom in a blue uniform and cap walking a white Lipizzan stallion along the center yard. Emma took a photo before the groom and horse disappeared into the stable. Each horse had a separate entrance to its own stall from this large atrium.

An older man came up to them. "Are you here for the stable tour today?" he asked.

Emma nodded and said, "My father, Hermann Maseman, used to ride here. Did you know him?" She was excited to possibly meet someone who may have met her father.

"*Nein*, I'm sorry. I only started here a few years ago."

"Is Rudolf Hinteregger still at the school? He was the chief rider at the time my father was here."

"*Herr* Hinteregger is retired now and has gone to work at the

Stud at Piber."

Emma looked at Sam, and then said. "We're going there in a few days to purchase breeding stock for my stables in America."

"If you wish, I could talk to our director to arrange an appointment for you to see him while you are there. My name is Josef Baeder."

"Oh, that would be wonderful!"

The older man took down Emma's hotel information, then led her and Sam to a small group of people waiting for the tour. There was a Japanese couple, a Spanish family, and a single African man. Emma listened to the different languages spoken amongst them, amazed at how these magnificent animals drew people together from all over the world.

A petite, young woman with short dark hair approached them. "*Hallo*. My name is Tanja Reiter, your docent for today." She asked if everyone could understand her in English and they all nodded.

"The Spanish Riding School was established in 1572 by the Habsburg monarchs," Tanja began. "They were the ones to choose the Spanish Lipizzaner breed for their intelligence, stature and temperament. The horses are born dark, almost black, but as they mature, they become totally white. In the 16th Century, the Habsburg line died out..."

As they entered the building, Emma was struck by the clean aisles and numerous, stately stalls these horses lived in. This was nothing like her place, and she decided to make a few changes to the interior of her stables when she arrived home. Each stall was made of tall, black wrought-iron fencing, topped with gold trim and posts, which allowed each horse to view his neighbor. Dark mahogany doors lined the aisle; and, at the top of each stall, was a plaque in black and gold containing the horse's name and year of birth. A few of the horses had their heads out, looking curiously at the group following Tanja. Emma saw that some were pure white and other, younger horses still had some gray markings. She smiled as she saw two horses nuzzling each other across the aisle.

"This is the oldest part of the school," Tanja continued. "The stable and the large riding hall were designed by an Austrian architect who studied in France. The upper story is for storage and offices, and guests can stay overnight. There are changing rooms for the riders near the tack room..."

Emma kept interrupting Tanja with questions, but the young girl simply answered and then quickly continued while they gazed into the large, pristine tack room.

"The school saddle, used during training, is black with a white *shabrack* - a European saddle cloth used on our Cavalry horses. The performance saddle of the High School of Riding is white, worn with either a red, green or gold *shabrack*, depending on the required performance. There are no stirrups on the jumper saddles - it is safer for the horse and rider..."

As they walked down the aisle, one white stallion, with the name CONVERSANO KITTY I above his stall door, stuck his head out to Emma. Conversano was the original blood line of her stallion, Gandolf! She reached out her hand to pet the horse's muzzle–

"Stop!" Tanja said, startling Emma and the horse. "Please do not touch the horses," she added softly with a smile. "It is not allowed."

"Why were some of the performance *shabracks* different?" Emma asked.

"The individual markings and fringes are used to show the status of each rider." Tanja leaned into Emma and whispered. "I can see that you have many questions, maybe we could go for a coffee after the tour, to save time?"

"Oh, I would love that!" Emma sighed. She saw Sam smile and nod in agreement.

Tanja continued towards the exit. As the last horse peeked out over his door, the African man asked in broken English why this adult horse was totally brown.

"One in two hundred horses stays dark. If it's male, it comes to Vienna. The school always keeps one dark horse in the stable as their good luck charm!"

****

Once outside, Tanja dismissed the rest of the group. Then, Emma and Sam followed her to the *Café Bräunerhof* on *Stallburggasse*, near the Hofburg Palace. It was very warm inside with many people chattering and laughing. Music by Mozart was playing in the background. Adding to the interior's charm were the small, marble-topped tables, and long booths standing flush against the oval-mirrored walls. A young man dressed in black trousers and white shirt seated them at a table with a bench seat.

"This is a very classic coffeehouse," Tanja said, taking off her coat. "I come here sometimes in the evening with my friends - for the music."

"It's lovely!" Emma sighed. "Thank you for bringing us here."

Sam excused himself to go use the restroom.

"Since you are a writer, Mrs. Parker, you might be interested to know that the famous Austrian author, Thomas Bernhard, sometimes came here for coffee - and to write."

"Please, call me Emma, and I'm not a writer. My father used to read Bernhard's work; but his books were in German, which I am sorry to say, I never learned."

"Oh, that is sad. Does your father live in America?"

"No, he passed away years ago, but I still have some of his things, including a few of his books. Unfortunately, after my father arrived in America, he was adamant that in his home we would only speak English."

"I've met other Americans who have said the same about their families," Tanja offered.

"My father was a sad man, when I was growing up." Emma wondered why she felt she needed to explain, and she thought of the bouts of her father's depression, except when he was working with the horses and his students. "He rode at the SRS before the war."

Sam returned, sat next to Emma, and picked up a menu. "Did you see the amazing pastries when we came in? This is going to be a tough decision."

"The apple strudel is my favorite," Tanja said smiling. "And, a cappuccino...or you may try our Viennese *Einspänner* coffee, if you wish, but it is very strong."

They placed their orders. Sam attempted to stretch his long legs out under the table, but found there was not enough room. Emma smiled, seeing that he was beginning to learn that the European people have a very different concept of space than Americans.

"What other questions do you have for me about the Riding School?" Tanja asked.

"Since we are in Austria, why is it called the Spanish Riding School?"

"Because the original stallions came from a Spanish breed on the Iberian Peninsula. They were a cross between Spanish, Arabian and Berber horses."

Emma eagerly pulled out her tablet and pen, taking notes. "Are any of the horses at the school used for breeding?"

"Yes, only the best are chosen to be returned to Piber Federal Stud in western Austria. Their temperament and intelligence are what makes them stand out from the others."

"We're going there in a few days, so that I can select some young horses for my breeding stock in Oregon. I have a Dressage riding school there. I'm very excited!"

After their drinks arrived, Tanja smiled and sipped her cappuccino. "I can see that..."

"Do you work outside of the school?" Sam asked, to give Tanja a break from Emma's questioning about the horses.

"No, I am studying at the university to become a translator - German into English. I still have two years, then I plan to open my own business."

"That's ambitious and impressive," Sam said. "Why did you become a docent at the Riding School?"

"It is an opportunity to work with people of different cultures and learn some of their languages." Tanja looked at her watch. "Oh, I must return to the stables for another tour, but let me give you my phone number and address so we can stay in touch."

Emma handed her the tablet and pen she'd been using so Tanja could note her information. "I hope that someday you will come to Oregon to see our part of the world. Thank you, Tanja. I am so glad we met."

"Likewise, and thank you for the coffee."

Emma gave Tanja her business card. The two women hugged and Tanja ran out of the coffeehouse.

"Would you like to order something else?" Sam asked.

"Oh, I'm too excited!" Emma laughed. "Do we have time to do a quick tour of the palace before the show?"

"I don't think so, maybe we can do that before we have to leave Vienna."

****

When Sam and Emma entered the baroque hall of the Hofburg Palace, the interior took her breath away. The striking ceiling and tiered seats were magnificent. One end was an arched seating area with red drapes and statuary, which, at one time, was where the royal family sat. Large crystal chandeliers hung over the neatly groomed arena floor. Two red pillars stood in the center. She noted in the brochure that grand balls used to be held here, but the hall was now only used for the horses.

The lighting in the riding hall was brilliant, with wall sconces and the gleaming chandeliers. A Johann Strauss waltz played as Emma and Sam found their seats. The atmosphere was austere, and the crowd seemed filled with excitement.

A hush fell as a man in a dark suit walked out to stand between the pillars. He announced the Lipizzan stallions and their riders. The School Quadrille, consisting of eight dazzling white horses, walked out of an arched door at the far end of the arena. Their riders were in formal dress: white shirts and breeches, with tall, black riding boots, dark tailcoats and white gloves. Their bicorne-style hats were like the one Emma had in her father's trunk at home.

All horses stepped in unison as they broke into two lines to perform the Steps and Movements of the Classical School section, each cantering along the outer edges of the arena. Their white saddles were striking against the red cloths, trimmed in gold. The most experienced riders had fringe on the cloth and bands to show their level of expertise, as Tanja had mentioned. Their movements were so synchronized, it was as if watching one horse in eight mirrors! At the end where they had entered, they merged into one line and walked in single file to the red pillars. As the first rider approached the posts, all riders reached up in unison and removed their hats in a salute to the Imperial Box, the royal family area. Once they were all through the pillars, they broke again into two lines in the *Passag*e, which was like a *Piaffe,* but with movement.

The audience applauded each time these performers continued different steps in true perfection: a *Half Pass,* where they moved forward and sideways at the same time, *Flying Changes,* changing each leading foreleg with every step, as if they were skipping, to the most beautiful music in the world.

Tears came to Emma's eyes as she watched these magnificent animals and riders effortlessly performing each Dressage movement, realizing her father had ridden here in his youth. She was sorry he did not share more about this part of his life, but was glad she was able to study under him, which brought her to her own career and passion. As the horses now left the arena, she looked at the program and saw the names of each rider.

She looked up as a composition by Franz Liszt came over the speakers and two riderless horses, with black cloths framed in gold thread, walked out. They were led by a handler holding long reins and walking on their horse's left side. One horse and handler walked to the front of the arena, while the other stayed near where Emma and Sam sat. The horse nearest them performed a *Levade*, standing on his hind legs for a few seconds. Then, the stallion jumped into a *Courbette*, a difficult movement as he raised up on his hind legs and jumped four times before his forelegs touched the ground. Applause drowned out the music for a moment.

Then, the first horse and rider astounded the audience by performing a *Capriole*, the highest movement in Dressage. The horse powerfully leaped into the air and kicked his hind legs out before he returned to earth. The announcer called this the *Airs Above the Ground*. The crowd exploded in appreciation as both horses were exited from the arena.

"Oh, my god!" Sam exclaimed. "How do those animals learn to do all this?"

Emma wiped more tears as the original eight returned to perform the final salute. She said softly, "With love, patience and passion."

****

They spent the next few days touring Vienna and the outlying areas. On their last night in the city, they took a *Fiaker* carriage from the hotel along *Kärntner Strasse* towards St. Stephan's Cathedral. They asked their driver to stop, and they walked to *Figlmüller's* for a *Schnitzel*, which Tanja had told them about.

While waiting in line, a man leaned towards Sam. "It is best if you only order one serving, because our Schnitzels are very large," the man said with a heavy accent. Sam thanked him.

Taking his advice, Sam and Emma were shocked when their meal arrived. The veal literally hung over the edge of a full-sized dinner plate. It was delicious!

Later, Sam took Emma to Mozart's House on *Domgasse*, where

the famous composer lived in the 1700's. They entered through a wide stone archway and were led to a small, round room - where a quartet was seated. Red velvet chairs were arranged in a half-circle around the lavishly ornate walls. Crystal chandeliers gave off a golden light. A few other couples joined the audience and then the doors were closed.

A hush fell as the musicians played the *Overture to the Marriage of Figaro*. The acoustics in the small room were amazing, and the music reminded Emma of her mother playing her cello with a smile on her face with pure joy. She was transported back to her childhood farm in Indiana, on a hot summer night - the night her father had died.

Afterwards, they walked around the outside of St. Stephan's Cathedral, with the incredibly lit, tall steeple piercing the night sky. The roof tiles were laid in a mosaic of a double-headed eagle, the symbol of the Habsburg dynasty. Sam and Emma stood in awe of the enormous building, which dated back to the 1100's. America's history seemed so young in comparison.

Then, they turned and walked down to see the blue Danube at night. During the day, it was a canal that joined the Danube and the Black Sea. But, at night, the lights danced off the water like a mirror as a boat passed under the bridge where Sam and Emma stood.

Sam pulled Emma to him, wrapped her in his coat and looked deeply into her eyes. He smiled and said, "You know what happens next…"

"Mhm," she cooed and raised her lips to his. "Something like this?" Her heart pounded as he deepened the kiss, making her knees go weak. She knew she'd never get used to the impact Sam had on her heart and her body.

They stood on the bridge for some time, enjoying the sights and sounds of the night in the city. Walking back to the hotel, they passed a small market still open, and Sam purchased some dark chocolate and a bottle of *Gemischter Satz*. He was surprised to learn that the grapes were actually grown within the city limits of Vienna.

****

When they returned to their hotel, the young woman at the front desk called them over. "I have a message for both of you."

She handed a piece of paper to Emma. "Mrs. Parker, a man by the name of Josef Baeder called to say that the director at the Piber Stud Farm will see you Friday morning at eleven o'clock."

"We will need a car," Sam said.

"But of course," the clerk smiled. "I will arrange for one to be delivered to the hotel that morning. The drive to Piber will take approximately two and a half hours."

Sam thanked the clerk and turned to walk towards the elevator.

"Mr. Parker," the clerk called. "Here is your message."

Sam took the note and saw it was from Jim Barolio in Oregon. Sam turned to Emma and handed over the key to their room and their purchases. "It's from Jim. I'll call from down here, if you want to go on up to our room."

Emma could see the concern on Sam's face. "Is it serious?"

"I don't know yet." He placed his hand on her cheek and smiled. "I won't be long."

Emma turned and walked into the elevator and pushed the button for their floor.

"Is there a phone I can use?" Sam asked the clerk.

"Yes, there is one at the far end of the lobby."

Sam entered the booth; the light came on as he closed the door. Giving the operator the information, he waited. Jim was helping Sam in a particular case of horse abuse at the Portland Meadows racetrack. When the phone rang back, he answered.

"Jim, what the hell is going on that you have to call me on my honeymoon?"

"I'm sorry, friend, but this case has escalated. We've already lost one horse at the Fleischer Stables, now another one is failing. When our track vet did some additional tests, they found an overdose of Lasix was used on the dead horse. But, this other colt is showing different symptoms, and the vet is stumped. I don't know what to do."

Sam thought for a minute. "This sounds like a case I had when I was at the Racing Bureau in Baltimore. It was at a farm in Kentucky."

"How do you want to handle this?" Jim asked.

"I'm not leaving my honeymoon over any damned horse!" Sam looked at the lobby, realizing how far away from Oregon he was and feeling helpless. "We're headed to Piber tomorrow to buy Emma's horses. When we're back in the States, we're flying down to Louisville from JFK before returning to Oregon. Emma wants to see her uncle. Maybe I could talk with Simon Day while I'm there."

"That sounds good. He might have more information that can help us."

"Yes, Simon's had more experience with these jerks who don't give a damn about their horses. I'll call you from Kentucky."

Sam hung up, and then walked to the open doors of the elevator. He'd had a lot of experience in compartmentalizing his life, and as the elevator slowly rose to their floor, he stuffed his anger into a corner of his mind. It would wait there until he needed it to solve this case.

****

Emma was waiting when he opened the door. She had lit some candles they'd bought earlier on their trip and was wearing the white negligee she'd worn on their wedding night. Sam smiled and took her into his arms.

"What did Jim want?" she asked.

"Nothing serious," he said, then kissed her passionately. "Mrs. Parker, I adore you."

He picked her up and placed her gently on the bed. All of his frustration was channeled away as he traced his lips down her throat and stopped just above her beautiful breasts. He smiled into her eyes, the soft light of the candle danced across her face. Her brown eyes grew darker as her breathing increased. He took one finger to slowly drop the strap of the negligee off her creamy shoulder, then grinned as she gasped when he brushed his lips across the top of her left breast. Her body arched up to meet his touch...

KENTUCKY

Late one night, shortly before the Aqueduct race, a man looked around Gallano Farm to make sure that no one was in sight. He crept into Divina's stallion stable, hiding just inside the door. The building was barely lit. One horse in particular, Mr. Divinity, walked up to his stall door and sniffed the air, then began to nicker as the man approached.

The man reached up a gloved hand, stroked the dark horse's neck and whispered to the animal. "Sorry about this, buddy."

He pulled out a plastic bag from his jacket pocket and force fed the dried contents to the horse. He said softly to the animal, "You won't feel anything for a while, boy."

CHAPTER FIVE

NEW YORK

George Mason lo oked overhead as he approached the stable in the backside at Aqueduct Race Track in Queens. He was glad the sky was clear and not raining, as it had been in Louisville. The Wood Memorial Stakes, one of the major pre-Kentucky Derby races, was scheduled for the next day. Aqueduct's track was nine-furlongs and could prove to be a fast race.

The aisle down the center of the horses' stalls was littered with bales of hay. Koenig's Spirit nodded his head and whinnied as George came up to rub his dark cheek.

"How did he travel?" George asked Fred, carefully looking over his colt.

"As well as expected. I'm glad we decided to fly him, instead of driving in a van for twelve hours or more. There are so many things that can go wrong when hauling horses."

"Has he had any signs of pleuropneumonia?" George asked, knowing the risk of what is called 'shipping fever' whenever his horses were transported for races.

"No, he's had enough time to settle here the last three days, so I'm sure he will be fine for the race tomorrow."

George nodded, trusting his trainer. He and Fred had been friends now for over twenty years.

"How was your flight?" Fred asked with a grin, knowing that

George had traveled on the same plane as Divina Gallano.

"It was very nice." First Class had been pleasant, sitting next to Divina. They'd talked about their racing experiences and their pasts, while sipping champagne. But, she was getting a little too familiar for George's taste.

Fred looked around. "Where is Mr. Divinity's stall?"

"At the other end of this barn." George looked down the long aisle, but was disappointed not to see Divina anywhere. Then he remembered. "As soon as we landed, she went to check into her hotel before coming to the track," he said, not sure why he felt he needed to explain anything to his friend. "I've been walking around awhile...to see the lay of the land here." George failed to elaborate that he needed some time to think, after spending so much time with Divina on the plane.

"We have an eight-horse field tomorrow," Fred said. "I'm sure Spirit will have no trouble with this group."

"Now look who's the optimist here!" George laughed.

A little while later, he was surprised to see Divina walk in, with sunlight shining down the aisle behind her. She had a white silk scarf wrapped around her head like those women in classic films. Removing her dark glasses, she smiled and waved to George. He walked up to her. "You look lovely, as usual."

"Well, thank you, Mr. Mason." She liked to use his formal name when others were around, in a professional sort of way. Hooking her arm in his, she led him to where Mr. Divinity stood. The tall roan colt pawed the ground in his stall as she approached. "Oh, I am looking forward to watching our horses race together again."

"I am, too." George glanced at the horse's legs. "Did you get settled into your hotel?"

"Yes, the Hotel Chelsea has always been my favorite in New York. Whenever my father brought me to the city, that's where we would stay. Maybe you could join me there for dinner this evening?"

"That might be arranged," George said, feeling a little apprehensive about revisiting a city that held so much of his past. "I will have to meet you there."

Mr. Divinity whinnied, and Divina walked up to the tall colt and rubbed his neck. "I have an odd feeling about this race, but I can't explain why. My trainer assured me there is nothing wrong with him, so we will see." She turned to George, "So, you will meet me at my hotel, say around six this evening?"

He looked around, and was surprised there was no one from Gallano Farm near Mr. Divinity's stall. He would never allow that to happen with his horses. Knowing he wouldn't be able to put her off, he said, "Unless you hear otherwise, I will be there."

Divina gave George a quick peck on his cheek, then sauntered out of the barn.

Fred walked up to his friend. "It's good our race doesn't start until mid-afternoon tomorrow. I want to exercise Spirit one last time before bedding him down for the night." When George didn't respond, he looked at the older man. "I have a hotel room reserved for us near the track," Fred continued. "We're on our own for dinner—"

"Divina's invited me to dinner in the city." George smiled and said, "So, you might not want to wait up for me!"

****

George hired a taxi to take him to the Hotel Chelsea in lower Manhattan. The chatty driver talked about his wife the entire drive, so eventually, George chose to ignore him and look out the window. He was amazed to see the differences between the neighborhoods of Queens and Brooklyn. Then, the Brooklyn Bridge came into view, with the tall buildings looming behind it. Once they were on the bridge, he quickly glanced to his left and saw the Statue of Liberty he'd seen from the ship when he'd arrived thirty-four years ago. That fateful day had changed his life forever.

As the car continued, George decided to stop obsessing about his past and considered what his evening with Divina had in store for him. She was such a beautiful woman, but he'd kept himself buried in his work and never allowed himself to spend much time alone with anyone but his staff and his friends in the horse world. He was a little nervous about what may happen tonight.

The taxi stopped in front of a twelve-story, red-bricked building, with cast iron balconies on each floor. "This hotel has been home of many writers and artist types for years," the driver said.

George smiled and paid the man, then stepped out, becoming aware that the air seemed more oppressive than out by the open track he'd just left. He walked into the lobby area and saw on the left a grand staircase of iron filigree and brass railing winding to the floors above and below. Looking down the stairwell, he was amazed at the architecture. Left and right of the entrance were two sitting areas, the furniture was a mix of antiques and some, more modern. Straight ahead was the reception desk. An older man, with a small goatee, was sleeping behind the counter. Just as George was about to walk up to him, someone called his name. George turned.

Divina stood in the opening of the sitting area to his left. She was dressed in coral silk, wrapped loosely around her lovely body. Her dark hair lay softly on her shoulders and her lips were a bright red. George took a long, slow breath and walked over to her, realizing that he may be in trouble - or he just might get lucky tonight!

He looked into the high-ceilinged room and saw numerous oversized paintings hung on the walls. A few people sat in over-stuffed chairs, either alone or talking in groups. Colorful Turkish area rugs lay on the tiled floor. There was a black fireplace to one side, with a bust of Shakespeare on the mantel.

"I thought I'd meet you here," Divina said in her sing-song voice, touching his arm. He felt an electric current surge through his body. "We're going next door to a little restaurant," she continued, as she picked up a shawl from a nearby chair.

They walked through the tall, arched doorway leading out of the hotel. George looked up and down Twenty-Third Street and shook his head at the tall buildings of various heights and colors. He could barely see a glimpse of the azure sky as the sun began to set in the west, and he wondered how people could live like this.

"Come on, George. I'm starving!" As they entered a restaurant adjacent to the hotel, Divina continued. "El Quijote has been here since the thirties, as part of The Chelsea. It has a full bar and Spanish Basque cuisine. I'm sure you will like it. Some of the entrees remind me of the foods the Spaniards brought to our islands in the Philippines."

They passed a bar that was lined with colorful bottles, lit from behind. Statues of the Spanish hero stood on the shelves nearby. George smiled to himself when he spotted a bottle of 1792 Kentucky Bourbon. As they followed a waiter past the tables, George saw a tray with two large, mouth-watering lobsters.

"I love it here!" Divina said as they were being seated at a table next to a wall of mirrors; small lamps with red shades gave off a soft light. The smells of spices, seafood and grilled meat were heavenly. They started with a Manchego cheese and olive appetizer. She had a white wine, and George ordered the 1792 bourbon.

"Aqueduct is a fascinating track," George began, slowly sipping his drink. "It's just eight miles from Belmont Park, the location of the third race for the Triple Crown..."

"I want to know more about you, George. When did you come to America?"

He looked down at his glass and said, "Here in 1937."

Divina saw George's face. "That was a hard time for everyone. Where is the rest of your family?"

George took another slow sip, letting the liquor burn down the back of his throat. "My parents were killed in the war," was all he said. He didn't want to talk about his brothers.

"Oh, I am so sorry," Divina said softly, placing her hand on his.

The last time he'd talked to her about his family, she'd touched him the same way. It didn't ease his pain. To change the subject, George turned his hand over to enclose her small fingers. "You have the smallest hands. I'm so glad you invited me here tonight."

After their dinner arrived, they talked about the upcoming race.

"This race will help establish our horses for the Derby," Divina sighed. She smiled slyly at George. "I wonder which of our colts will win."

"I wanted to ask you about that feeling you mentioned earlier today. What exactly is bothering you about Mr. Divinity?"

"I know my horse. But, when I looked into his eyes, it seemed there was something wrong with him."

"It's probably nothing - maybe a little stress from his transport. That's why I chose to fly Spirit here early. It gives him a few extra days to adjust to his new environment."

"I just hope mine is ready for the race tomorrow," Divina said, finishing her drink.

****

After they left the restaurant, George and Divina walked by a small, white church with tall stained-glass windows. The building was striking next to the red brick of the hotel, but it was dwarfed amongst the tall buildings around it.

"Let's catch a cab to Battery Park," Divina said, holding her hand up at the side of the curb. "There's a great view of the Hudson River."

A taxi stopped and the driver took them down towards the waterfront. As they got out, George stopped and looked again at the magnificent Statue of Liberty.

"Brings back memories for you, doesn't it?" Divina said, hooking her arm in his.

Then George saw Ellis Island and caught his breath as he remembered losing Hermann in the crowd of immigrants.

"My family arrived in San Francisco Bay," Divina said. "I will never forget seeing Angel Island...the detention center. It was disheartening. Our horses were quarantined."

They walked along the promenade.

"We were also detained," she continued, "and my father was interrogated. But, he had papers from our government, and eventually, we were released."

George thought of how simple his immigration had been, coming from Europe, compared to hers.

****

After walking awhile, they'd taken a cab back to the hotel. On the ride, George began to get nervous about what would happen next. When the driver pulled up outside The Chelsea, George asked him to wait. He turned to Divina and said, "I think it's time I return to the track–"

"Please, come up to my room for a nightcap," Divina said. "I don't want to be alone just yet."

He thought for a moment, then cancelled the driver.

As George followed Divina inside the building, he stopped when he saw a reflection in a mirror - a redheaded woman was wearing a green, hooded cape, her dark red lipstick was striking against her creamy face. She looked up as if she was looking directly at him. He was thrown back to his homeland, where he'd fallen in love for the first time - with Hannah Siemens, his brother, Hermann's, fiancé. George remembered the few moments he'd been with Hannah; the way she tossed her hair as she laughed, her soft skin, her smile. He knew he would never be forgiven for lying to his brother in order to convince him to cross the Atlantic to their new world, both men leaving Hannah behind.

"Come on, George," Divina called from the elevator.

He turned and smiled at Divina. But, when he looked back, the woman in the mirror was gone. Sadly, he stepped in beside Divina, and she pushed the button for the top floor. The doors closed and they rode in silence. He was becoming unsure of himself as they passed each floor.

Divina's room had a white marble fireplace, with a gilded mirror over the mantel. A Victorian-styled lounge sat in front of curtained windows. A floor lamp was the only light, and a mahogany desk and chair stood against one cream-colored wall.

George thought of the tiny dank room where he and his brother were to meet, if they were separated after their ship docked in America. He'd found the room, but Hermann had never arrived.

Divina draped her shawl over a chair, and opened the velvet curtains covering the long windows. The lights of the city brightened the room a little. One of the windows was actually a tall, glass door that led to a balcony. He walked over and looked down at the street below; surprised he could hear the city traffic through the closed door.

"Come, sit over here by me," Divina said, patting the chaise lounge she now sat on.

George was uncomfortable as he sat next to her - his body was too large for the small seat, and he kept trying to inch away from her as she clung to his arm.

"Isn't this nice?" she cooed, placing her head on his shoulder.

"Tell me more about Mr. Divinity–"

"George Mason!" she said, "I am trying to seduce you."

He quickly stood, remembering the years between their ages. "I'm old enough to be–"

"But, darling, my grandparents had a similar difference in their ages and it was not a problem." She stood and walked up to him. "Age is just a state of mind..." she said, smiling, leaning provocatively into him.

George thought of Hannah and said, "I'm very sorry, but I need to get back to the track." He quickly left, ignoring the shocked look on Divina's face.

****

The next day, George sat in the box seat of the multi-tiered grandstand at Aqueduct Race Course. He was dreading seeing Divina again after his quick exit the prior night, but knew he'd done the right thing. He wasn't ready to begin a romance just yet.

Fred walked up and sat next to him. "Spirit is ready to go. Stan's excited - this is his third race at this track."

As the horses began the parade before the grandstand, Divina entered the box and sat next to Fred, avoiding George.

Glancing between the two silent people next to him, Fred rolled his eyes. He'd been surprised to see George come in early last night. When he'd asked how his date had gone, George had refused to talk about it.

The horses were now in the gate.

"And they're off in the Wood Memorial Stakes," the announcer said over the loud speaker. "The horses are out of the gate..."

The crowd exploded as the field bolted down the track, four horses fighting for the lead. The field ran close together, and then three horses pulled ahead.

"As they come around the back of the field," the announcer continued, "Koenig's Spirit and Mr. Divinity fight for the lead."

In the last turn, George watched a bay and a gray horse gaining on the two colts in front.

"Come on, Mr. Divinity!" someone in the back yelled.

George turned, but couldn't see who it was. When he looked at the track again, Spirit and Mr. Divinity were now running neck and neck towards the finish line. Just then, a few yards from the wire, Divina's horse faltered and fell back. Spirit took the lead, followed by the two other contenders, who'd been pacing closely behind.

"Oh, no!" Divina cried. "What happened?"

After Spirit won the race, she ran out of the grandstand. Fred was jumping up and down with excitement, but George stood and watched Divina.

"Come on, George, we have to go to the Winner's Circle!"

George followed, but kept looking through the crowd. It seemed like the photographers would never stop taking pictures, as they stood next to Koenig's Spirit. The Wood Memorial Stakes silver plate, a three-footed platter, was handed to George while flashes went off all around them. He looked down and saw the engraved armorial in the center, with *Semper Fidelis* etched underneath.

"You did a fine job, Stan," George said, shaking his jockey's hand. He turned to Fred, handed him the platter and said, "I'll see you in the backside." Then, he left.

"This horse had everything to do with it!" Stan said to George's back, rubbing Spirit's neck.

"George knows that!" Fred said.

In the backside, George searched for Divina. Her horse was now cooled, washed and back in his stall. He overheard the track vet say he couldn't seem to find anything wrong with Mr. Divinity, and then he left to go test the winning horses.

Divina's face was distraught and she looked frightened. "I wish Seth were here. I'll have my horse checked when we get him home." She kept stroking her horse, who was still agitated and straining against the cross-ties in his stall.

George knew Seth Young had been with Divina for only a few years now. "Why didn't he come with you?" he asked.

She shook her head. "One of his daughters had an accident on her bicycle, so I insisted he stay with her."

"I can have my vet take a look at him, if you wish." George offered, as Fred joined them.

"That would be kind, but I'm sure my trainer will take care of everything." She looked around, and then asked, "Where is he?"

Fred said, "I saw Raul talking to a guy over by the Test Barn."

"Divina," George said, placing his hand on her arm, "is there anything I can do?"

"I'm sure he will be okay..." she began, then looked around.

One of her grooms entered the horse's stall and tried to calm the animal down. Fred watched closely.

"Please let me help," George insisted.

Just then, Raul Lopez joined them. He was a small man of Spanish decent who had worked for Divina's father since they'd arrived in Lexington. "Ms. Gallano, I just talked to the track vet. He said we can transport Mr. Divinity home whenever you are ready."

"All right," she said heavily. "That would be best." She then turned to her horse and continued stroking him, ignoring George.

Raul looked quickly at George and Fred. "Why don't you two go back to your winning horse and leave us alone!" he said angrily.

On the way back to Spirit's barn, George seemed sullen and pensive. To cheer him up, Fred said, "Spirit did a fine job. Johnny's cooling him down now."

George shook his head, trying to clear his mind. His horse had won today! He smiled and said, "Yes, in spite of everything else, I'm proud of that colt."

Fred glanced sideways at his friend and said, "I don't like the way Mr. Divinity was salivating so much, and his eyes were dilated. I hope he doesn't have something contagious!"

George nodded. "This is why I insist that our vet always travels with us."

They walked on in silence, and then Fred finally asked with a smile, "So, what happened last night?"

George sighed. "We had a very nice dinner and...we walked around the city."

"So, why did you come back so early? I didn't expect to see you until this morning."

"I was a coward..." George said in a soft voice. "I felt like I was cheating, even though–"

"I get it," Fred said quickly. He knew everything about George's past. "I can't say I'm not disappointed, but there will be other times."

When they reached Spirit's stall, the horse bobbed his head like he wanted attention. "Besides," Fred continued, "we have a winner on our hands!"

CHAPTER SIX

AUSTRIA

The morning sun filtered through the lobby of the Astoria Hotel, as Sam and Emma stepped off the elevator.

"I would've been sad if we had to leave because of that case in Oregon," she said as they walked to the concierge to wait for their car.

"There's no way I'd let that happen. You are too important to me, and going to Piber is one of your dreams." Sam hugged her. "I'm here to make your dreams come true! I know Jim can handle anything back there."

Emma saw the frown on Sam's face, even as he smiled. She knew he took his job seriously, and she admired his commitment. How different her life was since she and Sam had finally reunited; and now that they were married, she didn't want to change a thing in her life.

A small, orange Volkswagen bug arrived and they climbed in. Their rental was a two-door, like the ones she'd seen at home, but the back seat looked like it was built for small children. Emma smiled at the thought as she climbed in next to Sam.

She watched as he checked the dashboard, lights, and gearshift before he pulled away from the hotel. His motions were similar to his meticulous pre-check on his airplane. The rear engine of the small car hummed like a sewing machine. She looked at a map the concierge had given them that was thankfully translated into English. It also had the Viennese names listed, which would be helpful in reading road signs.

Once outside the city, they both relaxed. The countryside opened up with luscious green valleys encircled by mountains. They passed numerous small towns until they came to Graz, the capital city of the province of Styria. They decided to stop for a short break, finding a small café in a square called *Hauptplatz*. The blend of Baroque and Renaissance architecture was part of the charm of the city.

While they sat in the sunlight, Emma reached over and touched Sam's face. "You're letting your beard grow..." she said, feeling the short stubble against her fingers. "I like it."

"Good," Sam said smiling. After Paris, he'd decided that it was time for him to make a change. The beard was a start - he'd only had one once before in his life...

Later, they wandered the streets and came upon a fascinating, painted house with Baroque frescoes depicting the gods of mythology. When they became lost, the people were warm and helpful. An older man asked where they had parked. When they told him it was near a large cathedral, he smiled, pointed to the east and said in broken English, "Just listen for the bells. They will lead the way."

Once they were back in their car, Sam looked at the map to get his bearings. Emma went over some notes about the Piber Stud Farm she had brought with her.

"We're only about fifty kilometers from Piber now," Sam said, folding the map.

Emma smiled excitedly. "I can hardly wait to get there. This is unbelievable!" She looked at the papers on her lap; one was a letter, with the Piber Federal Stud Farm insignia on the letterhead - a large 'P' below a gold crown. "I've asked for a mare and a stallion to increase my Lipizzaner stock."

"Then, let's go get 'em!" Sam said and put the little car into gear.

****

After a while, as they came around a curve in the road, Emma caught her breath. The misty mountains looked as if they were painted in watercolors against the canvas of the sky. The Lipizzaner Stud Farm stood in the foreground with white buildings and red-tiled roofs amid green trees. A tall white steeple, with a red spire on top, towered high above the other buildings.

"This is so beautiful," Emma sighed. "I think I want to plant more trees around my stables at home now!"

Sam smiled and drove into the visitor's parking area. When they stepped out of the car, a young woman came to meet them, wearing gray slacks, blue jacket, and a European military-styled hat, with a red band and the Piber logo.

"*Hallo, mein* name *ist* Frida," she said with a laugh. *"Herlizch Willkommen Sie auf dem Lipizzaner-Gestüt Piber."*

"Hello, Frida," Emma said, offering her hand. "Do you speak English?"

"*Ja*, I speak English."

"My name is Emma Maseman." She quickly looked at Sam and smiled, "Emma Parker now. I have an appointment with Rudolf Hinteregger, about purchasing some horses for my stables in America. This is my husband, Sam."

"*Ja*, we've been expecting you. Follow me."

Frida led the way towards a three-story, white and tan Baroque building. They walked through an entryway that opened out to a large, arched courtyard, covered in grass. In the center and along each side were elaborately set, white-clothed tables and chairs. On the upper two levels, boxes of red flowers sat on the railings under each archway. A staff of white-coated, young people was busy setting the tableware.

"*Dies* is the castle, which houses our administrative offices, as well as our event rooms *und* a café. *Wir* have a wedding here later today. The season has just opened, so there may only be a few other visitors."

"It's a lovely setting, perfect for a wedding."

"*Ja*, this building was formerly an abbey for Brigittine monks."

"That explains the architecture," Sam interjected.

"Is Mr. Hinteregger waiting to see us?" Emma asked anxiously.

"*Ja*, his office is here to the right."

Just as they were leaving the courtyard, a tall, older man, with keen eyes beneath a full head of silver hair, walked up to them. He reached out a hand and smiled.

"*Hallo*, I am Rudolf Hinteregger. I assume you are Emma, Hermann's daughter?"

"Yes," Emma said, a little shyly. "How did you know?"

"You have your father's eyes, and your correspondence indicated the name Maseman," He looked at Sam. "And, this is your husband?"

"I'm Sam Parker. It's a pleasure to meet you, Sir." The two men shook hands.

"And you, as well." Rudolf turned to the young woman beside him. "*Danke*, Frida."

As she nodded and walked away, the man said to Emma, "Why don't you two come into my office?"

The spacious room Rudolf led them into was bright, with tall windows, high ceilings and mahogany wood paneling. The older man sat behind a massive desk and rested his elbows on the green, felt pad in front of him.

"Mr. Hinteregger," Emma began, "a friend of yours at the Spanish Riding School asked us to say 'hello' when we met - a Mr. Baeder."

"Ah, Josef and I were boys together in school."

"I am so pleased you have agreed to meet me, since–"

"Please, call me Rudi. Your father was one of my most outstanding students at the Spanish Riding School. I was Chief Rider there for many years, but have enjoyed my retirement here at the Federal Stud, where I am able to train the young stallions before they go to the School. I grew up in Graz and spent my youth in these hills."

Emma said, "I can't imagine what it was like to live here. It is so beautiful."

"*Ja*," Rudi said. "It was hard to leave while I worked in Vienna."

"I am pleased to know that you remember my father," Emma began. "I hope there is no problem with my request to purchase a stallion of the Neapolitano blood line. You see, I have a stallion from Conversano Regina, which my father purchased at a riding school in Verden. He performed there before he immigrated to the United States. He took the horse with him for breeding.

"Ah, that is what happened to Hermann." Rudi was quiet for a moment. Then he said, "And, Conversano is one of the six classic foundation lines of the Lipizzan stallions. Hermann made a good choice." Rudi looked out the tall window to his left, a wistful look on his face. Then, he smiled at Emma. "He always selected the best horses to ride at the school, as well. I understand you also wish to purchase a mare, *ja?*"

Emma nodded. "I want a broodmare. My stables are located in Oregon, and I wish to expand the Lipizzaner horse breed in America." Emma looked at Sam and couldn't understand why he was frowning at her.

Rudi opened a large, bound book on his desk and perused the handwritten notes on each page. "This is our current stud book, listing the birth of each foal here at Piber. I have chosen the best horses for you to select from. Do you wish to see them?"

"Oh, yes!" Emma sighed. She glanced over at Sam, who watched in silence, with a sullen look on his face. She knew this was her dream, not his, but he had always been so supportive of her.

As they walked outside, Emma said, "Rudi, I wish to ride my chosen stallion."

"But, of course." When they reached a paddock near one stable, he said, "Wait here a moment, and I will have them brought out for you."

Sam leaned towards Emma and whispered, "I'm not sure why he gets to pick the horses for you to see."

"Since Rudi knew my father, I trust his decisions."

"I'm not sure I do!" Sam said. "You don't know anything about this guy."

"No, but my father did, and he spoke highly of him."

Ignoring Sam's concerns, Emma rested her arms against the railing and watched Rudi walk up to a young man in a uniform similar to Frida's. Five stallions now roamed freely inside the paddock, some older ones had white coats, and others were a gray or even bay. As the two men talked for a few moments, she was surprised to see one stallion that stood out as he pranced with a long stride and strong legs. His shoulders were muscular, and he held his neck in a high arch - a very proud carriage. He stopped and seemed to stare right at Emma.

The young man walked among the horses, as Rudi came back to Emma and Sam.

"They are magnificent!" Emma sighed.

"Yes, they are the finest horses in all of Europe!" Rudi boasted.

Sam snorted softly, shoved his hands in his pockets, and looked out over the hillside. *Yes, they're beautiful,* he thought, *but nothing like my tall, sleek Thoroughbreds.*

"Rudi, I like that one," she said, pointing to the proud stallion that had caught her eye, the one with the dapper-gray coat. She was getting frustrated with her husband's attitude.

Rudi raised one hand to the young man. "Please have Neo saddled."

"I like that name," Emma said. "I always give my horses barn names, as well." She looked at Rudi and said, "I wish you could come to Oregon to see my stables. I now have two barns - one for stallions and geldings, and the other for mares and foals. I'm also adding a breeding shed." She knew she was babbling, but she wanted to impress Rudi. "There is a large, indoor arena, since it rains so much where we live. I'm excited to finally enlarge my Lipizzan stock. It's what my father always wanted to do."

Sam looked at Emma with confusion in his eyes and walked away.

"Sam?" she called after him, but he had disappeared around the corner of the stable.

Rudi asked, "Is there anything we can do for your husband?" He looked around, and then added, "There is so much more to see at Piber."

"I think he's just tired from traveling. We've been gone now for over a month, I'm sure he will be okay."

She and Rudi continued watching the other horses as they interacted within the paddock. While they waited for her stallion to be saddled, Rudi said, "You have chosen a good time to arrive here. Our summer season has just opened; during *Alpung*—"

"What is that?" Emma asked.

"It is the time the young horses are taken to the Alpine pastures for the summer. They spend three summers there, growing healthy and strong." Rudi looked at Emma and asked, "How many staff do you have at your stables?"

"Just one at this time, but I have a friend looking for more."

"Then, you will need a special handler, one who knows the Lipizzaners. I have arranged for a young man to travel with the horses to help you, if you wish."

"Oh, that would be wonderful!" Emma knew she had extra

funds in her budget for other staff.

"Let me go see what is taking so long," Rudi said and disappeared into the stable.

After a few moments, Rudi returned and said, "Here is Peter with your stallion, Neapolitano Toscana."

A different young man followed Rudi, leading the stallion she had liked. Peter tipped his hat to her. He was in his late twenties, tall and slender, with a nice smile.

"*Hallo*, I am Peter Norbert," the young man said, bowing with his arm across his chest. "I understand that I will be traveling to America with the Lipizzaners that you are choosing today?"

"Yes, if that is what you would like to do. I can really use the help, and would feel much better if someone the horses trust will be with them on the journey." She smiled and added, "Your English is very good."

Peter looked at the ground and blushed.

"When do you wish the horses to arrive?" Rudi asked Emma.

"My husband and I are still on our honeymoon..." She started, looked again for Sam, but was disappointed that he had not returned. "We will not be back in Oregon for a few days. Could the horses be shipped the following week, giving me time to prepare?"

"But of course. I will make all the arrangements. Peter will take Neo to an empty arena for you to ride."

As they followed the young man and horse, Emma said, "I continued my father's tradition of a Dressage riding school, as well as a small breeding program. I've been teaching for eleven years, after my father died."

"If I am not being too bold to ask..." Rudi said softly. "How did he die?"

Emma was silent for a moment. How could she tell this man her father had been murdered by his own brother? "He was hit by a car," she finally said, then took a deep breath and changed the subject. "I've had some students go on to the Grand-Prix level of Dressage."

"Very impressive!"

They passed a large riding hall, where she assumed they did most of their training. Then, as they approached an empty, smaller arena, another staff member opened the gate. Peter entered with the stallion and stood waiting, holding the reins. Emma walked up and gently placed her hands on the horse, his soft muzzle leaned into her.

She stroked his long neck and ears, looking him over. He sniffed the air, then bobbed his head and pawed at the ground, Peter held his bridle. She became silent and continued to allow the horse to get to know her, caressing him softly. She was sad that Sam was nowhere in sight.

She took the reins, mounted the horse and walked him around the arena to allow him time to warm up. For some reason, she began to hear in her head the solo guitar music of Paco de Lucia, one of her favorite musicians. Following the beats to the imagined song, with the slightest movement of her lower legs, she asked the horse to trot. Then, leaning her body slightly forward and her legs back, she was pleased to see him change into an extended trot, and felt as if the horse was rising with each step. She continued taking him through other movements in a sort of freestyle ballet, like her father taught her to do. It was like she was dancing with the horse to the music only she could hear. When finished, Emma praised him, then stopped the stallion near where Rudi and Peter stood.

"Only advanced riders are able to perform a ballet such as that," Rudi said, "...and, on a young horse you have never ridden."

"He's been trained very well." Emma smiled as she dismounted. "And, I've learned that all horses tend to want to please, with a little encouragement."

"I see Hermann's excellent riding skill in you," Rudi commented, "but you have some of your own talents, as well."

"Thank you, I received the gift from my father. He was my master."

"Now, let's look at the mares. There is one I think you will like - she is from the Pluto founding stallion line." Rudi nodded to Peter, who handed the stallion's reins to the other man in uniform. The gray horse was led away to be cooled and groomed.

Peter took them to the covered mare's stable, where the herd of numerous mares was gathered together. A few foals stood closely beside their mothers and watched them approach.

"These young foals will stay with their mothers until they are six months old," Peter told her. "Then, they are weaned and will join their respective herds."

Emma smiled at the small, dark colts and fillies, who frolicked around without a care in the world. Peter walked up to a mare and led her away from the herd with her halter as Rudi went to talk with another man across the arena.

"She's lovely!" Emma exclaimed, gently stroking the gray horse. The mare's coat was similar to Neo's, but it was lighter, and she had a long, white tail and mane. She had a strong conformation and proud stance. Emma looked back at the herd. "I can see why you wanted me to see her."

"This is Pluto Calma," Peter said, running his free hand down her nose. "She is among four mares who were not bred last year for the purpose of being offered for sale. Her colt from last year is now with his herd in the Alpine pastures. He is a fine animal. You may go up to the pasture, if you wish."

"I would appreciate that, but I will need to check with my husband." She looked around - still no sign of Sam. Emma liked this young man's manner. "How long have you worked here, Peter?"

"Since I was ten. My parents were killed in the war, and an older couple who lived near here took me in. They are both gone now, too." Peter looked away.

"I lost my grandparents in Germany during the war," Emma said sadly. "I never had a chance to get to know them." After a moment, she added, "How long will you be able to stay in America?"

"It doesn't matter," Peter said with a shrug of his shoulders. "I can stay as long as you need me."

Emma wondered how an immigrant on a working visa could possibly become a U.S. citizen, and decided to look into that as soon as she returned to Oregon.

When Rudi returned, Emma talked about previously agreed prices, and made arrangements for shipping the following week. "I'm glad to know that Peter will be accompanying the horses." She smiled at the young man. "I know that they will be in good hands."

Peter smiled and took the mare to her stall.

Emma looked around the area. "Rudi, while we have a moment alone, I would like to ask - do you know why my father left the Spanish Riding School? He never told me..."

****

Emma could see something was bothering Sam as they drove in silence. When they approached the village of Kölfach, they passed an interesting church spire that was square, with various markings and a golden 'onion' on top. As they continued through the winding streets, she said, "I'm hungry. Can we stop for lunch?"

"Here's a café that looks interesting," Sam said and parked the car near the garden.

Once they were seated at their table, a pretty waitress with long, curly, blonde hair came up to them with menus.

"*Guten Tag, Mien* name *ist* Elena," she said, smiling at Sam.

"Hello, Elena, do you understand English," Sam asked.

"Oh, *ja*, I do. What would you like to drink?"

Sam ordered a stein of beer and Emma, a glass of Riesling.

"We'll need a little time to look at the menu," Emma said. The waitress left.

"Going up to the high pasture was amazing!" Emma said, excitedly. "Calma's young colt was very handsome." They were not able to find Sam, so she had ridden up there alone. The herds were beautiful as they ran loose in the Alpine hills. Peter had pointed out the colt as he was playing with another young horse.

Elena brought their drinks, and they asked for sandwiches. After that, Sam didn't say anything. He just picked up a local newspaper that had been left on a nearby table and flipped through it.

"Piber was so exciting," Emma said, breaking the uncomfortable silence. "And, meeting Rudi. It was good to get to know someone who worked with my father. I was able to ride the young stallion for a little. He has such potential."

Sam continued to look at the paper, even though it was in German, just to avoid talking with Emma.

"Where did you go, Sam? You missed everything."

He closed the paper and set it aside. "I walked around the complex. Did you know they have their own blacksmith and farrier? There's also a chapel. While I was standing inside it, this calico cat walked up near the altar, stopped and sat down, then started cleaning herself. It was very surreal."

She noticed that he wasn't as interested as she was about her horses. "I was surprised you didn't want to–"

"This part of the trip was all for YOUR stables, Emma!" Sam said a little curtly. "That's all I kept hearing back there. I understood that from the beginning, but I felt like an outsider there."

The waitress returned with their food. "Elena," Sam asked, "do you have horseracing here in Austria?"

"*Ja*, at *Galloprennbahn Freudenau* in the *Prater* area of *Wien*. It is very old, and was damaged during the war, but is once again open. *Herr*, do you like horseracing?"

"Yes," he said, looking at Emma, "it's in my blood."

"You are a very, uh, how do you say - a very curious man." The waitress smiled and went back inside the café.

"I'm sorry, Sam," Emma began. "I didn't mean–"

"Let's just drop it," he said sharply and took a large bite.

"What is this renewed interest in racing now?" Emma asked after a few moments of more silence. "Is this for your work?"

"No," Sam said, pulling some cheese off of his sandwich. He wasn't ready to share his new passion with her just yet. "I've just been thinking about the upcoming Kentucky Derby. I'd like to stop at this track on our way back to Vienna."

"I think that could work," she said, hoping Sam would forgive her, if she went there with him. "As long as we don't miss our train," she added. "Remember, we're flying home in a few days. I'm looking forward to sharing my news with Uncle George."

"It's a good thing we flew the Shrike Commander to New York. I need to stop in Kentucky anyway before we go home - for work."

CHAPTER SEVEN

KENTUCKY

"How was your honeymoon?" Fred asked when Emma and Sam walked out of the small aircraft area of the Louisville airport.

"It was wonderful!" Emma sighed, almost wishing they were still in Europe. "I got to see the Lipizzaners in Vienna and at Piber."

They placed their bags in the back of the Jeep and climbed in. Fred looked in the rear-view mirror at Sam. "Are you glad to be back on U.S. soil again, Sam?"

"Yes...I can't wait to get back to Oregon."

Emma turned and saw Sam look quickly out the side window. She'd seen the change in him ever since they left Piber. He'd become sullen, only giving short answers to her questions on the plane ride. She knew they needed to talk, but decided to wait until Sam was ready.

As they rode up the long lane of Essen Farms, Emma got chills when she realized that this part of the Bluegrass country belonged to part of her family. She'd only known her Uncle George for a few years, because her father never talked about him. The long horse barns, with the golden dormers and cupolas, held some of the finest Thoroughbred racehorses in America.

As they pulled up in front of the large, white mansion, Emma saw a black Mercedes with the logo GALLANO FARM on the side door.

"Who's here?" she asked Fred.

"Divina Gallano, she owns a horse farm nearby." Fred looked at Emma. "She and George have become very close."

Emma wasn't sure how she felt about this news. George was a confirmed bachelor; at least that's what he told her when they first met in Oregon two years ago. That was when her life had been turned upside down.

George ran out of the house and hugged Emma in his large frame. "You are finally here! I am so glad you're safe." He looked over at his new nephew-in-law. "And, Sam, it is good to see you again."

"Hello, George," Sam said, shaking hands.

As Fred drove the car around to the garage, a petite, slender woman with dark hair came out of the house. She walked up to Emma and extended her hand. "You must be Emma, George's niece," she said with a slight accent in her voice. "I am Divina."

Emma was taken aback by this woman's beauty and wondered how any man could resist her. Divina placed Emma's arm in hers and led her into the house, talking as if they'd known each other forever. "I'll have George's housekeeper get your bags."

"I didn't know Uncle George had a housekeeper," Emma said, appealing to Sam with her eyes to say something.

"He does while I'm here," Divina said and the two women disappeared into the large house. A small woman with dark hair passed them to get the luggage.

"Let me help you, Jasmine," George offered, but the woman refused.

"I can do this, Mr. Mason. You go on with your guest."

"Sam, come with me," he said and walked towards a nearby pasture. "What did you enjoy on your journey?" he asked, clasping his arm around Sam's shoulders.

"I went to *Galloprennbahn Freudenau* racecourse, near Vienna. It was exciting to be back at the races again."

"Ah, *Freudenau* means 'joyfulness' in German. I've never been there, but I hear it is a good track."

"The first Austrian Derby was held there in the mid-1800, and it's a historical site." Then, Sam said, "I have to go check in with Simon Day about a call I received, while we were in Vienna. There's a case in Oregon that Simon may have some information for me. Can I take one of your vehicles?"

"Sure, Fred will get you the keys to the Jeep."

Just then, a dark flash ran passed them in the pasture near the house.

"Which colt is that?" Sam asked, nodding towards the young animal.

"Koenig's Spirit, my three-year old that is racing in this year's Kentucky Derby. Divina and I have horses vying for the trophy this year."

Sam knew George was talking about his passion to win the Triple Crown trophy, engraved with the three dates of each race won for the honored prize. It was more like an obsession.

The two men walked over to the fence. The colt was roan, with one white sock on his left hind fetlock. Sam was pleased when the youngster came up and sniffed his hand.

Without looking at George, Sam said, "I really appreciate that you kept your word - about breeding your stallion, Koenig's Wonder, with Classy Elegance - 'Ele,' as I like to call her. She's produced a fine foal." He paused, then turned and added, "I know you wanted to just give my mare back, but I felt better about buying her for the Claiming Price you'd paid at Del Mar."

"I understand why you needed to do that, and I respect you for it. I'm just glad that her foal was a colt. Koenig's Promise will do fine on the race track."

"Seeing the horseraces in Vienna, it was exciting to watch it all again—" Sam confided, then caught himself. He wasn't ready to reveal that at Piber, he had decided to begin racing again. "I called Mike McKenzie, at my dad's ranch in Eugene. He said that Promise's training is coming along nicely."

"I am willing to let you begin his yearling training," George bellowed, "but, I must insist Fred bring Promise here for his two-year training for the track!"

Sam looked at George, his hands on his hips. "That's never going to happen. We agreed he's my colt, and I'll train him the way my father taught me. He trained many champions." Sam could see the anger roiling inside of George, but he knew he had to stand his ground. And, he knew he'd said enough.

"We're flying back to Oregon tomorrow...to get ready for

Emma's new Lipizzaners," Sam said and walked towards the garage. He hadn't discussed it yet with Emma, but he knew he had to leave Kentucky as soon as he could - before he said something he'd regret.

****

Sam was still fuming as he pulled up in front of the Kentucky Horse Racing Commission Office. He tried to push his anger down, but every time he thought of George controlling Promise's training, it would rise again. He stomped into the building, almost knocking Simon Day over.

"Whoa, Cowboy," Simon said with a smile, his hands up in surrender. "What's got you all fired up?" Simon had called Sam 'Cowboy,' once he'd learned he was from the Northwest.

"George Mason!" Sam barked, and then stopped, trying to soften his words. "He's trying to control my life."

"Yep, that's George all right," Simon nodded. "Come on back and tell me all about it."

They walked through the banks of desks until they reached Simon's office. The two men went way back - to when they'd worked together at the Thoroughbred Racing Bureau. Sam sat in the green leather chair opposite Simon and said, "Look where we've landed since Baltimore - you here in Kentucky, me in Oregon, both working for the local Racing Commission offices."

"Yeah, I thought I'd never leave the Bureau. But actually, I like being here - closer to my family." Simon was quiet for a moment. Then he added, "My brother's health is not good." He leaned back in his chair, behind his large, oak desk.

"I'm sorry to hear that. I hope it's not too serious."

"How was the honeymoon?" Simon asked. He'd just learned that his brother's cancer was terminal.

"Wonderful, except we spent more time with the Lipizzaners than I liked. But, that's Emma's passion."

"What about you, Sam? What's your passion now?"

Sam looked at the pictures around Simon's office of some of the racehorses he'd helped in his career. "Racing...I want to get back in it."

Simon nodded, totally understanding. They'd been together a long time, and he could read this young man like a book. "So what's this case you talked about?"

"Jim Barolio, a guy you know, has been helping me with this while I've been away. It looks like a Lasix overdose." Sam looked at the now silver-haired man across from him. He'd started turning gray sooner than most men. "Remember that one we worked on together - the one at a farm near here?"

"I sure do," Simon said, shaking his head. "We never caught the bastard that caused that colt's death."

"Whose farm was that again?"

"I think it was in Lexington. I can pull the file and give you a call later."

"I'd appreciate it. We're flying back to Oregon tomorrow. You have my number there, right?"

"Sure do." Simon looked at his watch. "How about a beer?"

Sam knew his friend would want more than one. He grinned and said, "You're on!" He wanted to avoid going back to Essen Farms as long as he could.

****

Much later, Emma was glad to finally see Sam drive up to the Essen mansion and park the Jeep with the other vehicles. She'd been watching for him, trying to avoid Divina. As he walked into the foyer, she could hear George's booming voice in the den down the hall.

"Divina, dear, why don't you stay for dinner?" Emma's uncle said

"I'd love to!"

Emma grabbed Sam by the arm and pulled him into the parlor, shutting the door. "It's about time you got back here! I've been going crazy with that woman. She just won't leave me alone."

"Is that why you're hiding in here?" Sam said with a smile. He kissed Emma's forehead, the buzz from his beers still working. "I'm sure she's not all that bad—"

"Her voice is like Southern Comfort, all sweet at first, then burns as it goes down. She keeps asking me all these questions—" Emma stopped. "Have you been drinking?"

Sam held his wife at arm's length and looked into her eyes. "When did you ever drink Southern Comfort?"

She shrugged, ignoring the fact that he'd side-stepped her

question. "In college…once." She looked at Sam and said, "Uncle George told me we're leaving tomorrow! That's why I had to see you first. What's going on?"

"I got some new information...about the case...and I need to get back." He kissed Emma softly, feeling guilty about lying to both his wife and George. "I hope you can forgive me."

Suddenly, George burst through the door. "Here you two newlyweds are! Divina has agreed to stay for dinner, so why don't you come join us in the dining room."

Sam and Emma looked at each other, and then followed George down the hallway.

The long table could seat thirty people. Shining chandeliers hung above, casting rainbows on various crystal glass cases that stood on the outer walls. Four place settings gleamed at one end of the table.

"Here, Emma," George said, pulling out a chair near Divina. "You sit here."

Reluctantly, Emma sat down.

"You should have seen George in New York," Divina began, as she looked across the table where George sat. She touched Emma's arm. "He was so gallant and charming!"

Emma looked at her uncle, who was smiling at the woman next to her. *He's besotted by her*, she thought. *And, at his age!*

The main course of fried chicken, mashed potatoes, and green beans was served by the same small woman who helped them earlier with their luggage. When Emma tried to talk to her, the woman only smiled and quickly disappeared. Divina began talking about the Aqueduct race and her horse.

"Mr. Divinity just seemed off to me." Divina placed her hand on George's across the table and continued. "George was so helpful. He's been such a rock for me - so sweet and understanding."

Emma's stomach turned at the woman's syrupy words and put down her knife and fork.

After a while, Divina cooed as she got up, "Emma, dear, why don't you and I retire to the parlor and let the men talk. The staff will bring us some coffee."

Looking at Sam with pleading eyes, Emma also rose and followed Divina out of the room. She didn't remember her uncle having any 'staff', except for the people helping with the horses.

Divina placed her arm in Emma's as they walked together down the long hall. "I just love your Uncle George. He's the handsomest, most generous man I've ever known."

"I've only known him for a short while," Emma said, pulling her arm free when they entered the front room.

"Why, dear, what do you mean?"

"We just met two years ago."

"But, how is that possible? He's family!"

Emma didn't want to go into the details of her family history - why her father never told her that he and his brother came to America together. "I didn't know about him," was all she said.

"Well, in my family, we knew everything about everyone. There were no secrets—" Divina stopped, then turned away.

Just then, George came in, followed by Sam, who was carrying a tray. Emma watched as Divina took over serving the coffee, as if she was the lady of the house. Not sure why she disliked her, Emma turned and said, "Uncle George, have you heard from Karen yet?"

Stunned, George glanced first at Divina, then back at Emma. "No...I haven't."

Emma was pleased to see Divina looking jealously at her uncle.

"Karen Stinson's father was the prior owner of Essen Farms," George tried to explain, looking confused at his niece. "I hardly know her."

"I remember the McKenzie family," Divina said. She stared at George for a moment, then put down her coffee cup and started towards the door. "I think it's time I take my leave. Thank you, George, for a lovely evening. I'll see you tomorrow." She gave him a peck on the cheek, smiled at Emma and Sam, then walked out the door.

All three stood silent for a moment.

"Well, THAT was interesting," Sam said with a chuckle.

George turned to Emma and said, "I'm not sure why you had to bring Karen up just now. I thought we were having a wonderful time tonight."

"I'm sorry..." Emma started, seeing the hurt in her uncle's eyes. "I think I'm just tired from our long flight."

George's face softened and he placed his hand on her arm. "I understand. But, I have something I'd like to share with you two before you retire. I recently bought a Thoroughbred who was being abused. I want you to see him."

****

As they entered the smaller barn, Johnny Blair, the head groom, came up to them. Sam remembered him from an earlier time he'd been to Essen Farms. His dark skin glistened in the stable light.

"Sir, he's off his feed again. I don't know what to do with him."

"It will be all right, Johnny," George said. "I'll call Eric, I'm sure he won't mind coming by tonight." He turned and introduced Emma and Sam.

Johnny bowed and said, "Pleased to meet you." Then, he walked to the back of the barn.

Emma looked into the dark stall and saw the tall colt standing at the back of the enclosure. His head was hung low; he snorted and pawed at the ground. Her heart stopped when she saw the large welts on his sides where someone had beaten him. These were not marks made by a jockey during a race - they were done in anger, placed where the saddle blanket would cover them.

"His name is Lucky Storm," George said softly, "previously owned by Gordon Evers–"

"I know that jackass," Sam hissed. "Simon told me about him tonight..."

George nodded. "I've turned him in to the Commission, but he's threatened both me and Divina."

Sam looked around. "You might want to consider some additional security for a while, just to be safe."

"I've already taken care of that." George looked at Emma. "I just don't know what to do with this horse. Eric's waiting on some tests he ran, since the horse acts like he's been drugged. I don't think he can be used on the track again. He gets very aggressive and lashes out at his handlers."

Sam nodded, "These animals can cause havoc in a track's backside. I've seen too many like him in this industry."

Emma thought for a moment, watching the colt as he looked cautiously at her. She could see the pain in his sad eyes. After a moment, she said, "I have a friend in Oregon who works with abused horses." She turned to her uncle. "I could check with her when we get home, if you don't mind."

George sighed. "I was hoping you'd have a solution!"

****

Later, when Sam entered the guest bedroom, Emma was on the phone. "I know, Aunt Karen, you don't want anything to do with this farm. But, I need to talk with you. It's important..."

While Sam began to take off his shirt, he thought back to when he'd first met Karen Stinson. Her husband, Oliver, had known Sam's dad, but he was gone now, too.

After Emma hung up, she turned to him. "What took you so long to get back here?"

"Simon wanted to go get a beer. We got to talking about old stories, and I forgot the time." He decided to ignore the phone conversation he'd just heard.

"I was stuck here with Divina. All that woman could talk about was herself and her big horse farm."

Sam hung his shirt on the back of a chair, ignoring her. "So, you decided on your own again to take on another horse, without talking with me. You seem to be forgetting that we're a team here. We should have discussed it first."

Emma stared at Sam, surprised by his outburst. "That horse needs help, and I know someone who might be qualified to do just that."

Sam sat down on the bed and removed his boots. "And, another thing, your damned uncle was being obstinate about Promise's training - he thinks he's going to ship my horse here!"

"What are you talking about? I thought you planned to do our colt's training–"

"I am!" Sam dropped his jeans and got into bed, crossing his arms across his bare chest. "I've called the airport to have our plane ready early tomorrow. I want to leave here as soon as possible - Jim is waiting for me..."

"But, I hoped we could stay another day or two–" Emma started.

"We're leaving and that's final."

Upset, Emma walked out of the room. She went down the stairs, tears welling in her eyes. She wasn't sure where she was going, she just knew she couldn't talk with Sam right now. She'd never seen him so angry, but she wanted to try to understand him. She knew how forceful her uncle could be when he wanted something - she recognized that same trait in herself.

She saw a light coming from the den. Wiping the tears from her eyes, she turned into the now familiar room. George was sitting in one of the leather chairs, a glass in his hand, as he gazed into the fire.

"I thought I'd find you here," she said, glad that her voice didn't waiver. "I wanted to talk with you."

"Can I get you anything to drink?" he offered, not sure he was ready to hear what she had to say.

"No, I'm fine." She sat on the couch, curling her legs under her.

Quickly, George asked, "What did you think of Divina?"

"She seems like a very nice person," was all Emma was willing to say. She'd seen how smitten her uncle had been, and she didn't want to hurt him.

"We've only just started seeing each other - because of our interest in racing…and our horses. Her stallion was also sired by Koenig."

"I'm sorry that Sam and I must leave tomorrow morning. He has this case he needs to get back for…"

George was about to object, until he saw the sad look on her face. "You will return for the Derby in May, yes?"

"Of course, I wouldn't miss it for the world!" She looked away for a moment, and then said, "Besides, I have to get ready for the arrival of my new Lipizzaners from Austria."

"What was it like, the Spanish Riding School?"

"Oh, it was the most wonderful place. You should've seen the horses perform. They were magical. I met this young woman who took us on a tour of the stables. Someday, I hope she can come visit us."

George was silent for a moment. He took off his glasses and rubbed his eyes. Then, he looked at his niece and almost whispered, "Did you learn anything there - about your father?"

Emma nodded and sighed. "At Piber, I met Rudi Hinteregger, Dad's trainer at the riding school. He said Dad was sad to leave because he loved the school and riding so much. But, he told Rudi that his father had somehow let an obsession lead their family into great debt."

Emma knew that George would understand what that obsession was - the Friedrich painting, named *A Walk at Dusk*. It had sadly been the bane of their family. Her grandfather, her father, and both uncles had fallen under the painting's spell - and, all but one had died. When George wanted to destroy it, she'd decided that she was strong enough to place the painting into the Legion of Honor art museum in San Francisco, where it could no longer hurt anyone.

They sat in silence for a while, watching as the fire grew dim.

"I've been thinking," George sighed heavily, "...about going home - sometime in the future."

"But, this is your home."

"I mean to Essen - in Germany. Where our family began..."

George looked at Emma. "Do you think you might want to join me someday?"

Emma smiled and got up and hugged her uncle. "I'd love to!"

CHAPTER EIGHT

OREGON

As Sam turned their car up the winding road from Newberg, towards Chehalem Mountain, Emma looked over at her husband and sighed, "It's good to be home."

He'd apologized to her on the plane about his outburst at George's, and she had forgiven him. Emma knew how important Koenig's Promise was to him, and knew they could work out anything - as long as they did it with love.

When they drove into their lane, she smiled when she saw her gold and blue sign for RISING SUN STABLES. Her riding school had been her dream after she moved to Oregon six years ago from her parents' home in Indiana. Her best friend, Jennifer Carter, helped her find this property. But, Jennifer and her husband now lived in Montana, and they hardly saw each other.

Emma thought of her new breeding plans and hoped that her father would have been proud. She was itching to get her stables ready for the new Lipizzaners. She'd been cutting back the number of students ever since she'd made her decision. Then, she thought about where to put Lucky Storm, since he had so many issues, but felt that her new friend, Tracy, would be able to help her decide.

Sam parked in front of the large Colonial Revival home. Emma had fallen in love with this house the moment she saw it, since it reminded her of her childhood - the red-brick siding and white trim around the windows always brought her parents to mind. She stepped out of the car and looked with pride at her stables and arena. Gandolf, a tall, white Lipizzan stallion, stood in his outside run next to his stall. He whinnied when he saw her. His sire had been Conversano, her father's horse, who was now also gone.

She noticed Doc White's little black car parked near the stallion's stable. Tracy's truck was also there, with CMC painted on the door. Chehalem Mountain Center was Tracy's therapy clinic, located just on the other side of the mountain from Emma's.

"I wonder why Doc and Tracy are both here?" she said. "I hope nothing is wrong with the horses." Emma knew that Doc was now in his seventies, grooming his son, Ian, to take over his Veterinary clinic near Newberg.

A young man wearing a chambray shirt, jeans, and dusty boots walked out of the larger stable. Shane McKeegan waved. "Hey, you two, welcome back," he called as they stepped from the car. Grinning from ear to ear, Shane's red hair glistened in the sunlight. He ran up to them as a black cat named Shadow followed.

Sam hugged the boy. "Hi, Shane. How did everything go while we were away?"

"No problems. Doc's inside, checking the critters." He ran his fingers through his hair. "I have to say, Mrs. P., that mustang buckskin of yours is a pistol. Tracy's in there now, trying to calm him down."

"I hope he hasn't torn the stable apart," Emma said, laughing. She knew that Shane could handle any horse, but was glad he had help with Flash.

"Good to see you, Shane," Sam said. "Any college plans yet?"

Shane shuffled one boot in the dirt, and then said, "Nope."

Shane worked for Sam as an exerciser on Ele years ago, when he was racing her. When Shane graduated from high school last year, they'd talked about his future, but Shane would just shrug it off. Sam never stopped asking.

"Well, I hope you can stay on for a while," Emma said, scratching Shadow's head. The cat wove her small body around Emma's legs, purring loudly. "The new horses are due to arrive next week, and I can really use your help."

Sam started getting their bags out of the car.

"Can I help you with those?" Shane asked.

"Thanks, but I've got them."

"I'm going to see Doc," Emma said and steered Shane back towards the stable. "Tell me everything that's been going on..."

Shane began filling Emma in on what she'd missed, while Shadow followed. Emma got the cat when she'd bought the house, but she'd noticed that the feline preferred the stable to the house - now that Sam had moved in.

"...and Tracy's helped out a lot, too," Shane said, nodding to her red truck. "Sweet ride, huh? That Ford Highboy will haul anything you hitch to it." Shane opened the stable door and let Emma walk inside.

Emma had been friends with Tracy Newman since they'd met at a horse auction. Tracy created the center nearby and worked with helping abused or handicapped people, using horseback riding as therapy. Sometimes, she helped abused horses, as well. She was like a horse whisperer and could handle almost any animal.

"I want to start classes again in a few days," Emma said to Shane, walking into the coolness of the building, smelling the sweet aroma of hay. "Your dad's okay if I keep you for a while, right?"

"Sure, he'll let me know when he needs me. Oh, by the way, a new student came by yesterday - Nicole Hornsby. I gave her one of your brochures with the prices and everything, like you asked me to." He snorted and added, "She's a jumpy little creature."

"You know I want to cut some of my classes," Emma said.

"I'm sorry, I forgot. She said she'd come back tomorrow to meet you. She seemed pretty excited to get started."

Emma sighed and figured she would deal with the young girl later. Shane stopped at the tack room. She glanced inside the room and saw her father's tack trunk sitting on the floor. Visions of the magnificent white horses performing at the Spanish Riding School popped into her mind.

Smiling, she continued down the aisle, stroking and talking to each of the horses that stood with their heads over their doors. These animals were like children to her, and she'd missed them.

"Gandolf!" Emma said, walking up to the tall Lipizzan stallion. He nickered softly as she stroked his long neck. Her father had given him to her when she was young. She heard the two boarded horses whinny at the other end of the building, looking for attention through the strong, black mesh that she'd installed above the wooden walls of the stalls. It provided good ventilation, but also allowed each horse to see what was going on inside the barn. She thought of a few of the changes she'd decided to do after being in the Imperial Stables.

Just then, her veterinarian, Doc White, stepped out into the aisle from Sonny's stall, a gelding Lipizzaner, sired by Gandolf.

"Emma, my dear!" Doc exclaimed, a bit of a British accent still in his voice, and his gray, curly hair neatly combed. "It is so good to see you. How was your trip?"

She hugged the older man who'd sort of taken over the role of her father since they'd met. "It was unbelievable, Doc. We saw so many wonderful things, including your beloved London."

"Ah, well, I hope you had a warm pint for me while you were there. I miss my old pub in Windsor - the Bel and The Dragon." With a far-away look in his eyes, he continued, "I used to go there with my mates after a rousing game of cricket. It's right near the Thames River...and the Queen's castle."

Shane and Emma laughed, and then she looked across the aisle. Tracy stood inside Flash's stall, holding the reins of the buckskin as he pawed at the ground and nodded his head, neighing loudly in protest. Emma knew he was a handful.

Tracy came out of the stall and closed the door. She ran the back of her hand across her face to push back her long, auburn hair. "Glad you're back, Emma!"

"Hi, Tracy, good to see your helping with this monster," Emma said, then the two women hugged.

"I've had fun these past few weeks, helping Shane and Doc here."

"They're all fit as a fiddle," Doc smiled. "...although, we did have a small mishap with young Flash there." Doc winked at Shane as he walked up to Flash's stall.

"Mishap?" Emma asked, looking between the three people in front of her. "What kind of mishap?"

"Well..." Shane began, then Tracy jumped in. "He was just bored. I thought maybe I could take him over to my stables for a few days to see if I can use him in my work."

"I suggested it," Doc said, "since you will have your new horses arriving, after their quarantine."

"Well, I think that's a marvelous idea!" Emma was surprised she didn't feel more remorse over Flash leaving her stable.

She turned to Tracy. "I'm glad you're here...," Emma began. "My Uncle George has rescued a three-year-old Thoroughbred racehorse in Louisville. He was being abused. I've agreed to have him ship the poor animal here. I was hoping you could help me with him, too."

Tracy nodded, "No problem. Just let me know when he arrives." She looked at Doc and Shane, and then smiled. "Well, I've gotta go. I'll come back tomorrow to get Flash, if that's okay with you, Em."

"Great, I think I'm still circling the planet a bit, so tomorrow is good."

Tracy walked out of the stable.

"Well, I think it is time for me to go back to my clinic and see how Ian is doing," Doc said. "My son seems to be taking everything in stride, just as I knew he would." He looked a little sad for a moment, as he thought of his impending retirement. "Let me know when that young horse arrives, and I will come take a look at him."

"Thank you, Doc, for everything. I appreciate you so much." Emma hugged the older man again; she was thankful she'd found him all those years ago.

****

Back in the house, Sam sat down at the desk in the den and called Jim about the on-going case. He was tired and his shoulders ached from the tension between him and Emma.

"I talked to Simon. I'll fill you in later when we can talk."

"Good," Jim said. "When can you get back to the office?"

"I can be there in the morning. I'm beat right now."

"OK, see you then." Jim hung up.

Then, Sam called his friend, Mike, down in Eugene. He had been the trainer for Sam and his dad, and he was Shane's father.

"Good to hear your voice," Mike said with a bit of southern drawl in his voice. "How was the honeymoon?"

"Great, but I've missed Oregon." Sam stopped for a moment, then added, "How is Promise coming?"

"He's doing fine...lunging in the roundpen with the surcingle, and getting used to the flexible reins adding pressure to his bit. He didn't like it at first, but he's good with it now."

Sam didn't hear Emma walk in the front door just then.

"Sweet–" Sam stopped, remembering George's words and the anger started to rise again. "Mason wants to take over Promise's training when he's two!"

"What? Can he do that?"

"Over my dead body!" Sam stopped to calm his breath. He could hear Mike's sigh of relief over the phone. Then, Sam added, "I have to go into the office in Portland first thing tomorrow to talk to Jim, but I could drive to Eugene as soon as I can get away."

"What's your new young wife going to think about that?"

Sam thought for a moment. "She'll be fine. She's busy with her own horses right now. Besides, we have so much work to do to get Promise ready for racing next year. If that damned George Mason thinks he's going to ship Promise to Kentucky, interfering with my training plans, he's got another thing coming!"

Sam hung up, then looked up and saw Emma leaning against the doorway, her arms crossed in front of her.

"I have to go to the office in the morning," he said.

"I heard. When you see Jim, please tell him that riding classes will start soon. I want to get the kids going again before the new horses arrive. And, I need to talk to Jim about finding a new trainer."

"Mike needs me to come to Eugene to check on Promise, so I thought I'd drive down tomorrow afternoon, if that's okay with you."

"I know," was all Emma said, then she turned and walked up the stairs to unpack.

Later that night, as they were sipping wine in the den, Emma and Sam watched the flames in the river-stone fireplace. The tension between them had subsided. This was her favorite room in the house with the large, blue oval rug on gleaming wooden floors, tall bookshelves, and her desk, where she kept all of her training records. The rocker and red wing-backed chair had come from her parents' house in Indiana. She snuggled up to her husband on the long, leather couch, and looked up at the painting that now hung over the mantle that she'd painted from a photograph of her father and Conversano, performing in an arena in Verden, Germany.

"I can't wait to see how Promise is doing," Sam said excitedly.

"How long will you be in Eugene?"

"I'll be back tomorrow night." He thought for a moment, then said, "I'm sure glad George kept his promise about Ele."

"I always knew he would," Emma said.

"How did you know that?"

"He's like my father."

Sam looked into the roaring fire. His memory of Emma's father was at the Drake Hotel in Chicago years ago, when Sam had kissed Emma before leaving to go into the Navy to fly jets. He was young and didn't fear much, but the anger he saw in Hermann Maseman's face had scared him. Shaking the memory, he pulled Emma to him. "Remember our first night together here? It was just like this."

"Mhm," Emma sighed, leaning back into her husband's chest and felt his heartbeat against her rib cage. "This is right where I was."

They kissed for a few moments, and then Sam softly brushed his lips against her forehead. "Wait here," he said. "I have something for you!" He ran upstairs.

Emma shook her head, then took the dishes to the kitchen. *Well, that's not how I remember it!* she thought.

When they were both back in the den, Sam turned on the radio to a Portland jazz station, then pulled the chair up to the couch and sat in front of Emma. He opened the leather book he'd bought in Paris - a book of poems by *Saint-Exupéry*, a French writer.

"I was glad to see these were translated in English when I found it at that dealer's stand near the Seine River. Did you know this guy was a pioneer in aviation?" He leafed through the pages, then stopped and read sweet words of love.

Emma was transported to the time she and Sam had ridden horses to the hilltop on their property. They had found each other after twelve years had passed.

A woman's husky voice started singing, *The Look of Love*, over the radio. Sam laid the book down, stood and held out his hand to his wife. "Dance with me?"

Emma gladly stepped into Sam's arms as they slowly swayed together, their bodies melting into each other as the words drifted over them. She reached her hand up to his thick hair and ran her fingers through it, then slid her hand down to the back of his neck, grazing her lips softly across his cheek.

Sam pulled her closer into his body and kissed her. When the music finished, he whispered into her ear, "It's time for bed, Mrs. Parker."

CHAPTER NINE

The next day, Sam backed Emma's '67 Buick Gran Sport out of the garage and drove up their lane. It was a stream-lined car, with a black vinyl top and red pinstripe down each side of the gold-colored body. Em bought the Skylark when she arrived in Oregon. Now, she mostly drove their pickup for the riding stables, so Sam got the car.

I love this car, but I've gotta get my own damned truck, he thought.

At the road, he stopped and saw a 'For Sale' sign posted at the ranch across from theirs. He shoved aside the memories that flooded his mind about Joe Remsky, the guy who'd owned the ranch. Sitting there, he made a decision and wrote down the real estate agent's contact information. Then, he turned the car towards Portland.

The view was glorious in the early morning light. Layers of soft clouds hid the tops of the rolling hills. As he drove near the city limits, he could see the tall skyscrapers above the mist. Compared to some of the cities Sam had seen, Portland was a young city, split in two by the Willamette River.

He parked the car and walked into his office on the third floor of the Taylor building. Sally, Sam's secretary, looked up and grinned, pushing her glasses up on her nose. Her blonde hair was shoulder length now.

"Hi, Sally, what have I missed?"

She held out her left hand to show off her rings. "My wedding!"

"You and Bennie tied the knot while I was gone?!"

"We couldn't wait! You and Emma inspired us...," she said,

grinning. "It's about time you got back, though...Jim's been pretty grumpy lately."

Sam looked in the interior office, but didn't see anyone. "Where is he?"

"I'm here," Sam's friend said behind him, walking in. "I just got back from Portland Meadows." The two men walked into the next room. Jim sat down behind the desk, and Sam stood, looking at him.

"You're in my chair." Sam frowned a little.

"Well, it's been mine for a while now," Jim said, staying where he was. He and Sam had learned to fly together at a small airfield near Eugene. They were like brothers.

Sam sat down across from him and asked, "What's been going on?"

"Well, the crew is working on the track now to get rid of hidden ruts, caused by winter freezes. Those holes can do serious damage to horses, even causing them to have to be put down." He looked seriously at his friend, seeing that something was bothering Sam, but decided to keep the conversation light - for now. He chuckled and added, "The track's got a new ambulance. It's a damned black Cadillac hearse!"

"No way!" Sam exclaimed, trying to visualize the lumbering vehicle as it followed a field of horses racing down the track. He saw that Jim looked good, sitting there in this office. Sam realized if he was going to begin racing again, he'd have to do something about this job. "I had a chance to talk with Simon Day," he said. "He's going to check on a farm in Lexington that had a similar case using Lasix and will give us a call here."

"Great, I want to nail this bastard as soon as possible!" Jim said. "I had the track vet take more blood samples today on that second colt, since the first ones came back negative."

"You might want to have Kevin send them to Oregon State's lab in Corvallis. They'll do a broader search, since they have the veterinary school there." Sam looked at his watch and added, "Hey, I have to go to Eugene now...some stuff with mom."

"Is Joanne okay?" Jim asked. Sam's mom was a lot like his own.

"Yeah, but would you mind staying on the job here for a little while longer? I have something I need to do…"

Jim looked at Sam. "Sure, I'm starting to realize how much I missed it. Just let me know if I can help."

Sam nodded. "I'll fly down there, it'll take less time. My plane's at Newberg, and Mom's going to be waiting for me at the ranch."

Jim knew Sam would use the old, beat-up Chevy Impala the two of them kept at the Eugene airport for trips like this. "Give me a call when you get back," he said. "And, tell your mom 'Hi' for me."

Just then, Bennie Morris, Sally's husband walked in and kissed his wife. He was carrying his Pentax, which Sam knew he never went anywhere without. Some of his photos had helped Sam on an important case a few years ago.

"Hey, Bennie," Sam said. "I have a job for you..."

****

Emma sat at the desk in her den, proud of what she'd accomplished at Rising Sun. She rifled through the volume of mail that had accumulated since their trip, separating the bills from the other papers they needed to deal with. She was excited to see there was a letter from Tanja, the young docent at the Spanish Riding School. Quickly, Emma opened and read it. She was glad to see the young girl was contacting her, and felt that they could become great friends - even though they were continents apart.

Then, she picked up the phone and dialed her uncle.

"Hello," the voice on the other end said.

"Uncle George, this is Emma. I wanted to let you know we arrived home yesterday, and to thank you for letting us stay with you - even if it was brief."

"Oh, my dear, it is always good to see you!"

"When will Lucky Storm arrive here? I have my Lipizzaners coming in a few days."

She heard the hesitation in George's voice and knew it was because of their mixed reasons for their quick return to Oregon.

"I had forgotten about their quarantine requirement...." she added.

"The tests Eric ran on him showed that he was shot full of steroids. They'll take a while to wear off, but he seems a little calmer now. I'll have Fred arrange to fly him to you when you are ready. Will that be all right?"

"Perfect. I've talked with my friend, Tracy. She's excited about meeting him."

"That is good. He needs a lot of work, I'm afraid. Now, he is exhibiting outbursts of aggression. I just hope he will not be too much for you."

"No, Tracy knows how to bring these kinds of cases around. I want to help her, and I've seen her do her magic."

There was a pause at the other end, and then George said, "I'm taking Divina with me to the Arkansas Derby race at Oaklawn Park."

Emma now paused, then said, "Don't you think you're getting a little serious with Divina?"

"I'm not sure - yet."

"Just be careful!" Emma said. "I love you."

"I love you, too, *liebchen*." George hung up.

Emma leaned back in her chair, thinking of how glad she was to have her uncle in her life - now that the rest of her family was gone. She looked down at the calendar on her desk. "It can't be!" she said out loud, realizing that she'd missed her period. Usually, they came like clockwork at the first of each month. Then, she shrugged, figuring it was all the stress of traveling. *Everything will return to normal in a few days*, she thought to herself.

With that, Emma got up and walked down to the stables.

Tracy pulled up in her truck, hauling a horse trailer. Emma followed as she drove to the stables.

"Hi, lady," she called as she jumped down from the tall pickup. "I'm here to take Flash back to my center."

"He's ready and waiting," Emma said. "I am so glad you started your new program. I don't know of anyone else doing this type of therapy."

"It seems to be working. I've even been contacted by an friend of mine who was in the Marines, to see if I can help one of his buddies that came back from Vietnam all messed up. I guess the guy doesn't sleep and has major anger issues. Working with these horses has taught me it's all about trust and regaining confidence. I just hope I can help this veteran."

"I'm so proud of you!"

"Thanks, Em...I'm just doing my job."

They watched as Shane took Flash from his stall and led him into Tracy's trailer. They were both surprised how easily he loaded.

"He's probably just happy to be going somewhere," Shane said, laughing, as he closed the trailer door. Then, he went back to his room in the large stables.

"I'll call Peter later today," Emma told Tracy, as they walked to her truck. "I want to see how my new Lipizzaners are doing in quarantine - he's their young handler, from Vienna. He made sure the mare was not in heat before scheduling this - so the horses could travel together."

"Well, now," Tracy said with a smile. "He sounds intriguing. I'll help with hauling them here when they're released. I can rent a special transport van, if you want."

"That would be great! Oh, and by the way, my uncle will be shipping that Thoroughbred here shortly after that - the one I told you about." Emma looked at her friend, "I'd like to keep him here."

"But, my place is set up for guys like him!" Tracy said. "He could be too, huh, disruptive—"

"He can go at the end of the large stable, in Flash's stall, as long as you don't mind working with him here." Emma added, "I want to do this for my uncle."

Tracy thought for a moment. "We'll talk about this later, okay?"

Emma nodded.

"Well, I gotta go." Tracy hugged Emma and then drove off, Flash whinnying loudly from the trailer in protest.

Emma thought of when Flash came to Rising Sun. Her first husband had rescued him when they were rounding up wild mustangs in eastern Oregon. That was when she thought Ted was a good man...until he changed. *Just like his horse*, she thought, hating the black memories the animal always brought up. It was time for him to go.

After Tracy left, Emma was surprised to see a young girl coming down her lane on a bicycle. The girl got off, leaned her bike against the stable and walked up to her. She was a young, thin teenager, with short black hair and was taller than most kids her age. Just by her walk, Emma could see she seemed scrappy and strong-willed - a bit like herself.

"Hi, I'm Nikki Hornsby," the young girl said. "I want to take riding lessons...I came by yesterday."

Emma smiled. "I thought your name is Nicole."

"Yeah, it is, but I prefer Nikki. The grownups hate it."

"Where do you live?" Emma asked, thinking she must be from one of the nearby farms. They were a long ways away from any town.

"In Newberg, on the east side."

"But that's miles from here! And, you rode on your bike?"

"It's the only transportation I have, until I get my license. So, when can I start my lessons?"

Emma thought for a moment, and then said, "I'm sorry, but I'm not taking any new students right now. There's another Dressage training center opening near Sherwood–"

"But, that's too far away!" Nikki exclaimed. "You've got to let me ride here." The young girl looked at Emma with pleading eyes, then added, "I probably won't be in this area very long anyway...I tend to move a lot."

Seeing the girl's disappointed expression, Emma said, "Let me think about it. Would you like to see our horses?"

"Yes, please!"

Emma smiled. She liked the spirit in this young girl. "I have some new Lipizzan horses arriving soon from Austria," she said as she turned towards the stable door.

"Cool!" Nikki followed, looking around her. "I saw that traveling show of those horses perform at our fairgrounds once. That's why I'm here - I want to learn to ride like that."

Emma laughed. "You have a lot to learn, my dear! Let's go inside."

When they were inside the cool stable, Emma noticed that Nikki was not afraid of horses - she reached out and touched Gandolf when his head came out over his stall door, talking to him softly.

As they walked up to Sonny's stall, Emma scratched the horse behind his ears. "Do you have your own horse?" she asked.

"No, I was hoping you'd have one for me," Nikki said and rubbed the horse's neck.

"Sonny is the gentlest gelding we have here. I think he could work for you - if I decide you can take lessons. He is a six-year old Lipizzaner. When they're born, their coat is usually dark - sometimes even black. As they age, their color changes to this brilliant white. I'm sure you two would like each other."

Sonny nickered softly and stood still, letting Nikki get to know him. "Why was he gelded?"

The young white horse was her first success in breeding horses.

However, Sonny's aggressive behavior and low sperm count were inherited from his dam's bloodline, which necessitated his being gelded at an early age. Emma's hopes for him to be one of her stallions were lost. "He wasn't suitable for breeding," was all she said.

Just then, Shane came out of his room - the one next to the tack room. Emma looked at Nikki as she dropped her hands. She seemed to change in front of him - fear showing in her eyes.

"Hi, Shane," Emma said. "This is Nikki, the new student you told me about yesterday."

"You're the one I talked to," Nikki said.

"Yep, in the flesh." Shane had his hands tucked into his jeans pockets, and rocked back and forth on the heels of his boots. "Are you going to ride Sonny? He's the best training horse here. He hasn't bucked anyone off yet."

"I'm not sure..." The young girl took a few steps away from Shane, towards Sonny's stall door.

"Nikki," Emma asked. "How did you hear about my riding school?"

"Sarah Burkley, a...a girl I knew." Nikki didn't mention how well she'd known Sarah.

"Yes, I remember her. She took lessons here, until she moved."

"I really miss her," Nikki said with a sigh, stroking Sonny.

"Have you ever ridden a horse before?" Emma asked.

"Yes, lots of times, both Western and English. One of my previous foster parents, over by Wilsonville, had horses and taught me the basics of Dressage. But, that was two years ago."

"It's a little like riding a bike," Shane said with a laugh. "Once you've done it, you never forget."

Nikki turned to Emma and asked, "So, will you teach me?"

Emma smiled. "All right, then, as long as your parents agree to prices listed on the brochure Shane gave you, and they sign the release form. I hold two classes a week - on Tuesdays and Thursdays after school."

"I live with new foster parents. Their name is Mitchell - Maria and Walter." She looked away and said, "That's why I don't stay anywhere very long."

Emma's heart skipped a beat. Then, she said, "Well, before we can do anything, you'll need to have both of them take care of that."

"I'll see what I can do." Nikki looked again at Shane, and then said, "I gotta go."

"I'll give you a ride home–" Emma started.

"No, I'm good. See you later." Nikki ran out of the stable and rode off on her bike.

****

The old Eugene ranch house was built by Sam's grandfather - and not much had changed since then. He walked into the kitchen and found his mom was taking some dishes from the cupboard and placing them in a box. He was surprised to see his dad's white Stetson lying on the table.

"Hi, Mom," he said.

Joanna Parker turned and hugged her son. "Sam! How was your trip?"

"It was wonderful...unforgettable! You should see Austria - I think it was my favorite. The hills reminded me of Oregon."

"Look at you with that beard! You haven't grown one since–" She didn't finish because they both knew it was when Sam had lost his mare in a California Claiming Race. "Any plans for grandkids in my future?" she asked to change the subject.

"Oh, Mom, I don't know how I feel about kids..."

Joanna knew about Sam's traumatic experiences in Vietnam involving children and the scars they'd left behind. "I do know...Harold told me."

"Dad shouldn't have done that," Sam said in a soft voice. "I only shared that with him."

"And, I'm your mother and have a right to know! When life shatters something precious in our hearts, we just have to keep going."

Sam looked at his mom. He could see that she had made peace with her own loss. Sam had been young when his little sister died shortly after she was born. He hoped that someday he would find that same peace.

"Nevertheless, I'm glad you're here," she said, taking a deep breath. "I really needed to talk to you. Since your father's death...I've decided to start a new chapter in my life."

"What do you mean?"

"Well, for one thing, your father wanted you to have his hat."

Sam picked up the Stetson and put it on. "He wore this hat to every race track," he said, remembering how proud he was to go with his dad when he was racing his horses. Sam took off the hat, laid it back on the table - upside down. He knew the 'golden rule' of how to lay a Stetson on any surface to keep the brim's shape.

"I know," Joanna said. "He always looked so handsome in it - and so do you." She kissed her son on the cheek. "Also, he'd always said he wanted you to take the pickup."

"You're kidding? The '64 Chevy K10? Dad used to call it 'Big Green'!"

"Yes," she laughed, handing him the keys. "That monster takes up too much space in the garage."

"I've always loved that truck," Sam said, looking down at the worn, leather Chevrolet key fob. The silver medallion brought back memories of Sam and his dad riding together in that truck to the local airstrip, where Sam was taking flying lessons. "Thanks, Mom, I'll have to get it later, if that's okay." He pocketed the fob, then saw the look on his mom's face, sat down at the table and waited.

"No worries..." She pulled down a few more plates. "I have more news..." Now she turned back to her son. "I found a little apartment in town - near my friends. I moved there last month-"

"What?! Mom, why would you do that while I was away - without talking to me first?" Sam's need to protect his mom had grown stronger now that she was alone.

"It was my decision, not yours!" She sat down next to her son. "You know how much I hate driving into town every time I want to go shopping. And, I love that gallery at the university - their Asian art collection." Joanna placed her hand on Sam's. "Someday, I want to go to Asia."

"Asia? Where did that come from?"

"I've always wanted to travel. But, this place kept us here..." She looked out the window for a moment. "I've been thinking of selling the ranch, so I can buy a townhouse-"

"Sell the ranch?" Sam yelled as he jumped to his feet. "But, Granddad built it! We have so many memories wrapped up in this place."

"I know, but it's what I need to do - unless...you want it."

Sam was devastated. He thought for a moment. "God, I don't know...There's Emma's place...Promise's training - and, where would

Mike go? Emma's got these new horses now...they cost a bundle!"

Joanna watched her son. It broke her heart to see him like this, but she knew she had to - to get him to move on, as well. "I feel that you've changed with your new job up there - and Emma's plans for her horse farm—"

"It's Emma's dream." Sam stood, quiet for a moment, shaking his head.

"What about your dream, Sam? What happened to your passion for racing? When you were younger, you couldn't wait to be around racehorses! Ever since you lost Ele—"

"That was then, but Koenig's Promise will get me back there. I just don't know how...now. What will I do if you sell, Mom?"

She smiled and hugged him. "I'm sure you'll think of something!" She put on her jacket and picked up her purse and box of plates. "I'm going back to town...a friend wants to take me to the Farmer's Market. I love you!"

Sam walked to the stable, where he'd spent so much time as a kid. It was as if he was looking at it for the last time. He kicked a rock in the footpath, sending it into the river flowing nearby. He knew there was no way he could buy the ranch. *Damn*, he thought, *I'm going to miss this place!*

Mike McKeegan was grooming Sam's mare, Classy Elegance. Sam's parents had given Ele to him after he'd returned from Vietnam, and Mike helped train her for racing, but that seemed a lifetime ago now.

"Sam!" the older man said and dropped the brush into a bucket. "Good to see you!"

"Hi, Mike...you've gotten grayer." Both men hugged.

"And, wiser!" Mike's voice still had a southern drawl from his days in Kentucky.

"Did your mom tell you about the pickup?"

"Yes," Sam said, fingering the key fob in his pocket. "I'm going to need to work out a way to get it back up to Rising Sun."

"I'm sure we can figure something out with Shane one of these days. How soon do you want it?"

"I'll think about it and let you know." Sam walked up to the six-year-old chestnut mare and began stroking her. "Hey, Ele, how've you been?" The horse nickered softly and turned her head towards

Sam.

"She's doing just fine, and she's beginning to get her track legs back."

"Good, I want her to keep racing as long as she's fit. I know how much she loves it."

A sharp whinny came from a stall down the aisle. Koenig's Promise looked out over his door, the white star and blaze down his forehead shone brightly against his dark chestnut coat - the same auburn shade as his dam. When he'd first seen this colt in the breeding stall with his dam, Sam had fallen in love.

"Well, it looks like someone else missed you, Sam."

Sam laughed and walked to the young colt with the large brown eyes. He held out his hand to the horse's soft muzzle. "I've got great plans for you, young man...as long as I can figure out what I'm going to do next."

"So, you're mom told you," Mike said as he put Ele back in her stall.

"Yep, I can't believe it!"

"Do you think you'll be able to keep the ranch?"

"I doubt it. It's just so far from Rising Sun, and I don't want to interrupt Promise's training." Sam stopped for a moment and looked at the man he'd known since he was twelve.

Mike placed his arm around Sam's shoulder and said with a glint in his eye, "Till you iron it all out, son, let me tell you how Promise is coming. I think he's ready to start getting used to the saddle and girth. After that, we're going to need a rider."

Sam nodded and continued rubbing the animal's neck.

"I miss Shane down here," Mike said.

"Well, maybe we can work something out..."

Later, Sam walked back into the ranch house. He went from room to room, each full of different memories. Then, he heard a familiar chime, and he walked over to the eight-foot clock that his grandfather had made from scratch - a hobby he'd loved. The brass pendulum, visible through the glass door, swayed back and forth. Sam opened the door and pulled the weight to wind the mechanism. On a table nearby stood a wooden lamp Sam's father had carved out of an old oak tree that had fallen on the property. He sat down on the couch before the stone fireplace and wept for the loss of his dad...and now, possibly his past.

After a while, he walked into his old bedroom. Shelves hung on one wall, with trophies he'd won from baseball, model airplanes he'd built as a kid, and his ball cap with the Scorpion insignia for his squadron at Marana Air Base where he'd learned to fly jets. Finally, he realized that his life was no longer anchored to this place, but that he'd always have his memories wherever he was. He packed a box of keepsakes that he wanted, adding an old pair of boots he used to wear when he raced Ele.

On his way outside, he stopped in the kitchen and put on the Stetson. Then he said goodbye to Mike and left for home.

****

It was getting dark when Sam flew his plane into the Newberg airport and taxied to the hangar. A mechanic came out of the office, followed by a fat, fluffy tabby cat with long, white whiskers named 'Wendell.'

Sam placed his Stetson on his head, picked up the box and stepped out of his Shrike Commander aircraft, which he'd purchased during his job at the Racing Bureau in Baltimore. With one shoulder, he pushed the door shut.

"Hi, Smitty," he said to the mechanic. They'd been friends since he started keeping his plane at the small airport. Sam reached down and scratched Wendell's head, as the cat purred and rubbed against his pants leg, leaving long yellow fur on his black trousers. Sam quickly took his hand away, knowing that Wendell liked to bite and would never let go. With a wink and a loud meow, the cat sauntered off in search of someone else to scratch him.

"How was your mother?" Smitty asked, helping Sam get his plane into the hangar.

"She's fine...making a lot of changes." Sam didn't want to go into details about the chaos in his life right now.

"What've you got there?" Smitty asked, pointing to the box under Sam's arm. He'd seen the ball cap with the Marana Air Base name on top of the boots and trophies.

"Just some stuff from the old homestead."

"You were in Nam, right?"

"Yeah, I was stationed at Da Nang Air Base." Sam looked at

Smitty's hat, seeing that he'd served at Bien Hoa Air Force Base. He also saw the two gold stars, indicating that he'd served two different times in the same conflict. They'd never talked about their experiences overseas before. Sam set the box on a chair near the office door and asked, "When were you there?"

"Mid-sixties...I don't talk about it much. But, since you were..."

Sam nodded and waited, knowing how important it was to have someone understand.

Smitty leaned against a small Piper, pulled out a rag from his back pocket and wiped his greasy hands. "My personal service was nothing more than being in the wrong place at the wrong time - on the receiving end of our base being fired upon with over four hundred rounds of rockets, mortars, and small arms." He paused for a moment, then added, "I did what I had to do."

"Bien Hoa - they dropped Agent Orange from that base, didn't they?"

"Yep. They called it 'Operation Ranch Hand.' Lucky for me, I was a mechanic that worked mostly on the nose of those C-123s and avoided getting too close to that stuff." He shook his head, his eyes became sad. "Many guys weren't so lucky. I hated those damned barrels with the orange stripe in the middle - that's how that crap got its name."

Sam remained silent. Then, he was surprised to hear Smitty chuckle, rubbing the stubble on his chin.

"I used to be a hard sleeper - almost slept right through one of those attacks at the base. When I woke up, I hit my head on the rail of the bunk above me and knocked myself out for a bit. Eventually, I came to, grabbed my gun - no pants mind you - and ran outside." He was quiet for a bit, then added, "Now, anything wakes me up."

Wendell, the cat, came up and wound his body around Sam's leg. "Well, I'd better head home." He smiled and shook Smitty's hand. "Thanks for sharing. Maybe we can talk some more another time?"

"Sure thing." Smitty took his hat off, straightened his red hair and put it back on.

"See you next time." Sam set the box on the backseat of his car. Then, he got in, gently laid the Stetson on the seat next to him, and drove away up the mountain.

His thoughts jumped back to some of the missions he'd flown during that time in his life. He was first sent to Clark Air Force Base in the Philippines, then Vietnam. Some of those missions had left a deep hole inside of him, where they waited to surface when he least expected them. *We never forget*, he thought.

As the car came around the last hairpin turn, Sam saw Rising Sun Stables ahead. Then, he saw the sign in front of Joe's property again and decided to turn in. "No harm in looking around," he said to himself.

He remembered one time when he flew with Emma over both properties. Now, he realized that was when the need to get back into racing had grabbed him. Seeing that track in the woods behind Joe's barns had created the itch.

He got out of the car and walked around the outside of the locked house. Through a few windows, he could see that it was still furnished. Then, he walked to the largest barn, but he knew what was inside. Memories of that fateful night came flooding back when he almost lost Emma.

Suddenly, Sam couldn't breathe. On his missions in Nam, he was always in a plane. It was very different to fire on the enemy or drop a bomb from the air. But, shooting Joe point blank was something he'd never forget.

He started walking down through the woods to shake it off, then he came to the oval track. Joe had it built a few years ago to continue Koenig's Wonder's training, after the colt was stolen.

Sam sat down on a large stump next to the railing, his head in his hands. Then, his mom's words circled in his mind. '*What about your dream?*' she'd asked.

The full moon overhead made every white post visible, as he looked at the track in front of him. Now, he realized he'd allowed his own desires to take a back seat to Emma's ambitions for her place. *It is her horse farm*, he thought now. *Everything there is for her dream - not mine!*

Excited, Sam got up, climbed through the railing and started to pace around the dirt track. A few deer stood at the far turn. *That's not going to work!* he thought, realizing he was going to need a six-foot fence. Finding a herd of deer on the track while galloping a horse would be a disaster. "Hey!" he hollered and the deer scampered into the woods. Sam began to run, starting to see his silent dream coming alive again. He thought of when he first met George at Churchill

Downs, when he told Sam to keep his dream alive.

Sam yelled into the night, "And, that's exactly what I'm going to do!"

****

Emma was sitting at her desk in the den, working on a training plan for Nikki, when Sam came in, carrying a box and wearing the Stetson.

"How was your–" she stopped when she looked at her husband. "Wow, nice look on you, cowboy - that hat and beard."

"Thanks," he said, hugging her with one arm, jostling the box to one side. He leaned in and kissed her without removing the hat. "Mom gave me Dad's hat, and his old Chevy truck. I'll have to see when I can get the truck up here..." Sam set the box down on a side table, laid the hat next to it, then went over to the fireplace and poked the logs to get more flames. "Also, she's moved to an apartment in Eugene."

"Really?" Emma turned in her seat.

"And, now, she's thinking of selling the ranch so she can buy a place in town. I can't believe it - it's been in our family for generations!"

Emma walked up behind Sam and hugged him. She thought for a moment, and then said, "Well, I guess I can understand. That's how I felt after my mom and dad were gone–"

"You have no idea!" Sam snapped, stepping away from her. "This is not the same thing. My mom's not gone - she's just moved out!" Sam paced in front of the fireplace. He stopped and looked at Emma. "She asked me if I wanted to buy it."

"Oh, god, Sam. I just don't think we can afford it!"

Sam ran his fingers across his beard and continued pacing. "I don't know what I'm going to do about Mike and the horses. There's no way in hell they can come to your stables...And, now, I can't be there. It's too damned far for me to go to continue Promise's training." He stopped again and stared into the fire.

Emma stepped back, surprised at Sam's outburst. Silently, she now thought that maybe it would be best if her uncle did the horse training. "I'm sure we will think of something," Emma said, walking up to him again. "Maybe we could build another barn–"

"There's a world of difference between Dressage and racing," Sam said, turning to face Emma. "It takes more than just a barn to make a racing operation." He went to the box he'd brought back with him and began taking things out of it. "Never mind. I'll figure it out."

Emma watched him. He seemed to calm down as he took some pictures out and laid them on the table. There were a few of his mother, father and grandfather together in front of their barn. There was another one of Sam at a young age with his dad at a race track, his dad standing tall in his boots, jeans, white shirt and hat. Now, she understood about the hat - and the change in Sam's appearance.

Then, she saw a photo of Sam in his uniform with three Asian children, smiling in front of a Jeep. She asked, "When was this taken?"

Sam looked at the photo, then sat down on the couch and stared at the image for a moment. "We were part of Operation Rolling Thunder, flying F-105 Thunderchiefs. This was when I was in a small village outside of Saigon. Our troop started an orphanage there at a monastery."

"How wonderful!" Emma sighed, sitting next to him. "I'm so proud of you."

"There were so many kids orphaned in that country. We'd spend hours there when off duty. Later, we learned that some had American dads, who were killed in action."

A shadow came over his face. "One day, after returning to base, the guard at the gate yelled for us to get out of our Jeep. He'd seen a wire hanging down from the engine. The gate team checked the vehicle and there was a bomb under the engine compartment that was to have gone off when we started the Jeep...but a trip wire had fallen off and it didn't ignite. We were lucky, but that was when I realized that someone at the orphanage had placed it there. We never found out who did it, but it could easily have been one of the kids! That was the reality over there."

Emma remained silent, watching the muscles in Sam's jaw work as he remembered that time in his life. She knew there was no way she could ever imagine what he had gone through and was thankful that he'd survived. She started to understand this could possibly be one of the reasons he was uncertain about having kids of their own. She took him in her arms and held him close.

CHAPTER TEN

KENTUCKY

Koenig's Spirit had rider up and was walking onto the track at Churchill Downs for his early morning workout. He was being prepped for the upcoming Arkansas Derby. A man watched from the bleachers in the grandstand.

George and Fred stood at the railing, as their new exercise rider, Luke Tanner, cantered their horse alongside his exercise pony. The two horses jogged side by side until they came to the backstretch. Then, Luke gave his horse full rein. Spirit shot out in front of the other horse as he breezed the final stretch. Fred timed him with his stop watch.

"He's running easy and looks relaxed," George said proudly.

"Yes," Fred agreed, showing George the number on the watch. "Luke's been taking notes from Stan and it shows."

"Hello, gentlemen," Divina said from behind George. "I was watching your boy today. He looks really fit."

"Well, Divina," George said, turning to see the beautiful woman he'd been spending time with lately. Her yellow dress had a deep V-neck that showed off the tops of her lovely breasts. He cleared his throat and asked, "Are you exercising Mr. Divinity, as well?"

"No, Raul will bring him later. I called your home and learned that you were here, so I came to see if you would join me for breakfast at my country club." She looked quickly at Fred, smiled and added, "When you are finished here, of course. I have my car."

Fred looked away down the track. He didn't like to see her distracting George from their horse's training and wondered if she didn't have an ulterior motive.

"I would like that," George exclaimed. He nodded to Fred and the pair walked away.

Luke jogged Spirit back to where Fred waited. "Did you see him?" the young man asked, patting the tall horse's neck. "He was on fire!"

"Yes, he did four furlongs in a little over fifty."

"Awesome! Where's the boss going?" Luke asked as he watched the couple.

"To breakfast," Fred said sharply, then started walking towards the shedrow. Luke and Spirit trailed behind.

The man in the grandstand stood up and followed George and Divina.

****

As Divina drove her Mercedes to the front of Lyndon Hall at the Hurstbourne Country Club, a valet ran out to meet them and opened her door. "Hi, Ms. Gallano," the young man said, smiling.

"Hello, Jimmy," she said, handing him the keys and a tip.

George got out of the car and looked up at the large, three-story Gothic building. The red brick stood out against the black, wrought-iron railings and pillars. He knew this hall had been a part of Louisville's historic past since the 1800s. He saw the putting green nearby and said, "I didn't know you play golf."

"I don't, darling. Father became a fan when the course opened in the 60's. I just kept the membership up, because I love the social scene." Divina hooked one arm in his and they walked up the staircase to the entrance. "I'll bring you here next month before the Kentucky Derby. They have a marvelous Brunch, with the tables covered in different colors - like jockey silks. It's very entertaining."

George stopped when they entered the open hall, impressed by the black and white marble tile flooring, and a white spiral staircase that led up to the fourteen-foot-high ceiling. The Old English furnishings reeked of Southern elegance.

"Don't you just love this place?" she cooed and then led George to a dining room that looked out over the golf course. "Did you know that William Lynn, the first owner, was one of the founders of Louisville? It was named after King Louis XVI."

George was surprised to see the room was already half full by some of Louisville's elite crowd. Divina waved to a few people, then leaned in towards him, her dress plunging even more, and whispered, "There used to be Peacocks running wild here." She snickered and added, looking at a few elaborately dressed women, "some still are!"

The couple was ushered to a table by the bank of windows; the aroma of freshly baked bread filled the air. George realized he was famished. After they were served coffee and placed their order, he asked, "How is Mr. Divinity doing? Have you heard about his test results after the last race?"

Divina smiled sweetly, "Yes, Simon called and they were clear of any drugs! Isn't that wonderful? This means we will be going to the Arkansas Derby together." She laid her hand on George's.

Hesitantly, he took his hand away and picked up his cup. Sipping the sharp, dark coffee eased his dry throat. George didn't understand why he liked being in her company, yet still became nervous when she touched him.

OREGON

Emma lay curled in Sam's arms as the rising sun shone through their bedroom window. She watched the soft light creep across the walls of the room, then onto the Battenberg lace duvet at their feet. She stretched and said, "Good morning, Sam. It's another beautiful day in paradise."

Her father had used those same words numerous times to celebrate the joy of each new day. She liked to continue the tradition.

Sam opened his eyes, and then pulled Emma back to spoon against him. "What a marvelous way to start the day," he sighed.

She loved the feel of his warm body against hers and began stroking the long muscles down his arm, wishing they could stay like this forever. His fingers began caressing her skin under her silky camisole, one that he'd bought her in a little Paris shop on *Rue des Francs Bourgeois*. She pressed her body against his hand, his touch awakening her desire. Slowly, she turned to him and kissed his soft lips, moaning as he pulled her closer to him...

After they lay spent in each other's arms, Sam sat up and rubbed his beard. He was glad the hair was longer now, so it didn't scratch Emma's soft skin. "Why don't I go down and start breakfast while you shower?"

"What a lovely idea," she purred. As she watched him dress, she looked at the clock and yelled, "I've got to get ready!" She jumped up and grabbed some clothes. "Tracy's picking me up, so we can get Peter and my new horses. I can hardly wait!"

"This young man sounds like he's really dedicated to his job. I'm sorry I didn't get to meet him at Piber Stud." Sam finished getting dressed.

As soon as he left the bedroom, Emma ran to the bathroom. She'd felt slightly nauseous after their love making, but had held it at bay until he was gone. Throwing up again, she was worried that she had caught a bug, or worse yet - food poisoning. She couldn't be sick now, there was too much to do! She quickly showered, then dressed in jeans and a shirt.

In the kitchen, they sat across from each other.

"You're only having toast and coffee?" Sam asked. "Usually you're ready to eat a cow for breakfast."

"I'm good. I just think I might have picked up a twenty-four-hour bug. I'm sure it'll be gone by tomorrow."

Emma took her plate and cup to the sink. "I have a new student coming later this week - Nikki Hornsby."

Just then, the doorbell rang. Sam went to answer it and returned to the kitchen. "There's a lady and kid here. Were you expecting anyone this early?"

"No," Emma said, and then went to the front door.

"Nikki, why are you here so early?"

The older woman with Nikki stepped in front of the young girl. "I am Maria Mitchell, Nicole's foster mother. She tells me she wants to learn to ride horses here, is that correct?"

"Yes," Emma said, stepping back a little. "Please, come inside." She led the way to the den.

"Nicole said she wants private lessons," Maria said, pulling out the brochure. "But, I think they're very expensive. I'm not sure she needs private—"

"Maria…" Nikki said, her young face full of distress. "I wanted to talk to Emma about that."

Emma saw the sharp look Maria gave Nikki, which made the young girl cower. "Maybe we can work something out," she said in a soft voice to ease the tension. "Nikki…Nicole can be what is called a 'working student,' getting her private lessons and helping in the barn to work off some of her tuition." She wrote down an adjusted amount on a piece of paper and handed it to Maria.

"Oh, that would be wonderful!" Nikki sighed.

"I'm not sure…"

"Oh, please, Maria?" Nikki begged.

Maria thought for a moment, looking at the paper. "What will she have to do?"

"She can clean the stables and tack, for one–"

"But, that's menial work."

"It's what all the kids do…" Nikki sighed.

"Very well, I have the paperwork Nicole brought for me to sign," Maria said, digging in her purse.

"The release form must also be signed by her foster father–" Emma began.

"Walter is a salesman," Maria yelled, then calmed herself, looking around. "He's out of town a lot on business. I'll get him to sign it next time he's back." Maria picked up her purse and stood. "When do you start classes?"

"Thursday afternoon, around three-thirty." Emma saw both Maria and Nikki nod.

"I'll have her and the paperwork back then. Come on Nicole." The two left.

When Emma turned, Sam was leaning against the kitchen door. His arms were crossed over his chest. "That mother's a piece of work!"

"I know, my skin was crawling just talking to her. Poor Nikki!" Emma hugged Sam.

"Come on," Sam said, "we'd better get the stalls ready for those horses before Tracy gets here."

Once they were down by the stables, Emma told Shane, "Peter Norbert is arriving with the horses, so you won't need to come with us. He will be their handler here, as long as his Visa is good." She could see the hurt in the young boy's eyes. "I'm sorry, Shane, I should have told you earlier, but we got so busy since we returned. I'm sure we'll work something out."

"It's okay, Mrs. P.," Shane said, "I understand - these animals are very expensive. I'm sure this guy knows what they'll need..." Shane walked back into the stable.

Just then, Tracy pulled up with the horse van.

"Hi, Em, what a big day for you!" her friend said.

"Yes, I'm so excited!"

"Hi, Sam."

"Hey, Tracy," Sam said. He kissed Emma and said, "You'd better get going."

Emma climbed into the van and they drove off.

****

Later, Sam sat in the den, making his own plans. He decided to call his friend in Eugene to share his new idea.

"Are you going to buy this place?" Mike asked, referring to Sam's parents' property.

"I don't see how I can - it has over two-hundred acres."

"I may know a guy..."

"Keep me posted." Sam looked down at the notepad. "Hey, Mike, I've been thinking...I'll need a jockey, if I'm going to start racing. And, I want to get Ele ready for some upcoming races in California," Sam said. Now, he looked at Emma's calendar on the desk. "It looks like it's going to get crowded around here soon. Emma has a handler from Austria coming today with the Lipizzaners."

"It sounds like she's really gearing up for her breeding program now." Mike didn't say anything for a moment, and added, "What about Shane for your jockey? He rode for Harold...after you left."

Sam grinned. He was hoping Mike would say that. "I think he'd be perfect!"

Doc's black Morris Minor drove down their lane to the stables. In the past, Doc had been Sam's dad's vet. He'd moved his veterinary clinic to Chehalem Mountain and now worked for Emma. Sam thought, *It is interesting, how some people in your life sometimes circle around again.*

"Something's come up. I'll talk to you later," Sam said into the phone. He hung up and followed the small car to the stable.

Doc and Shane were standing outside of the tack room. "Hi, Doc," Sam said. "What brings you here today?"

"Hello, Sam. I told Emma I would be here when the new horses arrive." A young man walked out of one of the stalls and smiled at Sam. "Ah, you remember my son, Ian? He is going to be taking over my practice one day."

"Yes," Sam said, shaking Ian's hand. "Your dad and I have been friends for years." He was taller than his dad now, but he had that same curly hair.

"Isn't this exciting?" Doc said, rubbing his hands together. "I remember when Radcliffe, my Cleveland Bay, arrived here from England. He stood fourteen hands tall and was of the oldest horse breed in the County of York. They were bred for harness, you know, but over the years, were crossbred with Thoroughbreds. Sadly, he is no longer with us…"

Sam and Shane looked at each other and smiled, while Ian rolled his eyes in silence. They all knew that recently, when Doc started on one of his walks down memory lane, you just stood there and listened. That was part of his charm.

"Sam, how is Classy Elegance? Is she still at your father's ranch in Eugene? I've missed seeing her."

"Yes, Doc, she's doing well. Mike is getting her ready to race again and she's happy - she no longer weaves in her stall." Sam thought back to when Doc had told him that his mare did that when she was bored.

"Wonderful!" The older man looked at Sam for a moment. "Does this mean that you're going to start training horses again?"

Sam took a deep breath. He'd only been talking seriously about this with a few friends and wasn't sure how much to share - until he talked with Emma. "Don't know," was all he said.

When Gandolf whinnied, Doc said to Ian, "Let me introduce you to Emma's beautiful stallion." The two men walked down to the horse's stall.

While the older man and his son were occupied, Sam pulled Shane into the tack room. Softly, he said, "I just talked to your dad. How would you like to be my jockey?"

"What?!" Shane exclaimed.

"Shhh, keep your voice down. I don't want anyone else to know just yet." He looked around the door and saw Doc and Ian were now at Sonny's stall. "I'm going to take Ele to the track again and I need your help."

"You bet!" Shane said excitedly. "This work here has been good, but we both know it's all going to change soon. When do we start?"

"Sooner than you think!" Sam turned, then looked at Shane again. "Let's keep this between us for now. You can say your dad needs you in Eugene or something, if Emma asks - which is true."

"Sure thing. I'd better get those stalls ready."

It was about an hour later when the horse van pulled up outside. The four men walked out of the stable.

"They're here!" Emma exclaimed as she and a young man jumped down from the van. "Sam, this is Peter Norbert."

Sam shook his hand. "Welcome." Sam introduced Doc and his son.

"*Hallo*, it is very nice to meet you," Peter said, nodding to each man.

Emma pulled on Shane's sleeve to get him to move forward. "And, this is Shane. He's been taking care of the place while we were traveling."

Peter and Shane nodded to each other. Sam couldn't tell if there was some friction between them, but since Shane would be leaving soon, it really didn't matter. Sam looked at the young man with sandy hair and a high forehead. He seemed pleasant. Sam noticed that Tracy seemed to like him, since she smiled a lot more when she walked towards him.

All watched as Peter immediately went to the back of the large vehicle. He dropped the ramp and opened the doors. The two white horses stood side-by-side.

"Aren't they beautiful?" Tracy exclaimed. "I've seen fantastic horses in my life, but nothing compares to these two."

"Wow!" Shane exclaimed as Peter unloaded the mare first, slowly backing her out...her legs, tail and head were wrapped for protection. The stallion whinnied to her and became agitated. He began weaving and kicking, shaking the van.

"Whoa, Neo," Peter said, handing the mare's lead over to

Emma.

He slowly walked into the trailer, running his hand gently along the large animal's back and side. "Calm down now." He waited until the horse had quieted, then asked him to back out.

Once the two horses were unloaded, Peter looked around and said, "They will need to be walked for a while, after I have removed their pads. Then, they will want water and feed."

"I'll help you," Shane offered.

Peter nodded, and then looked at Emma "Which stable are they going to?"

"Calma is in the mare and foal stable over there," Emma said, pointing to the new stable. "Shane, you can take care of her. Peter, Neo will go over there, with the stallions and geldings."

Peter smiled and led the horse towards a grassy area near the larger stable.

Doc said, "Let me help you, young man. I want to hear all about your trip." They walked away, with Ian following.

Just before Shane took the mare, Emma said, "I'm not sure where Peter will stay yet."

"He can have the tack room tomorrow," Shane said, looking a little guiltily at Sam. "My dad wants me back in Eugene."

Emma stared at Shane for a moment. In the awkward silence, the mare became agitated. "Here," Tracy said, taking the mare's lead, "let me help you get this lady settled in." Tracy led the mare towards her stable.

"Well, if that's what you want to do, Shane," Emma finally said. "I'm going to miss you around here." She looked at Sam and said, "I guess Peter can stay in our downstairs guest room for tonight."

****

That night, Sam and Emma were in the den, sitting on the couch before the fire. Emma had her feet on Sam's lap.

"I can't believe Shane's going to be leaving." Emma sighed, leaning back on the pillow against the couch's arm. It had been a long, exhilarating day. "He's been a big help here."

"His dad needs him now," Sam said, looking into the flames. He wanted to tell Emma the truth, but instead, he said, "This would be a great opportunity for me to get Dad's truck - I could take Shane to

Eugene in our Skylark, then bring the truck back."

"How will we get our car back?"

"I'll think of something..." Sam began rubbing Emma's feet. He'd already started making his plans.

"Isn't Peter wonderful? He's so knowledgeable with the horses."

"Where is he now?"

"With the horses. He wanted to check once again to make sure they have everything they need." Emma sat up and curled her feet under her. "Uncle George's Thoroughbred should be arriving in a few days. Tracy will pick him up at the airport for me." She paused, and then added, "I want to stable him here and help Tracy with his recovery."

"Are you sure you aren't taking on too much?"

"No, I can handle this. Besides, Uncle George asked me."

Sam got up and stirred the dying fire. He turned and stood with his back to the warmth. "Did you see that Joe's ranch is for sale?"

"Yes...I saw the sign," Emma said, pulling her knees up to her chest. Sam didn't know about her nightmares about that place.

"It's a great location for a Thoroughbred racing operation..."

Emma was quiet for a moment. Then she said, "What about Uncle George's offer to handle Promise's training? Maybe that's the answer, if your mom sells the ranch–"

"What're you talking about?" Sam yelled angrily, his hands on his hips. "There's no way in hell I'm letting George train my horse."

Emma stared at him, unsure if she should say anything more. Sam turned and walked out of the house. After a moment, she could hear the car's engine start and him driving away. She'd never seen him so angry before.

CHAPTER ELEVEN

The following week, Emma walked out of their bathroom with a bottle of antacids in her hand. She was surprised she was still puking, but glad that Sam had left earlier for work. She didn't like him seeing her being so sick. His anger had started to simmer down, but she could tell there was still a rift going on between them. Her classes were starting again and she needed all the energy she could muster. *Maybe he's right*, she thought. *Maybe I need more help*. She looked in the mirror and shrugged, realizing it wasn't the first time she knew she was in over her head.

She got dressed, pocketing the bottle of pills, and walked down to the kitchen to make coffee.

While the coffee was brewing, there was a knock on the door. "Hello," Tracy called out. "Emma?"

"In the kitchen," Emma said as she watched the dark liquid drip into the glass pot. She looked at her friend as she entered the room. "Aren't you all dressed up today? Is that a new blouse?"

Tracy rolled her eyes. "I just wanted to look nice for–"

"Peter?" Emma laughed, taking two mugs from the cupboard. "I've seen you two connecting. I think he likes you."

"He's so cute...and shy. And, I like the way he handles those horses. You can tell he loves being with them."

"Well, I'm glad you've finally gotten out of those dusty jeans and started fixing up your hair. You spend too much time around your animals, and I can't imagine a nicer fellow for you."

"We'll see..." Tracy poured them coffee and sat at the table.

"My Uncle George is starting to date a woman in Kentucky," Emma shared. "I'm not sure I like her - for him. There's something about her..."

"I hope you aren't starting a match-making business!"

Emma ignored her and said, "He's taking her to the Arkansas race this weekend."

"I'm sure he knows what he's doing. His Thoroughbred is arriving here soon."

"Yes, I appreciate you coming with me to pick him up. I also have students coming later this afternoon."

"I still think you should let me take him to my place - you have enough on your plate."

"No, I want him here." Emma got up and took a few more antacids.

"Are you okay?" Tracy asked.

"Yes, I think this bug may be a virus, but I can't be sick right now."

Tracy was silent for a moment, then smiled and said, "I'm not surprised - with all the traveling you've done. You're bound to get something, somewhere..."

****

Sam was in the backside at Portland Meadows Racetrack, talking with Kevin Hansen, the track vet. He looked at the construction going on across the infield. "I'm concerned about the track since the fire last year, Kevin. Thank God there were no casualties, human or equine."

Kevin nodded and said, "Everything is on schedule. The new grandstand will be ready to open this fall. And, it won't disrupt the training season."

"There are a lot of good people worried about their jobs," Sam said, just as an older man joined them. He was robust with a bit of excess weight on his shorter frame.

"Hello, son," the man said, patting Kevin on the back, then saw Sam and nodded. "Well, if it isn't Sam Parker."

He shaking Raymond Hansen's hand. "It's nice to see you, again, Ray." Sam had known Kevin's father since he started at the ORC.

"How's my son doing?"

"He's perfect for the job. But, he has some large shoes to fill. We're going to miss you here."

Ray looked around the grounds. "I remember when this racecourse opened in '46. That was a shot in the arm for a lot of us after WWII; I came here to work when I was released from the Army. And, I was here when Meadows became the first racetrack in the country that held nighttime Thoroughbred racing."

"I think I heard about that," Sam said. "What're you doing these days, Ray, now that you've retired?"

"Every day is a holiday. Martha and I are living the good life!" The old man smiled, deepening the wrinkles in his tanned face. "We just got back from Arizona. She's even got me gardening now."

Sam laughed, then saw Jim wave at him from a distance. "Gentlemen, will you excuse me?" he said and walked away.

"What's up?" Sam asked Jim, who was standing by one of the barns.

"Sally told me you were here. I just got the results from the lab at OSU for that other colt," Jim said excitedly. "They couldn't find any of the usual drugs we see in horses, but one young chemist decided to check for poisons other than drugs."

Sam waited while Jim took a breath.

"There was Fiddleneck in his hay, the kind they call 'Devil's Lettuce'."

"I've heard of it," Sam said. "It contains alkaloids and can damage the liver. But, usually a horse won't even eat the stuff."

"Yes, that's what the chemist told me. So, it must have been force fed to the poor animal. I've asked around, but no one has seen anything or anyone suspicious near his stall."

"I wish we had some sort of surveillance cameras around these barns, like we had in the military," Sam said. "Maybe someday..." In the distance, Bennie was walking towards them. Sam smiled and said, "But, in the meantime, we have our own little spy."

Jim nodded and smiled. "I've told the other Commissioners and the Racing Bureau about this."

"Good. By the way, I don't think I've had a chance to tell you - Mom's selling the Eugene ranch."

"What?! Now what're you going to do with the horses?"

"Well...You remember that place across the road from Emma's?"

"The one owned by Remsky - one of the guys involved in stealing Mason's horse?"

"Yeah, I've talked with the realtor handling the sale. It has two good stables...and there's that oval track back in the woods."

"Wow that sounds perfect! You can get back into racing like you want...and you're still close to home."

"We could stop there and take a look before you go pick up the kids at Emma's."

Jim noticed Sam was now calling Rising Sun 'Emma's' and wondered if buying this other property was a good idea, but he kept it to himself. He looked at Sam for a moment. "What does Emma think?"

"I haven't told her yet..."

"My advice, man, is to never keep secrets from your wife!"

Just then, Bennie joined them. "Hi, guys. I'm ready to get to work."

"Where's your Pentax?"

Bennie looked around, and then pulled a sub-miniature camera about the size of a pack of gum out of his jacket pocket. "It's a German Minox-A. I like to call it my spy camera, when I'm on surveillance!"

Jim laughed. "Bennie, you know you're really not a spy–"

"But, I always feel like one when I work for you guys. I got the idea for one of these babies when Sally made me watch that movie, *Roman Holiday*. The news reporter in it had a lighter that was also a camera."

"Just walk around the backside," Sam said, "and take photos of anyone you see, especially around that barn over there." He discreetly pointed to one where three men were talking outside a bay horse's stall. "That barn seems to have the most problems."

"You got it, boss!" Bennie smiled and walked away.

****

At Rising Sun, Tracy backed her truck and horse trailer up, as Peter guided her. Once they were stopped, Emma stepped out of the truck. She could hear the horse screaming and kicking the insides of the vehicle.

"That monster made a lot of noise the whole way here!" Tracy said, walking to the back of the trailer. "I can see how he got his name – Lucky Storm. He's going to be a handful." She looked at Emma. "You're still sure you want him here, right? Now is the time to change your mind."

"I'm deadly sure. Remember, I tamed a wild mustang before."

"I know. That mustang has been a real asset at my ranch. Charlie, that veteran I told you about, came up last week to begin riding - it did my heart good to see him and Flash together. It was like that horse knew instinctively what the man needed." Tracy walked to the front of the trailer and opened the side door. "Yesterday, Charlie seemed to let go of so much anxiety, riding the horse around the arena. I could see they were creating a cohesive team in a very short time."

"What is your center like?" Peter asked.

"It's basically just a barn, some stables, and a pasture. But, it's really a place of learning and healing...I work with handicapped kids and adults, and people who have been abused. Now, I have veterans - people who were sent overseas during war time. My animals seem to help these people find a sort of peace with their own issues and pasts."

The Thoroughbred kicked the side of the trailer. "Ok," Tracy said, "I guess we better get him out of here." She gently placed her hand on the animal's neck. "I think we need to just call him 'Lucky.' It might build his confidence. What do you think, Peter?"

Peter blushed and opened the trailer's back door. Then, he looked at Tracy and said, "I think he will like that."

Tracy started to back the horse out of the trailer and he bolted forwards, almost knocking her over. She tightened his lead and yelled, "Whoa, boy." Digging in her heels, she brought him to a halt, but he tried to rear up inside the trailer. "Stop!" she said sternly, pulling on his lead, and he came down to stand in front of her. "I can see he needs to be retrained on trailers, which surprises me since he's a racehorse."

"We could back the trailer up to the roundpen and unload him there," Emma suggested. "We had to do that when we got Flash."

"Good idea," Tracy said. "That way he can get to know me and his new surroundings without feeling claustrophobic. Peter, would you mind closing the back of the trailer and move the vehicles?"

He nodded a little nervously, closed the trailer's back door, and walked to the cab of the truck. Once inside, he was pleased to see the gear shift and steering was on the same side as the vehicles in Austria. Slowly, he backed the vehicle up and stopped the trailer near the pen. He got out and helped Emma open the gate and the trailer's back door.

They stood to one side of the fence and watched as Tracy got back inside the front of the trailer. She removed his shipping wrap from his head, but left the ones on his legs. Then, she released Lucky, leaving his halter and lead line on. He looked around behind him. She waited until he slowly backed up on his own into the pen. He was a beautiful, tall gray animal, but with an attitude. He ran around the wide pen, kicking his legs and bobbing his head. His white mane and tail glistened in the sun.

Peter moved the truck and trailer away from the entrance to the roundpen, and Emma closed the gate.

Tracy walked in and stood in the center of the pen, letting Lucky trot around her. When he finally came to a halt, she slowly walked up to him, talking softly. He snorted, tried to move away, but she kept advancing until he let her get near.

"Peter," Tracy said, "would you bring me a lunge line and remove his leg wraps for me while I keep him quiet? Come in slowly."

The young man nodded and cautiously entered the pen. Tracy held onto Lucky's lead line, while Peter gently began to unwrap the coverings from the horse's right foreleg. Snorting, Lucky tried to bite Peter.

"No!" Tracy said sharply as she lightly flicked the end of the lead across the horse's nose. He seemed startled and stopped, but continued to snort. "Good boy," Tracy cooed, patting his neck. She fed the horse a treat. After Peter had removed all of the wraps, Tracy attached the long lunge line to his halter.

When Peter joined her by the fence, Emma said softly, "He just needs a gentle hand for a change."

"Snorting is his way of letting me know he doesn't like me - yet." Tracy said as she lunged Lucky awhile, waiting for him to calm down. The horse circled her, kicking and whinnying, throwing his head up against the line, but she continued to talk softly to him, until he finally trotted without agitation.

"Whoa," she said and was pleased to see him halt. Tracy slowly walked up to him, giving him another treat. He just stood there, watching her, his ears twitching in all directions. "Good boy," she said when he let her step up to him and pat his neck. "I think that's enough for today."

"I want to work with him next time, if you think that's okay," Emma said.

"Considering how far he came on his first day, I think that might work." Tracy began to lead Lucky out of the roundpen. "Let's see how you handle a little grooming, and then we'll get you settled into your new home, Lucky."

They were all surprised to see the animal stood well in his cross-ties for his grooming, but Tracy watched as Emma used a gentle hand and talked constantly to him. He didn't try to bite Peter when he helped.

"I think he's going to come along nicely here," Emma said and Tracy nodded.

Eventually, Lucky was led towards the double-wide stall Emma had chosen for him. The other horses watched, and Gandolf nickered. Lucky snorted in response. A whinny came from the mare's stable, and the big animal stopped. His ears swiveled towards the sound, and he whinnied in response.

Tracy laughed. "Well, it looks like he's made some new friends already. You're going to have to watch this one, though. I'm afraid he's a bit of a lady's man."

"He's not getting anywhere near my Lipizzaner mare, that's for sure–" Emma stopped when she saw the scars on his sides.

"I'm so sorry this had to happen to you, boy, but you're safe now," she cooed to Lucky. "No one is ever going to hurt you again." She gently ran her hand over his back and side, his flesh quivered at her touch. He snorted again and pulled away in fear as far as his lead would let him, then he stood and watched. Eventually, he hung his head down and nickered softly. Then, she released his lead and closed his stall door.

"Well," Tracy said, "I think that went well." She looked at her watch and said, "I've gotta get home. That Marine is coming back this afternoon."

Outside, Peter closed up the trailer, and Tracy walked to her truck. "See you tomorrow?"

"Sure," Emma replied. Peter waved, and they watched Tracy drive away.

"I'm going to check in on him," Emma said, then walked back into the stable. Lucky's head was out over the door when she entered, but he went to the back of his stall as she approached.

"It's okay, Lucky," she said softly to the animal. "You and I are going to become great friends...You'll see."

ARKANSAS

As their plane approached the Hot Springs airport, the large city spread out below them. Koenig's Spirit whinnied from his stall in the back with the change in the compartment's air pressure. George looked and saw Johnny Blair nod, indicating that all was well with his colt.

Then, George smiled at the young man across the aisle from him. Luke's head turned with excitement, as he tried to peer out of the small windows on each side of the plane.

"I've never flown anywhere before," Luke exclaimed. "I've never been out of Louisville...this is so awesome!"

When they landed and taxied near one hangar, Fred said, "Now the work begins."

A large horse van pulled up. The crew got busy unloading Spirit and all his gear, making sure they had everything they would need for the upcoming Arkansas Derby.

Their van pulled into the Oaklawn Park Race Track, and Fred showed their papers at the backside gate. The guard waved them through, giving them directions to their assigned barn.

"I wonder if Divina is here yet," George said.

"It's good we came a few days early." Fred got out of the truck, ignoring his friend. He hoped that George hadn't seen him roll his eyes earlier - he was getting a little tired of George's love life by now. "It'll give Spirit a chance to relax and get to know his surroundings."

Luke joined them and said, "These are some nice shedrows." One bay horse next to Spirit's stall whinnied and stretched his neck towards the young man.

"Get back here, Luke, and help unload our gear," Fred yelled.

George smiled as he watched Luke work, pleased that he'd

brought this young man into their family. He was a scrawny kid, but had strong arms and legs. He was quick to learn Spirit's temperament and drive. Luke lived with his mom in Louisville. His dad had been a jockey and died in an accident during one of his races. George knew Luke's passion was to also become a jockey, in spite of his mother's fears.

OREGON

Later, at Rising Sun, Emma was in the outside arena working with Amy and Josh Barolio, as they rode their horses that were boarded at Emma's stables. They came three days a week after school. Amy was practicing English riding, and Josh liked using a Western saddle that his dad used when he was a kid. Normally, Emma preferred working with students who were learning Dressage, but these kids were like family to her and she wanted them to learn the basics of riding from her. She'd known their parents since she and Sam reunited. Emma's heart leaped when she looked at these two kids. They weren't her biological family, but she felt as close to them as if they were, and liked it when they called her 'Aunt.'

A horse screamed from the large stable.

"Who's that, Aunt Emma?" Amy asked, as she brought her horse to a halt and dismounted. Josh brought his pony up to stand next to his sister.

"That's Lucky," Emma said, "a new Thoroughbred my uncle sent to me. He's here for rehabilitation therapy."

"What's that?" Josh asked.

"It's sort of like when someone breaks an arm or leg, they have to go to therapy to help learn how to reuse it."

"Did he break something?" Josh asked.

"No, he's just had his heart broken. I'm helping him to learn that not all people will hurt him."

"I love you!" Amy said, hugging Emma.

"I love you, Amy," Emma said, tears pooling in her eyes. "You too, Josh."

"Excuse me," Shane said behind them.

Emma turned to see Nikki and her foster mother, Maria, at the arena railing. Shane walked to stand next to Nikki, but Emma saw the young girl tense up and quickly move away from him.

"We're here for Nicole's first lesson," Maria said, handing Emma the release form.

"Yes, we're almost finished. Thank you, Shane, for bringing them here."

Shane nodded, and then walked away. Nikki relaxed a little.

Emma glanced at the form to make sure both parents had signed, and put it and the check into her pocket. She looked at Nikki and was pleased to see she was carrying a hunt cap and wearing riding breeches, tucked into tall, heeled boots. Emma turned to the Barolio kids. "Amy, Josh, this is another student - Nikki."

"Nicole!" Maria interjected.

"And, this is Maria."

"Hi," Amy and Josh said together.

Nikki only waved to the kids, but Maria seemed irritated. "I have a hair appointment soon. How long will this take?"

We will probably be an hour or so–"

"Perfect, I'll be back around five o'clock, okay?"

"Yes."

Maria turned and left as the kids watched.

"Nikki," Emma said, "I'm surprised Maria didn't want to stay and watch your first lesson."

"I'm not. She doesn't care what I do - as long as I stay out of her way."

Emma saw the look on Amy and Josh's faces. She clapped her hands to break the tension and said, "Okay, Josh, get back on your horse so we can finish your lesson."

"How come you have two names?" Josh asked Nikki, jumping back onto his pony.

"She likes to be called Nikki," Emma said. "Why don't you stay here with me, while I finish with these kids? Then, we'll begin your lesson."

They watched as the younger kids continued their exercises. Emma explained to Nikki, "Josh is six. He's just beginning to learn to ride. His pony is an American Shetland/Welsh crossbreed."

When Amy rode past them, Emma said, "She's nine and has been riding since she was five. She loves the English saddle and is doing Training Level Dressage exercises. Morgan horses have excellent temperaments for this type of riding, and Amy's Morgan is a fourteen-year-old sorrel gelding."

"That's how old I am!" Nikki said, eyes glued to the kids in the arena.

"Nikki, you will be starting with Introductory Level exercises, until I see how you respond to Dressage. You will be riding Sonny."

Just then, Sam and Jim arrived.

"I guess we can call it a day, kids," Emma said to Amy and Josh. "Take your horses to the stables to be groomed and fed. Nikki, you can go watch them while I talk to their dad."

The kids dismounted and all three walked to the stables, Nikki trailing behind the other two.

"Hey, sweet lady," Sam said, kissing Emma. "I missed you."

"I missed you, too!" Emma said, a little surprised at Sam. He was in a much better mood now. "Hi, Jim, has Sam been working you hard?"

"Not really, it's actually been fun to be back at the office. Where're the kids?"

"In the stables, grooming their horses. Let's go see how they're doing."

As they walked to the open stable door, Sam said, "I see your new student arrived. How did she do?"

Softly, she said, "Nikki is getting a private lesson after the kids leave."

As soon as they entered, Josh yelled, "Hey, Dad," dropped his brush and ran up to hug Jim. "You should've seen me and Buddy today; we were going in circles and everything!"

"Sorry I missed it, little man, but I'll make sure I'm here next time." Jim walked up to Amy and hugged her. "What did you do today, Pumpkin?"

"I learned to do a few of the movements on the next level today. Dressage is such a wonderful way to ride. I love it! And Sky followed my commands so well." Amy patted her horse, and then put him in the stall.

Out of the corner of her eye, Emma saw Nikki step back away from the group, avoiding standing near Sam or Jim, crossing her arms and tightening her jaw. The young girl was reacting to these men like Lucky had when Emma had first met him.

"Hey, Dad," Josh said, as he watched Shane lead his pony into his stall. "Did you know Aunt Emma is taking care of a hurt horse? He just arrived today and is back there all by himself." He looked at

Emma, "Can we go see him? Please?"

"I think that would be okay, but you have to promise me you will use soft voices and no fast movements. He's still pretty frightened."

"We promise!" Amy and Josh said in unison.

They all followed Emma to the other end of the long stable, Nikki trailing behind.

"Why is he kept here, away from the other horses," Josh asked in a whisper. "Won't he get lonely?"

"I'm doing this for his own protection - for now," Emma told the kids.

"What happened to him?" Amy asked.

"A mean man in Kentucky was hurting him," Sam said softly. Then, he looked at his wife with pride. "Aunt Emma will help him."

The gray colt immediately went to the back of his stall as they approached and stood with his head down, shivering, his ears laid back.

Josh said in a hushed voice, "What's his name?"

"I call him Lucky," Emma said. "He was trained as a racehorse, but his spirit was broken by that man Uncle Sam told you about. He'd started acting out - biting and kicking his handlers and jockeys. That's why they were beating him. They didn't understand that he was hurt and confused."

"Gee," Josh sighed. "That's terrible!"

After a while, Jim said softly, "Hey, kids, it's time we head home. Your mom's going to wonder what happened to us. Go get your gear and meet me at the car."

"Okay," Amy whispered, and she and Josh tiptoed back to the front of the stable.

"I'm going to talk with Jim for a bit, Em," Sam said. "Nice to see you, Nikki."

Now that they were alone, Emma watched Nikki relax and walk up to Lucky's stall. "People are stupid and can be so cruel," the young girl said so softly, Emma hardly heard her. Stepping closer, Emma could see tears welling in the young girl's eyes.

"Not all people, Nikki," she said. "He's going to need a lot of work. But I have a friend, Tracy, who is coming later to start some of his therapy."

Nikki kept looking at the horse. "Why aren't you doing it?"

"I will help, but Tracy is amazing with abused animals. She's been rescuing them for years and has an Equine therapy center near here. Maybe someday you can see her work."

Emma watched as the horse seemed to respond to Nikki's gaze, raising his head, looking directly at her and pricking his ears. It was the first glimpse of trust she'd seen in the horse so far and was surprised that he responded to Nikki so quickly. She made a mental note to tell Tracy about it later.

"I think we should start your lesson now. Let's go saddle Sonny. Then, you can ride him in the arena."

Nikki allowed Sonny to free walk as Emma watched her ride, knowing that she was being tested her on how well she and the new horse worked together. She tried to hold her hands steady as she asked the horse to work in a trot rising around the arena, the way Sarah's mom had taught her. She straightened her posture and checked her rein motions. She really liked the long, indoor arena, with the high ceiling, skylights, and windows along all the walls. It was so bright there, and she appreciated being in the light.

"How am I doing?" she asked Emma, smiling.

"I'm impressed. Now, please take Sonny in a medium walk around the arena, and then ask him to track right," Emma instructed, watching Nikki closely. Since Sonny was already trained in the Dressage movements, she was more interested in Nikki's equitation - her personal form. She was pleased to see the young girl follow her instructions. "Very good!" she praised.

Nikki was smiling as she sat proudly in the seat, glad to be riding again. This was the only time in her life when she ever felt in control and totally elated. The freedom she knew in riding, and sense of security, had been lost to her when the Berkleys moved to Alaska because of his job transfer - until now.

After a while, Emma said, "Bring Sonny to me and halt." When horse and rider stood before her, she patted Sonny on the neck. "Your ability to maintain your body position and use of body aids are good, but I want to work on streamlining your aids to make them more subtle. A judge should not see any movement from the rider during a competition."

Nikki nodded, "That's what Sarah always said I needed work on."

"Sarah?"

"Yes, Sarah Berkley, the...uh, friend I told you about the first day we met." She didn't tell Emma that Sarah's parents had taken her in as a foster child when she was ten. And, now, she was here with Sarah's first instructor - a dream come true.

"Oh, I remember." Emma looked at the young girl sitting on the white horse and realized how natural she looked. Nikki reminded her of herself as a young student. "Why don't you do two figure eights for me in a canter, with a simple change of lead. Then, return here to halt."

"Yes," Nikki said proudly, then turned Sonny back into the arena and followed Emma's directions. When finished, Nikki brought Sonny to stand in front of her.

"That's it for today," Emma said. She smiled when she saw the disappointment in Nikki's face. A student who didn't like it when a class was over had the potential to become a good rider. "I want you to visualize all you've done today; making notes in how you think you could minimize your body shifts to help Sonny go through the movements."

Nikki nodded, dismounted, and together they led Sonny towards the large stable.

After Nikki had Sonny's tack off and was brushing him in the aisle, Tracy's red truck pulled up outside and she walked into the cool building.

"Here's Tracy now," Emma said. "She's my friend I told you about, who is going to help Lucky."

Tracy and Emma hugged. "Hey, lady," Tracy said. "I'm here to take a look at our patient–" She stopped when she saw the young girl.

"This is Nikki Hornsby, my new student. She and Sonny just started today."

Tracy reached out a hand and shook Nikki's. "It's nice to meet you. You're in good hands with Emma. She's the best!"

Nikki nodded and resumed brushing Sonny.

"I have to go talk to Shane in the tack room," Emma said. "I'll be right back." She looked at Tracy and smiled, hoping she would get Nikki to open up a little more - she was such a private young girl.

"Have you ridden before?" Tracy asked Nikki, to get the conversation rolling.

"Yeah."

"Sonny is a great mount. He's patient and gentle–"

"I know."

Tracy watched Nikki brush the gelding's coat in silence. Then, as the young girl reached up to lift his mane, Tracy saw bruises on Nikki's arm when her shirt sleeve fell back. She didn't say anything, for now.

Nikki saw Tracy's face and quickly dropped her arm, pulling her sleeve down.

Tracy could see the fear in Nikki's eyes. It was similar to the looks she'd get from her animals when they were cornered.

Emma returned, and Tracy knew she could feel the tension. So, she started talking about Thoroughbreds to put Nikki at ease until Sonny was back in his stall. "Lucky is a Thoroughbred. The founding stallions of his bloodline were brought to England from the Near East in the seventeenth century, then bred with English horses to create these magnificent animals we know today. Besides horseracing, Thoroughbreds are used for polo and as hunters."

"In Dressage, too," Emma added, smiling.

"So, Lucky could be trained for Dressage?" Nikki asked, wondering to herself if maybe someday she could ride Lucky.

"Most definitely."

A car drove up and Emma looked out. "Maria's here to pick you up, Nikki."

"Thank you for the lesson."

"Come on, Nikki. We have to go!" Maria yelled.

"Okay, bye," Nikki said, waving as she ran out to the car.

After they left, Tracy turned to Emma and said, "Did you see those bruises on Nikki's arm?"

"What bruises?"

"I noticed them when she was grooming Sonny - some of them looked like they were fresh, others had started to change color - signs they'd begun to heal. I'm worried about that girl."

"I'll keep an eye on her and let you know if I find out where she got them."

"She probably won't want to talk about it. I was going to, but just her look shut me down. I've seen a lot of abused animals in my career - this girl has that same fear in her eyes."

"I wonder who could be doing that to her. Could it be kids at school?" Emma asked sadly.

"I'm sure she'll tell you - when she's ready." Tracy placed her arm around her friend's shoulder. "Let's go see Lucky." As they walked, she asked, "How are you feeling?"

"Better..."

In Lucky's stall, it took Tracy a few attempts before she was able to attach a lead line to Lucky's halter. "He sure is skeptical," Tracy said to Emma, as she led the gray to the roundpen. She was glad Peter had closed Lucky's door to his run and decided to join them.

The two watched at the fence, near where Lucky's saddle waited, while Tracy released the horse's lead so he could run freely around her. Lucky snorted whenever Tracy approached him. She stood in the center of the pen and said, "I'm going to wait and see if he will come to me." The horse bucked and threw his head back, as he raced around her.

"It's like you're having to start all over again," Emma said.

"Well, he's not some horse we found in the wild, but he does need to learn to trust again."

Eventually, Lucky came to a stop not far from Tracy. He snorted and tossed his head, but Tracy didn't move. She just held out her hand, holding the lunge line and a stick with a flag on a string in the other. "I want him to let me touch him again, to show him he doesn't need to be afraid," she said, slowly raising her hand as he walked up to her. Finally, Lucky allowed Tracy to stroke his forehead and neck. Then, she walked beside him and began touching his back and side gently with the flagged end of the whip.

"Good boy," Tracy cooed, then walked closer and trailed the flag down his legs. Lucky started and ran around the pen, then slowly approached her again. When Lucky just stood there, she backed away and waited. Then, when she touched him again with the flag and he didn't respond, she praised him and gave him a treat. She attached the lunge line and led him to where Emma and Peter waited.

"Let's see how he does getting saddled and if he'll let me ride him."

Peter went through the gate to help with Lucky's saddle, while Tracy held his lead. Lucky reared as Peter came near, but Tracy held him firm. "Whoa," she said, tugging strongly on the rope. Finally, the horse settled and allowed Peter to place the blanket, and then the saddle on his back.

The horse snorted a little, but stood while Peter worked with his girth. "What a good boy," she cooed again, stroking the tall horse's neck as she watched Peter. Once Lucky was saddled, she gave him another treat and walked him around in a circle to help him relax. Then, she lunged him with full tack on. When he didn't buck and came to a halt, she approached him and released the line. She held his reins and the stick in her left hand.

"Okay," she said, getting ready to mount him. "Let's see how you do." She began to step into the stirrup and Lucky reached around to bite her. Tracy flicked his nose lightly with the stick, "No!" she said sharply, then circled him again. They continued until he finally let her slide into the saddle. She praised him, but he reared, trying to dismount her. She hung on and eventually got him to slowly lope around the pen. "Good boy."

Tracy patted his neck and said, "I think he's going to come along faster than I'd expected. Without the pressure of training for the races - and getting beaten, he's going to be able to remember what it's like to just be a horse again."

Lucky was cooled and back in his stall, when Tracy and Emma walked down the stable aisle.

"Thank you, Peter, for your help," Tracy said.

"It was a pleasure to watch you work," he said shyly.

"See you next time."

As the two women walked outside, Emma said, "Shane is leaving to be with his father in Eugene. That just leaves me and Peter, but I want Peter to concentrate mostly on the Lipizzaners - not do the general chores."

"You're going to need some more help here. I know of some reliable workers - a sister/brother act. They've helped me at the clinic, but I have enough hands now and they can use the work. I'll send them over when you're ready so you can meet them."

That night, Sam was drying the dinner dishes as Emma washed them in the deep sink.

"Did I tell you that Uncle George and Divina are going to the next race together?" Emma said, handing a plate to Sam.

"I think it's great the old man is getting into the game. He's been single way too long."

"He's never been married, and I don't know he's ever really dated..." She didn't mention that her uncle had told her that he'd once been in love. But, that was a long time ago.

Sam placed the finished dishes into the cupboard and stood looking out the window at the large stable. George's Thoroughbred stood in his outside run.

"How's Lucky doing?" he asked.

"He's still watchful." Emma kissed Sam, running her hands down his back. "You should have seen Nikki and Lucky today. I think they have kindred spirits."

"What do you mean?"

"They seemed to have an instant connection with each other. Tracy saw it too." She decided not to tell Sam just yet about Tracy's concerns of Nikki possibly being abused - she wanted to talk to Nikki first.

"I'm concerned about you. Maybe Lucky should be at Tracy's, so she can work with him there? You have your Lipizzaners now."

"No, this is something I have to do. Besides, I'm getting more help. Tracy has some friends who are coming soon."

Sam hugged Emma closer and looked at her for a moment. Then, he said, "I have something I want to talk to you about. What would you think if I said I wanted to buy Joe's ranch–"

"What?!"

"It would allow me to bring my horses here, there's already stables and a track–"

Emma pulled away and paced in front of him. She ran her hands through her hair and said, "I don't know how we can do that. Not now!"

"Just think about it, okay?" Sam said and waited.

"No, I don't have to think about it!"

Sam shoved his hands in his pockets. "I'm driving Shane to Eugene tomorrow. We'll be leaving early," he said in a low voice and left the room.

Emma stood stunned. *What was he thinking?* she thought. *There's no way they could pay for something like that.* She shivered, remembering all the horrible things that had happened at that place - and the people connected with it. She couldn't imagine stepping foot on that property, let alone owning it!

CHAPTER TWELVE

Later the next day, Sam and Shane rode down the highway towards Eugene in the Buick Skylark. The two-door coupe was a sleek machine.

Sam thought of how he and Emma had left everything, but he knew that if he didn't purchase Joe's ranch, he'd be lying to himself - which is exactly what he'd done when he'd lost Ele. If he couldn't pursue horseracing, he knew he'd eventually disappear.

"Man," Shane said, "this car is awesome!"

Glad for the distraction, Sam glanced over at the young redhead sitting next to him. He saw himself in this boy, full of wander and joy. Suddenly, Sam wished he could do some things in his life over again. *And*, he realized, *maybe I can.*

"How fast will she go?" Shane asked.

"She has a three-forty horsepower engine and will top out at a hundred and five miles per hour, but I've never driven her that fast." Sam glanced at Shane, smiled, and then he accelerated.

"Listen to that engine!" the young boy exclaimed. "I want one of these."

"Well, if it's okay with your dad, you get to keep this car for a little while. I'm driving my dad's truck back up north today."

"No way!" Shane grinned from ear to ear, buffing the dashboard with his sleeve.

They drove on in silence, then Sam asked, "Shane, I appreciate you being my jockey."

"You know how much I love racing horses," the young man said. "And, Ele is such a great mare."

"Yes, but I still want you to think about college," Sam said, glancing over at Shane. "You're only nineteen now, and you have your whole future ahead of you. I don't think being a jockey is a profession - for you. You're so intelligent and have too much potential to waste—"

"I'm not wasting my potential, Sam! This is what I love. I'll keep doing it as long as I can, okay?"

"Okay," Sam said then continued driving. He was still going to gather some information on possible professions that might interest Shane, knowing the lad would someday get too big to be a jockey. Maybe he could find something in aeronautics, since Shane also liked speed and flying – just like Sam at his age.

When they arrived at Parker Ranch, they stopped near the garage. The green truck was sitting outside, and Sam could see it had been washed and waxed. They walked into the long ranch house.

"Anybody home?" Sam called out.

"In the study," Joanna Parker said.

When Sam entered the familiar room, he stopped when he saw all the boxes sitting around. It was like getting punched in the stomach. He looked around the bare spaces where mementos had always been. His mom and Mike were packing books. "Whoa, you two work fast!"

"When I make up my mind, I get busy!" Joanna said, kissing Sam on the cheek. "Grab a box and get started."

"Hi, Sam," Mike said. "I tried to stop her until you got here, but you know how she is." Mike hugged Shane. "Hello, son. Glad to see you."

"Me too, Dad." Shane said. "Sam says I can drive their Skylark...is that okay?"

Mike looked at Sam and saw his friend nod. "I can't take both vehicles back today, so Shane will be helping me out."

"I guess it's okay, but there will be rules!"

"Sweet!" Shane exclaimed. After Sam tossed him the car keys, Shane asked his dad, "Is it okay if I go see the horses?"

"Sure, I'll come with you." Mike and Shane left.

Joanna stopped packing and looked at her son. She could always tell when something was bothering him. "Are you upset that I didn't wait, son?"

Sam shoved his hands in his pockets and leaned against the cold stone fireplace. "Nah."

She walked over to him and placed a hand on his arm. "I know when things aren't right with you. What's up?"

He raked his hands over his bearded chin and sighed. "Em and I had a fight last night."

Joanna waited.

"I think she's getting too busy...and you know there's no way I can buy this place." He paced the room, then said, "I want to buy that ranch across from ours...for my horses."

"Did you go to sleep angry?"

He looked at her and blinked. "Well, yeah."

She shook her head. "How many times have I told you - never go to bed angry. You two have got to work this out." She patted his shoulder. "I'm sure you will." She turned to continue packing, and then stopped.

"Sam, I found a townhouse!" Joanna said excitedly. "It's over in the Cottage Hill district, near the University." She sat down in one of the large over-stuffed chairs. "I talked with a friend about the ranch property value and couldn't believe what he thought it was worth." She looked at her son, "You said something about buying the place across from Emma's."

Sam caught his mom's eye and sighed. "Yeah, but Em's against it. She said we can't afford it."

"Mike has a guy who's interested in this place. I guess he's always had his eye on it. Remember Malcolm Hoffman?"

"Sure I do." Malcolm had been a few years ahead of Sam in high school.

"Well, if we get what I think we will," Joanna broke in, "after the sale is final, I'll be able to buy my townhouse." She paused for a moment, then added, "I want you to have what's left."

He stood shocked for a moment, letting her words sink in. If she did that, he could possibly buy Joe's...if he could convince Em it was for the best. Sam knew his father had set up an excellent retirement profile, so the cash from the sale would be a bonus for his mom. A smile crept across his face. "It's a deal - providing you take some extra for yourself, Mom. I want you to have a nest egg for your travels."

"Agreed!"

The tall clock chimed. "Oh," Joanne said, "I have a bridge game to get to." She kissed her son on the cheek. "I love you, Sam." Then, she left the house.

Later, in the stable, Sam told Mike about Joe's ranch and his desire to buy it. He then shared what his mother had decided to do.

"Now, you can!" Mike said, smiling. "Does Emma know about your idea?"

"It's not her decision. She's going to be busy with her own plans...and now an abused Thoroughbred has come to Rising Sun. She won't have time to worry about what I'm doing," Sam said, trying to convince himself it would all work out. Everything seemed to be falling into place.

"What about your job at the Commission?" Mike asked.

"Jim seems to like taking over for me, so I may just let him have it again. I'll have to talk to the Board first." Sam paced the aisle. "That place is perfect, Mike! There's a big ranch house, a good stable, with a smaller stable nearby that can be used for Ele. And, there's a half-mile dirt track back in the woods."

"You've told me about it, but–"

"You know how much I love racing," Sam cut in. "Well, I figure it's time I get started again!" Classy Elegance whinnied, and Sam looked at his mare, her chestnut head bobbing over her door. He walked up to her and stroked her long neck. "Ele and I've really missed the track."

"And, Promise is in need of a rider now, too," Mike reminded Sam.

He turned back to Mike. "So, do you think you and Shane would like to move up there, and help me get her ready?"

"Heck, yeah!"

"Shane could drive the Skylark back up then." Sam looked around at the old stable, thinking of all the years he'd spent there. "This may be the last time I see this old place..."

Mike stepped over to Sam and patted his shoulder. "That may be true, but your memories here will never go away."

Shane was standing next to Promise's stall. "So, when can I ride this big guy?"

Sam looked at Mike and saw his friend nod. "I think right now is a good time to get started! Go get his tack."

"Wahoo!" Shane exclaimed as he ran to the tack room.

Sam grabbed the bridle hanging outside of the horse's stall and stepped in. "Ready to go, boy?"

The horse nodded. Sam patted the colt's neck and looked down at his legs, something his dad always did with his racehorses. He rubbed each joint, checking for heat. Then, he replaced the animal's halter and gently edged the bit into his mouth. Sam led Promise to the aisle and cross-tied him. "He's growing nicely," he said proudly. Running his hands over the colt's hind quarters. "Look at the power in those muscles."

"He's also tall for his age," Mike said, watching Sam closely. "I know I've been the trainer here for years for your dad; but now, I think it's your turn. I want you to take point on Promise's training."

Sam smiled. "I was hoping you'd say that, but you're going to help me, right?"

"Count on it."

"Here's his gear," Shane said, grinning from ear to ear. He now wore a helmet and carried the colt's saddle and pad.

Mike laid a saddle cloth and the pad onto the horse's back, rubbing him and talking to keep him calm. Then, he tightened the girth. This wasn't the first time the animal had felt a saddle on his back. Promise stood waiting, his eyes and ears alert.

"Shane," Sam said, "why don't you lead him to the roundpen and start lunging him to get him warmed up and relaxed with his tack on."

Promise followed Shane as if all this was normal. As he was lunged, he didn't buck or fight the equipment. His stride was smooth and strong, and he showed the confidence of an athlete.

"Good," Sam said, watching his colt trot around the pen. He stepped inside and took the lead lines, feeling the tension against the bit in the horse's mouth. Sam made a clicking sound and his horse arched his neck, his head held high as he broke into a canter.

After a while, Sam stopped Promise and walked up to him. He took the lead lines off and held his bridle. Shane was instructed to start jumping up and down next to Promise. Mike watched just inside the fence.

Sam said, "He needs to get used to someone approaching him like that before you actually get up. We want to keep him calm and happy to be doing this." Sam watched Promise's reaction. "Good boy," he said, stroking the horse's forehead.

After a few moments, Sam then said, "Okay, Shane, now jump up and lay over his back. Don't try to put your leg over yet."

Shane jumped up and lay across the saddle, while Sam walked Promise in a circle so he could get familiar with the weight. They repeated this motion a few times. Because the horse still seemed calm and relaxed, Sam halted the horse and told Shane to come down.

"I think he's ready for you to get in the saddle. What do you say, Mike?"

"He didn't bring his ears back or seem to protest so far, so I'd say go for it."

Shane smiled and Mike gave his son a leg up. Promise stood proudly, as if this was what he was meant to be - a racehorse with a rider. Slowly, Sam walked the pair around the pen, Shane did not put his feet in the stirrups at first. Sam nodded to Shane and gave him the reins. The young man put his feet in and walked Promise slowly in a circle. Then, he clicked his tongue and gently tapped the colt's sides, taking him into a slow trot.

"My god, he's a natural!" Mike said, standing near the fence with Sam.

Sam smiled with pride. "Yes, he is!"

The two men watched as Shane continued around the pen a number of times. Then, Sam said, "That's probably enough for today. Shane, why don't you dismount and go cool him down."

The boy jumped off the colt, praised him, and led him to the barn.

Sam smiled and nodded. "Keep that up for a few days and he'll be ready to work on the oval track." Happy with the progress of his colt today, Sam looked at his watch and said, "Well, I'd better head back. Keep me posted."

"Will do," Mike said.

Sam walked out into the sunshine and headed towards the truck...his truck now. It was a half-ton, Chevy pickup, with a Fleetside bed, which gave it a long, straight body. The driver's door creaked a little when he opened it. *That'll get some oil*, he thought, as he eased onto the bench seat behind the large, skinny steering wheel. He looked at the fawn-colored interior, running his hand along the dashboard. The smell of old vinyl and oil brought back so many memories. When he leaned back to get the key out of his pocket, his head bumped against the gun rack that hung along the inside of the narrow back window. He reached up and rubbed his head, and then he saw his dad's old, tan baseball cap hanging on one of the rack hooks. He took it down and smiled at the PARKER RANCH logo stitched across the cap. Shaking it out, he placed it on his head.

After he started the engine and put the truck into reverse, he laughed as his hand rubbed down the shaft of the gear shift. He could feel the indentation from his dad's pinky finger and remembered the way Harold would always hold it, with his thumb on the top of the gear shift, three fingers wrapped around the shifter, and his pinky extended down.

"Okay, Big Green, let's go to your new home."

****

Emma sat alone at her desk in the den, looking over her new breeding program. If they started breeding right away, since the gestation period is eleven to twelve months, Calma would have a foal by next spring. *Perfect timing!* she thought. She made a note to check with Peter the next day.

She stretched in her chair, still not well and overly tired. Looking at the clock, she was surprised Sam hadn't come home yet for dinner. She hated the way they'd left everything unresolved, but she had her work to do and their money was tied up right now. Those were her excuses, anyway.

Now, Emma looked down again at her calendar and rolled her shoulders to work out some of the tension in her neck. Leafing through previous dates, she saw a postcard stuck between the pages. It had a photo of their ship on the front, and she thought back to their honeymoon. The slow days on the cruise across the Atlantic had been timeless, with exquisite dinners, dancing, and moonlit walks on the deck. She sighed, realizing that life had changed so much since their return and thought, *is the honeymoon over now?*

ARKANSAS

Being one of the races for Kentucky Derby contenders, the Arkansas Derby was held at Oakland Park mid-April every year in Hot Springs. The grandstand was full on this cloudy day. Fred and Stan Gibson, George's jockey, were now in the track's backside, prepping Koenig's Spirit. The shedrow was busy with teams of men and women, getting their horses ready, as well.

A man watched in the shade of a row of trees by one of the barns.

"This is the last race Spirit will run before the big race in May," Stan said, looking around the neat shedrow outside of Spirit's stall. He was impressed by the condition of these tree-lined barns and always liked riding here.

"I've never seen a horse run like he does," Fred said, removing the last wraps on the young stallion's legs in a clockwise direction. "I don't want to jinx anything today."

Stan laughed, "Aren't we a superstitious bunch!" He pulled out a laminated four-leaf clover from his pocket. "I found this in the woods behind my parents' home near Fredericksburg when I was eight."

George walked up to join them. "What's this about superstition? I believe in making my own luck." He ran his hand down the horse's neck and front left leg. "How's our boy looking today?"

"He's ready and patiently waiting, as always." Fred patted Spirit's neck. "He's more like his sire than any other colt. I'm sure he'll have no problems on this nine-furlong track."

"I agree," Stan said. "Now, I'd better get ready and weigh in." He winked and walked off towards the jockey quarters. Johnny came up to start getting Spirit ready to walk to the paddock.

George nodded, looking proudly at his horse. He turned to Fred and said, "I've invited Divina to join us in our box for the race."

Fred pulled George aside, "I want to talk to you," he said in a low voice, as they stepped away from the busy shedrow. "Are you sure about getting so involved with her? Especially now that we're getting so close to the important races ahead of us. I need your focus here, at the track."

"I really like her," George said.

"Yeah, but can't it wait? We're really busy right now." Fred looked away for a moment, then back at his friend. He didn't like admitting that maybe he made a mistake. "I'm not sure she's the right woman for you."

"What? Why?"

"Because of her intervention in New York, pulling you away from the track like that. And again, the other day - when we were at Churchill Downs. Even though she's also in the racing world, I'm beginning to think she's too much of a diversion for you. I need you more concentrated here right now - at the tracks."

"But, you said I need a girl..."

"Maybe you should look for one who has the same goals as you."

Later, George and Fred sat together in the glass-enclosed, heated grandstand. As they had approached the building, George liked the center cupola and dormers on the roof - each containing a pole with the American flag flying in the light breeze. It was a grand building, commemorating a different time in architecture.

Thinking about Fred's words, George realized that maybe he was also feeling the same way. There always seemed to be something holding him back when he and Divina were together.

Divina joined them. "Hello, gentlemen." She waited until Fred got up to move so that she could sit next to George.

"I'm sorry Mr. Divinity is not racing today," George said, looking at the tote board, seeing the horse's name was now scratched. "What happened?"

"His tests were clear after the Aqueduct race." She glanced at the horses coming out onto the track. "But, since we brought him here, he's off his feed and doesn't seem right. So, based on Raul's recommendation, I pulled him out of this one. I didn't want to take any chances for the next race."

"Does your vet have any ideas?"

"Seth ran some of his own tests, but is waiting for results." She was quiet for a moment, then looked at George and asked softly, "After the race, when you return to Kentucky, would you please join me at my house? I have something I'd like to talk with you about."

"Yes, but it will probably be late." George smiled, but was a little concerned what was in store for him.

"That is no problem."

"Welcome, ladies and gentlemen," the announcer said over the loud speaker, "to the Arkansas Derby, one of the final chances for these horses to earn a space in the starting gate at this year's Kentucky Derby..."

All of the horses were now on the track. They paraded before the grandstand, did a turn and Spirit pranced next to his outrider as they approached the starting gate. Today was one of the largest field of horses in this track's history. One horse refused to go into the gate, so some handlers had to work to get him loaded. When all were in place, the bell rang and the gates flew open.

"They're off," the announcer called, "with Eclipse on Fire, taking the lead..."

The crowd roared as the horses raced down the track in a tight pack, but eventually leveled out with Eclipse on Fire still in the lead and Spirit in fifth place. Spirit never moved from that position until they came around the backstretch. Stan began to urge him on and in the last turn, he was in fourth.

"Come on, Spirit!" George yelled, watching as the horses started towards the home stretch. Spirit was on the inside with two other horses blocking him in, Eclipse On Fire ahead of the others.

Everyone went wild as the first horses neared the home stretch. Spirit moved up, but he couldn't seem to get away from the rail. He pushed a little harder and got to the outside, taking over second place, just as Eclipse On Fire crossed the finish line.

Divina turned to George. "I'm sorry he didn't win, but he definitely will go to the Kentucky Derby now." She kissed him on the cheek. "Call me when you get back home?"

"I thought we could go—"

"No...I don't feel well, so I will ride back with Raul, my trainer." She didn't explain that she'd been disappointed and worried about her stallion's condition through the entire race, but didn't want to show it in front of the men in the box with her.

When George nodded, she walked away. Watching Divina leave, he replayed the recent race in his head and slammed his fist onto the railing of their box. "Damn it, Fred! Why the hell did Spirit lose?"

Fred shrugged, placing his hand on George's shoulder. "Stan got locked in - you saw it. But, I'm not worried. Remember in '41, when Triple Crown winner, Whirlaway, came in second in his Derby Trial Stakes race? Spirit will still get a good position in the gate on his next big race."

George thought for a moment, then smiled and said. "Well then, I guess we have to get ready. If they can put a man on the Moon this year, I can win the Triple Crown!"

Fred and George entered the Oaklawn's backside and met up with Johnny Blair, who was walking Spirit towards the Test Barn. Immediately, George was grabbed from behind and thrown to the ground. Gordon Evers, the prior owner of Lucky Storm, punched his fist into George's left eye.

"Go get security!" Fred yelled to another groom, then ran to pull Evers off of George. Johnny quickly took Spirit away from the commotion.

"Because of you, you son-of-a-bitch, the Racing Commission has removed me from the Derby race!" Evers spat in George's face, straining against Fred's grasp. "This could end my career."

"Your career ended when you decided to abuse animals. You brought this on yourself, you arrogant imbecile."

Evers' face turned almost purple with rage and he tried to pull free, but the guards ran up and grabbed him.

"Arrest this man!" George said, trying to calm his breathing, as he brushed the dirt off his shirt sleeve and wiped the blood from his face with his handkerchief. He tossed the bloody cloth into a waste bin and said, "Evers should be banned from every racecourse. He's a menace to society!"

As the guards pulled him away, Gordon Evers vowed, "You're a dead man, Mason!"

****

Later, in Oaklawn Park's backside, the man looked around to make sure no one was watching. He walked to the shedrow where Koenig's Spirit had been stabled and pulled George's bloody handkerchief out of the bin. In the faint light, he smiled when he saw the initials 'GM' embroidered on it.

"Perfect," he whispered to himself and placed the cloth in a paper bag. Then, cautiously, he walked away from the shedrow.

KENTUCKY

At Gallano Farm, Divina was standing in her parlor, looking at her wedding photo. It had been ten years since her divorce - and also her estrangement from her sister. She missed Tala, because she was the last of her family here in the States. She did have an aunt and uncle still in Manila who wrote to her periodically. But, they were so far away. Divina needed family near her now.

Just then, she was glad to see George's car as he drove up to her house.

He knocked and Jasmine let him in. "Miss Divina is in the parlor, please go in."

When George walked in, Divina saw his bruised face. She rushed to his side and gently placed her hand on his cheek. "What happened to you?"

"Evers attacked me in the Oaklawn backside after you left. He's in jail now, and I'll be pressing charges."

Divina poured him a drink, as George paced around the room and talked about the race. "I was hoping to go to the Kentucky Derby with no losses," he said. "But, Fred said not to worry..."

"I'm sure Fred knows what he's talking about. He's a good trainer." Divina handed George his glass, then she sat down on the settee. "George, why did you leave my hotel?"

"What?" He stopped and stared at her.

"The Chelsea - in New York?" She looked down at her hands, then back at him. "I'd hoped you were interested in me."

"I am..." George started, then cleared his throat and took a big gulp. "It's just complicated with me..."

"I'm not looking for love, just someone I can grow old with." She got up and walked to the windows that looked out at her softly lit garden. "I loved my husband. He swept me off my feet...then, he broke my heart."

"How did he do that?"

"He ran off with my sister," she blurted out, and then she wrapped her arms around herself. "I learned to harden my heart to avoid that kind of pain again." She paused for a moment before she asked, "Are you seeing someone else?"

There was a commotion in the hallway and Seth, Divina's vet walked in. He stopped when he saw George. "I'm sorry to interrupt;

Simon Day is on his way with our test results." These really were from his tests he'd done after New York, when Simon's came back clear. Seth still believed there was something wrong with Mr. Divinity.

"Do you want me to leave?" George asked, thankful for the interruption.

"No, please...I want you to stay," Divina said.

They saw a car drive up and stop. In silence, they all waited until Simon walked in. Divina went up to him and held out her hand.

"Hello," she said, smiling nervously. "Can I mix you a cocktail?"

"No thanks," Simon said. "I'm still working."

"Simon," George said, shaking hands with the man who once tried to arrest him for drugging his horse.

The people in the room watched as Simon looked down at the papers he had in his hand. "I have the test results from the ones Seth requested...Ms. Gallano, I'm sorry to report that Mr. Divinity was poisoned–"

"When?" Divina said, sinking onto the settee.

George sat beside her. "I thought you said–"

"It must have been given to him before he was transported to Aqueduct," Simon explained. "I need to talk to all of your staff."

"What was the drug?" George asked.

"It wasn't a drug," Seth said. "It was a plant - called Locoweed."

Simon broke in. "We couldn't find anything at first, but Seth here was the one who discovered it."

Seth nodded and said, "The urine test I did showed traces of Swainsonine, an alkaloid from the Locoweed plant. It's toxic to horses."

"But where did he get it?" George asked.

"I don't know." Seth looked at Divina and added, "Locoweed is not found in this part of the country, but I saw it once when I went to Vet school in eastern Washington. Most of the symptoms don't appear for a couple of weeks. That's when the horse seems to go crazy - thus the plant's name. It's–"

Just then, there was a loud commotion and one of her grooms ran into the room. "Ms. Gallano, we have a problem with Mr. Divinity! You must come..."

Everyone followed the groom to the brightly lit paddock and saw the screaming horse racing around in a frantic circle, like he was being chased by some vicious animal.

"I let him out, like Mr. Lopez wanted, so the horse could exercise..." the groom said to Divina, "but, then, he just went...loco!"

She looked around, but didn't see her trainer. "Where is Raul?"

"He left right after I let the horse out. We don't usually do this at night, but I follow his orders."

The horse shook his head while he ran, like he was trying to remove his halter, and he began bucking, his piercing screams filling the air. When he stopped, he reared and pawed at the sky.

"Seth," Divina screamed, "do something!"

The vet immediately got his kit and pulled out a syringe. He yelled to the other men, "We have to tranquilize him. Get some rope to try and catch him." It took all three men to bring the horse to a halt. Mr. Divinity stood, agitated and straining against the ropes, as Seth moved in to give him the injection. "Let him go," Seth called, stepping back. They released the ropes and ran out of the paddock. The horse continued running around, until the medication started taking effect, slowing him down. Eventually, the animal stood to one side of the paddock, his breathing erratic and heavy, and sweat poured off his coat.

"Is there anything that can be done for him?" George asked, placing an arm around Divina.

Simon and Seth both shook their heads. Simon said, "There's no antidote—"

"I can start him on sedatives and laxatives," Seth jumped in, "to see if we can flush out some of the poison in his system. But, it may be too late. We'll have to keep him very quiet...and, he will probably get worse before he gets better." Seth looked sadly at Divina. "I'm afraid your stallion will never be able to race again...and will possibly be unable to be used for stud. Locoweed can cause sterility in horses."

Suddenly, Divina looked very tired. She said, "I think I want to be alone."

CHAPTER THIRTEEN

OREGON

Early one morning, Sam and Emma lay in their bed, snuggling after making love. Her head laid on Sam's bare chest, as she ran her fingers over his skin. "I'm so sorry we left everything up in the air," she said. "It hurts when we can't work things out."

Sam kissed the top of her head. "Me, too. My mom always said - don't go to bed angry, so I promise we will never do that again. I love you too much to hurt you in any way."

Emma looked up and said, "I love you, Sam. I know I can be a handful sometimes–" She quickly put her hand to her mouth, got up and ran to the bathroom, closing the door after her.

"Em, are you all right?" Sam asked on the other side of the door.

"I'll be out in a second..." Emma washed her face after throwing up and walked back into their bedroom.

"I think I caught a flu bug somewhere." She tried to smile. "What a way to break up a perfect moment, huh?"

"You need to go see your doctor," Sam suggested, hugging her against him.

"You're probably right. I'll call Dr. Blake and schedule an appointment. He's the new doc at the clinic in Newberg." She didn't mention her missed period.

Sam got dressed and went downstairs to start coffee.

Emma took a shower, then sat on the bed and called her

doctor's office. She was surprised they had a cancellation and she could get in later that morning. She didn't have any classes, so she took the appointment.

As she was getting dressed, Emma still believed it was just a virus.

She only drank black coffee at breakfast, while she watched Sam eat his pancakes. "I can't believe how fast your parents' ranch is moving!" she said, looking out the kitchen window at her stables.

"Yeah, I think it was all meant to be. Mom's closing tomorrow and is getting her new townhouse at the end of next week. She's so excited." He looked at his watch, picked up his plate and put it in the sink. "I have to fly down there to help her, I hope you don't mind."

"Not at all. I just wish I could come with you, but I was able to get an appointment today at the doctor's."

"I hope you're feeling better," he said, kissing her. He looked into her eyes and knew he had to ask. "Have you thought any more about me buying Joe's place?"

"No."

"I could bring Mike and Shane up with the horses - it'd be perfect to continue Promise's training–"

"No!" Emma said.

Just then, Peter walked in from the stable. "Good morning!" he said. "I'm starting to like this Oregon weather–" he stopped when he saw the look on Sam and Emma's faces. "I'll just get some coffee and go to work."

"Peter," Emma said, not looking at Sam, "I need to go to town this morning. I'll come to the stable in a minute so we can go over our schedule."

Sam knew his wife needed a little more time, so he kissed her cheek, then turned and left.

****

Emma sat in her doctor's office in Newberg with a thermometer in her mouth. The room was white, stark and cold as she sat on the end of the examination table with a paper cover over her lap

"What symptoms are you having, Mrs. Parker?" the nurse asked, removing the thermometer.

"I've been nauseous for over a week now. I'm sure this is just a bug."

"You don't have a fever, but the doctor will be in shortly." She took Emma's blood pressure and pulse. "When was your last period?"

Emma told her. "Just before I went on my honeymoon - to Europe."

Then, Dr. Blake entered. He was a man in his late fifties with sandy hair and a small pouch around his middle.

"Emma, it is good to meet you."

"Hello, Doctor."

"I hear you haven't been feeling well."

"Yes, I must have picked up a virus somewhere. My husband and I went on a cruise and toured Europe...I probably picked up something then."

He looked over her chart. "Well, I would like to run a few tests, just to be on the safe side," he said, listening to her heart and lungs. "In the meantime, I think you should get some rest."

"But, I just purchased some new Lipizzan horses for my breeding program, and we have to start soon."

"Rest and lots of fluids, young lady!" Dr. Blake ordered.

"Yes, sir."

"I'll call you when I have the test results."

"Thank you." Emma waited for him to leave, feeling apprehensive about the outcome.

****

When she returned home, she decided to look over their budget to see if there was any way she could help Sam, even though she really didn't want to buy that property. Emma shook her head when she realized how much she was going to have to pay Melody Hunt to work for her. They agreed to let her younger brother, Tommy, work for riding lessons.

Tracy called. "Hey, the Hunt kids are here at my place and want to know if they can come by to see what they need to do for you. I had planned to start working on Lucky today, too. Is that okay?"

Emma agreed and hung up. *Rest,* she thought, laughing. *That's not going to happen!*

As she walked down to the stables, she was surprised to see Nikki there, petting Sonny.

"Hi," Nikki said. "I know it's Saturday, but I was hoping I could ride Sonny for a bit." After the morning she'd had at home, Nikki needed to get away.

Emma noticed that the young girl seemed a little agitated. "Are you all right?"

Nikki turned away, rubbing her arm, then said, "Yeah, I'm fine." She looked back at Emma. "So, can I ride? Just for a little while? Please?"

Emma smiled. "Saddle him up! You know where everything is now."

Nikki ran to the tack room, but stopped just outside the door. She looked inside, then went in when she saw it was empty. After a moment, she walked back out with Sonny's blanket and saddle. Emma watched as Nikki fumbled a little, getting the saddle just right, so she stepped in to help her.

After Sonny was ready, Nikki led him to the arena. Emma watched as she mounted and started walking him around the outer rail, slowly working him up to a canter. As Nikki rode, taking Sonny through some of the gaits she'd learned, Emma noticed that it seemed to calm the girl.

As Nikki felt Sonny's body move under her, she began to let the anger go. Earlier, her foster dad, Walter, had been in one of his moods and woke her up, yelling at Maria that his eggs weren't just right. Then, she'd heard him throw his plate against a wall, and he'd begun to hit Maria. Nikki had pulled the pillow over her ears to block out Maria's cries, but she could still hear. Afraid he was going to come to her room, she'd quickly dressed and ran out the back door. She knew she'd be safe at Emma's.

"I'll be right back, okay?" Emma said.

Nikki nodded and smiled, happy to be here. This was the one place left to her where she could feel free and alive, not always looking over her shoulder - afraid.

Emma wasn't sure why she walked back to the tack room to get the riding crop. Somehow, she just knew it was the right thing to do. When she returned to the arena, Nikki was now walking Sonny again.

"Bring him over here and halt," Emma said.

Nikki followed directions, and then asked, "Should I dismount?"

"No, I have something for you." Emma held out the crop. "My father gave this to me when I was a young girl, and I want you to have it."

Nikki looked surprised. "Really?" Few people in her life ever gave her anything so nice. The Berkleys had been the only other ones.

"Yes, and I'm going to show you how to properly use it - with gentle kindness."

After a while, Tracy drove in, followed by Melody and Tommy Hunt. Melody drove a yellow Gremlin with a white stripe down each side. Emma smiled, thinking how ridiculous their car looked. When she'd first met these kids, she'd learned that Melody was a senior in high school. She had long, blonde hair and was going to college in the fall to Oregon State to study to be a veterinarian. Tommy, Melody's younger brother, was ten years old. He was very energetic and loved horses.

"Nikki, it's time for a break. Take Sonny to get some water and come back in a few minutes. We'll continue then, okay?" Nikki walked Sonny to a trough outside the large barn, cautiously watching the new kids. She knew Melody only as one of the 'cool' girls who ran around in a gang of other seniors.

Emma walked out to meet her new staff. "Welcome, kids." She swept her arms wide. "Glad to have you aboard."

"Wow, this place is awesome!" Tommy said, looking around. "I can't wait to get started."

"Well, then, follow me." Emma led the way to the main stable and opened the large door. "This building has the stallions and a few geldings. Most are my own horses, and I have a couple of boarders now."

As she walked down the wide aisle, Tommy peeked into all the stalls. He pointed to Neo and said, "Whoa, look at that dude!"

"This is Neapolitano Toscana, my new Lipizzan stud."

"He's very handsome!" Melody said. "I've never seen anything like him before."

"He came from Piber, the famous Austrian farm that breeds the Lipizzaners who perform for the Spanish Riding School in Vienna."

Peter walked in and Emma introduced him. Then, she said to the kids, "Peter will go over your chores for me. I have a student waiting."

"Cool!" Tommy exclaimed, as Emma and Tracy walked out of the stable.

"How's Lucky doing?" Tracy asked.

"He's settling down, but I haven't had much time to work with him yet. I've been so busy and still not feeling up to par." Emma saw the concerned look on her friend's face and added, "I went to see the doctor today. He says I'm fine."

"Well, that's good news." Tracy smiled. "Why don't you go finish with your student."

Emma stopped and lowered her voice. "It's Nikki. She just showed up out of the blue and wanted to ride Sonny. I think something's bothering her..."

"Maybe I'll come watch her ride; do you think that would be okay?"

"We can see. I'd appreciate your input."

They walked back to the arena. Nikki was standing next to Sonny, talking softly to the gentle horse. Sonny seemed to be leaning into Nikki somewhat, as if he knew she needed a hug. Emma smiled, remembering how Gandolf used to do that for her when she was upset. *He's just like his sire*, she thought to herself.

"Nikki, Tracy's here to work with Lucky, but she wanted to see you ride. Do you mind?"

"No, it's okay." Nikki stepped away from Sonny, nodding to Tracy. "Look at the riding crop Emma gave me!" Then, she turned to Emma and asked, "Can I start again?"

"Go ahead," Emma said. "This time, I want you to trot him through a few figure eights."

"Okay." Nikki mounted and walked Sonny to one end of the arena, then flicked the crop gently on one side to work him up to a trot, slowly pulling the reins to lead him into the figure.

"I'm impressed!" Tracy said as she watched Nikki. "She's come a long way."

"She's a natural," Emma said. "It's like she was born to ride horses. And, I think it's good therapy for her."

After a few turns around the arena, Emma called to Nikki. "Okay, I think that's enough for now."

"Can I watch you work with Lucky?" Nikki asked.

Emma thought for a moment, then said, "Why don't you go see if Melody will cool Sonny down and groom him," Emma said. "Then you can meet us in the paddock."

"Okay!"

Later, Emma and Nikki watched as Lucky was lunged in the outside paddock next to the arena. Tracy stood in the center with a long lead line and a lunge whip trailing in the dirt behind Lucky as he circled around her in a gentle lope. Once in a while, he'd buck or rear his head, but Tracy pulled him back in line each time. She softly talked to him the entire time, letting him know he wasn't going to get away with any of his old habits and that he was safe. Eventually, he became calmer and followed her directions.

"Can I ride him?" Nikki asked, as Tracy led Lucky to the paddock fence.

"I'd rather wait to see how he responds to my therapy before anyone rides him."

"He's settling down nicely," Emma offered.

Nikki stepped up to the paddock and held her hand through the fence.

"Be careful, he likes to bite!" Tracy cautioned, continuing to hold his lead line.

Nikki still held out her hand. Lucky brought his head up, then walked slowly up to the girl and sniffed. Tracy and Emma watched as Lucky allowed Nikki to rub his neck - the two youngsters putting their foreheads together, understanding.

CHAPTER FOURTEEN

One week before she would be leaving for the Kentucky Derby, Emma was lunging Neo in the enclosed arena, to allow him to warm up before she rode him.

In the distance, she could hear Elvin Coffee's old tractor plowing the field near the stables and thought that he was early this year, but they were having an unseasonably warm spring. Ever since she bought the property, she had a deal with the old farmer that he'd continue to work the land if he would give her hay for her horses. She turned her head when a movement to her left caught her eye. Peter walked in and was watching her and the stallion.

"He is a fine animal and will bring many foals for you, Mrs. Parker."

"Please call me Emma. We're going to be working closely with the horses and there's no need to be so formal. I want you to feel welcome here at Rising Sun. This is your new home."

"*Danke*, Mrs. Parker," Peter said as he nodded and smiled. He refused to call her by her first name - it wasn't how he had been raised.

"Do you miss Austria?" she asked, looking sideways.

"Sometimes. But, coming here with the horses has been a blessing, and I'm so grateful. America is amazing, and the people in the Northwest that I have met are open and friendly."

"Like Tracy?"

Peter smiled and nodded to the horse, who was now standing

still. "I think he's finished lunging for now."

"I have a little more to do with Neo," Emma said to Peter and pulled the horse towards her. She removed the lunge line.

Just then, Melody's yellow Gremlin drove down the lane and parked near the stable. Tommy jumped out first and ran to the arena. Melody followed, wearing breeches and a green turtleneck that set off her long, blonde hair.

"Hi kids, you're early today," Emma called.

"Teacher's Day, so we came here," Melody said, smiling at Peter.

"Cool, huh, Mrs. P.?" Tommy said.

Emma was surprised that he used her same nickname that Shane had used, but she liked it.

"Neo's a great horse, isn't he?" Tommy seemed to bounce in place with excitement.

"Yes, he is," Emma said, smiling.

"Hey, Peter," Melody said, looking sideways at the young man.

Emma noticed that Melody seemed to have a crush on him. *Tracy has some competition,* she thought, smiling.

She mounted Neo and started to walk him around the arena. Emma used her legs and reins to canter the horse in a figure eight, then went around the arena in a *Flying Change.* She crossed to the center and brought the horse into a *Piaffe,* where he trotted in place.

"Wow, how did you do that?" Tommy asked excitedly.

"Someday, I will teach you," Emma smiled, then cantered Neo to the outer edge.

Peter talked about the history of these beautiful animals. "The Lipizzan horses were originally bred for the military - enabling their rider to wield his sword, while using only his legs to command the horse."

"Awesome!" Tommy exclaimed.

"For the past four hundred years," Peter continued, "they have been trained at the Spanish Riding School in Vienna, Austria. I come from a village near there, where the Piber Stud is."

"How long are you staying in the States?" Melody asked, smiling at Peter.

"I'm not sure, it depends on Mrs. Parker...and my work Visa—"

"When do I get to learn to ride like that, Mrs. P.?" Tommy broke in, bored with the grown-up talk.

"You'll need to start learning on an English saddle first, Tommy," Emma said, "Maybe we can begin tomorrow, after your chores are done - if that's okay with Melody." Emma looked at his sister and saw her nod in agreement. "Okay you two, it's time you get to work."

In the aisle of the large stable, Peter finished grooming Neo and put him back into his stall. He checked to see how Melody and Tommy were doing, then, he and Emma walked to the mare's barn and talked about her plans for the breeding program.

Pluto Calma stood in her stall and whinnied when they entered. The mare was calm in her new surroundings, but Emma was concerned that she could get lonely - being the only horse in the building.

"We could start breeding early next month, and Calma could foal next April," Emma said, glad that she had installed two large foaling stalls in the new mare's barn.

Peter smiled and said, "If Calma does not come into her natural cycle next week, we can induce estrus. I'm sure Dr. White will assist us."

"There is another Lipizzan barn near here. Maybe we could encourage them to bring their mares to breed, as well, since we have two fine stallions. And, I'd like to keep at least one of her filly's to continue the line."

"*Ja*, I think that is a good idea." Peter rubbed the mare's neck.

Emma looked at Peter and added, "Tracy's coming here this afternoon to work with Lucky." She saw the young man blush. She really liked seeing these two people together. "I think she likes you."

Peter shook his head, but grinned. "I think she is amazing - the work she does."

"Yes, she is." Through one of the barn windows, Emma saw Sam drive up.

"Sam's home," she said and walked out to his truck. She could see he was preoccupied.

"Hi, Sam," she hugged him with one arm.

"Can I talk with you, Em?"

The couple walked towards the house, but didn't go in. Sam put his hands in his pockets and said, "Mike told me the sale of Mom and

Dad's ranch is finalized. I guess the guy paid cash. She's giving the keys to the new buyer in a few days."

"So soon?"

"Yeah." Sam stopped and took one of Emma's hands. "Em, Mom said I get the rest of the money, now that she's made the arrangements to buy her new place." He waited for a moment, deciding whether he should tell her about the offer he'd made. Then he knew what he had to do. He said, "I've been talking with a Portland realtor about buying Joe's ranch–"

"You've already talked to a realtor?" Emma blurted out. "Why didn't you say anything?"

"Em, I've been talking with you. But now, with this money coming in, it won't be a problem. There's nothing to stop me..."

Emma turned away and looked up at the hill where Sam had proposed to her two years ago. She'd thought at that time that she'd lost him again, but then he came back with an engagement ring. She looked down at the rings on her finger and wondered, *what is happening to us?*

"You know I want to race again," Sam continued. "And, Jim's been missing the ORC job, so he's thinking of taking it back. You're busy here with what you love, which I know nothing about. I race Thoroughbreds - it's in my genes. Shane wants to be my jock... He paused and looked at the ranch across the road. "I think it's my turn."

Emma thought for a moment, then said, "I'm still not sure it's a wise investment for us right now." She didn't tell him her real reason - the nightmares about Joe.

Upset, he said, "I've got a case to work on." He turned and left.

****

Sam was alone in the Portland office. Jim was at the track, and Sally had gone home. The phone rang, and he answered it. "Oregon Racing Commission."

"Is this Mr. Parker?" the voice said on the other end of the line.

"Yes, this is Sam."

"This is Kendra Jones, of Winderly Realty. I called that interested party after you left my office. He has accepted your offer!"

Sam sat back in his chair, not sure how to respond. "That was quick." He'd seen properties move fast before, but this was unreal.

"The seller wanted to unload that property as soon as possible."

The agent hadn't disclosed who the seller was, but Sam didn't really care. He figured it was some relative of Joe's, who he had no desire to meet.

"I'll make the arrangements for you to sign the papers and give you a call." the agent said.

He thought for a moment. All this time, he'd figured Emma would support him on his dream, but now he wasn't so sure. The day before, when he'd put in his offer at the agent's office, Kendra knew about the money coming in from his folks' ranch. That was when Sam had decided to put the property in his own name.

"Remember, I'm the primary buyer," he said over the phone.

"Yes, your wife's name will not be on the sale. The property will be yours alone."

"Thank you." Sam hung up and leaned forward, a large grin forming across his face. He thought...*my property! I like the sound of that*. He picked up the phone again and dialed. "Mike, pack everything - you're coming up here!"

"Already?"

"Yep. If it were me, I'd start now."

"We already have." Mike hung up.

Sam stood and looked out the window at the city's skyline, wondering how he was going to tell Emma about all this. He didn't understand her reluctance; but, hadn't she made all her plans about Rising Sun without him? He rubbed his hands through his hair. Then, he thought that if he could find out more about Nikki's situation with her foster parents, it might ease his news of the ranch.

He looked up the Children Services Division in McMinnville and made a call. When he was finished, he grabbed his jacket and walked out of the office.

****

"Come on, Tommy, we gotta go see Grandma!" Melody yelled as she stood near her car at Emma's place. Her little brother came running out of the large stable.

"I wish we could stay and watch Tracy on Lucky today," the little boy said.

"Me, too. But, Grandma's waiting." The two said goodbye, got into the Gremlin, and drove away.

Emma waved to the kids, then joined Nikki and Doc as they watched Tracy ride Lucky in the paddock. Nikki was there for another lesson, since Maria had agreed to more classes each week. Emma noticed that she still kept a bit of distance between her and Doc as they stood at the railing.

This was the first time the tall gray Thoroughbred trotted proudly with Tracy on his back without his usual outbursts. He was now acting more like a contented horse.

"Horses are sensitive animals," Tracy was saying as she asked him to canter. "They respond better to a lighter, gentler touch. This poor guy is finally beginning to trust me." She took him through different gaits, praising him at each switch, then changed rein in the other direction.

"How long have you been in the foster program?" Doc asked Nikki. Emma listened for her response.

The young girl was quiet for moment, not sure how or why she should answer him. *Who does this old man think he is, prying into my business?* Nikki thought defensively. But, Doc didn't push, he just waited. Then, after a few moments, she said in a small voice, "Since I was in kindergarten."

"Oh, my word," Doc said with compassion, glancing at Emma. "I'm so sorry. That must be hard for you."

Nikki shrugged. "I'm used to it now."

"Where are your parents? Your real parents?"

"I don't know. It was so long ago."

Doc looked at her in surprise.

"I don't want to talk about it," Nikki said, focusing back on Lucky.

Emma wondered how children became wards of the court - what would their parents have done to cause them to lose their kids. She decided to look into it on her own, when she got the chance.

Peter walked out and joined them.

Then, Emma said, "I want to give him a try." She slowly stepped into the paddock and waited. She had been spending time talking and petting Lucky since he'd come to her place - even feeding him apples once in a while. Now, she hoped he'd maybe let her ride him.

Tracy nodded and slowed Lucky to a walk, then brought him over to the side of the paddock and dismounted. Emma stretched out her hand to let the horse sniff and stroked his long neck. "Good boy," she cooed, then took the reins as Tracy walked up to hold his bridle.

As Emma gently mounted Lucky, he stood calmly without reacting, except for looking back at her. Slowly, she walked the big horse around, patting his neck and praising him. Then, she took him into a canter. They rode like this in silence for a little while longer, and then she brought Lucky to a halt and dismounted near where everyone stood. "What a good boy," she praised.

"This is exciting!" Tracy said. "He's getting used to us." She turned to the people standing next to her. "It's amazing how quickly he has responded to us. I was afraid we were going to have more of a fight on our hands."

Emma heard the stable phone ring in the tack room and watched as Peter went to answer it. Then, he called out, "Mrs. Parker, the telephone is for you."

Emma handed Lucky's reins to Tracy and walked to the large stable.

The air was cool as she walked inside and picked up the phone. "Emma Parker."

"Dr. Blake here. I have the results of your test—"

"What kind of virus do I have?" Emma asked. "You can prescribe something for it, right?"

She was surprised when her doctor laughed. "This is bigger than a virus, my dear," he said. "Emma, you are six weeks pregnant. Your baby is due in December. I want you to come in next week to go over..."

She didn't really hear the rest of the conversation. She realized she had been holding her breath, then exhaled long and slow. *Pregnant*!

"Mrs. Parker? Did you hear me?" Dr. Blake said over the phone line.

"Oh, yes, thank you," Emma said, her excitement rising. "Thank you!" She hung up.

She stood for a bit, stunned and glad that Peter had gone back to the paddock. She wanted to savor this moment, alone. She thought back and knew she must have gotten pregnant either before or shortly after they left for their honeymoon - probably on the ship crossing the Atlantic. She thought, *I've got to tell Sam!*

"You okay?" Nikki asked, standing just outside the tack room door.

Emma looked up and smiled. "Yes, dear, I'm fine." She placed her arm over the girl's shoulder and walked with Nikki outside the stable. Then, she said, "I have to go up to the house for a few minutes. Will you help Tracy with Lucky?"

"Sure thing." Nikki nodded and ran back to where Tracy stood.

In the house, Emma was so excited as she dialed the number for Sam's office. She couldn't wait to tell him. When Sally answered, Emma said, "Hi, Sally, this is Emma. Can I speak to Sam?"

"I'm sorry, but he just left. He didn't say where he was going. I'll tell him you called when he checks in."

"Thank you." Disappointed, Emma hung up. She needed to tell someone, so she dialed her godmother in New York.

"Karen, speaking," the voice on the other end said. Emma smiled at her aunt's greeting. She'd always said that on the phone since she'd known her.

"Hi, Aunt Karen."

"Hello, Emma dear. It's so good to hear your voice."

"I have some news...Sam is out right now, so I have to wait to tell him, but I wanted to—"

"Honey, slow down. What's going on?"

Emma took a deep breath, "I'm pregnant!" she yelled into the phone. "But, you can't tell anyone until I talk to Sam, okay?"

There was a silence on the other end of the line. "Aunt Karen? Are you still there?"

"Yes, dear, I'm just trying to absorb it all—" Karen stopped. Thoughts of her own lost child flooded back to her, the memory still too raw.

Emma listened for a moment, but was surprised that her aunt seemed less excited about her news.

Then, Karen finally said, "I'm so happy for you. When is the baby due?"

"December - I can hardly believe it!"

After she hung up, Emma decided to call her best friend, Jennifer. They'd met at art school ages ago in Chicago. Emma had studied painting, but Jennifer's passion was photography.

Her friend's husband, Jason, answered. When Emma asked to talk to Jennifer, he told her that she was in Africa on a photo shoot.

"She'll be back in about a month," Jason said. "She's going to call me this weekend...can I give her a message?"

Emma chose to wait. She said goodbye and went back outside. Walking down the path from her house, she saw that the clear sky seemed bluer and the colors of the flowers were more vibrant than ever before. Life was as it should be! But, as she neared her friends, she decided to wait to tell anyone else until she had a chance to let Sam know that they were going to have a baby.

Tracy still had Lucky in the paddock, and Nikki was stroking the gray's neck as he stretched his head against the fence. The young girl didn't seem to have noticed that Doc was now standing next to her. Emma walked up to join them, trying to act as if nothing had happened.

"Can I ride Lucky?" Nikki asked Emma. "He looks okay to me today."

Looking at her friend, Tracy could tell that something was up. But, Emma nodded and Nikki crawled through the fence.

"Now, remember to walk up to him slowly," she cautioned the girl, "and put out your hand for him to sniff."

Nikki followed Tracy's directions. Lucky placed his soft muzzle in her hand, then she slowly reached up to stroke his forehead. "Good boy," she cooed, like she'd seen the others do. "We're going to be good friends."

Emma looked at Nikki - she'd said the same thing to this horse when he'd arrived.

Tracy held his reins as Nikki mounted the tall gray horse. Then, she attached a long lead line and handed the reins to Nikki. Horse and rider walked around the paddock. Lucky whinnied softly, like he was happy he and Nikki had this time together.

All watched as Tracy worked with the pair. "They instinctively protect themselves, so use a soft rein and gentle pull...that's it."

"You're not going to get hurt," Nikki said to the horse, patting Lucky's neck as he let her ride him in a slow trot.

Nikki and horse seemed to immediately settle down and become one with each other.

****

Sam entered the Children Services office in McMinnville and approached the half-round counter, where various women sat. Two women were talking. Then one hugged the other and said, "I love you for helping me." The women left the area, and Sam looked around him. A young woman with red hair sat at the other end of the counter.

"May I help you?" she asked with a smile.

"I have an appointment with Lynn Chamberlain. Sam Parker."

She looked at a calendar on her desk and said, "I will let her know you're here."

Sam walked around the lobby for a moment, thinking that this was an interesting place to work. The staff seemed happy, in spite of some of the circumstances of the cases they probably had to work on. Some kids ended up here because the court had to take them away from their parents - maybe like Nikki. But, he was here to find out.

He looked out the bank of windows and watched the rain coming down in sheets, thankful he was now inside. *Wait five minutes and the sun will come back out*, he thought to himself with a chuckle. That's what most Oregonians say when the weather turned bad - it was constantly changing.

A young woman with jet black hair, pulled back in a bun, and beautiful dark eyes came out to meet him. She offered her hand and said, "Hello, Mr. Parker. I'm Lynn."

He followed her to an interview room. On the phone, he'd learned that she was assigned to Nikki's case for the foster parent program. He was surprised to see the size of the file Lynn laid on the desk between them. Nikki was such a young girl.

"I've been Nicole's caseworker here at CSD for two years," Lynn began, "But, I know the woman she had before me, she's retired now." She tapped the file and added, "And, I have all of her case notes."

"She likes to be called Nikki," Sam said and saw the caseworker smile as she gazed down at the file and made a note.

"Why are you here, Mr. Parker?"

"I am the Director of the Oregon Horse Racing Commission," he started, hoping his title would make an impression. "And my wife,

Emma, is teaching Nikki to ride horses at her Rising Sun Stables - a Dressage training center on Chehalem Mountain near Newberg." Sam stopped and wondered if he should lie to this woman. Emma didn't know he was here, but he took a chance. "She wanted me to check to see if there is anything that would prevent Nikki from taking riding lessons." Sam knew this was a lame excuse, but he hoped to learn more about the young girl.

"I can't really give out any—"

Sam cut in, "Walter and Maria Mitchell have signed a release form, so I know they are her foster parents." He took a breath. "I was just wondering how long Nikki's been with them."

"I'm afraid most of her information is confidential," Lynn said, then looked up at Sam and saw the expression in his eyes. It was similar to a pleading parent, hoping to get their child back. She sighed and said, "All I can say is that she went to the Mitchells less than one year ago. Nicole...Nikki is their first foster child." She looked back at her file and added sadly, "She has been in our program since she was five."

He stared at the woman across from him. "If she's been in your program that long, how many other foster homes has she been assigned to?"

Lynn said, "I can't reveal anything more—"

"What happened to her parents?" Sam asked quickly. "Why was she put in the foster program to begin with?"

"I'm sorry," Lynn said, closing the file. Then, she looked at Sam again. "But, I can tell you that she is an angry child with trust issues. These kinds of kids tend to run away, when they don't like something at their current placement."

She stood and opened the door. As she escorted Sam out of the building, Lynn added, "That's all I can say - for now."

KENTUCKY

George and Divina sat together at Gallano Farm, watching the moon rise over the stables through the large windows.

"Mr. Divinity's not getting any better," Divina said. "I'm not sure of the future of Gallano Farm. I can't handle this alone."

She got up and paced in front of the large windows. "I was young when I got married. He was handsome and charming." She sighed and turned to George. "Have you ever been married?"

"No." He looked away for a moment. "I was in love once...but she died in the war." He wasn't ready to tell her about Hannah, just yet. He didn't know if he'd ever be ready.

"I'm so sorry." She sat down next to him and placed her hand on his knee, "It was such a terrible time. Many loved ones were lost."

They sat in silence for a moment, each with their own memories.

"I haven't been in love since my marriage," Divina finally said. She looked at George. "I sort of thought that maybe that might change when I met you."

There was a knock on the front door and Jasmine's voice could be heard down the hallway. "Hello, Mr. Day. Miss Divina is in the den."

George and Divina looked at each other. Then, just as the man walked in, George stood. "Hello, Simon," he said and shook his hand.

"Hi," Simon said, and then turned to Divina. "Ms. Gallano, we may have a suspect for the poisoning of Mr. Divinity."

"Who is it?" she asked.

"Darrell Fisher, one of the guards at Churchill Downs—"

"I know him," Divina exclaimed. "He was a friend of my ex-husband!"

CHAPTER FIFTEEN

OREGON

Nikki was doing so well riding Lucky around the paddock, first in a trot, then a canter. Both the young girl and the horse seemed to be enjoying themselves as they continued.

"That's it," Tracy said, still holding the lunge line, in case she needed to intervene. "Keep his reins gently pulled back like that, so he doesn't run away with you. Remember, he is a race horse!"

"This is so fun!" Nikki said, smiling. "I like him...and I think he likes me, too." She patted Lucky's neck.

"Head up, heels down," Tracy told Nikki. "Keep your weight in the saddle..."

Just then, the tractor in the field backfired, startling Lucky. He stopped and reared up, throwing Nikki off.

Tracy went to the horse as Emma and Doc ran to Nikki.

"Whoa, boy," Tracy called, pulling on his lead and steering him away. She tried to calm the animal down. "It's okay," she said to him at the other side of the paddock. He spun in circles as the tractor backfired again, but Tracy held him firm. She was glad when she saw Peter run in to help her.

"Nikki," Emma cried. "Are you hurt?" She brushed away the dirt from Nikki's face.

When Nikki tried to sit up, Doc stopped her. "Lie still, you could have broken something." He looked into her eyes to check her pupils. Confirming there were no signs of head trauma, he ran his hands along the young girl's limbs, checking for broken bones.

"I'm fine!" Nikki said, trying to sit up. "Don't touch me!" she yelled as she pushed the man's hands away and scrambled to get up.

"Lie still until Doc has had a chance to check you," Emma said sternly, firmly holding Nikki. "We don't want you to cause any more damage."

"I'll take Lucky to cool down," Tracy said and left the paddock with the animal. He nickered softly, looking back at Nikki as he was led away.

Nikki lay still, cringing at Doc's hands as he slowly sat her up. He lifted her blouse to check her back, frowned, then he let it fall back into place.

"Can I get up now?" Nikki asked, tugging the material tight around her.

"I think she will be all right," he finally said. "Maybe a little sore and bruised...but nothing is broken and she doesn't have a concussion."

"I want you to come to the house to lie down for a while," Emma said to Nikki, as the young girl brushed the dirt off her pants. "I'll have Peter call Maria—"

"No! I'm okay. How is Lucky?"

"I'm sure he's fine, but, you understand we have to call Maria," Emma insisted. "She needs to know about your fall, and will want to come pick you up." She looked at Doc. "Is she okay to move now?"

"Yes, but I'd like to keep her under observation until her parent arrives."

"Foster parent!" Nikki exclaimed. She started walking towards the house, brushing more dust off her clothes.

Doc followed as Emma asked Peter to call Maria. "Her number is listed on the board by the phone in the tack room."

Once they were in the den, Nikki reluctantly laid down on the couch. Doc kept watching her, checking her pulse. "You have to stay awake for a few hours," he said, "in case of any possible head injury."

Nikki pulled away from him. "I'm fine!"

"How did you get those bruises on your back, Nikki?" Doc asked softly. "They aren't from the fall today...they're a few days old."

Nikki looked at Doc, and then turned away. "I fell during gym class at school," she said, shrugging nonchalantly. "It's no big deal." Just then, Nikki looked up and saw Emma standing in the doorway.

Emma stepped into the room, sat at Nikki's feet and touched her leg. "When I was about your age, I fell off Gandolf." She looked at Doc, then back to Nikki. "At first, I was a little afraid to ride again, but eventually, you have to get back on - if you really want to ride."

"It's not the first time I've fallen off a horse," Nikki said, trying to smile.

Tracy came in. "How are you doing, kid?"

"Fine - is Lucky okay?"

"Yes, but I shouldn't have let you ride him yet. It's my fault–"

"No," Emma said. "It was the tractor that spooked him. She and Lucky were doing so well together."

After a few moments, a car sped up the drive. Maria had arrived, and Emma went out to meet her. "We're in here," she said and led the way back to the den.

Maria went to Nikki, but didn't touch her. She glared down at the small girl lying on the couch, "See why I didn't really want you taking these stupid riding lessons? I knew you'd get hurt–"

"I'm not hurt...and it was an accident." Nikki stood up slowly and put her hands on her hips. "I want to keep taking lessons."

"We'll see about that!" Maria turned and glared at Emma. "How did this happen?"

"A tractor backfired, startling the horse she was riding. Dr. White here said she is all right."

"She doesn't have any broken bones," Doc interjected. "I cautioned her to not sleep for a few hours, just to make sure her head is okay."

"I know you, you're not even a real doctor," Maria exclaimed. "You're a vet!"

"Yes," Doc said, "but I am also a medical practitioner. I just specialize in animals."

"My god!" Maria whirled on Emma. "I don't know what my husband will do!"

Tracy stepped forward and said, "I'm sure he'll understand–".

"We can't tell Walter about this, he'll go crazy!" Maria said, wringing her hands. Then, she turned to Nikki and yelled, "Nicole, get in the car."

Nikki looked around the room, then tried to smile at Emma.

"Now!" Maria barked.

Slowly, Nikki left the room with Maria following her, continuing to rant on about what Walter would do - if he knew...

"Wow," Tracy sighed, "I thought I was a hard ass. She takes the cake."

Doc laughed, trying to ease the tension in the room. "She'll calm down after she sees Nikki is okay. Maria's working on adrenalin right now."

"I'm just surprised to see how protective she was," Emma said. "Up till now, she seemed as if she didn't really care what Nikki did."

Doc cleared his throat. "I found some older bruises on Nikki's back today." He looked between Emma and Tracy with sad eyes.

"I saw some on her arm the other day when she was brushing Sonny," Tracy added. "She dismissed them, but I've seen bruises like that on kids who were being used as a punching bag."

That evening, Emma hugged Sam as she lay against his chest. The fire in the den was roaring now and cast a warm glow around the room. She sighed and said, "I told you about Nikki falling..."

"Yes, is she okay?"

"Maria hasn't called, but Doc thought she was not injured too badly." She snuggled closer to Sam, holding him tightly. "After she left, he and Tracy both told me that they saw bruises on her back and arms, but Nikki insisted she'd fallen at school. Doc said they weren't from any fall–"

"What!?" Sam exclaimed, sitting upright.

"Tracy thinks Nikki is being abused." Emma sat up and hugged herself.

Sam stood up and began pacing the room. "If I ever get my hands on whoever is doing this–"

"We don't know this for sure, yet. It's not like we can start accusing anyone–"

He stopped and looked at Emma. "I've been talking to the Children Services office about Nikki. They said she's been in their program since she was five."

"Oh, my god!" Emma sighed. "No wonder she's so guarded."

"I'll go talk to them again tomorrow and let them know." He continued to pace, then said, "Em, I need to–"

"Wait!" Emma said and walked up to him. "I love you so much..." she began, holding his hand. She knew that in spite of this turmoil, she was going to have to tell Sam, but she couldn't bring herself to tell him everything. "Sam, I'm pregnant."

She held her breath, knowing how conflicted he was about having children. When she saw his eyes light up and he smiled, she exhaled. He hugged her carefully, then asked, "When is it due?"

"December. We may even have a Christmas baby." She kissed him and said, "I know about our mothers' pasts...and you've had some bad experiences with children, but I'm sure we can work this out together."

Sam looked up at the ceiling for a moment, then back at Emma. "I may just need a little time to adjust..."

"I totally understand. Just please talk to me, if you have any doubts." Emma hugged Sam, then said, "I think I got pregnant around the beginning of our honeymoon, maybe even sometime on the ship."

Sam smiled and kissed his wife, "You were able to finally relax from all this work."

"When we were in Paris, I was sitting in the *Sacré-Coeur*, wondering about us having children." She looked up at her husband. "I heard a voice that told me everything will be all right. So, I know it will."

He hugged and kissed her again, then said, "Why don't you call George and let him know he's going to be a great-uncle." Then, he left the room.

Sam walked into the kitchen and pulled down a bottle of bourbon from the cupboard. Pouring a short glass, he took a long swig, letting the liquid slowly burn down to his stomach. He shook his head in disbelief. *A baby!* he thought. He took another swig and saw his hand shake a little. Yes, he was afraid, but also excited. He just wasn't sure which emotion was going to win out.

He sat at the kitchen table and looked out the side window at the ranch across the road - at his ranch, his dreams. Sam knew he couldn't tell Emma about it yet - not now that she'd dropped this bomb on him. Suddenly, he thought of Vietnam, remembering those terrifying events...

KENTUCKY

Simon turned on the tape recorder and looked at the man sitting across from him in the interrogation room at his Commissioners office. He cleared his voice.

"Interview with Darrell Fisher, by Simon Day..."

"Why am I here?" Darrell asked, looking cockily around the small room, with gray walls and no window.

"Because I need to talk to you," Simon said. He'd brought Darrell in for questioning in connection with the poisoning of Divina Gallano's stallion. He looked down at his file, stalling a bit in hopes to make the man nervous. It was one of the tactics he'd found useful in the past.

"How long have you worked at Churchill Downs as a security guard?" Simon asked.

Darrell looked right and up at the ceiling. "Fifteen years."

Simon made a note in the file and asked, "During that time, do you have certain barns in the backside that you're assigned to watch?"

Darrell looked at Simon as if he was an alien. "What the hell does that have to do with anything?"

"Just answer the question."

"No, I get different assignments at the track each day."

"How often are you assigned to the backside gate?" Simon asked, based on some sightings that were reported by certain people he'd talked with recently. One time in particular was of interest.

"I don't know - maybe once or twice a week. Why?"

Simon decided to switch tactics. "Do you work at any other racetracks?"

Darrell sat quietly for a moment. "Do I need a lawyer?" he asked.

"You haven't been charged with any crime. We just need you to answer a few more questions."

"Well, sometimes, I moonlight over at Keeneland - when they get short-handed."

"Did you hear about what happened to the stallion at Gallano Farm?"

Darrell's eyes went wide and said "No!" as he loudly cleared his throat and fidgeted in his chair.

Got him! Simon thought and smiled. These were telltale signs of someone telling a lie.

"Where were you on the night of April, 9th?" This was the night before the Aqueduct race in New York.

It took a while for Darrell to answer, but then he slowly smiled and said, "With Gordon Evers."

OREGON

It was dark when Nikki walked into her house. She'd gone for a walk to clear her head after her fall. Immediately, she could tell by the silence that something was up. It was never quiet here.

As she entered the kitchen, Walter sat at the table and stared at her. Maria stood frightened by the refrigerator. Nikki could see the tears and black eye on the woman's face.

"I was called at work today," Walter yelled at Nikki. "Do you know why?" He looked at his wife, "Because that bitch at that riding center decided I needed to know that you'd fallen off a goddamned horse!" His fist slammed on the table, making Maria jump and cry louder.

"Shut up, bitch!" he yelled at his wife. "Stop that bawling."

"Leave her alone!" Nikki cried, tears starting to stream down her face.

He turned on Nikki and raised his hand. She cowered, covering her face. "Don't you tell me what to do, you little mongrel. I should've never agreed to take you on. If it weren't for the money...You've been nothing but trouble since you came here."

He smacked Nikki on the side of her head, causing her cheek to slam against the wall. Her head ached even more now.

Slowly, she stood up, took a deep breath and said, "You're just a stupid bully, like the ones at school!"

Walter grabbed Nikki and dragged her into the living room.

"No!" Maria screamed and followed.

"You're never going back to that damned place again, you hear?" he spat at Nikki. "Now, I'M going to teach you a lesson!"

He threw her on the couch, a pain running through her back as she fell on something hard. She reached back and wrapped her fingers around the riding crop that Emma had given her. Just as Walter came near her, she brought the crop up and hit him across the face as hard as she could. He staggered back, giving her enough time to get up and run out the door.

"Walter, stop!" she could hear Maria's screams as she ran down the road, crying, still clutching her crop.

Shaking, Nikki ran to Miller's Gas Station. They had a telephone booth outside. She prayed there was enough change left in the coin slot, like she'd found on other times when she needed money.

"Thank you!" she sighed, holding the coins in her hand. Her fingers shook as she dialed Emma's number and waited, her breath coming in quick pants that hurt her chest. She tried to slow her breathing down.

"Hello?" Emma said on the line.

"Emma, this is Nikki...I, uh, I won't be able to get to class for a week...because of my studies."

"Are you okay, Nikki? I've been worried about you since the fall."

Nikki ran her hand against her aching head.

"The fall from the horse was nothing!" she said and quickly hung up. She couldn't bring herself to tell Emma what was really going on.

Slowly, she sank down in the booth and put her arms around her knees. She still held the crop in her hand, her whole body shaking now. Nikki knew what was waiting for her when she went back home.

CHAPTER SIXTEEN

A few days had passed since Emma told Sam about the baby. She walked down the hall from their upstairs bedroom and paused at the open doorway of her art studio. She stepped into the room and looked around at the array of unfinished canvasses, paints and brushes. Since she'd moved here, she'd started so many paintings, but since the one of her father and Conversano, she'd been unable to complete anything else.

Emma started thinking about some baby names that had come to her in the night.

Sam walked up behind her and put his arms around her. "Good morning," he whispered in her ear.

She turned and hugged her husband, kissing him softly on the lips. "I love you, Sam."

"And, I love you, and our baby." He looked around the room. "What're you doing in here this time of day?"

"I was thinking...this could be our nursery."

"But, what about your art? This was always a special room for you."

"Painting was more my father's passion for me. He felt it was more dignified for young ladies than working with horses."

"How wrong was he?" Sam laughed. "I'm sure he'd be proud of you for the work you're doing here."

She sighed. "I hope so."

Sam looked out the bank of windows and saw his ranch, the

house and stables just waiting for him to begin.

Emma saw the serious look in his eyes and asked, "Sam, what's the matter?"

"I was going to tell you before, but the news of the baby trumped mine." He hesitated, took a deep breath. "I bought Joe's ranch–"

"You did what?" Emma stepped away from him.

"I got the call...that my offer was accepted."

"Without telling me?" Emma paced the room. "I thought we were going to wait until we could discuss it further."

"I've tried to talk to you about it. You're busy here...and I have to move Mike and the horses up–"

The phone rang. Sam stared at Emma, then went downstairs to answer it.

Emma looked around the studio - the sweet moment now shattered. She turned, closed the door and went downstairs.

"That was Jim," Sam lied, as Emma entered the den. He didn't tell her it was the real estate agent saying he could pick up the keys today.

"Just go!" she yelled, and Sam left.

On the drive into the city, Sam stopped at a little coffee shop in Newberg. After picking up his order, he used a pay phone outside and called Mike. He'd already given Mike the go-ahead days before.

"I'm getting the keys now," Sam told his friend. "When can you be up here?"

"We've been waiting for your call. We'll meet you at the ranch this afternoon."

"Okay, see you then."

Sam hung up and belittled himself because he felt so selfish - even though he still believed that he was doing the right thing.

****

Emma stormed to the stable and went into Gandolf's stall. She was glad Peter wasn't there, so she could be alone with her friend. She flung her arms around her horse's neck. The stallion stood still, allowing her to cry into his mane. The pair had done this numerous times in their lives together, each understanding what the other needed.

"I can't go over there," Emma sobbed. "Not after all that happened..." Her mind was flooded with images of the nightmares that haunted her of that night, and meeting her Uncle Franz for the first time - seeing the greed in his eyes when he showed her the Caspar Friedrich painting that caused his death.

Just then, she heard footsteps and quickly wiped her eyes.

"Are you okay, Mrs. Parker?" Peter asked.

"Yes," Emma said, wiping her nose on her sleeve. "I just came to see how Gandolf was doing."

"We can go over the breeding plan later," Peter said, then went into his room and shut the door. He was nervous when he'd found her crying and hoped it was nothing he had done. He really liked it here and would be sad if he ever had to leave.

A few moments later, Tracy arrived. By then, Emma was calmer and wanted to put their argument behind her. She walked out to meet her friend.

"Hey, Em," Tracy called, jumping down from her truck. "Hi, Peter." she said, when he came out and joined them. She then glanced at both of them. "What's up?"

"*Hallo,*" Peter said, then looked at Emma and placed his hands in his pockets.

"Well..." Emma began, a little embarrassed. "I want you two to know that Sam and I are expecting a baby."

Peter stared at her with a sigh of relief.

"Hot damn!" Tracy exclaimed and hugged her friend. "I'm so excited for you. When's the little bundle coming?"

"December."

Peter finally smiled and said, "*Wunderbare,* Mrs. Parker! If you wish, I will help with the lessons until you are ready to resume them. I used to train the young horses at Piber."

"Thank you, Peter. That is so sweet. But, would you please call me 'Emma'?"

He looked at Tracy and blushed, then turned to Emma and said, "I will go check on Calma...it is time for her exercise."

As they watched Peter walk away, Tracy said, "Dang, he's got a cute butt!" She then turned and asked Emma, "Have you decided on any baby names yet?"

"I just told Sam last night. If it's a girl - I want to call her Sophia, after my mother."

"That's so pretty, and if it's a boy?"

"I don't know yet. That's all I've come up with so far." Emma turned and looked up the lane.

Tracy stood with her hands on her hips and said. "Okay, spill - what else is up? Your eyes were all red when I got here."

Emma sighed. "You know me so well...Sam bought the ranch across the road. He's moving his dad's racing operation up here - horses, Shane and his dad. The whole lot."

"What's so bad about that?"

"He did it without talking to me!" She knew this wasn't the truth.

Peter walked out of the mare's barn with Calma.

Tracy admired his strong hands as he led the horse to the outside paddock. She sighed and turned to Emma. "Well, I've always thought the difference between men and women is that we ladies like to talk things over, chew on it awhile, and then make a decision. Most men I've known just jumped in and got wet before they'd thought it through." Then Tracy added, "At least Sam won't have to keep going back and forth between here and Eugene."

Emma looked at the dreaded place. Then, Tracy's words sunk in. "I hadn't thought of that," she said, a spark of hope filtering into her heart. "I'm just afraid - you know what happened with the last owner of that ranch..."

"Yes, but that's all in the past, and Sam will be building new memories there."

"You're absolutely right!" She smiled and hugged her friend. "Thank you!"

"Glad I could help!" Tracy said, smiling. She looked at the man and the mare in the paddock. "Let's go watch Peter in action, okay?"

The two women walked to the fence and admired the beautiful mare as she lunged around the sandy-haired young man. Peter had placed double reins on Calma, like Emma had seen at the Spanish Riding School, so he could walk behind the horse and control her as if he were riding her. He asked the horse to change between a working trot, a rising trot, then back to a working trot with only the use of the reins. Then, he changed reins and the mare continued in the opposite direction.

"It's going to be interesting to watch him teach," Emma said.

"Yeah," Tracy sighed. "He's so good with his hands..."

Emma laughed and bumped her friend with her shoulder. It was good to feel the weight of Sam's decision fall away, and she could see more clearly into their future.

Tracy looked at Emma. "Um, I came here to see if it's okay if I work with Lucky some more. Since he threw Nikki, he's going to need some extra time getting back on track."

"About Nikki - she called to say she was going to have to postpone classes for a week. She said it was because of her studies."

"I wonder if it's really homework that made her stop," Tracy said.

"Me, too," Emma said, sadly.

Peter then said to the mare, "That is enough for today, Calma." He looked and was embarrassed when he saw the two women watching him.

"You're going to be a fine trainer here," Emma said.

The young man smiled.

"I'm going to bring Lucky in, when you're finished," Tracy said.

"Then, I will take Calma back to her stable."

Emma and Tracy watched Peter as he removed the long lines, then led the mare out of the paddock. Then, the two women went into the large stable to get the equipment.

Later, Peter and Emma stood outside the paddock as Tracy led Lucky inside. The horse was wearing full tack. Peter looked down and frowned when he saw the CO_2 fire extinguisher that sat at Emma's feet.

Today, Tracy asked Peter to place an empty barrel to one side of the paddock. "I want to see how the horse reacts to obstacles." Lucky was on a long lunge line, which Tracy held in her left hand. She had a whip with a flag in her right.

"He let me tack him today without a fuss," Emma said.

Tracy laughed as Lucky bucked a little. "He's acting like an old guy getting used to his suspenders." As she lunged the horse awhile, he was back to pulling on his lead a little, but slowly seemed to relax again. He became cautious anytime he came near the barrel. Each time as they circled, Tracy would take him closer to the obstacle. Then, she brought him to a halt and walked him up to it and let him sniff it. She walked him back, and then led him up to it. He hesitated and went around the barrel.

"No," she said gently. "I want you to go over it." Once again, she led the animal to the barrel, but continued walking. After a few tries, he eventually jumped over it. "Good boy!" she said.

She lunged him, avoiding the barrel this time. "Let's see how you do with unexpected noises," Tracy said to the horse. As he seemed to relax again, she flicked the whip, making a popping sound with the flag on the end. Lucky startled, but continued to lunge. "Good boy," she cooed, then repeated this until the horse stopped responding to the noise.

"She is amazing!" Peter sighed, standing next to Emma.

Emma looked at the star-struck young man and said, "Yes, she is."

"Okay," Tracy said, lunging Lucky. "Now it's time for louder noises - like the one the tractor made the other day."

Emma picked up the extinguisher and said, "Are you ready?"

When Tracy nodded, Emma pulled the handle and a loud blast sounded. Then, she released it. Lucky reared and screamed, startled.

"Whoa," Tracy called to him. "You're okay, boy. That mean machine won't hurt you."

Lucky finally settled and lunged again. Then, the two women continued, until the horse stopped reacting to the unexpected noise.

After a while, Emma handed the extinguisher to Peter and said, "Well, I have some work to do. Thanks, Tracy!" she called and walked to the house to leave the two lovebirds alone.

****

Tracy and Peter walked up the aisle, after putting Lucky back into his stall.

"He probably will be okay with noises now, after today's work," she said. "I just hope Nikki will want to ride him again soon. I think she and the horse need each other."

She stopped at Peter's room and looked in. "So, this is where you live?"

"*Ja*," he said. Surprised to see her just walk in, he followed her.

Tracy sat on the twin bed and smiled. The walls were covered in a dark siding, with no pictures, but there was an empty gun rack. An armoire stood against the side near a window that looked out towards the outdoor paddock.

"This is a small room, but nice," she said, placing her hands around one knee and leaning back. She was hoping he'd notice how her hair fell off her shoulders, trying to entice the man. "Do you like it?"

He nodded. "It reminds me of an American cowboy's room that I saw in the films in Vienna."

Peter sat nervously on the chair next to a wooden desk.

Tracy got up and walked around the room. There were pictures on the desk next to him of two different couples, and one of Peter holding the lead of a white stallion in front of a large stable. "Where was this taken?" she asked, pointing to the one with the horse.

"At Piber, the Lipizzan stud farm in Austria."

"Do you miss it? Austria?" She had such a crush on him from the moment she'd met him, but this was the first time they'd had a chance to be alone and talk like this.

"Sometimes," Peter said. "Those other two photos - one is of my parents and the other is Mr. and Mrs. Schmid, the couple who took care of me after my parents died...Luka was a blacksmith at the Piber Stud Farm, and he got me a job there when I was young." He looked sadly at Tracy. "I have no family left there now."

"Did you know that Emma has been looking into you becoming a citizen, so you can stay here?" She walked around the room.

"*Nein*! She never said anything."

"I think she just wanted to see what was involved first. I'm sure when she knows more, you two can talk about it."

He went to Tracy and asked, "Would you like me to stay here?"

Tracy placed her hand on his cheek and kissed him softly. "Yes."

Peter closed the door.

****

Sam drove into his new ranch and parked near the house to wait for Mike. He grabbed his notebook and baseball cap on the seat next to him and stepped out of his truck. He looked across at Rising Sun, feeling a twinge of guilt that the road now separated his and Emma's horse worlds. But, this is what he needed to survive.

He unlocked the ranch house. The air was musty, so Sam opened a few windows. Looking around the large open room with the fireplace, he decided that he'd need to replace the old, tapestry couch and chairs, but would keep the walnut tables and antique, roll-top desk. He walked through the entire house, noting it had three furnished bedrooms. The place had been left as if Joe was going to walk back in at any moment. Sam went back into the large room.

Sitting down at the desk, he checked the phone to make sure it was connected. Getting a dial tone, he dialed the number for CSD and asked for Lynn. When the receptionist told him she was out, he left his office number for her to call. Leaving a message about Nikki's possible abuse wasn't something he wanted to do.

Sam looked at his watch as he hung up and decided he had time to start on his training program. He thought of each step his dad would do with a young colt. With each notation, his excitement grew as he realized his dream was finally coming true. He leaned back in the chair and rubbed his hands over his face. Placing his ball cap on his head, he got up and went outside.

He walked past the paddock, then into each of the barns, making sure all was ready. Classy Elegance and Koenig's Promise were moving up here today. His dad had a couple of horses left: O'Leary's Bluff, a favorite bay stallion, was too old to race, but he'd brought many wins in his racing days. O'Leary could turn out to be a fine stud for Sam's stables. Stanford, a five-year old gelding, was a good exercise pony on the track. Seeing that all was ready, Sam took a moment to visualize Koenig's Promise going to the Belmont Stakes in two years. Thinking about his own future helped him push his fear of a baby aside...for now.

After a while, Mike honked as he pulled his truck into the lane, hauling the large four-horse trailer. Sam heard a loud whinny and walked out to meet them.

"Welcome to your new home," Sam said, shaking Mike's hand. "After we get the horses settled, I'll show you around." He looked in the back of Mike's pickup, loaded with boxes. Then he saw his two family heirlooms he treasured - his grandfather's clock and his dad's oak lamp. "Mom didn't want these?" he asked, pointing to the two special items.

Mike snickered and said, "Nah, she said they didn't go with her new decor and knew you'd want them. I can take these across the road later–"

"No, I want to keep them here."

Just then, Shane drove the Skylark into the lane. Sam could hear the loud music playing from the car's radio, even with the windows rolled up. The young man turned off the engine and got out of the vehicle, grinning from ear to ear. "Man that was so cool!" Shane said. "I've never had such a great time."

Sam held out his hand and waited. Reluctantly, Shane placed the car keys in his hand. "Maybe you can borrow it from time to time," Sam said as he pocketed the keys.

"Wow that would be great!"

"Let's get these horses out of the trailer," Mike finally said.

The men busied themselves unloading each horse carefully and placing them in their stalls. "Ele goes over there," Sam said to Shane, pointing to the smaller barn. "It's perfect for when I start breeding her."

****

After they were finished with the horses, Mike and Shane grabbed their bags and followed Sam into the house. "You two can fight over who gets which room. I really don't care."

Shane looked in each room and yelled, "This one's mine!" He threw his bag on the bed and returned to the open living room.

"I was going to make coffee, but didn't have time." Sam looked down at his boots, then back up at his friends. "I've got some news—"

"More than this?" Shane laughed.

"Emma and I are going to have a baby - due in December." Before the two could respond, he quickly added, "I've already told Mom she's going to be a grandmother."

Mike and Shane looked at each other. Then with a big grin, Mike said, "Congratulations! I bet your mom's excited."

"Yeah, that's great news," Shane said.

Sam was surprised they'd taken the news better than he had. He wanted to the talk about something else, so he asked, "Mike, do you think Ele's ready to race again?"

"I'm sure of it!" Mike said. He saw that Sam didn't seem excited about the baby and was a little concerned. But, they had plenty of time to work all that out.

"I think I need a new name for this place," Sam thought out

loud.

Shane said, pointing to Sam's hat. "What about the name of your dad's place?"

Sam took off the hat and looked at the logo. "Great idea! PARKER RANCH it is!" He knew the sale of his dad's ranch didn't include the rights to the business name.

Mike nodded. "Harold would be proud."

Sam grinned and said, "You two want to see the track?"

They walked down the trail into the woods behind the large stable. As they came out into a clearing, Shane whistled. "Dang, this is nice. Who built it?"

Sam looked around at the dirt track and said, "The previous owner - Joe Remsky."

"Remsky?" Shane said, then shivered. "I remember that dude."

Sam remembered him too, even up to the point when he'd had to kill him.

Mike saw the look on Sam's face and said, "This will do nicely for training, right?"

Sam nodded; thankful his friend had changed the subject. "I'm going to be spending more time here with the horses now. Besides, the Board okayed Jim to take over at ORC again. I still have a key to the office, but he'll call if he needs me. I've been away from racing too long now..."

Shane broke in, "I thought it was so you could be with Emma."

"That too," Sam said smiling. "You know, as an investigator, it's made me more aware of how stupid owners and trainers are in horseracing only for the money."

"What are you in it for?" Mike asked, even though he knew what the answer was.

"To watch these horses do what they love - run!" Sam thought for a moment. "First, I want to get Ele ready for the next Santa Anita Race. And then, we're prepping Promise for the Triple Crown!"

****

It was an hour later when Sam entered the ORC office in Portland. There was a note from Sally on the desk with Nikki's caseworker's number. He saw that Lynn had only called a few minutes ago, so he sat down and dialed. He was glad that he was alone, so he wouldn't be overheard.

"Lynn, this is Sam Parker. I thought you should know that my wife told me she saw some bruises on Nikki."

He heard Lynn sigh, and then she said, "This isn't the first report we've had. She seems to fall a lot. We've had other phone calls like this, but it usually comes to nothing."

"But, will you at least look into it? Maybe it's some bullies at school," Sam urged.

"I'll see what I can do. But, please...tell no one else about this until we have had a chance to investigate."

CHAPTER SEVENTEEN

KENTUCKY

The early morning mist was thick, swirling around the young athletes' legs as they entered the famous track with the Twin Spires. Fred had brought a few extra horses today from Essen Farms to workout with Koenig's Spirit, to challenge him in preparation for the upcoming Kentucky Derby.

George stepped up to the railing next to Fred. "We have some spectators."

The two men looked around them. Men and women stood either in the grandstand or along the rails - reporters and touters, each trying to get a scoop on whether Spirit would be the favorite to win in the following Saturday's race.

"Well, our boy will give them something to talk about today," Fred said, smiling.

"Just don't give everything away," George cautioned him.

"I know what I'm doing!"

The two watched as their horses cantered past the grandstand, and then went into a slow gallop around the first turn. Spirit looked strong and confident, his head held high as he paced alongside one of his stable mates, their steps synchronizing in a beautiful dance. When the field reached the backstretch, Stan stood in the stirrups and leaned forward, giving Spirit the signal to let go. Fred, and others watching, began their stop watches. The two horses pulled away from the pack, creating a gap of three lengths, then four, then five.

"Okay, Stan," Fred said softly to himself, "take charge and keep him there..."

Spirit stayed in the same position as they came around the last turn, Stan holding the reins to check the strong animal. Looking behind him, the field of horses was still following at the same pace. Smiling at the last post, he gave the horse his head again to cross the finish.

"Perfect!" George smiled. "We have a great team."

Stan trotted Spirit back to where his trainer stood. "Well, what do you think?"

"That was just as I wanted you to do," Fred beamed. "Now, go cool him down."

After Stan and the other jockeys led their steeds to the shedrow, George and Fred were swamped with reporters. The touters, people who made money from tips on horses, eavesdropped nearby, taking notes.

One woman reporter asked, "It's tragic about Mr. Divinity not racing in this year's Kentucky Derby. Any comments you care to share, Mr. Mason?"

"Yes, it is tragic," George answered, but didn't say anymore.

"Are you still dating Ms. Gallano–"

Fred jumped in. "Let's keep this about racing, shall we?"

"Your boy put on a good show this morning, Mason." one man said. "But, is he ready to go up against Gary Nash's, Return Thunder, in the Kentucky Derby?"

Stepping back a little from the microphone shoved in his face, George smiled and said, "I guess you'll have to wait and see."

OREGON

Emma was in the nursery, sitting in a rocking chair that her mother had at their home in Indiana. Slowly, she began to rock, thinking of the times her mother would hold her and sing to her in that same chair. Memories of her young childhood were vague, but sometimes flashes of images would surface at the oddest times. This was one of those moments. Softly, she began to sing the lullaby her mother had written for her, "Go to sleep, little girl. May your dreams all be pleasant..."

She hummed as she looked around the soft, yellow walls, the wallpaper trim she'd chosen at a store in Portland laid on a table nearby. Emma considered all she could do with the trim, jotting down a few notes on a small pad. Then, she smiled when she saw the framed painting of the *Sacré-Coeur* she'd found in Paris that now hung in her baby's room.

"Mrs. Parker," Emma heard Peter call from downstairs. His voice was raised a bit, which indicated he was worried about something.

"I'm up here in the nursery, Peter," she said, pocketing the notepad and pencil. "I'll be right there."

Emma hurried down the stairs and stopped when she saw his face. "What is it?"

"It is Lucky - he is, how do you say...acting up again. Please hurry." Peter ran out of the house. Emma followed, grabbing an apple off the kitchen counter.

Before they entered the large stable, Emma could hear the horse's screams. As she ran into the building, Lucky was rearing in his stall, his hooves hitting the walls hard. Just then, she saw Shadow skitter out from under the stall door, chasing a mouse.

"Whoa, boy," she said, trying to soothe the horse. "It's okay, Lucky. I'm here." She continued to talk to the horse as she went up to his door and held out her hand with the apple in it. "Come here, it's all okay..." She looked down and saw that he had blood on one of his front legs. "Peter, get the kit - he's bleeding."

Peter ran to the tack room.

"Lucky, come here, boy," Emma continued. He stood still in his stall, breathing heavy and snorting. She looked him over and saw the cut on his left foreleg wasn't very deep. "You're acting like a juvenile, young man...it's very unbecoming." Emma knew that it really didn't matter what she said, as long as she used her soft voice. Slowly, Lucky walked up to her hand, sniffed, nickered, and took the apple.

"Scared of a little mouse," she said, stroking his long neck, "and I was ignoring you. I'm sorry. I've been occupied with my new baby."

Peter walked up slowly, surprised to see the animal so quiet now in his stall. "What did you do?" he asked Emma. "Why is he so calm?"

"He was startled when the cat was chasing a mouse in his stall.

We need to make sure all of our feed and tack are kept in mice-proof bins." She stroked Lucky's forehead. "Also, I think Lucky wants more attention. After all, he is a racehorse. He's used to people near him all the time, treating him like a prince."

"Maybe he is missing Tracy?" Peter asked.

Emma could hear the hope in his voice. She nodded and said, "I think Nikki, too." Emma watched as Lucky bobbed his head as if agreeing with her. "I'll go call them both and see if they can come over this afternoon. Will you start working on his leg and make sure he didn't damage any ligaments?"

"*Ja*, Mrs. Parker."

"Peter, please call me Emma."

"*Ja*, Mrs. Parker," Peter said, smiling.

Emma laughed and patted the horse. "I'll go get your girls here, Lucky. Okay?"

The horse whinnied again and she left.

Emma walked back to the house and called Tracy. "Peter and I think Lucky needs to see you - and Nikki."

"Peter said that?" Tracy said over the phone.

Emma laughed. "Yes, so when can you get here?"

"I wish I could come right now, but I have three students coming. We won't be finished until later this afternoon. Will he be okay until then?" Tracy asked.

Emma smiled and said, "Sure. But, who do you mean, Lucky or Peter?"

"Both!" Tracy laughed and hung up.

Emma then dialed Nikki's number. She knew that Sam had reported Nikki's bruises to her caseworker, but that was last week.

When Maria answered, Emma said, "Hello Maria, this is Emma. How is Nikki doing?"

"Fine."

"Is she ready to come back for more riding classes?"

Maria was quiet for a moment, and then said, "I can bring her over this afternoon - after school. I know how much this means to her."

Emma agreed and hung up. She let out a heavy sigh. Talking to Maria always made Emma uncomfortable. She wasn't sure why.

****

Later, Emma stood on the porch as Maria and Nikki drove up. She was pleased to see that Nikki was carrying her riding crop. "Hello," she said as they came near. "I'm so glad to see you both. Would you like to come in for refreshments?"

Maria's smile faded and she looked nervously around her for a moment. "No, I have to get back home before–" She stopped for a moment, then added, "I'll come pick you up later, Nikki." Maria got into the car and drove off.

"That's interesting!" Nikki said, standing on the porch with her hands on her hips. "She's never called me that before. I guess Maria's starting to stand up for me..."

"I made some lemonade - would you like some before we get started?"

"Sure."

They walked into the kitchen and sat at the table.

"Where's Sam?" Nikki asked.

"He's at his ranch across the road, working with other Thoroughbreds, like Lucky–"

"His ranch? Why isn't it yours, too?"

"Sam's passion is Thoroughbred racing...and mine is different. We each have our own interests - we've had them since before we met."

"Huh," Nikki said, sipping through her straw until the liquid was gone. "I don't think I've ever known a couple like you - each doing what you love."

"It's important in a relationship that we never lose our own dreams - the ones we brought to the marriage. I believe that helps many couples stay together."

"Has Sam always been a trainer?"

"No, he also worked with the Oregon Racing Commission. He was the director, until recently."

"What did he do there?"

"Investigate cases where horses were being abused just to win a race. That's what was happening to Lucky in Kentucky before my Uncle George took him away from that nasty man. Sam would sometimes go to tracks all over Oregon."

Nikki looked down at her empty glass. "My foster dad

sometimes works at Portland Meadows–"

"I have some great news," Emma said, interrupting her. She gently placed her hand on the young girl's arm and said, "I'm pregnant!"

Nikki stared at Emma, then pulled her arm away and nervously asked, "Does this mean you won't be able to continue my classes?" She'd been with some foster parents before who decided they didn't want her anymore when they found out they were expecting.

"Oh, not for a long time," Emma assured her. "The baby isn't due until December. Besides, this isn't like other jobs where women take maternity leave. I live and work here, and Peter will help–"

"I don't trust him," Nikki said.

Emma then told her about Peter's past. "He's a very gentle and patient young man; and, I trust that he would never do anything to hurt anyone, especially you."

"Why me?"

Emma smiled. "He told me once that he thinks of you like a little sister."

Nikki looked out the window towards the stables. "I don't have any brothers or sisters."

"I'm so sorry, but I know how you feel. I was an only child, too." She didn't mention her brother who'd died in infancy before she was born.

"Your life is nothing like mine!"

Emma sat quietly for a moment, trying to envision how her own life would have been different if she hadn't had her loving parents, but she couldn't. "Why don't you tell me what it was like for you, so I can understand?"

"I don't really like to talk about it."

Emma sat back in her chair and looked at the young girl across from her. "I know about your bruises," she said softly. "Is everything okay at home?"

Nikki didn't respond, just looked out the window.

Taking a sip of lemonade, Emma shared a story: "I once knew a girl at my college in Chicago who was being verbally and physically abused by her father. I could always tell when something had happened to her - because when she'd come back to school, she was quiet and guarded. She wouldn't talk to me, but I kept assuring her I was her friend. Then, one day, during our second year together, she came to me and confessed. She told me that she'd finally realized that nothing was going to change, until she could stand up to him."

Emma gently touched the young girl's arm again. "I am your friend, Nikki. If you ever need to talk, I am here for you."

Nikki fingered the riding crop and said, "I don't know why you're telling me this. It has nothing to do with me." She stood up and said, "Can I go ride now?"

Emma got up and took the empty glasses to the counter. "Let's get Sonny ready!"

As Nikki and Emma walked towards the stables, Nikki asked, "Can I see Lucky first? Is he okay?"

"Yes, I think he missed you."

When they entered the long stable, Emma watched as Nikki walked up to Lucky's stall.

"Hi, boy," Nikki said, holding out her hand to be sniffed.

Emma smiled and watched as Lucky walked up and nickered softly, placing his muzzle into Nikki's palm. He seemed at ease and stepped even closer, so the young girl could reach up and scratch behind his ears.

When Nikki saw the bandage on his foreleg, she asked, "What happened to him?"

"He injured himself when he was kicking his stall this morning. I told him he was acting like a teenager." Emma laughed. "But, I think he was just lonely."

"I know how he feels sometimes..."

Nikki thought about what Emma had said. She couldn't tell Emma about the other night, when she'd fought Walter off with the crop. She'd felt so alone in that phone booth, hoping that he'd go out drinking. When she did get home, he was gone. She had a chance to talk to Maria about what he'd been doing to both of them. Thinking of Emma's words, Nikki finally decided that she needed to get up enough nerve to tell her foster mother that it had to stop - THEY had to make it stop!

Emma watched as a shadow fell over Nikki's face as the young girl stroked the tall animal's neck. After a few moments, she said, "If we don't get going, you won't have time to ride."

Peter came out of the tack room, as Emma and Nikki came up the stable aisle.

"*Hallo*, squirt," he said awkwardly, "where have you been so long?"

Nikki smiled for the first time at Peter. "Squirt? I'm not short!" she said, attempting to stand taller.

Peter looked a little embarrassed. "I'm sorry. I've heard Shane use that term before and thought it meant something different. I'm still learning the English idioms." Then, he eyed Nikki and smiled, "But, you are shorter than me."

Emma was glad to see Nikki seemed a little more relaxed around Peter. These two were acting like siblings, so Emma stood back and let them work together.

"Are you riding today?" Peter asked Nikki.

"Yes."

"I'll get your saddle for you while you lead Sonny out of his stall."

"Okay." Nikki ran to Sonny's stall, put on his bridle, then opened the door and led him out. She cross-tied him in the aisle and ran her hands over his almost white coat. "You are such a handsome horse," she cooed.

"I'll meet you in the arena," Emma said and walked out of the barn. As she left, she heard Nikki asking Peter if he knew about the baby.

Tracy drove up and parked outside the stable. She was wearing an oversized, tan Carhartt jacket that Emma knew had belonged to Tracy's dad.

Emma saw her friend's purple fingers and laughed. "Treating your horses' hooves without gloves again, I see." Everyone in the horse world knew that Gentian violet, used to treat Thrush, always stained your hands.

"Guilty. How is Lucky?"

"He's much better, now that Nikki is back. Peter was right - that silly horse missed his young friend."

"Yeah, those two connected pretty quickly. I'm not surprised." Tracy looked around. "Where's Peter?"

"He's helping Nikki saddle Sonny. When he's done, you two can go check Lucky."

Emma laughed when Tracy smiled, winked at her and turned to open the stable door.

Nikki walked out, leading Sonny. "He's inside," she said to Tracy with a chuckle.

"He, who?" Tracy asked.

Nikki rolled her eyes and said. "Grown-ups!"

Then, she and Emma walked with Sonny towards the arena.

"Hey, Em," Tracy said, "After I see how Lucky is doing, is it okay if I take Peter to see my riding center?"

"No problem," Emma said, smiling.

****

"My place is on the north side of this mountain," Tracy said as she drove. "It's really not far from Emma's."

As the truck came over a rise, Peter saw the sun shining on the snow-covered Mt. Hood in the distance to the east. He had been impressed with it when he first flew to Oregon, but still, the one mountain did not compare to the Alps near his home in Austria.

"How long have you been doing this profession?" he asked.

"I've had my center now for three years," she said proudly. "Therapeutic horseback riding is relatively new to Oregon."

Tracy turned a corner and there were apple and plum trees in bloom. They continued now through rolling hills of fir trees and a cedar grove until she began to slow the truck. As she turned into her lane, Peter looked down and saw a rock with CRC etched on it.

"What does CRC mean?" he asked.

"Chehalem Mountain Center," Tracy said and parked near a large red house and barn. The two-story, older, cottage-style house had white trim and three dormers on the roof.

As they stepped out of the truck, Peter were surprised when they were met with cries from turkeys and chickens. Then, he saw the hen house beside the barn. One chicken had gotten out and was frantically running back and forth, trying to get back in. An older black cat sat on the drive to meet them, and two younger kittens ran out of the barn to play with the older one.

"This is where I do most of my work," Tracy said, pointing to the large barn. "Sometimes, I will take my horses to a client, but I prefer they come here."

"Why did you choose this type of work?"

Tracy thought for a moment, wondering how much of her past

she was willing to share, then said, "I had someone help me once... I learned how much horses have to give and what good listeners they are."

Just then, a silver car drove in and parked near Tracy's truck. A pretty blonde woman emerged, wearing some makeup and a business suit. Her younger daughter got out and they walked towards them.

"Hi, you two!" Tracy called. She introduced Peter, then placed her arm around the young girl's shoulders and said, "Megan is one of my volunteers who helps me around here when she can."

Peter saw that Megan had the same color of hair as her mother, but she wore it long and pulled back in a ponytail. She wore a purple sweatshirt and black vest, and her jeans were tucked into a pair of Justin boots. He recognized the boots' logo from a time he'd spent at a farm store in McMinnville, while he'd waited for a feed order.

The young girl smiled and said, "I came here once for a friend's birthday party when I was six, and I fell in love with horses here."

"Birthday party?" Peter asked, looking at Tracy.

"I've held parties here for local kids for years. They get to have a fun celebration with the horses."

"She can only stay for a half-hour today," Megan's mother said. "She's on the High School Equestrian team and has Master Showman classes."

"What is that?" Peter asked.

Megan explained, "I teach 4-H kids how to show their animals."

"What is 4-H?"

Tracy said, "It's a club for young kids to learn leadership and responsibility, through working with their farm animals. They show them at county and state fairs."

She turned to Megan and her mom. "Peter is from Austria, helping Emma Parker with her new Lipizzan horses."

"That's awesome!" Megan exclaimed.

Peter was a little embarrassed. He smiled, then looked around. "Tracy, you have a beautiful home."

"Thank you," Tracy said a little shyly. "It still needs work, and it'd look better with a little paint."

"Don't we all!" Megan's mother said, patting her cheek. Then, she got in her car and left.

Megan went to one of the barns to start mucking the stalls, while

Tracy and Peter walked around the main barn. When Peter saw the large stalls with two sliding doors, he said, "Are these foaling stalls?"

"No, I took the middle wall out so the animals have more room when they're inside. I don't like keeping animals in tight places. It's not right."

There was a ramp for handicapped people. Off to one side was a family waiting room, with a couch, TV, and toys. "I have a few kids and adults in wheelchairs, so their drivers or families can wait in here while we do our therapy." They walked on, and then Tracy added, "I'm taking a speech therapy class, because sometimes I work with non-verbal kids."

A bark came from one of the stalls. When Megan opened the sliding door, a tan collie ran out to greet them.

"This is Whisper," Tracy said, laughing. "She thinks that her job is to herd the other animals, so I sometimes keep her in here to give the others a rest." Immediately, Whisper started barking and ran out of the barn.

Peter leaned against the fence and looked in the large, indoor arena. "How many students do you teach?"

"It depends..." Tracy's voice calmed when she began talking about her training as she looked into the arena. Peter had to lean in to hear her. "While riding, these kids learn about relationships - and themselves. Horses bring out our desire to be social, if we will only learn to listen and talk to each other. Animals show us so much about ourselves. Their inner sense knows exactly what's going on with their rider and what they need - like some of the veterans I've helped with depression and anxiety.

"I try not to focus on their traumatic experiences. It's almost like Zen; I let them become mindful of their surroundings. They start with grooming and getting to know their horse. Then, the next week, they go on to walking, and eventually riding. Their focus becomes so intense; the transformation is amazing to watch."

They heard a horse whinny and Tracy said, "Come on, let's go see the horses."

When they walked outside, two cream-colored horses stood in the fenced pasture with a couple of small donkeys.

"They're Norwegian Fjords," Tracy said. "These two have the gentlest nature, like golden retrievers in the horse world. They're breed is perfect for what I do."

Just then, Whisper ran through an opening in the fence and started barking, chasing the horses. One horse bucked and raced around the pasture.

She laughed. "They're just playing with each other. They do this every time they're together." Then, Whisper started chasing one of the donkeys, who started braying. "It's good exercise for all of them."

In the distance, Peter could see a large pond, with grassy edges and a few benches placed nearby. Red-winged blackbirds flew in amongst the reeds, and the surface of the water mirrored the landscape around it.

"I created that pond as a tranquil area where peace resides," Tracy said in her soft voice again. "Nothing bad can happen there."

****

As Emma watched Nikki ride Sonny in a rising trot around the indoor arena, she was wondering how she was going to tell her about the upcoming trip to Kentucky.

"You've put the letters out!" the young girl exclaimed. "Do I get to work with them today?"

"Have you seen anyone ride with them before?" Emma asked.

"Yeah, I watched when Sarah did some of her Dressage tests at the Fairgrounds."

"Good, then you'll understand my directions. If you get confused, just raise your hand and we'll see what you need." Emma looked down at a test in her hand she'd used as a young rider. The paper was yellowed and dog-eared, but memories of her own beginning days with Dressage made her smile.

"Walk to A, facing X, and halt," she said, watching as Nikki followed. When rider and horse were in place, she said, "Normally, during a test, you would enter the arena at A. At A, in a rising trot, follow center line." She waited until Nikki began. "At C, track right...Now, at B, circle right 20 meters...Good!" Again, she waited. "At F, canter to K...At K, go to X and do a simple lead change."

Once Nikki changed her lead, she reversed direction and repeated the movements going the other way. When horse and rider had completed the steps, Emma looked again at her paper. "Down center line, and halt at X."

When Nikki was in position, Emma added, "Do you know how to salute?"

"I think so..." Nikki took Sonny's reins in her left hand. Holding the horse still, she let her right hand drop straight along her body and inclined her head in a slight bow.

"Exactly!" Emma exclaimed. "I'm very proud of you."

Nikki beamed and patted Sonny's neck. "Good boy," she said softly to the horse.

"You're advancing much quicker than I expected. We may have to add a few more movements for you during your next class."

The lesson was over and Sonny was back in his stall. Emma and Nikki walked to the house. The two waved as Peter and Tracy drove in.

Emma turned to Nikki and said, "My Uncle George has a colt racing in the Kentucky Derby in Louisville, so Sam and I are going there in a few days."

Emma was surprised to see Nikki start to cry. "You can't go! Please...please take me with you!"

"Honey, I'm sorry, but that's impossible - since we're not your parents."

Nikki wiped the tears from her eyes and stared at Emma. "I wish you were."

Emma took out the notepad and pencil from her pocket and wrote down George's name and phone number. "You can call this number anytime." She looked at the two people staring at them. "And, remember, Peter and Tracy will still be here for you."

Just then, a car sped up their lane and stopped in a cloud of dust.

"Oh, no!" Nikki exclaimed. "It's Walter!" She looked at Emma with fear in her eyes. "He's my foster dad. What's he doing here? I thought Maria was going to pick me up."

The car door slammed and a big, burly man stormed towards them. Emma was glad that Peter and Tracy were there.

"What the hell did I tell you?" he yelled at Nikki. "No more lessons!" He threw her bike into the trunk of the car.

"But, Maria said I could–"

"Get your butt in the goddamned car." Nikki ran and got into the backseat.

Peter held both hands up and said, "Mr. Mitchell, I am sure

Nikki–"

Walter pushed Peter aside and turned to Emma. "Nicole is done here - do you understand? I don't want you near her again, or I will sue the lot of you!"

"We can work this out, if you would just calm down–" Emma began, but Walter had turned on his heel and walked to the car, slamming the door after he got in.

Nikki looked out the window and waved to Emma, tears streaming down her face as their car sped away, gravel flying under the wheels.

"Whew, what a jackass," Tracy said. "He reminds me of some of the owners I've had to rescue horses from."

Emma stood shaking. Walter reminded her of her ex-husband.

****

That evening, as Emma sat on the couch in the den, she had her arms wrapped around her legs. She was still shaking as memories flooded back to her of the night her ex-husband had beaten and raped her. It was about this same time - just before the Kentucky Derby.

Sam walked in and stopped when he saw her. "Hey, Em, are you all right?" He sat on the couch beside her and hugged her. "What happened?"

"I met Nikki's foster dad today." She looked away and tears began to stream down her face. "He's a lot like Ted..."

"Did he hurt you? Damn it, I should've been here–"

"You couldn't have done anything. And, I wasn't alone - Peter and Tracy were both here. I didn't think he would do anything stupid with witnesses. But, he won't let Nikki continue her classes, and he threatened to sue–"

"He doesn't have a case! I'll go talk to him–"

"No! It will all settle out. I'm just afraid for Nikki...she was heartbroken; almost frightened when I told her we were going to Kentucky. I wish we weren't leaving now."

"We have to go, for George. But, I could have Jim do some checking up on Walter Mitchell while we're gone." Sam was quiet for a moment. Then he added, "Lynn Chamberlain, Nikki's caseworker, called me today. She said we're not to worry about Nikki's bruises.

Lynn went to her house and didn't feel she's in any danger."

"That poor kid! Isn't there anything we can do?"

Sam looked at his wife, his heart swelling. "I'm not sure, but I'm going to try like hell." He kissed Emma and added, "Lynn said she'll check in on Nikki while we're gone, and I gave her George's phone number."

Emma sighed and relaxed a little. "Thank you, Sam. I really appreciate you."

Sam looked at his wife. "Em, I'm sorry I blind-sided you with the purchase of Joe's place. I know I should have waited until we'd had a chance to talk more about it, but racing is in my blood–"

"I know, honey, but there's something I haven't told you." Emma stared into Sam's eyes and confessed, "Sometimes, I've had nightmares of that night when I was attacked by Joe - and that awful Karl Strauss. They'd used that place, plotting to take Koenig's Wonder...and me out of the country. Ted was killed there. Sometimes, it feels like it's happening all over again..."

"Why didn't you tell me?"

"I thought the nightmares would go away...someday."

Sam was a little hurt, but decided to let it go. He hugged her. "I wish you would've told me before, but now I understand."

Emma took a deep breath and smiled at her husband. "Today, when I told Tracy about you buying the place, she said that we can now build new memories - with the horses and your dreams coming true. And, now that you're getting the extra money from your parents' sale, I think it will be good for us."

"I promise we will make happy memories there."

They kissed and held onto each other, feeling their love growing deeper by the moment. Emma leaned into him, the strength of his body laid against hers, arousing her.

Sam rose up on one elbow, gently touched Emma's face and looked into her eyes. "Is it okay..." he asked, "with the baby?"

She smiled and pulled him closer. "Absolutely..."

CHAPTER EIGHTEEN

KENTUCKY

It was late afternoon when Emma looked out the window of their plane at the land spread out below them. "I love flying with you, Sam. The world looks so different from up here." The farm houses, barns, and neatly-plowed fields of land reminded her of her childhood home. "Where are we now?"

Sam looked at his watch, checked the area below, and said, "Southern Indiana."

"I thought some of those farms looked familiar."

Laughing, he said, "All farms look alike from the air. We'll be flying over your family's old place in a few minutes." He looked at his wife and asked, "Do you miss it?"

Emma thought for a moment of her parents, both gone now. It had been a while since she'd allowed herself to think of them and how much they had meant to her. Her mother was such a beautiful person, kind-hearted and talented. Emma would sometimes feel in her heart her mother playing the cello in the summer Indiana evenings. And, Emma was forever thankful to her father for teaching her everything she knew about horses and Dressage. With pride in his eyes, when she was riding through a difficult exercise on Gandolf, he always encouraged her to do her very best.

"I miss Mom and Dad," she said softly and leaned her forehead against the plane's side window.

Grandview came into view, the town where Emma grew up. "There's the old church...and the diner!" she exclaimed.

As he circled the area, Sam remembered the summer when he'd gone there to look for Emma. He'd been afraid he'd lost her forever.

"We'll be landing in Louisville in a few minutes," he said, turning the plane to the southeast, calling in to the airport tower.

Emma could see the ribbon of the Ohio River below as it snaked through the land. "I can't wait to see Uncle George. This is my first Kentucky Derby!"

"Really?" Sam said, glancing at her. "My first was when Koenig's Wonder won..." He took her hand and kissed it. "That horse brought me back to you."

Emma smiled and placed her hand on his cheek. "I always knew that someday we'd find each other."

A large horse farm to the west of the city came into view. "Is that Essen Farms?"

Sam looked out the window and saw that they had passed the airport and were still heading east. Counting the stables with red and gold cupolas and then seeing the large, white mansion, he nodded. He banked the plane back west towards the airport. As he approached the runway, he cut the gas to slow the engines. Keeping the nose up and the plane level, he landed on the tarmac and taxied to the parking area for small planes. A ground crewman led them to an empty tie-down space, then Sam turned off the engines.

After they'd picked up their rental car, they drove towards Essen Farms. When they passed Churchill Downs, Emma could see the tents, trucks and trailers already in place for the next day's crowd. News vans, food venders and florists vans were parked everywhere.

"I'm glad we came the day before the Derby," Emma said. "It will give us a chance to catch up with my uncle."

As they drove up the long, tree-lined lane of Essen Farms, Sam saw a black horse grazing alone in the newly green pasture. The first time he'd been to Essen Farms, snow had covered the ground. A few other dark horses were grazing in the white-fenced pasture near the stables.

George walked out of the nearest stable to greet them. "Hello!" he bellowed, hugging Emma and kissing her cheek. "I've missed you."

"I've missed you, too, Uncle George."

Sam saw that George was avoiding him, since he'd been the reason they'd cut their last visit short. "Hi, George, it's good to see you," he said, trying to rebuild the bridge between them. He held out his hand to the older man and waited, relieved when the older man shook it.

In a nearby pasture, the solo horse walked up to the fence and whinnied.

"Ah, here's Koenig - the sire that began our line of stallions," George said proudly.

The tall, dark horse whinnied again. Sam saw the white star and blaze down Koenig's forehead and realized that was where his own colt got those markings, from his grandsire. Suddenly, he couldn't wait to get back to Oregon.

George held Emma at arms' length and asked, "How are you feeling? I was so happy to get your news of the baby."

Emma looked at Sam. "We're pretty excited, too." She took one of George's arms and started walking towards the house. "Let's go in so we can talk about it." Sam got the bags from the car and followed them.

They entered the tall, white mansion, the air warm and welcoming in the dark entry. Sam never got over how tall the ceilings were in this place.

"Should I put these in the same room as last time?" he asked, pointing to their luggage. With a grin, he added, "Or should I let the housekeeper take them?"

George rolled his eyes in embarrassment and said, "I only have a housekeeper when Divina is here. She brings hers along with her. Your room is on the left at the top of the stairs..." He offered to help, but Sam was already headed up the wide stairwell.

"How long can you stay?" George asked his niece.

"The day after tomorrow, I'm afraid," Emma replied. "I have students coming that I have to prepare for." When she saw the sad look in her uncle's eyes, she kissed his cheek and added, "I'm going up first to unpack and freshen up, and then I'll meet you downstairs, okay?"

George smiled and watched proudly as his niece ascended the stairs.

In the den, Sam and George were talking and drinking bourbon before the roaring fire.

"Where's Fred?" Sam asked, looking around the trophy-filled room and dreamt of his own den looking like this someday.

"He's at Churchill Downs with Spirit, getting him ready for the big day. He should be here shortly."

"As we were flying over Louisville," Sam began, "I was telling Emma about Koenig's Wonder winning the Derby. Remember when I came here when he was born?"

George smiled and took another sip. "Yes...you were still in the Air Force - flying jets, as I recall."

"Yes," Sam looked into the liquid in his glass. "I went to Indiana to find Emma after I left here."

"And, did you?"

"No, the farm had been sold by then, and I thought I'd lost her forever." Sam tried to shake off the melancholy and said, "Did you know I named my mare after Koenig's dam?"

"So that's where Classy Elegance came from," George said, smiling. "I always wondered about that. How is Ele?"

"She's good, Mike's getting her ready to race again soon."

Fred walked in, poured a drink, and sat on the long leather couch. "All is well at the Downs," he said, taking a long draw of bourbon. "Johnny is staying with Spirit, keeping a sharp eye on him tonight."

George thought of the night years ago when Karl Strauss had drugged Wonder's sire, Koenig, just before he'd won the Derby. That man had torn his family apart, and George had vowed he would never forgive him. He wondered now where Strauss was.

"George," Fred was saying. "I was telling you what Eric saw at the track - Evers was back."

"I thought he was banned from Churchill Downs!" the older man yelled, slamming his fist on the arm of his chair.

"Well, someone let him back in. I talked to security before I left, but also alerted Johnny. Our grooms won't let anything happen to Spirit."

"How's Spirit doing?" Sam asked, to ease the tension in the room.

Fred smiled and said, "He's ready! That colt can't wait for tomorrow."

Sam looked over at George. "You know I've been talking about racing again..."

George nodded, Emma had told him on one of their weekly calls.

"Well, I just bought the ranch across from Rising Sun - you know - the one with the track in the woods?"

"Yes, the one where my brother shot me–" George stopped, memories of that fateful night flooded back to him. He'd thought he'd lost his younger brother in Germany in the war. But, he'd been wrong.

"I'm using that track to train my horses. I'm no longer working for the Racing Commission, so I have more time now. Promise is coming along nicely. I can see that he has a lot of Koenig's Wonder in him!"

George was still upset that Sam wanted to train Promise, but Fred's glance stopped him from saying anything more.

Just then, Emma entered the room.

"Hello, Emma," Fred said, then stood up and set his glass on the liquor cabinet. "Well, I'd better go check on the horses." He turned, gave a warning glance at George, and left the room.

"Have you been talking about horses all this time?" Emma asked, laughing. She sat down on the end of the couch near Sam's chair.

"Pretty much," Sam said.

George beamed at his niece, "Have you decided on any names for the baby yet?"

Emma looked at Sam "Sophia, if it's a girl," she said, "after my mom." She hadn't had a chance to discuss this yet with Sam, but was glad when he smiled.

"Sophia Joanna - after both of our mom's," Sam added with a nod.

"Perfect," Emma agreed.

"And, if it's a boy?" George asked.

"We haven't decided just yet," Sam said quickly.

George thought for a moment, then said, "What about Harold - after your dad, Sam?"

Emma and Sam looked at each other. She smiled and nodded to Sam, "I think that's a wonderful name."

"We'll think about it," Sam said, a shadow coming over his face.

He wasn't sure if he wanted his kid to constantly remind him of losing his dad every day.

"Uncle George, you should see Lucky - that's what we call the Thoroughbred you sent to me. He's doing so well, and Tracy thinks his progress is really coming along. I can't wait to start training him in Dressage–"

"Retired Thoroughbreds are sometimes good at that," Sam interjected.

Emma nodded and continued, "He's even started trusting one of my young students, Nikki. We just learned that she may have also been abused–" She put her hand on the arm of the couch and looked quickly at Sam. "Is it okay if I share this with him?"

Sam patted her hand and said, "We just have to be careful who we talk to about it, so please keep this to yourself." He explained to George, "Nikki is in a foster home. Recently, I've been talking with her caseworker, and we're concerned about her - the kid is only fourteen."

"I'm sorry to hear that," George said. "It is sad to hear about children - or animals for that matter - being intentionally hurt."

"I agree," Emma said, yawning. "Well, it's been a long day, so I'm going up to bed. I can't wait for tomorrow, I even bought a special hat for the day!" She kissed Sam, then her uncle, and left.

George looked concerned. "It seems like a lot is going on there in Oregon. Is Emma okay?"

"She's good," Sam assured him. "We have extra hands now, and I always keep an eye on her..." Sam stood and stretched, then said, "I'll say goodnight, as well."

Unconvinced about Emma, George watched as Sam left the room.

****

The next day, in the backside of Churchill Downs, the place was alive with activity for the 97th Kentucky Derby. Horses were being prepped and pampered for The Run for the Roses.

As Emma and Sam walked along the shedrow, she had to place her hand on her wide-brimmed hat to keep it on her head. She'd chosen red and asked the clerk to place a gold ribbon around it, since those were George's racing colors. When they came up to Spirit's stall, George was talking with a small man with sandy hair and muscular forearms.

"Stan, you've got to remember to give him his head when he comes out of the gate. He needs to be ahead of the field from the beginning. We don't want a repeat of Arkansas today."

"I know what to do, George. This isn't my first race–" Stan stopped when he saw the couple approach.

George looked over his shoulder and smiled. "Emma...Sam, this is my new jockey, Stan Gibson." He turned to Stan, "My niece, Emma, and her husband, Sam Parker."

"Parker?" the jockey asked, shaking hands. "I know that name."

"I used to work for the TRB in Baltimore."

Stan nodded, "Ah, you're THAT Sam Parker! You're famous around here."

Sam looked confused. "Famous. Why?"

"You solved the Koenig's Wonder case!"

"Ahem," George said. "You'd better go get ready, Stan."

The jockey sighed, "Okay, George. You're the boss!" He saluted and walked away.

Just then, Divina joined them, her dark hair blowing in the slight breeze between the shedrow. Her two-toned orange and yellow, organza hat hardly moved, and Emma was surprised that she was wearing white gloves.

"George, darling, I wanted to wish you luck," she said as she kissed his cheek. Then, she saw the others. "Oh, Emma, it is so good to see you again."

"Hello, Divina." Emma stepped back a little to avoid a hug, not quite sure that she liked how familiar the woman was to her uncle. "Is your horse also racing today?"

Sam knew about Mr. Divinity's poisoning. Simon had called him. He was about to say something when Divina and George exchanged glances.

"No..." was all she said.

George said quickly, to ease the tension, "I think Koenig's Spirit is going to set a new track record today!"

Divina smiled and mouthed a 'Thank you' to George. Trying to act as if nothing was wrong, she put her arm in Emma's and said, "Let's go to George's box and wait for the men to join us. I have so much to talk to you about."

Emma looked pleadingly at Sam, but he was busy talking with Fred now, so she went along.

****

"What a lovely day for the races," Divina sighed, sitting down in one of the chairs in the grandstand box, sipping the mint Julep she'd been handed when they entered. Emma looked at the crowd through a pair of binoculars. All around them, the air was buzzing with excitement and color. Women wore expensive dresses and elaborate hats, covered in ribbons and flowers. The men were dressed in their finest suits, some wore top hats.

"I didn't want to say anything - in front of all the others," Divina said sadly. "Mr. Divinity will not be racing today because he was poisoned."

"I'm sorry to hear that," Emma said. "It must be so hard for you..."

Divina ran her gloved hand through her long hair that fell over one shoulder. "Yes, it is."

Emma was about to tell her about the baby, when Divina blurted out, "I think I may possibly have to sell my farm!" She nervously looked around her to see if she'd been overheard, but most of the nearby boxes were still empty.

"What?" Emma exclaimed. "But, why–"

"I'm not sure, yet. Oh, please don't breathe a word of this to George. I just needed to share my thoughts with someone...and I'm so alone here anymore."

"I won't," Emma said, and then sat quietly for a moment, thinking of what else she could say - but there were no words.

****

In the paddock area, George and Sam walked along as Fred led Spirit towards his assigned stall. Johnny carried Spirit's saddle, pad and blanket. Spirit pranced excitedly next to Fred, pulling on his lead line. Sam could see the young horse was anxious to get started.

The place was frantic with photographers and reporters, interviewing the owners and trainers about their horse's chances in the race. George tried to avoid the vultures as much as possible.

As Johnny saddled Spirit, Stan walked up in his white breeches, the red silk jersey, with the gold 'V' in the center, was shining in the late afternoon sun. The jockey reached up and patted Spirit's neck. "We're ready, boy, aren't we?" he said softly. Then, he turned to the horse's owner. "George, do you have any more words of wisdom for me?"

"Just watch that last turn for anyone coming up on you."

"Got it!"

Sam shook his head. He wasn't sure about George's strategy, but then, he was going to train Promise differently - more like his dad used to.

****

Emma was glad to see the men arrive at their box in the grandstand before the start of the race. Her heart fluttered to see Sam looking so handsome in his boots, dark jeans, blazer, and his white shirt and Stetson. He leaned over and kissed her softly as he sat down.

"How is Koenig's Spirit?" Divina asked, making sure George sat next to her.

"He's set to run!"

"Afterwards, I'd like all of you to come to my farm for refreshments," Divina cooed. She looked quickly at Emma and smiled. "I want you to see where I live."

Just then, horns started playing *My Old Kentucky Home* and the crowd stood and sang along. The horses paraded passed the grandstand and were loaded into the starting gate. Then, after a brief pause, the long-anticipated bell rang, the gates flew open, and the horses sped forward in a tight pack as they thundered by the crowd.

"The field is breaking up," the announcer said, "with Eclipse on Fire, the Arkansas Derby winner, Return Thunder, and Koenig's Spirit leading the pack."

All watched as Spirit started moving to the outside and ran around the other two. When they approached the backstretch, two horses were now in the lead: Koenig's Spirit and Return Thunder, a bay with four white socks. Eclipse on Fire was falling back with the other horses as they began to stagger into position behind the leaders. Approaching the last turn, Spirit started to move ahead.

"At the rail is Koenig's Spirit, in the red and gold colors..." the announcer's voice bellowed over the roar of the crowd.

Emma was caught up in the elation and anticipation as she watched these magnificent animals compete with each other. Spirit was now being outpaced by the bay stallion as they came around the last turn, the rest of the field of horses falling behind.

"Come on, Spirit!" she yelled along with the others.

"Their coming to the wire!" the announcer said, "Koenig's Spirit's on the move..." George's colt inched forward in a burst of speed and crossed the finish line first.

"It's Koenig's Spirit for this year's Kentucky Derby!" The crowd went crazy. Emma looked at Divina and was surprised to see her excitement for George's win.

"And, ladies and gentlemen, we have a new track record..." the announcer said.

"Well, we have much to celebrate, now!" Divina yelled. She took George's face in her hands and kissed him on the mouth. "You need to go get your trophy, darling." She looked at the others in the box, "And, I will see you all later at my home." She disappeared into the crowd.

George stared after her. "I wanted her to come with me...," he said. Then, he turned and said, "Emma, Sam, please join us."

Fred led the way to the Winner's Circle as a blanket of red roses was gently placed over Spirit's neck. Stan beamed as he sat on the tall horse, posing for the photographers. George congratulated his jockey on a great success, then he gently stroked the stallion's sweaty neck.

Emma couldn't believe she was standing here, where so many other horses had stood in the past, after winning this prestigious race. She smiled for the cameras and stroked Spirit's cheek. Then, she looked over at Sam and saw how natural he seemed. She wondered if she and her husband would be sharing a win like this for his horses someday.

One reporter pushed a microphone into George's face and asked, "Will Koenig's Spirit be ready for Pimlico, Mr. Mason?"

George smiled for the cameras. "In two weeks, Koenig's Spirit will be first to cross the finish at the Preakness Stakes!" he predicted.

****

After the race, all arrived at Gallano Farm. Jasmine, Divina's housekeeper, met them at the front door and led them into the large parlor that was already filled with the most elite people in the Kentucky horseracing scene. Bustling waiters and caterers wove through the crowd with trays of filled Champagne glasses and canapés. Long tables, mounted with numerous dishes of food, sat against one wall.

Sam and Emma were the last to arrive. Emma smiled as she watched him carefully hang his Stetson on a hat rack near the door, making sure the brim didn't touch anything. She was surprised to see all the other people that were there to congratulate George. Emma thought, *Maybe she's not as alone as she thinks!*

Divina buzzed around the crowd, kissing and hugging everyone.

"That boy of yours is going to take you to Pimlico's Winner's Circle, Mason!" one man bellowed, slapping George on the back.

George thanked him and walked towards Emma. "I don't know half of these people!" he exclaimed. "And, I thought I knew everyone in Louisville."

"Maybe Divina runs in a different circle than you," Emma whispered. She wondered if the party would have gone on, even if Spirit had lost the race. She was about to tell her uncle what Divina had said, but Sam walked up with a bourbon in one hand and a glass that looked like soda water in the other, which he handed to Emma. "What a spread!" he said. "That Burgoo and cornbread look good."

"Burgoo?" Emma asked.

George chuckled. "It's a stew made with barbequed meat and vegetables, served with Kentucky's finest cornbread." He saw a couple over by the bar. "Excuse me, I need a drink."

When George left, Sam added, "There are even desserts called the Derby Pie and Bourbon Balls, which I'm going to try later."

"This is ginger-ale!" she said after tasting her drink. "It's really good."

"Glad you like it. Can I get you something to eat?"

"No, I'm good for now...maybe later." Emma still hadn't recovered her appetite, but thankfully, the morning sickness had stopped.

Sam walked towards the large buffet.

She looked around the room and saw the bank of windows.

Drawn to the lovely flowers outside, Emma decided to visit the garden...she needed some fresh air. A tall Japanese Lilac bloomed just outside the door with fragrant, white flowers. She continued up the path, glad for a moment of peace. She didn't know that she was being watched.

It was growing dark when everyone left the party, except for George's group. The caterers were clearing the buffet and picking up glasses and plates throughout the house. George and Divina were hovered together in one corner, talking. Sam knew that Fred had gone to one of the barns to talk with the stable hands, so he walked into the next room, which was now empty. A black, grand piano sat in one corner.

Through the window, Sam smiled when he saw Emma sitting on a bench in the garden. He waved to her and she came in to join him. A wedding photo on the piano caught his eye, and he stared at it for a moment.

George had his arm around Divina's waist when they walked up to where Sam and Emma now stood.

"It is time to go back," George said. "Fred will meet us at the car." He turned and the group walked towards the front door.

Outside, George hugged Divina, then kissed her. "Thank you for doing this."

Divina smiled in delight. "It was my pleasure."

****

The man in black stepped into the shadows as he watched the last guests drive away. Divina stood under the soft porch light, her dark hair glistening. Seeing her slender body sent shivers through him. His anger rose as he decided what he must do. He needed to destroy her - like she had him. But, he just had to be patient a little longer.

CHAPTER NINETEEN

OREGON

It was raining when Sam and Jim walked across the grassy infield towards the backside of Portland Meadows Racetrack. A couple of horses were going through their morning exercises at the other side of the now muddy track.

"I watched the Kentucky Derby on TV," Jim said as drops of water fell off the brim of his Air Force ball cap. He'd been in the same training unit with Sam in Arizona. "That was pretty exciting!"

"Yes," Sam began. "It was a great victory for George. Now he's getting his horse ready for the Preakness Stakes."

Just as Sam was about to tell his best friend about the baby, Jim broke in, "Hey, I forgot - Bennie brought his photos to the office a couple of days ago. There were some interesting shots he wanted to talk to us about. He said he'd meet us there in twenty minutes."

A black hearse pulled up next to them and the dark window lowered. Mat Perez, the track physician, called out, "Hey guys - like our new wheels?" Mat was taking his residency in Ophthalmology at OHSU and worked part time for the track's medical team.

Sam laughed and said, "I bet this makes the jockeys nervous." Sam saw Mat's young assistant in the passenger seat grin from ear to ear.

"How've you been?" Jim asked, leaning against the Cadillac.

"I'm great!" Mat said, his dark-rimmed glasses sliding down his nose. "It's been pretty slow, which is a good thing."

"Have you seen Kevin?" Sam asked.

"Last time I saw him, he was at the test barn." Mat looked over at his assistant, who just shrugged his shoulders.

When Sam saw a rider take a tumble, he pointed down the track and said, "You'd better go!"

The hearse sped away, as the outriders raced to catch the riderless horse.

The barns in the backside of Portland Meadows held rows of stables, back to back. Some were in need of paint and repair. Sam was surprised to see a goat tied just inside one barn near the tack room.

"I've never seen a goat here before," he said to his friend.

"You'd be surprised what some grooms bring to this place. They're a superstitious bunch." Jim chuckled and shook his head.

In one barn, some of the horses looked out over their stall doors, nibbling on feed in netted bags. As a groom walked past one dark horse, the animal laid his ears back and tried to bite him. But, the groom quickly stepped out of the way. One stallion had a blue tetherball hanging outside the door. He was known as a 'cribber' - a horse who got bored easily and liked to chew on everything. Sam thought, *they're just like children!* The ball was a plaything.

As the two men approached the test barn, they overheard Kevin Hansen, the track vet, talking to a tall woman who was frantically taking notes.

"In my novel," the woman said, "I want my information to be as accurate as possible. That's why I asked for this interview. If you'd like, I will mention you as one of my experts in my acknowledgments."

"Well, in that case," Kevin said smiling, "as you can see, this is where we do the post-race tests. Mostly, the winning horses are the ones tested; but I also watch for horses that have been winning, yet did poorly in the last race - or vice versa. I examine them here, looking for injuries or signs of lameness. Sometimes, a trainer will try to distract me so I don't see that their horse is a 'bleeder,' one who bleeds from his nostrils. It's usually a sign of EIPH - exercise-induced pulmonary hemorrhaging.

"Basically, we draw blood and get a urine sample. Most attention is on a horse's left side. I always like to take blood from the offside, because trainers hate that." Kevin showed the woman just how he did the procedure, demonstrating with his hands in the air. "I put pressure on the jugular vein with my left and take the blood sample with my right. After that, the test is labeled and sealed in our office. The horse's urine is taken by a technician, but getting a horse to pee can take hours." Kevin chuckled. "A few of our guys claim that by whistling or singing, they can get a horse to pee faster. Generally, we're the last ones leaving the backside at night because we're waiting on a horse."

Just then, the riderless horse was being led into the testing area, still breathing heavily and his coat covered in sweat.

"Well, I have to go to work now," Kevin said.

"Thank you so much for taking the time to talk with me," the woman said, shaking his hand.

Jim and Sam stepped up next to Kevin and the three men watched as the woman walked towards the back gate. "Are you getting famous, Kevin?" Jim snickered.

"Nah, just helping a writer get her facts straight. What can I do for you two?" he asked as he walked towards the small office to get his equipment.

"We're looking into the colts from the Busch Training Stables and Fleischer Stables," Jim began. "Can you check your records and give me a call if you see anything suspicious in their tests prior to the last month?"

"Sure thing – I'll do anything for you boys who protect these animals." Kevin waved and went into his little office.

Sam turned and said to Jim, "Well, let's go check those photos."

As he and Jim started walking towards the back gate, Sam stopped and looked at his friend. "Oh, by the way, Emma is pregnant."

Jim grinned and let out a yelp. "Hot damn! It's about time." He slapped Sam on his back and said, "So when's the happy event?"

"December, I think." It was the first time Sam had allowed himself to be a little excited about the news. He didn't like blurting it out like that, but telling Jim seemed to make it more real. They both had similar experiences in Vietnam, so he knew that Jim understood what this meant to him.

As they neared the back gate, Sam said, "I've been thinking about renting a few stalls here when I bring Ele and Promise up to get used to the larger track. Promise is going to also need some starting gate training."

"I'm glad to see you getting back into racing," Jim said.

"Me, too!" Sam glanced to his left and saw a man selling equestrian supplies, liniments and balms.

"Want a coffee before we go?" Jim asked.

"Sure." They stopped in the backside café, and ordered two coffees to go.

While they waited, Sam looked around the room. Colorful tapestries and photos of jockeys on horses hung against the dark, paneled walls. Music from a jukebox filtered through the air as a few people sat near the windows in the green, vinyl booths. Sam knew some were jockeys. A few were playing cards, but one small man was telling a story about one of his past races. When their coffee was ready, Jim thanked the clerk and they left.

****

"I love you more," Sam heard Sally say just as he opened the door to the ORC office. "No, I love you more..." Bennie cooed, then jumped off the desk as Sam and Jim entered.

"You two love birds need to get a room," Sam said.

Sally giggled and straightened her hair. "We have a room!"

"Bennie, Jim said you have the photos—"

"Right here, boss!" Bennie rifled through some papers on Sally's desk, then handed an envelope to Sam.

While the two men looked at each photo, Bennie told them some of the gossip he'd overheard at the track.

"Man, the stories I heard today. One groom, who works for Busch's stables, said they've been trying some new herbal poultice that's made out of wild yam to reduce inflammation in a horse's joints." Bennie winked at his wife. "Honey, before you know it, they'll be using that great smelling night cream you get at the drugstore on horses." Sally laughed.

Sam stopped at one picture. He thought he knew the man standing next to one of the trainers in front of that same stables. "I think I know him." Sam showed the photo to Jim and Bennie, pointing at the image.

Bennie nodded. "A trainer told me that's the guy who brings extra tack and supplies to the backside for sale at Meadows."

Sam nodded to Jim. "I saw him there today. I thought the track owners wanted to put a ban on vendors back there."

"So I was told." Jim handed the photos to Bennie, who put them back in the envelope and set them on Sally's desk.

"Thanks, Bennie," Sam said. "You've been a big help..." He looked between Sally and her husband, as if he wanted to say more, but he only sighed.

"I have some errands to run." Sam looked at his friend, and realized that this was no longer his office. "See you all later," he said and left. He wasn't sure why he couldn't bring himself to tell the young couple about the baby.

****

At Rising Sun, Emma placed her hand on her stomach where their child was beginning to grow and smiled as she gazed around the nursery. She'd always loved the lighting here, but she didn't miss painting anymore - she had so much to look forward to. She'd stored her art supplies in the attic, thinking that someday her child might be interested.

Looking at the wallpaper border that now hung around the room at eye level, she saw how the images of the flattened world were captured on the blue background. Animals and landmarks from every continent were included: elephants and camels in Africa, the Eiffel Tower in France, Pandas and the Great Wall in China, the Statue of Liberty near New York. She smiled when she saw it even had fir trees in Oregon. Rain now pelted against the windows.

Carefully, she cut out individual images from a leftover strip of the border, like jet airplanes and cruise ships, tigers and kangaroos. Then, she separated each continent. These loose pieces she pasted to the white closet door of the nursery.

Emma looked at her watch.

Just then, she was surprised to hear Nikki call out from downstairs, "Anyone home?"

"Come on up, Nikki, and see what I've done to the nursery."

The young girl ran up the stairs two at a time and turned into the baby's room. "Wow, this is so cool!" She shrugged out of her wet coat, went to the crib and gently picked up the stuffed white lamb.

"Since our travels to Europe, Sam and I wanted our child to see the world, just as we had." Emma pointed to a small cut out piece she'd pasted over the light switch, "See, there's a compass so she...or he will never lose their way."

Nikki hugged Emma. "I wish you were my mom! Your baby is so lucky."

"Do you remember your parents?" Emma asked, walking to straighten a small blanket lying over the rocking chair.

Nikki was silent for a moment, then hugged the lamb and said, "...I remember a blue, stuffed pony."

Emma's heart fluttered at the thought of that being her only childhood memory. She walked to Nikki and put her arm over her shoulders. "Do you still have it?"

"No, I don't know what happened to it." Nikki put the lamb back in the crib.

"Wait, I thought Walter wasn't going to let you continue your lessons."

Nikki shrugged. "I'm not here for a lesson...I just wanted to see you. Maria said I could." The young girl walked around the room, looking at the colorful world on the banner.

All of a sudden, a heavy cloud outside darkened the small room and the air seemed thick, making it hard to breathe. To Emma, it felt like a premonition. She shook her shoulders and said, "Let's go see the horses," and led the way downstairs. "I have a little work to do with Neo, my new Lipizzaner." Emma remembered the last time she'd had a feeling like that...

Nikki stood in the enclosed arena and watched Emma ride the white stallion. She was in awe of Emma's ability to get this animal to follow any command she gave him, no matter how slight. She hoped that one day she would be able to ride like her.

"When I rode Neo at the Piber Stud Farm," Emma told Nikki, "I noticed that he was having some difficulty doing a *Shoulder-In*. That's what we're going to work on today."

The horse began trotting, and then Emma brought him into a collected trot around the arena. Once they were at a long wall, she changed her seat bone and leg position to get him to move both forward and sideways. "You have to make sure your shoulders are parallel to his and that his hind legs move in a straight line."

"Wow," Nikki sighed, watching the pair gracefully pass her.

Slowly, the horse cantered, then Emma turned him from the far corner towards the center. Here, she asked him to go into a movement where the horse changed his leading leg during the moment of suspension when all of his hooves were off the ground.

"Oh, my god, it's like he's skipping! What is that called?"

"A *Flying Lead Change*," Emma responded.

"How did you do that?"

Just then, Emma cried out and held her hand over her stomach. "Nikki!" she screamed and fell off the horse, hitting the ground hard and was knocked unconscious.

Nikki ran to her, crying "Emma, Emma!" Nervously, she looked at the stallion, which was now standing at the other side of the arena. Frantically, she shook Emma's shoulders. "Wake up!" She looked around and yelled, "HELP! PETER, HELP!"

Peter came running into the arena and stopped when he saw Emma. "What has happened?" he asked as he ran to them.

"I don't know," Nikki cried, tears streaming down her cheeks. "She just fell off Neo...she won't wake up - and she's bleeding!"

Peter looked around to see where Neo stood, and then he saw the blood on Emma's breeches. "Oh, dear Lord!" he exclaimed. "Stay here with her; I will call for an ambulance."

He grabbed the horse's reins and ran with him towards the stables.

"Call Sam, too!" Nikki was, now sobbing.

Sam arrived home, just as Emma was being placed into the ambulance. "Emma!" he cried, but one of the EMT's stopped him. "That's my wife!" he yelled.

"She's regained consciousness, but we have to get her to the hospital."

"She's pregnant!" Sam told the young man. "I want to ride with her–"

"No!" Nikki screamed. "I don't want to stay here." She looked nervously at Peter. "Please don't leave me here..."

"We have to go, sir," the medic said. "She'll be at Newberg Hospital."

"Okay. I'll be right behind you," Sam said, nodding. He watched as they closed the doors and sped away with sirens blasting.

"Nikki, I'll take you with me."

Nikki hugged Sam for the first time. He wrapped his arms around her, and then looked at Peter. "Call her foster parents and tell them where we are."

"*Ja,*" Peter said, "I will call Tracy, too." He ran to the stable.

****

Sam and Nikki followed the ambulance in his truck.

"What happened?" Sam asked the frightened girl next to him.

"I don't know - she was riding Neo when she just fell. I've never been so scared in my life." Nikki was more frightened now than she ever was with Walter.

When they arrived at the hospital, a nurse told them that the doctor was with Emma now. "You can sit in the waiting room. Dr. Blake will be out as soon–"

"But, how is she?" Sam insisted. "Will she be all right?"

"I can't say for now," the nurse said. "Just wait over there, Mr. Parker."

Sam sat down and looked around the room, the white, sterile walls seemed cold and impersonal. A young couple sat away from them, talking. One older man was near the windows, he seemed to be looking for someone. Nurses bustled passed as they went from their station to other wings of the hospital. Each time a pair of large double doors opened, Sam could hear machines beeping.

"I hate hospitals!" Nikki said as she sat next to Sam. Then, she got up and started pacing.

Sam was going to tell her about the last time he was in a hospital, but since his dad had died, he decided to keep it to himself. "When were you in a hospital?" he asked.

She sat down again. "Last time Maria had to come here."

"Maria?" Sam said, looking at the young girl next to her. "What happened?"

Nikki was quiet for a moment. She was sorry now that she'd brought it up and wasn't sure what to say. Then, she used the usual reply, "She fell..."

A doctor came out of one of the doors, but he went up to the couple. Sam was glad he couldn't hear what the doctor was saying. It seemed like hours went by, but he knew it had only been about twenty minutes.

Just then, a man walked into the hospital. Nikki grabbed Sam's arm. "It's Walter," she said in a small voice.

"Nikki, what the hell are you doing here?" Walter Mitchell bellowed, making everyone in the room look at him. "I thought I told you—"

"Emma fell...and Sam brought me—"

"Come on, you've no business being here!" He glared at Sam.

Walter tried to grab Nikki, but Sam stopped him. He thought he recognized him.

"Wait!" Sam said, standing between Walter and Nikki. "She just wants to know how Emma is—"

"I don't give a damn! I'm taking the girl home—"

"Haven't I seen you before - at Portland Meadows?"

"Sam is the Racing Commissioner," Nikki said proudly, but then cowered when she looked at her foster dad.

Sam was about to correct her, until he saw the look on Walter's face - the look of an angry, caged animal. He wanted to know why.

"I never go there," Walter said. "You must be mistaken." He grabbed Nikki and dragged her out of the hospital.

Sam started to follow them, when a doctor came into the room and called his name.

Turning, his heart stopped. The look on the doctor's face was grave. Slowly, Sam walked up to him. "Is Emma okay?" he asked.

"I'm Dr. Blake, Emma's new physician. She's going to be fine...she did suffer a slight concussion when she fell, but, the paramedics said she was only unconscious for a short while."

"Can I see her?"

The doctor began to lead Sam back through the double doors. "There's something I need to tell you..."

After they were alone in the hallway, Dr. Blake stopped near one of the patients' doors. "I'm sorry to tell you that Emma miscarried." He waited for a moment, and then added, "Under general anesthesia, I performed a D&C to remove any tissue remaining inside the uterus, but she will need to remain in the hospital overnight for observation."

Sam didn't really hear what the doctor said after he'd told him

Emma had lost the baby; he just stared at the man in silence.

"I'm sorry for your loss," Dr. Blake said. He opened the door, "You can see her now."

Slowly, Sam walked inside the white, sterile room. Emma seemed to be sleeping and looked so small in the large bed, covered with blankets and machines and wires all around her. Every so often, one of the machines beeped. Sam felt as if he were in a trance, walking in slow motion as he went to her bedside. He touched her hair, almost afraid to hurt her. Then, he saw the tear stains down the side of her face.

"Em," he whispered, "I'm here. Can you hear me?" He kissed her gently on the forehead.

She slowly opened her eyes. The sadness he saw ripped him apart. "I lost the baby," she said in a small voice.

"I know, honey...I'm just glad you're okay." It was true. Sam was so thankful that Emma was not seriously hurt - or that he hadn't lost her. She was more important to him than anything else in the world.

Emma held onto Sam tightly, sobbing. "Dr. Blake said that... he said...I'm unable to carry children to full term."

"Oh, Em, it's okay. There are other ways to have kids - when we're ready." His heart broke to hear her sobs. "Let's not talk about that now."

They clung to each other as if they were drowning in the ocean, trying to grasp at any chance to breathe again.

After a moment, Dr. Blake walked in.

Sam asked, "Do you know if we were having a boy or girl?"

"I'm sorry, but it was too soon - we really can't say at this point." Dr. Blake pulled Sam aside and said softly, "In miscarriages, the embryo is too small."

His words cut into Sam's heart like a hot knife. *What the hell am I supposed to do now?* he thought. He looked at Emma, then back at the doctor. "Thank you for all of your help."

Then Dr. Blake went up to Emma. "I'll be back later to check on you," he said, and left the room.

Emma started to cry again.

Sam walked up to her and took her in his arms.

"I always felt the baby was a girl," she sighed. "Sophia Joanna...that was her name."

CHAPTER TWENTY

Later that week, Emma sat in her bedroom, trying to rest. The curtains were drawn shut, keeping her in darkness. She still felt like she was drowning when she closed her eyes, and her headaches were getting worse. It had only been a few days, but nothing seemed real.

"Can I get you anything?" Tracy asked softly from the doorway.

Emma looked up, her hand still on her head. She hesitated a moment, then simply said, "No, thank you."

"Your Aunt Karen is arriving tomorrow. I've never met her–"

"She'll know what to do!" Emma sighed, slowly nodding her head. "She'll know."

****

In the den, Sam sat at the desk with a glass in his hand, staring at the phone. He knew he had to call George, but he just couldn't bring himself to do it. He'd already had to call to tell him about the baby...but, this seemed harder - more final.

He took another sip of bourbon, and looked at the clock in disbelief. "Nine in the morning!" he said out loud. He'd never had a drink this early before. He thought for a moment." That's noon in Kentucky." He finished his drink, and dialed.

George finally answered.

"It's Sam. Emma wanted me to call to let you know that we've decided on a...a sort of memorial site on the property...for Sophia."

George was silent on the other end. He'd heard the hesitation in Sam's voice. "How are you doing, Sam?"

Ignoring his question, Sam continued, "Emma would like you to come...it will be in two days. Can you be here?"

"Yes," George said. "I'll make the arrangements."

Sam hung up. He slammed his fist on the desk and picked up his glass. Finding it empty, he walked out to the kitchen to pour another. Looking out the window, he stopped and set his glass down. "Work!" he said out loud. "I need to train my colt."

He left a note by the bottle and walked out.

****

The next day, a taxi drove up to the house and Karen got out. She looked up at the blue sky, wondering what in the world she was going to say. Tragedies like this were never easy for her, and she'd had her share of them.

Tracy came out and said, "You must be Emma's aunt."

"Yes, I'm Karen. I'm not really her aunt, but her mother and I were such good friends."

"I'm Tracy, by the way. Emma and I are good friends, too." Tracy babbled on as the taxi driver removed Karen's bag from the trunk. "I've been with her since..." Tracy stopped, and then looked at Karen. "Emma said you could stay in the downstairs guest room. She's resting upstairs."

Karen smiled, paid the man and he left. Then, Tracy led the way into the house, carrying the bag. "Why don't you go on up to see her, it's the last door on the right."

"Thank you for being here," Karen said, touching Tracy's arm. As they passed the den, she asked, "Where's Sam?"

"He's at his ranch across the road - I found his note in the kitchen." Tracy didn't tell her about the bottle and empty glass she'd also found. Sam had hardly said two words to her today, and he didn't come back the previous night. "I'll be in one of the stables, helping with Emma's horses," Tracy said as she took the bag to the guest room.

Karen walked into Emma's bedroom, tapping softly on the opened door. "Hello, dear."

"Aunt Karen!" Emma said, and then tears poured down her cheeks. She was hugging the stuffed, white lamb she'd bought for Sophia.

Karen hugged her goddaughter and let her cry - the soft lamb squeezed between them.

"The doctor couldn't tell us if it was a boy or girl," Emma sobbed. "So, I decided it had to be a girl. We were going to call her Sophia...after Mom."

"Your mother would have loved that," Karen said softly. "I'm so sorry this had to happen to you. Such a loss."

Emma took a deep breath and wiped her eyes. "I know it probably sounds silly, but I want the memorial for little Sophia on the hilltop on our property. - it has a special meaning for me." It was like she was on autopilot, wanting to handle everything as if nothing had happened - trying to move forward before she collapsed. But, still, it felt like she was wading through a rushing river, the current pushing her back with each step. "A pretty marble lamb arrived yesterday with no note."

Karen picked up the little stuffed animal. She was surprised to see it when she came in, since she was the one who'd found the stone lamb in New York and had it shipped here - for Emma, and the baby. "I did that," she said. "It's Italian marble."

"You!? That was so sweet." Emma blew her nose and hugged her aunt. "I don't know what to do now..."

Karen could see that Emma was close to hysterics. "Rest, dear. That's what you should do."

Emma stared at her reflection in the Bentwood mirror across the room. She lay back against the pillows, exhausted.

****

Sam was glad that neither Mike nor Shane were around when he walked into his stable and stood in the large, open door. Parker Ranch was his dream, but now he only felt sadness.

His mare, Ele, peeked her head out over her door. Slowly, Sam walked up to her and wrapped his arms around her neck. He wanted to sob into her mane and cry for their lost child, but no tears would come. He'd been so damned afraid of the idea of having a kid - and now, look at them. They were never going to have any kids of their own. *If only I'd been there...* he thought. *Maybe I could have done something...*

"You okay, Sam?" Mike asked behind him.

Sam quickly turned. "Sure," he lied. "Emma has company, so I thought we could get started again with Promise's training. Can you get him ready to take to the track? Is Shane here?"

Mike watched his friend closely. He could see the pain in Sam's eyes, but totally understood. Men grieve in different ways, and he'd seen Sam grieve before. He knew his friend would use work to push his pain aside - until the day it surfaced to punch him in the gut. Mike hoped he'd be there when that happened.

"You got it!" he said to Sam, and walked to the tack room in the larger stable.

****

"I made us some tea," Karen said as she entered Emma's dark room, carrying a tray. She set it on the table next to the bed and helped Emma sit up. Then, she opened the curtains to let the sunshine in.

"Have you eaten anything? I brought some scones I found in the bread box." Karen placed a napkin across Emma's lap, then poured a cup of tea with a little milk, just as she knew Emma liked it. "Your mother had that bread box on the farm in Indiana - I remember it because I gave it to her."

"Yes, that's why I kept it." Emma looked at Karen. "You were always like a sister to Mom - that's why I think of you as my aunt." She took a sip, letting the warmth of the tea seep through her body. She placed her hand on Karen's. "And, you're my godmother. I'm so thankful you came."

"I'm happy to be here," Karen smiled and sipped her own tea. She offered a plate with a scone and was glad to see Emma take a few bites. "You'll feel better after you've eaten something. It's important to keep up your strength."

After a few moments, Karen decided it was time to reveal her own secret, if it could help Emma to realize she wasn't alone with her grief. "Did you know I had a child?"

"No, why have I never met–"

"I was just sixteen when I got pregnant...It was during my first year at the Conservatory - with a young boy in my class, before I met your mother...But, I was forced to give the child up - my parents were so embarrassed." Karen held up her hand before Emma could say anything. "Let me finish...I was sent to an orphanage - in Italy, and a nun took my baby from me right after it was born. I never got to hold my child, either. So, I totally understand what you are going through..."

Emma only stared at her aunt in disbelief, that they both had suffered a similar loss.

"I'm not sure you knew," Karen continued, "that I was never able to have children with your Uncle Oliver. After we were married, we learned that he'd received an injury in college football, which made him sterile. It was all so tragic, since we really wanted children. But, then, you came along," Karen said, touching Emma's cheek, "and you became the child we always missed. That's why I doted on you so, my dear. I love you so much."

Emma felt a little comfort in knowing that she was not the alone in this. If her aunt could survive, so could she. Emma clung to Karen and cried - for the loss of both of their children.

****

Later, Karen was alone in the downstairs guest room, sitting on the bed. It was a modest little room, with an old vanity and mirror sitting against one wall, an armoire against the other. In a corner sat one small Chintz-covered club chair, with a floor lamp next to it.

She began to unpack, then sank down into the chair and sobbed. She had never told anyone, other than Oliver and Emma's mother, about her lost child. She knew exactly what poor Emma was feeling.

Wiping her eyes, she decided that it was finally time to confront her past. She went to the den and dialed her mother's number in Boston.

KENTUCKY

Near the mare's stable, the man watched as Divina returned home. He stepped back into the shadows. Seeing her again only fueled his anger, justifying what he planned to do. He knew it was time.

When all was quiet, he walked into the barn. Charito nickered softly as he approached her stall. She came forward as he held out his hand and rubbed her neck. "Sorry, old girl," he whispered.

He mixed some dried foliage with hay and fed it to her. He knew the poison would take only a few hours.

Just before he left, he threw something into one corner of the mare's stall.

CHAPTER TWENTY-ONE

OREGON

The dreaded day arrived. Most of their family and friends were going to be there. Emma stared into her gaping closet. *What do you wear to your child's memorial?* she wondered and broke into tears. Then, she saw that Karen had placed a dress for her over the chair next to the mirror. She knew Sam had gone to the airport to pick up her uncle. Everything was ready - so Emma had no excuse, but to get dressed.

Finally, she looked at her reflection again. Her hair was twisted into a bun and she looked pale, but there was nothing she could do about it. Tears started to flow. She opened her dresser drawer and pulled out a cotton handkerchief that her mother had embroidered with colorful pansies - her mother's favorite flower. Wiping her eyes, she walked out of the room.

In the hall, she stopped. Downstairs, she could hear the muffled voices of Tracy and Joanna talking with Karen. She couldn't face them just yet, so she slowly opened the nursery door and walked in. As soon as she entered, she knew it was a mistake. She collapsed into the rocking chair and sobbed.

After a while, there was a knock at the door. "Emma, honey," Karen said. "Can I come in?" Without waiting for an answer, she opened the door, stepped in and closed it again.

She walked to Emma and knelt down. "It will be okay," Karen

sighed, moving a strand of hair that had fallen across Emma's face. "I know it seems like it won't right now, but with time - it will. We just have to get through today, okay?"

Emma nodded, wiped her eyes, blew her nose and stood. "Oh, I've ruined Mother's handkerchief," she said, looking at the soggy cloth in her hand.

Karen took it and pulled another one from her sleeve. "Here's one that your mother made for me."

Emma hugged her aunt. "I am so lucky to have you, and now my Uncle George in my life. You both are all I have left of my family."

"George?" Karen asked, looking puzzled.

"He owns Essen Farms in Kentucky. I only learned about him a couple of years ago - before Sam and I were married–"

"George Mason is your uncle?!" Karen exclaimed. "I thought your family name was Maseman."

"Uncle George's name was changed at Immigration when he came here from Germany with my dad, but he still goes by Mason for his business."

Karen looked disgusted, "Just like he changed my family's farm from McKenzie to Essen."

Emma remembered Karen talking about McKenzie Farms back in Chicago years ago. Now, she finally made the connection. "Essen Farms was your father's horse farm in Louisville?" she asked.

"My father should have given that damned place to me, not that foreigner!"

"I thought Mom said you went to court over that dispute years ago. Didn't you meet George then?"

"He never appeared! It was all handled by my father's attorney."

"If you could've come to our wedding, you would have met him then."

Karen touched Emma's hand. "I'm so sorry I couldn't be there. You know I was dealing with Uncle Oliver's death in that car crash."

Emma nodded and thought about her past - the loss of her father and mother, Sam's dad, and her other uncle, Franz. *How many lives are gone,* she thought. *And now, my own child.*

Then, she heard Sam's voice downstairs and knew they were back from the airport. She sighed. "Let's get this day over with."

The wind had started up, as Emma and Sam walked to the top of the hill of their property. *How this place had so many other lovely memories*, Emma thought, *but now it would always be a place of sadness.*

She stopped when she saw the white lamb gleaming in the sunshine, sitting on a black stone slab. Everyone gathered together under the large oak tree.

"We are here to commemorate Sophia Joanna Parker, a small soul that only had a short beginning..." Emma would forever remember the words George said as he droned on - it reminded her of when she'd stood at her parents' graves during each of their funerals. She was glad that Sam had chosen her uncle to read the words she'd written for their daughter.

She looked around at the other people who had come to share this tragic day: Jim Barolio and his wife, Nancy; Doc and Ian White; Peter and Tracy; Mike and Shane; and Sam's mother, Joanna. Emma wished her friend, Jennifer, could be here, but she and Jason were in Australia on an anniversary trip. Jennifer had been with her when she had to bury both of her parents.

Then, Emma saw Sam's face. He looked like a bomb about to explode, but was trying hard to keep the fuse from igniting it. His world had also been turned upside down. She placed her arm in his and held on tight...hoping she would not collapse.

"She never had a chance..." her uncle was now saying. Emma felt herself slowly crumble inside and bent over in pain, the kind of pain one has when a leg or arm has been amputated - the limb is no longer there, but it still aches.

Joanna walked up to her and placed her arm around Emma's waist. She looked over at Sam and tried to smile.

"I can't do this–" Emma started.

"I know," Joanna said softly. "I'll get you home and into bed. Sam will make excuses. I'm sure everyone will understand." She helped Emma to the car.

****

After the memorial, George and Karen rode together. He'd been struck by her beauty the moment he saw her. He was surprised to learn that she lived in a Brownstone in New York City, since her mother had a house in Boston.

"When was the last time you were at the farm?" he asked.

"I haven't been there since I was twelve years old," Karen told him. "I was sent to Prep school, then the New York Conservatory..." Her words trailed off, she didn't need to share everything with this man. She was upset that she was paired with George for the drive up the hill to the grave site. *What a tragic day*, she thought, *and it's not getting any better.*

George had always wondered what brought Bob McKenzie to give him the horse farm before his own daughter. Now, as he parked the car in front of Emma's house, he decided to know why. "I was shocked when your father–"

"Excuse me," Karen said abruptly and stepped out of the car. "I want to go see how Emma is doing."

"Of course," George said as he watched her walk into the house.

Inside, Karen met Sam on the stairs. "Please get a taxi for me," she asked softly, looking back as George entered. "I need to return to New York as soon as possible."

"I can take you–"

"No, you need to be here."

Sam looked away for a moment, then said, "If that's what you want..."

The curtains were again drawn and Emma's bedroom was dark, except for a small lamp on the night stand. Karen walked over to her, lying in the big bed with the lace comforter draped over her. One arm was over her eyes, as if to block out any possible light. Karen could hear her soft sobs, knowing how deep Emma's grief ran.

"Dear, I have to go–"

"No!" Emma looked up. "I need you–"

"You have Sam...And, all of your friends here will help you. I can send Joanna back up, if you want." Karen thought of her call to her mother the previous night and said, "My mother called and wants to see me." She didn't like lying to Emma, but couldn't tell her it was because of her anger at George that she was compelled to leave so abruptly. She couldn't stay in this house with him still in it!

Emma stared at her, tears streaming down her already wet cheeks.

Karen wiped Emma's tears and hugged her. "Please call me - you can come stay with me any time. I'm sorry, but I must leave..." She pushed a lock of hair behind Emma's ear. "Someday, you will find a way to transfer the love of your own child to someone who will need you - like you and I did."

****

After most people had left, George was in the kitchen helping Nancy Barolio finish the dishes. She'd seemed surprised he'd offered, but it was something he could do to keep his mind occupied. He didn't want to think about what this day had meant.

"Nancy," George asked, setting a plate in the cupboard, "how long have you known Emma and Sam?"

"I first met Emma a few years ago when Sam brought her to McMinnville, where Jim and I live. Before that, I was in the Navy, stationed at Marana Air Base the same time as Sam - that's where I met Jim."

Tracy entered the room. "We can handle the rest, George," she said, taking his dishtowel from him. She picked up a tray with three glasses and Sam's bottle of bourbon. "I think the men are in the den. Why don't you take these and join them?"

Just as George approached the door, he overheard Jim talking to Sam about the cases at Portland Meadows.

"I found the name of the owner of that horse in the photo Bennie had...it was Owen Busch."

"That's the stables Bennie talked about using natural products on his horses." Sam said. "Could they be the ones behind the Fleischer colt's poisoning?"

"I don't know - that one was a Lasix case. But, I'll do some more digging."

George could see the anger stirring in Sam as he stood before the unlit fireplace, his hands in his pockets. Both men looked up as he entered.

"Owen Busch," George said, setting the tray down on the coffee table. "I know that name, but I forget now why."

"Would you let me know if you remember more about him?" Jim asked, handing him one of his old business cards. The job title and contact information was still the same.

"Yes." George began to fill the glasses and gave one to each of

222

them. "The ladies thought we could use this," he said to take the tension out of the room. He watched as Sam slugged the entire contents in one large gulp.

"How are you doing, Sam?" George asked, putting his hand on his shoulder.

Sam shrugged his hand off. Glad the bottle was on the tray, he poured more. "I'm fine," he said, then drank the second glassful.

Nancy appeared at the door and said, "Jim, we have to go pick up the kids at the babysitter's."

Jim set down his unfinished drink and looked at Sam. "You're going to be okay. Call me if you need me." He patted his friend on the back, and then left with his wife.

George sat down in one of the large leather chairs. He sipped his drink, then said, "I am so sorry for your loss, son—"

"I'm not your son!" Sam snapped, then ran his hand through his hair and sighed. "Sorry, it's just been a hard day...I don't want to talk about it."

"I know." George sat quietly for a moment, and then said, "I'd like to see Ele while I'm here." He saw Sam look up at the ceiling.

"Emma's friend, Tracy, is still here," George said, knowing Sam was probably concerned about leaving Emma. "I will tell her where we're going, we won't be long."

****

The clear air was refreshing after the stifling, warm house. The two men walked up the lane to Sam's new ranch in the soft afternoon light, and George noticed how tired Sam looked.

"Are you getting ready for the Preakness Stakes?" Sam asked to make conversation.

"Most definitely!" George said, then he looked up. He felt a twinge in his left arm, where his brother had shot him in this very same place, years ago. "How many acres do you have?" he asked, trying to forget that night.

"Ten, but most of it is still woods." Sam was glad to be out of the house and thinking about something other than their baby. He took a deep breath and said, "There's a track back there - I'll take you, if you want to see it."

"I would like that. How is Promise doing?"

"He's right on track - he's had a rider up now for over two weeks. You met Mike McKeegan today. He's my manager, and he says Promise is ready to go to Portland Meadows track for more training."

Sam led the way to Ele's stable. As they walked in, Classy Elegance poked her head out over her stall door.

George stepped up to the mare. "Hello, lady, you look wonderful." He ran his hands over her coat, gently talking to her. The horse nickered in response.

"Mike's getting her ready to race soon, too," Sam said, feeling a little jealous at his horse's reaction to this man.

"It sounds like you have big plans here." George started to walk out of the stable and looked around. "Where is my colt?"

"He's MY colt!" Sam said sharply, following George outside. "Shane's exercising Promise, down at the track."

"Today?"

"The work never stops," Sam said, paused, then added, "I'm training him to be ready for the Belmont Stakes in '73–"

"I still think Fred should be the one training Promise, since Koenig's Wonder's his sire–"

"Like I told you before - I'm training Promise!"

Sam and George stood toe to toe, angrily yelling at each other.

Just then, Mike ran up and hollered, "Break it up, you two!" He looked between the men who were about to attack each other. "I could hear you down at the track. This is not the time, nor the place."

Sam and George stepped away from each other.

"Only Kentucky farms produce Triple Crown winners–" George began.

"I beg to differ," Mike said, holding both hands up to stop Sam from saying anything. "Remember the horse, Assault? He won in '46 and was trained in Texas..."

Sam nodded and finally smiled a little. Mike always knew how to diffuse arguments between him and his dad in the past. And, he was sure that today's disagreement with George was over much more than horses. It was a way to release some of the pent-up tension.

"Let's go watch Promise exercise," he said and led the way towards the woods.

George was surprised to see the density of the trees on Sam's property - the mix of fir and oak trees. A large, three-point buck stood on a small rise a few yards away from them as they walked towards the clearing ahead. When they came out from under the canopy of trees, a pair of hawks circled overhead, their cries piercing the silence. George stopped when he saw the large, oval track that completely surrounded the clearing, fenced with high oak posts.

They stepped inside the gate as Shane was slowly trotting Promise around the track, warming him up. Then, the lad took him into a canter for half the length of the oval. On the backstretch, he let the horse take the lead. Promise ran with pure joy, like he was on some open mountain range.

Mike whistled, and Shane gently slowed the young colt, leading him towards his dad.

"He's a fine looking animal!" George said, reaching up to pat his neck. "And, he's quite tall for his age."

"Yes, and, as you can see, he loves to run," Sam said with pride. "I have some tricks up my sleeve that Kentucky trainers never thought of!"

Shane trotted, and then walked Promise around the track to start his cool down, the fading sunlight gleaming on the auburn horse's coat. Then, when Sam gave a wave to the pair, Shane walked the horse back and off the track, following the trail to the stables.

After watching the men and boy work with the young stallion, George began to see how serious Sam was and that Mike was a good manager. He decided to wait and see.

As George and Sam walked back towards the stable, he said, "I'm happy to see you following your passion."

Sam only nodded and kept walking.

Once they were outside the building, George added, "Be careful that you don't use your work to hide your feelings. You've had a big loss, and Emma needs you - especially now."

Sam kicked his foot in the dirt. "I'm just so angry...I don't understand how it happened or what we're supposed to do now."

George sighed. "Sometimes, we never know what causes this sort of thing. Usually, it happens to someone else. But, when you experience it, you just need to love each other and continue living one day at a time. I'm sure everything will work out."

****

Later, George was alone, sitting in the den at Rising Sun while a small fire was ebbing in the hearth. Sam had gone back to his ranch - using the excuse that he needed to check on his horses again.

A step on the stairs creaked and Emma appeared in the doorway, dressed in her nightgown and robe. She looked pale and distraught, but smiled a little when she saw him.

She sighed and sat down beside him on the long couch, then placed her arm around his and laid her head on his shoulder. "I'm glad you're still here."

George patted her hand. "Yes, I will stay until you tell me to leave - if that's what you need."

"This is all like a bad dream. I keep hoping I'll wake up soon and it won't be real."

George just sat and listened.

She looked up at her last living relative on her dad's side of the family.

"Sam has always been afraid of children," she said. "But, I thought we were through all that when I learned I was pregnant. Now he won't have to worry about it - I can't have kids."

"I think Sam is avoiding the reality of your lost child," George said. "He didn't want to talk to me about it, either. But, maybe, you two can share your feelings and move on...it will just take time." He turned Emma towards him and said, "When I lost both of my brothers, I thought the world had ended for me. But, then, I found you! We are what's left of the Maseman family, and I cherish every moment we have together."

Emma looked at George, but couldn't bring herself to say any more about loss or death or time. Finally, she asked, "How's Divina."

George stared into the fire, "She's just a friend."

"How did you like meeting Karen?"

"She was pleasant, under the circumstances. But, I don't think I made a very good impression."

George thought of the first time he'd seen Karen McKenzie years ago at Arlington Track, when he'd hidden in the shadows.

"I'm going to bed," Emma said. Then, she kissed him, "Uncle George, you don't want to end up alone. It's time you find a wife!"

Later, Sam had returned and George retired to the upstairs guest bedroom. He looked around the room and remembered the last time he'd been there – it was after Franz had died. The walls were still blue, and the daybed he'd used was there. He now sat in the overstuffed chair and allowed himself to think of his past and how he'd lived alone through most of it. A wife and family had not been his destiny.

Then, Hannah came to mind. *I've loved only one woman*, he thought to himself. *But, she is a ghost who will never age for me.*

His guilt kept eating at him for not looking for her when he returned to Germany after the war to search for his parents. His family was gone now, except for Emma.

"Maybe it's too late for me now," he said to himself, when he finally realized that he could never love Divina – not the way she needed him.

He heard a phone ringing. After a few moments, someone came running up the stairs. He was surprised when they stopped and there was a knock at his door.

"George," Sam said, "that was Fred. Divina's mare was found dead."

CHAPTER TWENTY-TWO

BOSTON

The next day, Karen arrived at her mother's house, which had belonged to her grandparents. Mollie McKenzie moved there after Karen's father died, leaving the Kentucky horse world behind her. The white clapboard house was built in the early 1900's in the Jamaica Plain district, but Karen never really liked it. There were too many rules.

She walked into the foyer and dropped her bag on the hardwood floor.

"Mother, where are you?" Karen called out, then she heard footsteps from the back of the house.

"There you are," Mollie said, placing a small jeweled hand to her silver hair, her crisp blue eyes shining in her lined face. Karen was amazed to see that even in her nineties, her mother's stature was queen-like. There were no hugs of affection, which Karen never expected.

"You don't have to yell like some commoner." Then, Mollie turned and said, "We'll have tea in the parlor," as she walked down the hall.

Karen followed her mother into the blue room with antiques and over-stuffed furniture that had been there for hundreds of years. Nothing had changed. When she was small, Karen always thought this should have been called the music room, since there was a piano and an old Victrola. But then, she remembered that music was limited to only certain hours of the day and this room was used mostly for receiving guests.

The maid brought in the tea tray and smiled at Karen.

"Hello, Annabelle, I hope that you are well," Karen said, aware that her mother hated her familiar chatter with the servant. Whenever they'd visited here, she would spend most of her time in the kitchen with Annabelle, listening to her stories of England. She was brought to America when she was a teenager by Karen's grandparents to serve as Mollie's nanny and never left. Unfortunately, her mother was taught to only see Annabelle as an employee.

"That will be all," Mollie said abruptly, waiving her hand. Annabelle smiled at Karen, curtsied, and left the room.

Karen's mother chatted about her friends and the bridge games she loved so much. Then, she began reminiscing. "My parents introduced me into Boston's high society, you know. We Appleby's were a revered family here..."

Karen listened to the familiar stories and thought about her maternal grandparents. She wondered what her mother's life was like as a child in this house, but then she thought of her own cold, loveless past. As they sat on the sofa, after the tea had turned cold, Karen finally changed the conversation to her reason for coming.

"Mother, I'm here to ask you about the child that was taken away from me..."

Mollie stared at her daughter, then sighed. "Oh, Karen, it was for the best–"

"How could you do that to me?"

Her mother got up and pulled a cord to summons the maid. After the tray was removed, she said, "I refuse to talk about it. Remember, you were away studying music in Europe–"

"That was your own lie you told your friends..." Karen blurted, "And yourselves."

"Well, that's all in the past now." Mollie walked across the room and opened a drawer of a large Chippendale desk. "I have two tickets for tonight's symphony. Would you like to join me?"

Resigned, Karen accepted, knowing that her mother was not going to continue the discussion. That's what their family had always done when something ugly in their past was brought up - they buried it and moved on, as if it never happened. "But, we're not finished."

****

It was after intermission and the second half had begun at the Boston Symphony hall. Karen first fell in love with the orchestra and classical music here as a child when visiting her grandparents. The first half was some pieces by more contemporary composers. One in particular Karen didn't like, the atonal sounds had grated on her nerves. It was as if the composer was trying to create unheard notes for his composition in an attempt to write something new. She wondered if the man was tone deaf and sympathized with the musicians.

Looking around the hall, she was still amazed at the beauty of the building, built in 1900. The stage, which had the elaborate pipes for the famous organ as the backdrop, was surrounded by a silver filigree casing that led up to a gilded shield at the top center. The vaulted ceilings, covered in decorated beams, added to the lovely acoustics.

The orchestra was now performing a symphony by Vivaldi. Karen was transported to her time at the music conservatory in New York. She used to sit next to Sophia, Emma's mother, in the cello section. Sophia was just beginning when Karen returned. They were so young then and had their futures ahead of them. Sophia was much more talented and rightfully received the appointment to first chair. She was also much more serious than Karen, but that didn't stop them from becoming fast friends.

Watching the Boston Symphony now, Karen smiled as she closed her eyes and imagined her cello in her hands. She always smiled when she played for the pure joy of the experience. Often, at the conservatory, she would look over at Ethan O'Brien in the bass section and see that his eyes were closed and he was smiling, just like she did.

She had found a kindred spirit in Ethan. Vivaldi was their favorite composer, and they would sometimes rehearse together for a concert. She remembered how Ethan's hair fell down over his forehead during an energetic piece, his dark-rimmed glasses giving him a handsome, sort of rogue look – like an actor in a movie.

During one of their private moments in Ethan's flat, they'd practiced Vivaldi's Cello concertos. When Karen played a solo

Concerto in E minor, their senses and sexuality were heightened. When she played the last note of the composition, the young couple looked at each other, slowly laid down their instruments, and fell into each other's arms. Karen was still a virgin then, but Ethan was more experienced. He had shown her what it was like to feel unconditional love through every pore in her body, his fingers moving softly as if he were playing a love song on her skin. She had gotten pregnant during one of those sessions.

Karen now opened her eyes and found that she was looking to the right of the stage at the bass section. She started when she saw that one of the men's movements seemed somewhat familiar, especially the unusual way he held his bow. She grabbed Mollie's opera glasses and gasped as she looked at the man close-up. The similarities were uncanny, even though this man's hair was graying at the temples. *Could this be him?* she wondered.

She grabbed her program and strained to read the names of the orchestra members until her mother handed her a small flashlight. Karen's heart stopped as she read that the First Chair Bassist was Ethan!

Slowly, she sat back in her seat and sighed, aware of her mother's sideways glance, realizing that she'd been holding her breath for some time.

For the rest of the concert, Karen did not hear the music as she watched Ethan, while images of that time long ago floated in her mind like scenes of a movie, disjointed and fleeting: Ethan refusing her calls when she'd learned she was pregnant; her parents sending her to Italy; the nun at the orphanage taking her child away and later telling her it had died. A month later, Karen had returned to her parents' home in Kentucky, numb and depressed, unable to cope or find joy in anything. She never left the house, until it was time to go back to the Conservatory.

The music stopped and the audience applauded, bringing Karen back into the present. As if awakening from a deep sleep, she looked around her in a daze.

"Come on, Karen, it's time to go," Mollie said, slowly rising from her seat.

On the way out of the concert hall, they were stopped by numerous people who knew her mother. While Mollie and friends chatted on, Karen caught sight of Ethan walking out. He was handsome in his tailcoat and tuxedo pants. She wondered if he ever wanted to know what happened to her - or if she should tell him about their child.

Just as she started to walk towards him, a pretty blonde woman and two children ran up to him. Karen stopped and watched as they hugged, and Ethan picked up the little girl in his arms. Her eyes filled with tears as she watched the small family leave.

****

Alone in her mother's parlor, while Mollie was changing and Annabelle was making tea, Karen sat in a maroon-velvet wingback chair and looked at a dying fire in the brick fireplace. She stirred the embers, adding a soft glow to the room.

The furnishings reminded her of her grandparents. Photographs of them and her mother as a child, and ones when Mollie was younger, sat on the old, upright piano. Karen was not surprised to see there were no photos of her father.

She found a recording of Vivaldi's concertos, which she had loved as a child. Opening the old Victrola, she put the single-sided record on the spindle, turned the crank a few times, and gently placed the needle on the spinning disk.

While the music filtered through the room, she saw her family's old Bible on a shelf under the cherry antique side table next to her. She opened the book to the first page and looked at the lineage of her family through the years. She smiled when she found her name and her marriage to Oliver, but then was saddened to see there were no births listed.

As she began to thumb through the large book, a yellowed letter fell onto the floor. Karen picked it up and saw that it was written to her mother from an orphanage in Italy, south of Florence - the *Santa Maria della Scala.*

Karen slowly opened the letter. Her hands began to shake as she read it. Anger rose inside of her - the type that could lead to someone doing something they'd later regret. The lies she'd been told, the injustice of it all!

Her mother walked in, wearing a nightdress and soft, purple velvet robe. Annabelle followed her with the tea tray.

Impatiently, Karen waited until the tea was poured and Annabelle left.

"Why did you not tell me about this?" Karen blurted out to her mother, holding up the letter.

Mollie's face went pale. "Where did you find that?"

"In this old Bible…" Karen stood with one hand over her heart. "Why would you keep this from me - lying about my child - making me think that it was dead all these years?" The nuns never told her whether it was a boy or a girl.

"It was for your own good."

Karen put the letter in her pocket and announced, "I will never forgive you for this!" She turned and left the room.

Pacing in her old bedroom, Karen wanted to break something. She'd never been so angry in her life. Looking around at the four-poster bed and the painted, white fireplace, brought back memories of her childhood with her grandparents. In spite of their strictness, they had always provided a room for her. She and her mother visited often, because Mollie never really liked Kentucky.

Karen started packing, the letter now lying on her bed. She couldn't wait to get out of this house. At first, she thought she would book the next flight for New York; but, slowly, she sat down on the bed and picked up the letter. She noted a telephone number on the orphanage's letterhead.

What would I say if I called? she wondered to herself. *Do you know where my child is now?* She shook her head, knowing how futile that seemed - after all these years. But…she knew she had to try.

Checking the time zone pages of the phone book, she saw that Italy was six hours ahead of Boston's time. She looked at her watch. Remembering from school that nuns arose early for Morning Prayers, she picked up the telephone and dialed. While waiting, she rehearsed in her mind what she would ask…

Pronto, an older woman's voice said on the other end.

"Hello," Karen started, and then hesitated. "Do you speak English?"

"Yes."

"Is this the *Santa Maria della Scala* in Siena?"

"Yes."

"This is Karen…uh…McKenzie. I apologize for calling so

early...but, I was there over forty years ago...to have a child. Would you be able to help me find information about that birth?"

There was a long pause at the other end. Just as Karen was about to ask if the woman was still there, the voice said, "I'm afraid we do not have those records."

Once again heartbroken, Karen gave the nun her address in New York. "Please contact me if you learn anything." Then, she said, "Thank you," and hung up.

For the first time in her life, she allowed herself to hope that someday she would find her lost child.

KENTUCKY

George had caught the first overnight flight to Kentucky. It was early morning when he landed, and the first thing he did was call Divina. Jasmine told him to come over immediately.

When he and Fred arrived at Gallano Farm, Divina was in the mare's barn with Seth, her vet, and Simon Day. The mare lay on her side, legs stretched out in front of her.

Fred touched the mare and said, "She's stone cold!"

"I came as soon as I heard," George said to Divina. He was exhausted from the long flight, but he pushed that all aside when he saw how distraught she looked.

"She was my prize mare, born here from one of my father's broodmare's bloodlines - the last of her lineage. She was my hope of this becoming a breeding farm, and...she was in foal. Now, that is all over." Divina wrung her small hands and paced. "I don't know what I am going to do!"

Seth drew some blood, then said, "I'm going to do a necropsy here. I want to get some answers as to what would have caused this."

Divina looked at Simon and asked, "How could this happen?"

"I'm not sure," Simon told her, as he took the sample from Seth. "I'll get this to the lab right away, and we'll have the results in a few days." He looked at Seth and George. "I also got some samples of the mare's feed. I'll be in touch," then he packed his kit and left.

George turned to Divina. "Why don't we go back to the house. Seth and Fred can take care of all this."

Divina placed her hand on the mare's cold neck. "Goodbye, Charito."

As they walked into her house, she asked, "What would you do, George?"

"I don't know," was all he could think to say. He'd had experiences of people working on his staff who sabotaged his horses' chances of winning, but never anything this drastic.

She led the way into her study and walked right up to the bar. She poured a stiff shot of bourbon, drank it down, and then asked George if he wanted one. When he nodded, she poured more and carried both glasses to where he sat.

She looked around her. "This place is all I have left, but it is no longer the grand horse farm my father built. And, now this..."

George waited.

"Maybe I should sell–"

"What? No!"

"I've been thinking about it for some time...ever since the problems with Mr. Divinity began. But losing my mare is the last straw." She sipped her drink now, looking out at the stable through the large windows. "I think it is time."

"But what will you do?"

"I do not know yet." She stared at George over the rim of her glass. "Do you think you might want it?"

George stood and began pacing the room. "This isn't the answer, you don't just give up after–"

"I've been here most of my life." She looked around. "This is my home." Then, she looked down at her hands. "But, I received a letter from a family member that I didn't even know I had - a cousin on my mother's side, who is still in the Philippines. She told me about my aunt and uncle's recent passing...my cousin is the only family I have left–"

"What about your sister?"

"Tala? I don't know if she's dead or alive - I never hear from her."

"You have your horses insured, right?"

She stood and walked over to George, touching his arm. "I haven't told you about my financial problems that resulted from some bad investments my ex-husband made - before he left. That's why I had planned to change this into a breeding farm." She stopped for a moment, and then continued, "I've been struggling for years now, and the insurance would only make a dent in my debt."

George took her into his arms and held her close. She felt so small and helpless against him. He stroked her dark hair and softly said, "Take some time to think about it."

****

After everyone was gone, Seth walked into the stable. Two grooms were there, talking about how they were going to get her body out of the stall.

"Don't worry about that tonight," Seth said. "We'll deal with it in the morning."

He said goodnight, and the grooms walked to their quarters near the tack room. Seth entered Charito's stall and stood looking down at her lifeless body. He knew this horse was the last hope of keeping Gallano Farm alive, but with Mr. Divinity's illness, and now this additional tragedy of losing the mare and her foal, it was all just too much. He had no idea what the future held for him, either.

Just as Seth turned to leave, something white in the corner of the stall caught his eye. He picked it up and saw it was a bloody handkerchief. He pulled a rubber glove from one of his pockets. As he carefully placed the cloth inside the glove, he noticed some initials embroidered in one corner.

"I have to see Simon Day, right away!" Seth yelled to the grooms, and he left.

CHAPTER TWENTY-THREE

OREGON

Days later, after the memorial, Sam and Emma were not talking. He hardly ever spent much time at Rising Sun during the day now - sometimes he wouldn't even come home at night. He used the same old excuse - his horses. Emma was depressed all the time, but she couldn't help it. All she could do was cry herself to sleep. She refused to eat, even though Tracy came over each day and tried. Emma missed Nikki, but there was no energy to do her classes. Amy and Josh had moved their horses to another training stable, so Nikki was the only student she had left. Thankfully, Peter and the others helped with the horses.

She sat in the nursery, holding the stuffed lamb and rocked in her mother's chair.

"Hello," Emma heard Doc's voice from downstairs. "Emma?"

She didn't answer, just slowly closed her eyes and hoped he would go away. Then she heard Tracy and Doc talking below. After a while, both of them came up the stairs and entered the room.

"Emma," Tracy said, sitting on a chair next to her. "I called Doc - I was worried about you."

Slowly, Emma turned and Doc walked up to her, taking her hand in his. "You have gone through one of the worst possible things in the world, my dear. Is there anything I can do for you?"

When she shook her head, he said, "I want to see Sam."

She looked out the window and said, "He's across the way, at his ranch. Please leave me alone."

****

Sam stood in the aisle of his horse stable, staring at nothing. Mike and Shane were getting Promise ready to go to Portland Meadows.

"You want to come with us?" Mike asked Sam. When he didn't answer, Mike looked at Shane, then back at Sam. "We could use your help here."

Shane shook his head, but said nothing. He led Promise out of the stable.

"Put him in the trailer, I'll join you in a minute," Mike said to his son, then walked up to his friend. At a loss, he asked, "How's that case going at Gallano Farm?"

Sam seemed to come out of a daze and asked, "How do you know about that?"

"Remember, I used to work at various farms in Lexington and Louisville before I moved to Oregon. I know about the Gallano family."

"What do you know?"

"Abian Gallano was from one of the oldest families in the Philippine Islands. They created their equine empire over centuries of careful breeding and training." Mike was glad to see Sam listening to him again. "I met his daughter, Divina, when she was little. It's tragic what's happening to her now."

Doc walked into the stable. "Sam, I want to talk with you." He saw Mike and said, "Oh, hello, Mike, it is good to see you again."

"You haven't changed a bit, Doc!"

"Oh, yes I have," Doc laughed. Then, he lowered his voice and said, "I'm pleased to see that you are here for Sam. I know how much you meant to his father."

Mike looked between Sam and Doc, then said, "I'm going to head to the track."

Sam sat down on one of the bales in the aisle. "What do you want, Doc?" he asked. "I didn't call you."

Doc slowly sat down across from Sam. "I know that you are hurting right now, but Emma needs you–"

"I'm too busy to talk," he snapped. He jumped up and walked to Ele's stall. "We're getting Ele ready to race again, so I think you should leave."

"I was with your dad when they lost your brother...I know how hard these times can be. But, shutting everyone out is not the answer." When Sam did not respond, Doc got up. "If there is anything I can do, please let me know." He placed his hand on Sam's shoulder, then walked out.

Alone again, Sam opened his mare's door, led Ele out and cross-tied her in the aisle. He decided to groom her, hoping that if he kept his hands busy, he wouldn't hit something - or someone. He should have gone with Mike and Shane to watch Promise at the track. Mike had told him his colt was handling working with other horses on the bigger track like a pro, but he was still skittish with the starting gate. Sam really wanted to see if he could help, but he was frightened. He'd only felt this much fear when he was in Vietnam. Somehow, he needed to find a way to shake it off.

Slowly, he ran the brush over Ele's sides, even though she didn't need it. The more he brushed, the more he began to think about taking her to the next Santa Anita race - in California. *Maybe that's it,* he thought. *I just need to get out of Oregon - to focus on racing.* His excitement started to rise as he began planning what he needed to do - he had to get Mike onboard so Shane could come with him. They'd already had the boy up on her at the track, testing her speed and performance. Sam knew she was ready, so there was nothing holding him back. For the first time in a long time, he began to feel alive again!

It was growing dark when Sam came out of the stable. He walked down the trail through the woods. Near the track, he stood and tried to breathe in the night air, but his chest felt like there was a tight band strapped around it. He looked up and saw several shooting stars and remembered one night when his dad had told him they meant that a soul had died. Tears finally came to his eyes as he wondered which star had been Sophia's...

****

Alone one morning, Emma wandered aimlessly around her

house, unable to focus on anything. Today was the first time she'd gotten dressed. She tried to look at her breeding program, but had quickly pushed it aside. Then, she'd gone to the kitchen, opened the refrigerator door and closed it again. Nothing looked good or held her interest for very long now. She looked around the room and saw clean dishes stacked on the counter, but she ignored them. Instead, she poured a cup of coffee and grabbed a small cookie from a plate Tracy had left for her.

Sam had left for California a couple of days ago. When he'd come home to pack, Emma tried to talk to him about Sophia, but he'd refused. All he wanted to talk about was taking Ele to the races. For the first time since her miscarriage, Emma had gotten angry. She'd told him that she didn't care what he did, as long as he didn't stay here. Her last words to her husband kept circling in her mind. Sadly, she now thought, *What if something happens to him, and those are the last words I said?* She shook her head as her anger returned. "I don't give a damn what happens to him!" she yelled out loud. Slowly, she sank to a chair and sobbed.

"Emma?" she heard Nikki call from the foyer. "Are you in here?"

Emma quickly wiped her eyes. "Nikki?" she said, walking to the hallway. "What're you doing here?"

"I rode my bike over to see how you are—" Nikki saw Emma's face, then the cookie in her hand and asked, "Are there any more of those? I'm famished."

"Yes, come into the kitchen." Emma walked back and took the plate of cookies to the table. "Do you want some milk?" she said, then put her hand to her head. "I think there is some here..." She opened the refrigerator and sighed with relief. "I have milk."

"Sure, that would be great." Nikki watched Emma, afraid that she might say something wrong. Emma looked pretty fragile right now, so unlike herself. She knew what had happened with the baby - Tracy told her.

"Where's Sam," Nikki asked Emma.

"He's...at the races. How have you been?" Emma asked, lowering herself onto a chair. "I'm sorry I haven't been able to do classes yet, I just..."

"It's okay," Nikki said, chewing on a cookie. *Maybe if I distract her,* she thought. *That always works with Maria...* After another bite, she said, "I miss you...and Sonny and Lucky...but I have so much going on at school right now. I may even try out for cheerleading. I'm not sure yet. The squad had a girl drop out after one month and they need another."

Emma looked up and smiled for the first time in a long time. "Cheerleading?"

"Yep," Nikki smiled. "On the first day, you have to be able to actually do a cheer! I have a new friend, Becky - this is her second year and she's helping me learn an easy one they've used before. It's sometimes confusing, but I really like it. I'm not very good at tumbling yet. I can learn."

"I'm sure you will."

"Oh, and we're getting ready for the Spring Semi-Formal dance."

"A dance? That sounds like fun. Do you have a date?"

"Nah, I'm just going to go with my girlfriend and see what happens. I don't even know how to dance."

"What are you going to wear?"

Nikki looked at her hands, then back up at Emma. "I'm not sure yet. We don't have a lot of money–"

"Please let me help you!" Emma said emphatically. "We could go shopping - when is the dance?"

"This next Saturday. Are you sure this would be all right?"

"Yes, I would love to, as long as it's okay with your foster parents." Emma surprised herself when she jumped up and started putting things away into the cupboards. She stopped and turned to Nikki. "I'll call Maria and see what she says."

"Oh, Emma," Nikki said, hugging her. "That would be so wonderful!"

"Why don't I take you home - we'll put your bike in my truck. We could ask her then."

"Okay." Nikki knew that Walter was out of town.

Just as they were about to load the bike, Maria drove up. Emma was surprised to see the panicked look on her face. "Hi, Maria, we were just about–"

"Nicole, we have to go." Maria grabbed Nikki's bike and quickly shoved it into the trunk.

"But, Emma and I–"

"Now, Nicole!"

Emma watched Nikki get into the passenger seat. The poor girl looked frightened. Then, they left.

She stood for a moment, stunned and confused. They were going to have so much fun. It was always a delight to have Nikki here. Emma had finally felt something more than her own despair, but now it was back.

Slowly, she walked down to the stables. Looking around her at the empty paddocks and arena, she realized that her life didn't seem to really be moving forward for her now. *Sam's life has*, she thought. She took a deep breath and made her decision.

As she entered the large stable, she called out, "Peter?"

The young man came out of his room. "*Ja*, Mrs. Parker?"

"I have to leave for a few days."

"But, where are you going?"

"I'll call you as soon as I know."

When Emma entered her house, she went to the den and dialed her Aunt Karen's number.

"Karen, speaking," the voice on the other end said.

"Hi, Aunt Karen...would you mind terribly if I came to stay with you for a few days?"

"Emma, honey, is there anything wrong?"

She stopped for a moment, and then said, "No...I just need a change. I can be there tomorrow, if I can get a flight out tonight."

"Absolutely! Just let me know what flight number you'll be on. And, Emma, dear," Karen added, "I love you."

"I love you, too!" Emma hung up.

She then called Tracy to ask her to help Peter take care of the horses. She told her where she was going, but asked her not to tell anyone just yet. Tracy offered to take Emma to the airport, once she'd booked a flight. When Tracy asked her where Sam was, Emma only said, "He's living it up in California!"

After she was able to get a seat on the next plane to New York, Emma ran upstairs to pack. Before she went into her bedroom, she stopped at the closed door to the nursery. Slowly, she opened it and stepped in. Immediately, she felt the stab of pain in her stomach like she'd experienced at her baby's memorial. It still hurt too much.

Quickly, she closed the door and went to her bedroom, randomly throwing some clothes into her suitcase. Just before she closed her bag, she saw the journal her aunt had given her for her eighteenth birthday. *For your dreams*, Karen had written in it. She added it to her bag.

Emma stopped to look around the room and saw some of Sam's things lying around - a shirt and belt hanging over the chair, an older pair of boots under the armoire. *If he can run away*, she thought to herself, *then so can I.*

KENTUCKY

Gordon Evers sat in his office. He didn't like Darrell sitting across from him, trimming his fingernails. But, the man had proved useful.

"Mason's only offering the minimal value for Gallano Farm," Evers said, looking at the piece of paper on his desk with the real estate agency's logo on the letterhead. He wasn't surprised to see that Divina was selling her horse farm and that George Mason was interested.

"If he wants that farm," he added, "he's going to have to pay more than it's worth - especially if he's also buying her horse stock."

Darrell stood and looked over Evers' shoulder. "I can't really see him paying more," he said, shaking his head. "But, I'm sure if you make a better offer, that real estate agent won't mind."

Evers thought for a moment, then said, "I don't want that damned place. I just want to drive the price up...It's one way I can get revenge." He sat back and smiled. "Anyway, I'm sure Mason will pay."

There was a long pause, and then Darrell asked, "What makes you think he'll counter your offer?"

"George Mason likes to win!"

NEW YORK

Emma arrived at JFK airport in the early morning hours. It had been a non-stop, five-hour redeye flight, and she was dog tired. She'd been unable to sleep on the plane, trying to make some sense of her life, but she still felt so empty inside.

As she walked out into the airplane's gate area, she was glad to see her aunt waiting.

"There you are!" Karen said, hugging her. Then, she held her at arms' length and looked at her. "Let's get your bag and take you home, so you can get some rest. You look exhausted."

"I appreciate this so much," Emma said.

"Does Sam know you are here?"

"No," was all Emma said.

Silently, they walked through the long airport towards the baggage claim area.

****

When they arrived at Karen's Brownstone in the Crown Heights district, Emma was surprised to see that some of the buildings had been painted different colors. Karen's was the original stone, with a stoop leading to the entrance, and three stories of bay windows on the front.

Once she was settled in, Emma now sat on the floral Damask couch in the study and took off her shoes. Karen brought in some tea and sat across from her. Silently, she waited, knowing that Emma would open up when she was ready.

After a few moments, Emma began to cry. "I feel so lost! I go through the motions each day, but I'm not really there doing them. I'm like a robot. I've stopped everything, I ignore the horses and...everyone..."

"You've been through one of the worst ordeals anyone should experience."

"But, I thought I'd be better by now. Sam is no help! He was more interested in his racehorses; he even sleeps at his ranch." Emma stopped and sighed. "I just couldn't stay home any longer - there were too many memories..." She wiped her eyes with the handkerchief Karen gave her. "I went into the nursery before I left - it was horrible - like the day I lost my baby."

Karen sat quietly again and sipped her tea, letting Emma take her time to find her words.

"Yesterday," Emma continued, picking up her cup, "Nikki came to see me. She was so alive and excited about trying out for cheerleading...and a dance coming up." Emma paused, took a sip, and then went on. "We were just going dress shopping when her foster mother came to get her. Nikki's foster dad is such an ugly man, and I'm afraid for the poor girl..."

Karen set her teacup down and sat next to Emma, taking her in her arms. She knew a little about this young girl in Emma's life from Tracy. "Do you think he is hurting Nikki?"

Emma pushed a lock of hair back behind one ear. "I'm not sure - but we've seen some bruises—"

"What? When?" Tracy had not told her about this.

"At my farm, but she always makes excuses that they were from a fall. I don't really believe her, now that I've seen her foster dad's temper."

"I'm not sure getting involved is the right—"

"But, Nikki is sweet...and...I feel so close to her. I don't want anything bad to happen to her."

"She's not your child, Emma," Karen said. She knew her words would hurt, but Emma needed to see the reality. "I think you're transferring your love for your baby to Nikki, especially now that you're hurting so much. You have to be careful."

Emma thought for a moment, then sighed. "You're probably right. It's just so hard when Sam is gone so much, or won't even say Sophia's name."

"Don't worry about Sam - he is grieving in his own way, just as you are. I know that he loves you."

"I'm not so sure anymore."

Karen softly took Emma's hands in hers and smiled. "Well, after you get some rest, why don't I take you to see some of the city sites later today? Have you been in New York before?"

"Only to land here at the airport, then take the ship for our cruise to Rome - on our honeymoon." Emma stopped, then shook her head. "I can't believe that wasn't very long ago."

****

As the sun was beginning to set, the skyline of New York was stunning. Emma sat across from Karen at a table in the Rainbow Room on the sixty-fifth floor of the RCA building, near the Rockefeller Plaza. She looked around at the elegantly set, cloth-covered tables, filled with candlelight, shining crystal, china and silverware. The tables surrounded a revolving dance floor, which had a giant star in the center, made of different colors of wood inlay.

"What a beautiful place," she sighed. "And, look at that view!" She took her aunt's hand across the table and said, "Thank you! I really needed this today. What an exciting city. I'm surprised Sam and I never spent time here on our way to Europe."

At the mention of Sam's name, Emma dropped her hand to her lap. "There were a lot of things I think we could have done differently."

"Not tonight, dear," Karen cooed. "We are celebrating your first night in New York!" She looked at the menu and asked, "What shall we order?"

Emma glanced over the list, overwhelmed by the choices. Then, she closed it and said, "Why don't you order for both of us?"

When Karen nodded in agreement, Emma put her chin in her hand and gazed out the large banks of windows, watching the light and shadows change as the sun lowered in the sky. *It's still light in Oregon*, she thought, remembering that in New York, they were already three hours ahead. Emma caught her breath as she saw the Empire State Building's lights came on.

After Karen placed their order, she talked about what happened to her, after she left the Conservatory. "I found a fabulous job working at an art gallery on Fifty-Seventh Street. That's where I met Oliver." She took a sip of water, then continued. "He was my knight in shining armor! We were married two years later and began traveling around the world."

As her aunt talked, Emma imagined some of the places she had seen on her honeymoon, then she grew sad at the thought of Sam and her there together - it all seemed so long ago now.

"I have to go to Italy someday," Karen said wistfully as she gazed out the window. She reached over and took Emma's hand. "The world will never be the same for us, my dear."

****

The next morning, Emma was sitting in Karen's dining nook, sipping coffee and reading through her journal. She read through the page she'd written about when she'd first met Sam in the betting area at Arlington Race Track. He was so handsome, and she was naive. She had noted about how he'd laughed when she'd asked him if he was a touter - a person who sold information about a horse to someone before they made a bet.

She turned to the back, to an empty page after her notes about their honeymoon. She took up her pen and entered Sophia's name and what her tiny attempt at life had meant to Emma. Tears welled as she wrote. Finally, one tear fell onto the page, blurring some of her words. She put the pen down, blotted the smeared ink and closed the book.

"What's that?" Karen asked when she entered the room. Looking over Emma's shoulder, she exclaimed, "Oh, I gave you that journal!"

"Yes," Emma said, wiping her eyes.

Karen sat down and looked at her niece. "I have an idea. You know that the Preakness Stakes is coming up in a few days. I have a friend who's racing his horse. We've been friends since Oliver and I were married. Gary went to college with Oliver at Columbia University, and he has a reserved box in the Pimlico grandstand. Would you like to come with me?"

Emma remembered that her Uncle George would be there. She was glad to have something to look forward to. "Yes, I'd love to!"

Karen looked down at the journal. "Do you think Sam will be there?" she asked.

Jutting her jaw into the air, Emma said, "Frankly, I really don't care!"

CHAPTER TWENTY-FOUR

KENTUCKY

George sat in his office at Essen Farms, going over the necessary paperwork needed for the upcoming Preakness race. He was having Koenig's Spirit flown early to Pimlico Race Course. Excited, he leaned back in his chair and envisioned what it would be like for his horse to cross the finish line first. He'd been waiting for this day for some time.

He looked at a photo sitting on his desk of Emma and Sam that he'd taken when he was in Oregon for their wedding. Those two kids deserved each other - they were so in love. The tragedy they'd recently gone through should never be experienced by anyone. He shook his head, thinking of the death of their child and what it had done to the loving couple. The last time he saw Sam, the poor man was using his work to avoid thinking of his loss. And, Emma, George didn't know for sure how she was taking it.

He'd called Rising Sun Stables to check in on them, but Peter told him they both were gone and didn't know where they were. George wondered if Peter had been told to say that - to avoid prying people. He frowned and thought, *I'm not just people! I'm Emma's uncle!*

Just then, Fred came in and sat down in the leather chair across from the large desk. "Spirit's all set for Baltimore." When George didn't respond, he asked, "Are you really serious about buying Divina's Farm? The price has gone sky high with another offer. Did you ever find out who the other potential buyer is?"

"No, and I don't care." George thought for a moment. "I wouldn't put it past Gordon Evers to be the one - he did say he'd get even with me."

"Divina has a few good horses left, but I'm not sure we–" Fred began.

"Her lawyer is there now waiting for me to sign the papers."

"But, where are we going to get the extra hands–"

"We will keep Divina's current help, if they wish to continue there. It will become part of Essen Farms." George heaved himself out of his chair, handed Spirit's papers to his friend and walked towards the door. "I'll be sorry to see her leave," he said, "but I think she is doing the right thing."

****

"Everything seems to be in order, Mr. Mason," the older lawyer said at the end of the long table in Divina's study. The afternoon light was beginning to dim as the sun set low on the horizon. He pushed the papers and pen towards George, "If you will just sign..."

George turned to the woman sitting next to him, who looked so sad. He placed his hand on her arm and said, "Divina, are you sure this is what you want? This farm has been your home for many years."

She slowly glanced around the room. "I have given it much thought. It is no longer the place where my family is. I must go..."

George nodded and said, "I plan to keep all of your employees here, if that is what they wish."

"Oh, I was hoping for that. Some of them worked with my father." She looked between the two men. "I'm afraid Raul has resigned as my trainer. So, you will need to find someone else..."

"I understand." As George signed the papers, he silently wondered if that man hadn't played a part in the evil that had destroyed Divina's prize horses.

"These will be filed tomorrow," the lawyer said. "Possession will start in five days." He rose, gathered the paperwork, and then shook both George and Divina's hands. "Thank you. If there is nothing else, I must get back to my office." The lawyer looked at each of them, then picked up his briefcase and left.

"God, I need a drink!" Divina sighed and went to the bar. George got up and sat on the couch against one wall. She poured two doubles, and then returned to sit next to George. "I hope my father forgives me..." she began.

"I'm sure he would understand. Each of us carries something for which we hope to be forgiven."

She looked at George. "What forgiveness are you seeking?"

George looked into his drink, and then said, "I lied to one of my brothers - before we got onto the ship coming to America..." He took a sip and continued, "He died before I got the chance to ask him to forgive me."

"I'm so sorry," Divina said, placing her hand on his thigh.

George stood up, took a longer drink, then said, "Divina, I wish that I could have returned the affection you seemed to have for me. I've always wanted to be just friends - because I am still in love with someone else." He set his glass on the coffee table and took her hands in his. "I'm sure that we will see each other again before you leave for the Philippines - before we have to say goodbye."

OREGON

Sam turned his truck and trailer into the lane of his ranch. "It's good to be home," he said to Shane. They both laughed when Ele whinnied in agreement from the trailer behind them. Sam thought back to when Emma had said those same words after their return from their honeymoon and was surprised to feel a twinge of guilt. Now, he couldn't wait to tell Emma about Ele's wins!

Mike came out of the house and waved to them. "Good to see you back!" He looked at Sam as he climbed out of the truck and saw he was wearing the same getup that his dad always wore to the races. "Like your new duds," he said to his friend.

"Well, a new game requires a new image." Sam smiled as he put his Stetson back on his head.

Shane jumped out. "You should've seen her, Dad!" he exclaimed. "She was on fire - she won every race!"

"I'm sure it also had to do with the great jockey she had riding her," Sam laughed. "Shane knew exactly what she wanted."

Mike beamed with pride. "Didn't I tell you he's perfect?"

"You sure did." Sam looked across the road to Rising Sun and said, "I think I'll go tell Emma–"

"She's not there," Mike said solemnly.

"What? Where is she? When will she be back?"

"I checked in with Peter after she'd called here - looking for you." Mike looked between Shane and Sam. "She didn't leave a message, and Peter wouldn't say, even if he knew."

"What the hell?" Sam sighed, leaning back against the dusty truck.

Mike shrugged, and then said, "Jim called and said he needs to talk with you. I'll help Shane get Ele settled, if you want to go." He threw Sam his keys, "You can take my truck."

Sam nodded, then walked to Mike's GMC and drove away.

****

Sam was actually glad the ORC office was empty when he arrived. Jim had been doing a great job taking over for him. He looked out the window across the city, and the Willamette River that wove through it. Then, he sat down at the large desk and was surprised to see a note for him to call Nikki's caseworker. It was a week old.

He picked up the phone and dialed.

"Lynn Chamberlain," the woman's voice on the other end said. "How can I help you?"

"Lynn, this is Sam Parker. I apologize for the delay, but I just got your message. I've been out of town. Is anything wrong with Nikki?"

"No, she seems fine, but I was a little worried about her when I received a call from her school. She had been missing some classes. But, now her attendance is good again."

"I wish you could give me more about her past." He hoped there was something he could do. "Both Emma and I are concerned about her."

"I know." There was a pause, then Lynn said, "I'm not supposed to tell you...but you had asked before. And, now I feel you should know that Nikki has been placed in fifteen different foster homes since the court took jurisdiction."

"Fifteen?!" Sam exclaimed. "God, why so many?"

"The more troubled a child is, the more likely they move from family to family. She did spend a year with one nice family; but sadly, they had to move away."

"Can you tell me about Nikki's birth parents? Do you know who they are?"

Sam took notes as Lynn said, "The records are confidential, but...in this case...I can only say that her birth mother is still alive - the father died in a car accident just before Nikki came to us." Sam made a mental note to see if her real parents had a criminal record.

The woman was silent for a moment, and then added, "I'm still looking into that other thing you asked me about. Just let me know when you're ready..."

He thanked Lynn and told her he'd have to get back to her in a few days and hung up. He leaned back in his chair and let out a heavy sigh.

Then, he saw the envelope on the desk with Bennie's pictures. He picked it up and began thumbing through the images again. He stopped at one photo of a man and woman, standing near a barn in the Portland Meadows backside. Sam recognized Walter and Maria Mitchell. Not really knowing why, he put the photo in his coat pocket.

"Hey, Sam," Jim said as he entered the office. He tossed his hat on the filing cabinet to his left. "Glad you're back, but you're in my chair."

"Did you ever hear back from Kevin about those stables' test records?"

"Yes, he said there really wasn't anything he could find, but–"

Just then, the phone rang. Jim answered, then rolled his eyes and handed the phone to Sam. "It's Simon...for you."

Sam held the receiver so that both men could hear Simon's voice.

"Hi, Sam, are you coming to the Preakness Stakes this weekend?"

"Don't know, Simon. What's up?"

"I'm calling about that Lexington Lasix case I was going to check on. Interestingly, it was connected to Gallano Farm."

"That's a hell of a coincidence," Jim said.

"I thought so, too," Simon agreed. "And, the test results for Divina's mare are in - that poor animal was given Oleander! One leaf of that stuff will kill a horse." Before Sam or Jim could say anything, Simon added, "And, we have some evidence pointing to George

Mason as a suspect!"

"What?!" Sam exclaimed. "What evidence?"

"I can't tell you right now - we're still working on the investigation, but–"

"Have you arrested George yet?"

"No, I'm going over to question him before he leaves for Baltimore."

Sam looked at his friend and said, "Then, I'll be going to Maryland."

****

It was late when Sam entered the Portland nightclub. After Simon's call, he needed a drink. He was glad when he'd stumbled onto this place near the waterfront. But, now, sitting near a small dais, all he could think about was Emma.

He watched as couples danced to music being played by a Jazz group - a young woman, singing, accompanied by a guitarist and saxophone player. She sang in French, but then translated the second verse into English. The song was about her great love. The woman's long, brown hair and red-rimmed glasses framed her beautiful face, and her lovely voice filtered over the noise of the bar.

Sam thought of Emma, wondering where she was now. He remembered the night he'd seen her years ago in a similar Portland club. It was their second encounter, but he'd never stopped loving her from the moment he met her in Chicago - when she was just eighteen.

The saxophone player began a different tune and the woman now sang the lyrics to *Who Can I Turn To?* As Sam heard the words, images of times with Emma flashed through his mind: When they'd walked along the waterfront in Chicago, and when he proposed to her on the hill at Rising Sun in Oregon. Sam grew sad as he recalled that the hill was now their child's memorial site. Suddenly, he couldn't breathe. It was like all the air had been sucked out of the room. Quickly, he left some money on the table and stepped out into the night.

As he walked along the waterfront, silent tears ran down his face as he now understood what Emma was going through. He realized that he'd secretly looked forward to their baby's birth, in spite of his fears. Grief grabbed his heart as he sat on a bench and finally allowed himself to truly mourn for his lost child.

Finally, Sam took out his handkerchief and wiped his eyes.

He got up and walked out onto the same bridge where he'd kissed Emma years ago. As a small boat appeared, he leaned out over the dark water and watched the white-capped wake glisten in the moonlight. He looked up at the stars overhead and said a little prayer for his Sophia.

Now, he thought of his dad's words - *Racing is my second love - my family is my first.* Suddenly, Sam realized that if he didn't do something, he could lose Emma, too.

CHAPTER TWENTY-FIVE

BALTIMORE

Pimlico Race Course opened in 1870, and was named after an old tavern in London. It was called *Old Hilltop*, because of a small rise in the infield. The first Preakness Stakes ran in 1873, just two weeks after the Kentucky Derby. It was the sight of the 1938 famous race between Seabiscuit and War Admiral.

George was excited and nervous at the same time, pacing before Koenig's Spirit's stall in the backside of Pimlico track. "Are you sure we've thought of everything, Fred? You brought Spirit's lucky saddle blanket, right?"

Fred laughed and placed his hand on his friend's arm. "Calm down, George. We have everything, and he's set." He pointed to the tall stallion, looking calmly up and down at the other horses in the shedrow. Beautifully-colored baskets of flowers hung on the outside of each building. "He looks happy. You know that if there was anything wrong, he'd be weaving his head right now - like he does when he's stressed out. This horse seems to have a sixth sense about this race."

Breathing a heavy sigh, George smiled and nodded. "I'm glad we've got Stan as our jockey, and that Spirit's had some time to work out on this track before the race." He looked at the cloud-covered sky and frowned. "But, I don't like that there's rain predicted."

"It's going to be okay," Fred assured his friend.

"Before I left Louisville, Divina gave me her new address in the Philippines," George said a little sadly. "She is there by now...I hope she finds happiness again."

"I'm sure she will." Fred looked around, then said, "If you're going to stay here for a moment, I'm going to go check on Stan." George nodded, and Fred left for the jockey's quarters.

Just then, Sam walked up to the stall. "How's your boy this morning?" he said, stroking the horse's long neck.

"Sam, it's so good to see you." George hugged his nephew. He could see the dark circles under Sam's eyes, but decided to let it go for now. He looked at his horse and said, "Spirit is doing fine."

"I won a couple of races with Ele at Santa Anita last week," Sam said, smiling. "She's still got it!" He looked at George and asked, "Did Simon Day get hold of you before you left Louisville?"

"No, we left early. Why?"

Sam shrugged. "It's probably nothing." He didn't want to jinx today's race with bad news.

George looked around. "Where's Emma?"

"I don't know," was all Sam said, a shadow crossing his face.

"What do you mean?"

"When I got back to Oregon...she was gone."

George didn't like this. He tried to think of places she might be, but nothing came to mind. He realized he didn't know his niece very well, and he needed to rectify that soon. "Did she leave any word?"

Sam only shook his head. Just then, it began to rain.

****

The man walked into the Pimlico track backside, and waited until the starting gate was in place and ready.

"Hey, Maylord," someone called, but the man didn't recognize his assumed name at first.

"Maylord."

The man turned and saw the guy who'd gotten him on the gate crew, and then he smiled. "Yeah...I forgot." The two men walked together with their heads close. "You got me in the starting stall I wanted, right?" the man asked in a whisper.

"Sure thing, just as you asked. You going to tell me–"

"None of your damned business!" the man said, and then walked away towards the toilets.

Inside one of the stalls, he checked the hidden device in his pants pocket, which was no bigger than a lighter. He smiled to himself, thinking of what he had planned.

When the call came out for all starters to go to the gate, he walked out through the already sloppy track to stall Number Four - Koenig's Spirit's gate.

****

The Pimlico grandstand was filled with spectators, both in the upper boxes and the uncovered bleachers out front. Some people stood below with umbrellas opened over their heads as the rain muddied the track. White tents in the infield surrounded the gazebo that was used for the Winner's Circle; 'Pimlico' was spelled out in colorful flowers nearby.

"I can't believe this," Sam said, as he walked next to George and Fred. "The last time I was here, I was investigating a jockey who shocked his horse to make him run faster. We suspended his ass and had him arrested, because those devices are prohibited at American racetracks."

"Bob McKenzie brought me here," George said, reminiscing, as well, "when his colt, Bold Red, was headed for the Triple Crown—" He stopped mid-stream when he saw the back of the woman sitting in the box next to his - her red hair gleaming, even though there was no sun shining. When the woman turned towards them, he said, "Karen?"

The woman looked up and smiled, "Yes?" Then, when Karen saw it was George Mason, a frown crossed her brow. "Oh, it's you!"

She quickly turned away to talk with her friend, Gary Nash, owner of Return Thunder, who was also racing today. "Gary, I see that your horse's odds make him a favorite to win today."

Karen's friend nodded with a smile.

"He was second in the Kentucky Derby," she continued.

"I have a feeling he's going to win today!" Nash boasted, after seeing George Mason standing across from him.

The three men sat down in the box next to Karen, just as Emma walked up to join her.

Sam jumped up. "Emma!" he called to her. "I didn't know you

were going to be here."

Emma ignored Sam, turned to George and asked, "Is Divina joining you, Uncle George?"

Sam looked as if she'd slapped him in the face. Slowly, he sat down.

"No," George said, "she sold her farm and has returned to the Philippines."

Emma stared at her uncle in disbelief, then sat next to Karen.

"Good afternoon, ladies and gentlemen," a voice over the loud speaker said as the horses entered the track. "Today is the 96th running of The Preakness Stakes, the second jewel in horseracing's Triple Crown."

The crowd roared.

Karen's friend leaned in towards Emma and said, "The history of Pimlico Track is priceless. You know how the horses cross under the wire at the finish line of every race?" Emma nodded. "Well, supposedly, in 1870, a jockey on a colt named *Preakness* ran in the Stakes - that's how this race got its name. Back then, a silk bag of gold coins was hung from a wire stretched across the track at the finish line. When the jockey won the race, he was given that bag, awarding him the *purse* money after he and his horse had crossed *under the wire*. A lot of racing terminology came from that event."

Emma looked over and enjoyed seeing the look of jealousy on Sam's face.

Just then, the announcer said, "We're ready for The Run for the Black-Eyed Susans, which are the state flower of Maryland!" All eyes turned towards the track, watching the beautiful animals parade before the grandstand. Stan's red jersey and helmet stood out amongst the other colors. The sky cleared as they were being steered toward the starting gate.

The man led Koenig's Spirit into his starting stall and disconnected the lead line. Holding onto the horse's bridle, he nodded to the jockey and whispered something to the horse. After all the horses were loaded, just before the gates were opened, the man discreetly used the buzzer on Spirit's left flank, causing the animal to bolt through the front gate.

The crowd gasped and shouted as the horse and jockey ran down the track, only to be stopped by an outrider. The announcer commented on Spirit's false start as he was led around the gate. Two crewmen cradled behind the horse to push him back into his stall, where the man was again waiting. A couple of seconds passed, then the bell rang and the gates flung open.

"And, they're off!" the announcer said. "Return Thunder and Eclipse on Fire, taking the lead..."

The field of horses burst down the track in a tight pack. All eyes watched as they leveled out until, a few yards later - Spirit began to lag behind, kicking his left hind leg out behind him. Screams from the grandstand rang out as Stan pulled him up, then jumped off. The track vet and other handlers ran out to help him. Unsure what to do, Stan held Spirit's reins as the large horse stood there with his injured leg suspended - the one marked with a white sock. Spirit was carefully led towards the front of the grandstand, out of the way of the other horses still racing in the backstretch. Before the starting gate was pulled to the infield, the man had disappeared into the crowd and left Pimlico.

The men in George's box raced down to join the others standing near Koenig's Spirit.

"What happened?" George yelled as he ran across the muddy track to his horse. When he came up to Spirit, he could see the pain in the animal's eyes. "Where's that horse ambulance?" he said, looking down at the injured leg.

"Here come the other horses," Fred said, and he and Sam held tight onto Spirit's bridle to keep him still.

They watched the field of horses coming around the last turn. All they could do was stand there and watch as they finished the race that Spirit had been a part of - a very tragic moment in the life of a Thoroughbred.

"Return Thunder has won!" the announcer said, but the crowd was no longer watching the race - their focus was on what was happening to Koenig's Spirit.

Once the other animals were clear, the equine ambulance pulled up to where George's horse stood in obvious pain. People at the edge of the track were screaming, watching as the men slowly helped Spirit into the trailer.

Fred held the horse's hock of his injured leg to avoid more damage, as Spirit stood in the van on his three good legs. His body trembled as other men placed a sling around him. His vet, Eric Muldoon, and the track vet worked on a makeshift splint to stabilize the horse's damaged hind leg. Johnny Blaire now stood at the front of the trailer, holding Spirit's bridle, talking softly to the injured animal, as Fred walked to where George stood watching.

"Before we get him on the plane," Eric said, "I'll give him a stronger sedative, to make him more comfortable for the flight home. He's quiet now, but anything could spook him. I'll see you guys at the airport."

George nodded, and then he and Fred hurried towards the backside, followed by the media. "Sam," George said softly, "Pack up everything - I want to get out of here as soon as possible. And, Fred, call Hagyard to let them know we're coming."

"You got it!" Fred said, and then he and Sam broke into a sprint. A crowd of newsmen ran towards George as he continued walking.

"The horse will have to be put down, right?" the first reporter asked.

"No!" George stopped. "We will do everything we can to make him comfortable."

"Where will Koenig's Spirit be taken?" another reporter asked.

"To the Equine surgery at Hagyard in Lexington, Kentucky," George said, and continued walking. "He will get the best care there."

"What do you think happened to your horse today, Mason?" the first reporter blurted out, shoving a microphone towards George.

"I don't know, I just hope he will be okay." George sighed, then added, "Another year without a Triple Crown winner!"

"Some say this was caused by over-aggressive training methods. What do you think?" the same reporter asked.

George turned on the man. "I would never allow anything to be done to harm one of my horses - by anyone. Now, go away!" He then called for help from the backside security.

The guards commanded the media out of the area.

"Uncle George!" Emma exclaimed as she and Karen caught up with him. She hugged him. "I'm so sorry—"

"I have to go now, dear, but will you come back to Essen Farms? I wish to talk with you."

"Yes, I'll come as soon as possible." Emma sadly watched as her uncle walked away, looking so confused and hurt. She and Karen followed him to where Fred stood.

As they walked, Emma turned to her aunt and said, "I hate to see Uncle George like this - do you mind going with me to Kentucky?"

"I'll go - for you...but I refuse to step foot on Essen Farms."

Sam came up to George and Fred. "The track officials want to talk with you two before you leave. I'll stay here and finish packing this up, if that works for you."

George placed his hand on Sam's shoulder. "Thank you, son."

Sam looked at Emma, then asked George, "Can I hitch a ride with you back to Kentucky? I don't have my plane this time."

George nodded, and he and Fred walked away.

Sam approached Emma and said softly, "I need to talk to you!"

"I can't right now," Emma said, then left with Karen.

Hurt and confused, Sam finished getting Spirit's tack ready.

"If only she'd let me talk to her," he said to no one.

While he stuffed equipment into the travel bins, he thought of the book he'd brought along to read on the DC-10 – the one he'd purchased in Paris. A particular poem had struck him – the one about the importance of two people looking together in the same direction. It's what he hoped for him and Emma now. He just had to figure out a way to tell her.

CHAPTER TWENTY-SIX

KENTUCKY

That evening, Karen drove their rental as she and Emma neared Essen Farms. "I owe Gary for lending us his private plane and pilot to fly us down here."

"I'm so grateful to him...and to you," Emma said, looking at her aunt. "You've been so wonderful to me." She turned to watch the white fence pass by the window. "Uncle George said to meet him here."

"Remember, I'm only doing this for you," Karen said, looking nervously as she turned into the long lane that led up to the mansion. "But, I'm not staying here! I'll go to a hotel in town."

"Can I stay with you?" Emma asked, wanting to avoid Sam. She was sure he came here with George after the race. He'd looked so sad and desperate at the track, but she just didn't have the strength to face him yet.

"It's been over forty years since I was here," Karen said, taking a deep breath as she parked the car near the entrance of her childhood home. She stepped out of the vehicle and looked around at the familiar settings - the long stables with the dark, green roofs, the pastures with beautiful horses grazing, the tall columns rising in front of the Colonial house. She sighed. "I think some memories are best left buried."

George opened the door, "Welcome! I am so glad you came."

"Is Sam here?" Emma asked, looking behind her uncle into the large foyer.

"No, he went to see Simon Day. Hello, Karen," George said, taking her hand.

Karen pulled her hand away. "George," she said abruptly, and then walked in.

The house was cool inside, and the smell of furniture polish brought her back to years when she'd run through those doors with the excitement of a child. The door to the parlor on her right stood open and she stopped in her tracks. *Nothing has changed,* she thought. The same red chairs stood exactly where they always had been. Her mother used to love to entertain in that room, feeling like the queen she'd always thought she should have been. Karen smiled to see the two Ming vases still stood sentinel on each side of the tall windows. The only thing different was that the long, red-velvet curtains were not open. Her mother would never have allowed that.

"Are you okay?" Emma asked.

Karen looked at the two people standing near her. "Yes...I'm just surprised to see that this room is still the same."

"I wanted to leave it as I found it when I met first came here," George told her. "It was perfect then - and it still is."

"Is there anything we can do for you?" Emma asked as she and Karen followed George into the long foyer. She watched her aunt glancing around, smiling like a kid in a candy shop - especially when she looked up at the shining chandelier. She was so glad she'd been able to get Karen to come with her.

"Eric and Fred are with Spirit at the equine center," George said sadly. "His surgery went well," he lied, with sadness in his eyes. "Their surgeons are the best. He will have to stay there for a few days...I was going to the center shortly, if you would like to join me."

"Yes," Emma said, looking quickly at Karen. "I'd like that." She wondered what her uncle was not telling them.

"Is Henry with him, as well?" Karen asked.

"Do you mean Henry Phillips?" George asked. When she nodded, he said, "No, I'm afraid he died a few years ago. Eric

Muldoon is our vet now."

Karen seemed saddened by the news, like another part of her past had fallen away.

"Why don't you come into the den for a few moments before we leave," George said as he led the way down the hall. When he entered the room, he watched as Karen walked to look at the trophies and pictures of their horses who'd won races in the past.

One photo struck her - she and her mother stood next to her father in the winner's circle with one of their colts. "Oh, this was taken when Kentucky Wind won the Derby! I was only eight." Tears came to her eyes as she remembered that day.

****

Later, when George walked into the Haygard's surgery with his niece and Karen, his heart broke when he heard Spirit's cries. Dr. Jack Reed, the surgeon, stood to one side of Koenig's Spirit. He wore a tan coat over his clothes, his strong arms were crossed in front, as he watched the assistants adjust the sling in the recovery stall around the dark horse's belly. Spirit's hind leg was now wrapped in a more permanent splint, and he looked frightened and confused as he was awakening from the anesthesia.

"Hello, Jack," George said, shaking hands with the large man he'd known and respected for years.

"George!" the surgeon's face lit up when he smiled, and the two men shook hands.

"Ahem," Karen said.

George turned to the two women behind him. "This is my niece, Emma Parker, and...Karen McKenzie."

"Karen Stenson now," Karen said, shaking the surgeon's hand. "I'm Bob McKenzie's daughter."

"Oh my goodness," Jack said smiling, causing the wrinkles at the sides of his eyes to deepen. "I haven't heard that name around these parts in a very long time."

"I know," Karen answered, looking sharply at George.

George avoided her eyes and asked, "Is it okay if I talk to Spirit?" When the surgeon nodded, George stepped up to his horse, stroked his head and used a soft voice. "I'm here, boy, you're going to be okay. Settle and stay calm." The horse immediately quieted down, and nickered softly as he leaned into George's touch.

Emma watched as her uncle was able to ease Spirit so quickly and realized that some of that calmness around horses was also in her blood.

"He's doing very well," Jack said. "I was able to use an arthroscopic surgery to remove the chip fragments in his fetlock, avoiding any further damage to the cartilage. But, I'm afraid I had to fuse the joint to stabilize it." He stopped and looked at George with compassion. "As you probably know, this will cause permanent lameness, and he will not be able to race again."

After a few moments, George heaved a heavy sigh and said to the surgeon, "I'm just thankful you're here to help save him. So many people have advised me to euthanize him, but he deserves more than that - as long as he is comfortable."

Karen knew the severity of this news, having spent so much time with her father in the horse barns. She looked around at the gray walls and bright lights. A plaque on one wall held the credentials of this man. "How long have you been the surgeon here, Dr. Reed?"

The doctor smiled and said, "Call me Jack...I interned here and never left."

Fred and Eric talked as they entered the area. "I'm not sure how he's going to take–" Fred had started to say, until he saw George.

"Hello," Eric said to Karen, extending his hand. "My name is Eric Muldoon. I don't think we've met. I'm George's veterinarian."

Karen took his hand. "Do I detect a bit of Irish in your voice?"

"Yes, born and raised in Dublin. I came to America ten years ago."

"What brought you here?" Karen asked.

"The Bluegrass country!"

As George watched Karen and Eric talking, he was surprised that it bothered him so much - he hardly knew Karen!

****

Sam was sitting in Simon's office in downtown Louisville.

"Before you say anything," Sam said, "in George's defense, I asked him at Pimlico if you'd talked with him. He said he'd taken Spirit to the track early."

"I know, but I still have to see him. This is serious!"

"He's got bigger problems right now."

Simon nodded, his face grave. "I saw the race on television, and that looked like a nasty break. What's George planning to do with Koenig Spirit?"

"If I know George, he'll fight for that horse's life."

"August Parr, our friend from the Thoroughbred Racing Bureau, was at Pimlico."

"He's still working there?" Sam said, thinking of his days working for the TRB after he'd thought his life was over.

"Yep. He looked at Koenig's Spirit on the track - before they took him off. August saw an area on the left side of the horse's hind quarters, where the hair looked like it had been singed. The animal may have had some kind of electrical shock device used on him. It must have happened at the gate - which could be the reason he bolted."

Sam sat up on the edge of his seat. "Before I left Pimlico, I got a list of the starting gate crew." He handed a sheet of paper to Simon.

Looking down at the names, Simon made a note next to a couple, and then handed the list back to Sam. "I recognize most of these guys, except the ones I marked."

Sam checked the list again himself. Then, he added, "I also found a Louisville news guy who had a video camera near the starting gate area. I've arranged for him to bring it here now."

While they waited, Sam said, "You know you can count on me to help with this investigation...and Gallano's mare."

"Ah, don't mention THAT one!" Simon sighed. He got up and closed the door to his office. "I was beginning to think Gordon Evers was behind all this - until now."

"What evidence did you find on George?"

"I didn't find it - it just came to me." Simon handed Sam a plastic evidence bag containing a handkerchief. "Divina's vet, Seth Young, found this in the mare's stall."

Sam looked at the cloth inside the bag, turning it over in his hands. He quickly looked up at Simon and said, "GM? You don't think–"

"I don't know what to think." Simon took the bag and placed it back in his desk drawer. "I can't rule out the fact that George Mason could be involved!" He looked at Sam and added, "You know you can't tell anyone about this, right?"

"Yeah, I know," Sam said.

"On that tip you gave me, about Kentucky marriages - I didn't find anything for Mitchell. But, you got me thinking...so I checked on Divina's marriage and divorce papers." He handed Sam a newspaper clipping with a photo. "She was married to a Walter Maylord; the certificate was witnessed by her sister, Tala—"

"Maylord?" Sam asked as he jumped up and grabbed the list again. He then handed it back to Simon. "Look at this!"

"I'll be damned!" Simon said.

Just then, there was a knock. A young man in his twenties walked in with a camera and what looked like a suitcase attached. "Mr. Day?" he asked as he placed the equipment on top of some papers on a table next to one wall. When Simon stood up and nodded, the young man said, "Andy Fisher, at your service."

They shook hands, and Sam was introduced.

Simon looked at the equipment and asked, "What's all this?"

"It's what I used at Pimlico. It's pretty great how compact they're making video cameras now. This one's called a Sony Porta-Pak."

"What am I supposed to do with it?"

"Here, I'll show you." Picking up the camera, Andy turned it on and demonstrated how they could see the actual footage taken at the track. The men hovered over the small screen to watch the black and white images.

"There's no sound yet," Andy explained. "But, someday, I bet there will be an even smaller, hand-held video camera without the pack - maybe even with color!"

"I'm glad this was pointed at the starting gate!" Sam exclaimed.

In the video, the crew members walked to the gate, leading their horse into the designated stall. Sam knew that Koenig's Spirit had gate number Four, so he kept his eyes on the man approaching it.

"Can this be stopped?" he asked.

Andy nodded and paused the tape.

"Damn!" Sam swore and looked quickly at Simon. "I think that could be Walter Mitchell - the guy I've been investigating in Oregon!"

"But, what does that have to do with Baltimore?" Andy asked.

"They could be related..." Sam started to take off his jacket and stopped. "Man, I forgot I had this," he said as he pulled out the photo from his pocket. He smiled and showed the image to Simon. "Here's some evidence for you! This was taken by a friend of mine in the backside at Portland Meadows racetrack in Oregon. The woman is Maria Mitchell. I met her at Emma's farm. But, look at this guy," he said, pointing to the man in the photo.

Sam looked at the two men and added, "He's Walter Mitchell - aka Walter Maylord, our guy in the Preakness starting gate!"

"I can't believe this," Simon yelled, comparing the photo to the video screen.

Sam continued to stare at the photo. There was something about the woman's face that kept bugging him - and then it clicked. He picked up the newspaper clipping. "And, I'll bet you a hundred bucks that this woman in my photo is Divina Gallano's sister."

****

Karen and George sat in the sunshine on the patio outside his house at Essen Farms, as Emma brought out a tray with a pitcher of iced tea and some glasses.

"I'm so sorry for your loss," Emma heard Karen say. "I understand how serious Spirit's injury is to you."

"Here," George said, jumping up and grabbing the tray from his niece. He didn't want to discuss this right now. "Let me help you." He set the tray on the small, round table between them, and then filled each glass.

"Karen has been sharing some memories of the farm with me," he said, smiling as he handed Karen a glass.

Emma could see her aunt was still uncomfortable being around George and at Essen Farms.

Sam drove up and walked into the house. Emma was glad he had not seen them, but she saw he was excited about something. Quickly, she jumped up and said, "Aunt Karen, I think we'd better go." She turned to George and smiled, "Thank you for everything."

"But," George said, standing, "I thought you were staying here."

"No, we're going to the Seelbach Hotel in town," Karen said, placing her handbag under her arm.

"I'm going with her," Emma said, "and please don't tell Sam where I am. I'll explain later." She kissed her uncle and they left.

George stood for a moment, stunned at their abrupt departure. He'd been enjoying his time with Karen. Sadly, he picked up the tray of drinks and walked back into the house. After taking the tray to the kitchen, he found Sam in the den, pouring a shot of bourbon. "I'll take one of those," he said, then closed the door.

Sam turned around, chugged his drink, then handed one to George. "I need to see Emma—"

"She's not here," was all George said.

Sam looked confused. "But, I thought she was coming here."

"What did Simon have to say about the events at the track?" George said to avoid having to explain where Emma had gone.

Excitedly, Sam poured another drink, but sipped this one. Then, he said, "We're not sure yet, but Simon and I think Spirit's starter may have been involved in all this. August Parr, a guy I used to work with, thought that Spirit probably kicked the left side of the gate as he shot out the first time, which may have caused his fetlock injury." He was about to tell George about Divina's ex-husband and sister, but caught himself, knowing he couldn't discuss Divina's case with George. "Simon's still looking into it." He looked at George and added, "This is confidential for now, okay?"

George nodded, and then paced the room, wishing that he could strangle the bastard with his own bare hands.

"How's Spirit?" Sam asked.

"He's going to be lame," George said sadly.

"What?" Sam exclaimed, setting his drink down. "Why?"

"His joint had to be fused to enable him to use that leg again. Spirit will get to spend the rest of his life in a pasture...but at least he's alive." George slumped down onto a chair and finished his drink. Then, he looked at Sam and asked, "What the hell is going on between you and Emma?"

"What do you mean?"

"She won't tell me anything. What did you do?"

Sam sat in the chair across from George. "I don't know...ever since we lost Sophia...I think we've drifted apart." He stood up and said, "I really want to work things out." He turned away and leaned one shoulder against the fireplace mantle. "But, Emma won't let me."

George sighed and got up. Walking over to Sam, he could see how exhausted his nephew was. "I know that you two love each other...and how much family means to you both. Just give her some time." He patted Sam's shoulder and said, "Why don't you stay here tonight - you can use the same room you did the last time you were here. We can talk some more in the morning. Everything always looks better after a good night's sleep."

Sam suddenly yawned. "You're right...I think I'll turn in."

Alone now, George thought of Karen again. Listening to her talk about living here when she was young only reminded George of what he had gained at her expense. She should have been able to live her life here, not sent off to some boarding school or wherever it was her family had chosen. And, then, when he thought of how her father had literally given this farm to him - instead of his own daughter, George's blood began to boil. He'd always loved Bob McKenzie like a father, but now he knew what that father did to his own family.

He thought of Hannah. All these years, he'd believed that she loved him as much as he loved her, but it was his fantasy. For the first time in his life, he admitted to himself that she had loved his brother - not him.

George remembered what Emma told him when they were back in Oregon. He smiled at himself and thought, *Yes, it is time I let go of the ghost.*

OREGON

It was dark when Nikki rode up to her house on her bike. The game ran a lot longer than she'd expected. Afterwards, Becky and the other girls on her cheerleading team wanted to go out for Cokes and fries, and she was surprised when they'd asked her, too. Nikki didn't like lying to Becky's mother, telling her that she had called Maria. But, the last time she did that, Maria told her she couldn't go. Nikki liked the new friends she was making, and Becky wanted to know all about her riding lessons. Since Sarah left, Nikki really never had a close friend...until now.

As she put her bike against the garage and walked towards the house, she became frightened when she saw Walter's car parked outside. *He wasn't supposed to come home until tomorrow*, she thought.

Even before she opened the door, she heard Maria's cries. "I'm sorry, Walter, I don't know where she is."

"You are my biggest mistake - leaving Divina - for you. You're nothing like her! You and that brat have ruined my life!"

Then, Nikki heard the back door slam shut. She cautiously

walked in and softly closed the front door. When she entered the kitchen and found Maria, alone and badly beaten, she exclaimed, "That bastard!" She got a wet cloth to wipe Maria's bleeding mouth.

"Nikki!" Maria said, looking frantically around her. "You have to leave. He's in one of his moods. I don't know what he'll do - I've never seen him like this..." Slowly, she tried to stand, but her knees buckled and she fell back to the floor. "He didn't mean to hurt me. I know he didn't..."

Just then, Walter came back in and pulled Maria to her feet. "I thought you said she wasn't here–"

"I just got home!" Nikki said, stepping in between the two people who were supposed to take care of her, the people who were role models as parents. She decided to lie. "I was at cheerleading practice–"

"I told you that you weren't going to do that, because it costs too damned much!" Walter yelled at Nikki.

"You're a pathetic monster," Nikki screamed. "You can't hurt me anymore!"

Walter grabbed the young girl by the hair and pulled her into the living room. Maria screamed and tried to follow.

"When I get home, I expect you two to be here! I'm the master of this house–"

"That doesn't give you the right–" Nikki began.

"Shut up, you little bitch!" he said, as he slapped Nikki across the mouth. "I'm going to beat that stubbornness out of you!" Each time Walter yelled at her, he slapped her until she fell onto the couch.

"I don't want you going to that horse farm ever again, you hear?" This time Walter hit her with his fist, throwing her head back against the hard wood on the arm of the furniture.

Nikki screamed and looked across the room. She saw Maria standing in the kitchen doorway, watching as Walter beat her until she fell unconscious.

CHAPTER TWENTY-SEVEN

KENTUCKY

The next morning, Emma sat at their hotel suite's desk, sipping coffee. The Seelbach held a lot of Louisville's history, which opened in 1905 and was one of the city's grandest hotels and architectural achievements in French Renaissance design. When they'd arrived last night, she was stunned by the hotel's expansive lobby, with the large palms that stood next to wide pillars, and the high-ceilinged skylight. The elaborate, wide staircase was split at the top, and continued to each side of the second level, where their suite was.

She was glad that now she had a few moments alone. As she opened her journal to the first page, her aunt's words jumped out at her. Tears welled in her eyes as she was flooded with memories of her and Sam. She fingered the gold locket that he'd given her in the dark theater in Chicago and wondered now about some of those dreams she'd allowed her younger self to believe in.

As she read her own notes, she heard a woman's voice coming from a radio in the next room, singing a ballad about a boy and lessons learned.

Emma thought of seeing Sam again yesterday - her feelings were all mixed up. She was relieved that he was okay, but she was still angry at him for leaving her - when she needed him the most. Losing Sophia had taken so much away from her, but he never let her talk about her. It was like he didn't even care.

Karen came in and said, "Did you know some believe that this hotel is haunted–" She stopped when she saw Emma and went over to hug her. "What's wrong, sweetie?"

"I can't get my baby out of my mind," she said, sobbing now. "And, Sam has been no help."

Karen handed her a tissue from her sleeve.

"Thank you," Emma said, wiping her eyes. Then she looked up. "I don't think I told you that I can't have any more children, due to that fall I had when I was young."

Karen sat next to her. "I remember that accident."

"I've always wanted to have kids, but...I'm not so sure Sam did."

When Karen was sure Emma had said all she'd wanted to, she sighed. "I'm so sorry this happened to you, sweetie, but I know that you still love Sam. And, yesterday, I saw how much he loves you. Time will heal and you two will find a way to move forward. All will be as it should be."

Emma stared at her aunt. "What did you say?"

"All will be–"

"I know - it's just that when we were in Paris, I was sitting in the *Sacré-Coeur*, and I heard a voice say that very same thing!"

****

As Karen drove towards Essen Farms, she said, "Oliver was the love of my life, and I miss him so much. If only that drunk driver hadn't killed him!" She paused, and then added, "But, lately, I've been feeling pretty lonely..."

When they parked at the mansion, Emma stepped out of the car. She looked at one of the nearby pastures and said to Karen, "Look!" They saw a dark colt, jumping and running towards them. He whinnied softly, and Emma and Karen laughed to see the wonderful joy in such a young horse. They didn't know that this colt, sired by Koenig's Wonder, was George's next hope for the Triple Crown in two years.

The tall door to the mansion opened and George stepped out. "Good morning, ladies," he said happily.

"You must have good news about Spirit," Emma said and ran to hug her uncle.

"He was doing much better earlier this morning when I went to see him. Eric thinks that he might be strong enough to come home next week."

"That's wonderful!" Karen said. She was surprised to feel more comfortable here today.

Sam came out and stood next to Emma. "Can we talk?" he asked softly.

When she nodded, Karen and George stepped into the house and closed the door.

The young couple walked up the lane, towards where the young colt stood. As they came near, Sam could see he was about the same age as Promise.

"I have to apologize to you..." Sam began, tripping over his words. "I've been terribly wrong. I shouldn't have left when I did - I wasn't there for you. Em, I'm so sorry."

She stopped and turned to him. "I really needed you–"

"I know, I was being selfish and forgot what was important - us, together."

She smiled a little. "Yes, I think we both were..." She placed her arms around him and touched his strong back. "We've been through an awful experience. But, we're strong and I know we were meant for each other. I love you so much."

Sam hugged her close to him. "Oh, God, thank you! I love you more than you know." He leaned down and kissed her.

****

Karen and George stood in the parlor of the house and watched as the two young people in their lives seemed to be working things out and starting to heal.

"Oh, that warms my heart," Karen sighed, her hand over her heart. "I was beginning to worry about those two."

George looked at her. "I had faith in Sam. He's a good man and I knew he'd work things out in his own time."

The phone began to ring, and George went to answer it. "Yes, I will get her," he said, then laid the receiver down, but didn't hang up. When he turned around, he had a grave look on his face.

"What is it?" Karen asked.

George quickly went outside and said, "Emma, you have a phone call - hurry."

Emma came running and followed George into the house. "Who is it?" she asked, but he said nothing. Karen and Sam stood near them in the parlor.

"Hello?" Emma said into the phone.

"Oh, Emma, I am so glad I found you!" the voice on the other end said.

"Doc? What's the matter?"

"It was hard to track you or Sam down, until I talked to Mike McKenzie. He told me Sam was going to the Preakness, so I figured George Mason was a good option—"

Emma interrupted him. "Doc, why did you call?"

"Is Sam there, too?"

"Yes."

"You both need to return to Oregon immediately - Nikki has been hospitalized!"

After Doc explained a little more, Emma hung up and said, "Sam, do you have your plane here?"

"No, why?"

"We have to go home - now!"

****

At the Seelbach hotel, Emma frantically packed, while Sam called down to the reception desk for a taxi to the airport. "You don't need to drive us there," he insisted to George.

Emma came out of the bedroom with her bag. "Our plane leaves in twenty minutes," he told her, "and, Jim will meet us in Portland."

"We'll call you as soon as we know more about Nikki," Emma said, kissing her two favorite relatives in the world. Then, she and Sam left.

George and Karen stood in the quiet hotel suite, wondering what to do next. Feeling a little awkward, he cleared his throat and invited Karen to leave the hotel and stay at Essen Farms - until they hear from Emma and Sam. "After all, it was your home once."

Karen thought for a moment. "Yes, I don't want to be alone right now."

"You can stay as long as you like," he said. "I'll wait downstairs in the lobby so you can pack your things. There is no hurry."

****

When they arrived back at Essen Farms, George led the way to Karen's old room.

As she stepped in, she gasped. "This is just as I left it. It feels like I've gone back in time." She saw the dolls sitting on a toy chest, as if they'd been waiting for her. She began to laugh. "I think I've outgrown this room."

"Yes, I think you have, but Bob didn't want it changed - in case you returned."

Tears came to Karen's eyes as thoughts and memories of her father surfaced. "All in all, he really was a sweet man, wasn't he?"

"Yes, I always thought so." George moved to one side of the room, allowing Karen to enjoy the moments of her past. "He was always good to me...I had lost my family after I came to America. Bob became my family."

"I'm sorry I turned away from him so long ago. I was angry—" Karen stopped, and then she sighed. "I think I'll use the guest room while I'm here, if that's okay."

"You can use any room you wish," George said, smiling. He carried her bag, followed her to the next room on the left, and set the case on the bed. After an awkward moment, he said, "I'll go fix us some drinks in the den. Will that be all right?"

"Yes, I'd like that." Karen turned and looked at herself in the large, beveled-glass mirror on the dresser. "I'll only be a moment."

She took a bit longer than a few moments in the bedroom, hanging up her clothes in the large, cherry armoire. Slowly, she sat on the bed and wondered what in the world she was doing here. In spite of her fears, she had always loved this house. And, George didn't really seem like the monster she'd thought he was. Finally, she checked her hair and makeup before going downstairs.

When she entered the warm room, she almost felt as if her father was still there. *Yes*, she thought to herself, *I really have missed him - and I need to make peace here.*

The two sat down next to each other on the leather couch and stared at the wall of trophies. "He spent more time in this room than any other one in the house," she told George. "I loved coming in here when he was sitting before the fire in the evening. It felt so warm and safe..."

George smiled. "Yes, I felt the same."

Sipping her drink, Karen's thoughts turned to Emma. "Have you ever met this young girl that they're running off to see?"

"Nikki? No, but Emma has told me about her. I think she and Nikki have become very close while the child was taking riding lessons. It sounded like her home life is not very pleasant."

She nodded and said, "Emma is very protective of her, and rightfully so, I hear." Then, she raised her glass towards George. "Well, here's to them all finding happiness."

"I'll drink to that."

They tapped their glasses and finished their drinks.

Karen took off her shoes, turned in her seat and curled her legs up under her. She ran her fingers through her long hair and said, "Since I grew up on this farm, I could tell you a few things about training a racehorse..."

OREGON

Emma thought the flight back home was taking forever. Sam held her as she explained why she'd gone to New York. She'd just needed to get away - the same as he did - to escape the sad reminders of what they had lost.

"I want us to work together - as a team," Sam said. "Even though we have our own interests, we can support each other, as we've done in the past. We have a strong bond - our love. Nothing can ever change that."

Emma smiled and touched Sam's cheek. "As long as we do everything with love, we will be all right." She kissed her husband as the plane began to approach the Portland airport.

It was dark when they landed, but they were glad to see Jim was there to meet them. He took them to where his small Cessna waited, and then they flew on to Newberg - where Nikki was in the hospital.

"I had Nancy drive your car to the airport for you," Jim told Sam as they entered Newberg.

"Thank you, Jim. I owe you one. We'll call when we know more."

****

Sam and Emma quickly drove to the hospital. When they finally arrived, they were relieved to find that neither of Nikki's foster parents was there. Emma went to the nurse's station and asked about her.

"We only have a Nicole Hornsby, is that who you mean?" the nurse asked. She was a large woman with graying hair.

"Yes," Emma said as she glanced down at the log and noted Nikki's room number. "How is she? Can we see her?"

"I'm sorry, but unless you are a relative, you cannot go in there."

"Let me make a phone call and see what I can do," Sam said, asking where a phone was located.

"You can use the pay phone down the hall, sir."

Sam walked away as Doc and Tracy entered through a door from the cafeteria.

"Oh, thank God, you two are here!" Emma sighed. "Do you know how Nikki is?"

Doc patted her arm and said, "I've talked with Robin Blake, the ER doctor. Nikki is conscious, but weak."

"Conscious? What happened?"

"You need to sit down, Emma," Tracy said, leading her to a bank of chairs. The only other person in the room was a large woman, asleep in a chair against one wall.

After she sat down, Tracy and Doc sat on either side of her. Emma was glad to see Sam returning, and the other woman woke up and left.

"We think Nikki was attacked..." Tracy began. "Maria called the farm looking for you. She'd told Peter that an ambulance was coming to their house to take Nikki to the hospital. Her husband got on the phone and told Peter her injuries were because of Lucky, and he demanded the animal be put down." Tracy looked at Doc and added, "That's when I called Doc, and we came here."

"But," Doc added, "I knew she had not been to your place for a few days...and, when I saw her, Nikki's bruises and lacerations were not from any animal."

"When did you see her?" Emma asked.

"When they brought her into the hospital," Tracy said. "We

arrived at the same time as the ambulance."

"I was glad to see Robin was working in the Emergency Room when we arrived," Doc interjected. "We've known each other for some time, ever since I started helping his wife with her Morgan, Tucker, for his regular checkups." Doc looked around to make sure they would not be overheard. "I've been talking with him about a hypothetical case of abuse–"

Tracy added, "Earlier, we overheard him questioning Maria, but when she saw us here, all she said was that Nicole had fallen."

"Had she been violated?" Sam asked angrily, not sure he wanted to know the answer.

Doc said, "Robin said no, thank God! She'd had some internal bleeding and would need a laparoscopic surgery to remove her appendix. He told us they'd caught it before it ruptured, and she'll have minimal scarring."

Tracy added, "He also said she's young and will heal quickly."

"When can she be released?" Emma asked.

Tracy said, "Maybe tomorrow." She looked at Doc, then added, "She'll have a few weeks' recovery at home after her surgery, and her other bruises will be sore for a few days."

"Bruises?" Sam asked.

"I'm afraid she'd been brutally beaten–" Doc began.

"Damn!" Sam swore. "I have to make another phone call," he said, then walked to the pay phone down the hall.

"I can't believe this has happened!" Emma said, wringing her hands in her lap.

Doc placed his hand over hers to quiet her. "She is in good hands now, and I'm sure the staff won't let anything else happen to her."

When Sam returned, he said he had to go to his office on an emergency. He looked at Emma and said, "I won't be long. Is that all right with you?" When she nodded, he quickly kissed her and left.

Tracy looked at Emma. "I have to get back to the farm and see if Peter needs any help. Will you be okay until Sam gets back?"

"Yes, thank you for being here."

After Tracy left, Emma watched the nurse get up and go down one hall. She turned to Doc. "I know you probably have a million things to do, Doc. I'm good here; I can talk with Dr. Blake when he comes out again."

"If you're sure you don't need me, dear."

"Yes. And, thank you."

Emma waited until Doc was out of the hospital. She looked up and down the hallway, and checked to make sure the nurse's station was still empty. Quickly, she snuck through a double door to the patients' area and found Nikki's room.

Softly, she opened the door and gasped. The small girl lay in the bed, her face black and blue, her head wrapped with gauze covering one eye. There were ugly, dark marks on both of her thin arms that lay on the white blanket.

"Nikki," Emma said softly. "It's Emma...are you awake?"

Nikki moaned...her voice raspy. "Emma?"

"Yes sweetie. I'm here..." She gently touched one arm. "Is there anything I can do for you?"

"I really didn't fall."

"Does Maria know?"

Nikki refused to answer.

"Did Walter do this to you?"

Nikki turned her face away, tears streaming down her red cheeks. Slowly, she nodded her head.

Angry, Emma said, "I'll be right back. Someone needs to teach that man a lesson!"

"No!" Nikki screamed.

****

As Emma sat in the back seat of the taxi, she looked in her little address book she always carried and saw the address for Nikki's house. "And, hurry!" she told the driver angrily.

When the taxi arrived at the gray cottage in need of repair, Emma walked in without knocking. She found Maria in the kitchen, alone, obsessively scrubbing the counter top. She was bruised, with one black eye, and her mouth was bleeding.

"Maria," Emma said, "You should go to the hospital–"

"No!" Maria yelled. "You don't understand. He just made a mistake - he should've never married me, then none of this would've happened–"

"I'm calling the police. Neither you nor Nikki deserve this–"

"NO!" Maria screamed. "You can't...

Just then, Walter walked into the room.

"What the hell are you doing in my house?" he yelled. Emma watched Maria cower and run to one corner.

"You're such a weak bastard," Emma said, "that you have to hit women and children to feel like a man. I'm going to get Maria some help–"

As Emma tried to pass him, Walter grabbed her roughly by the arms, bruising her skin. "Those bitches deserved what they got!" Then, he attacked Emma.

****

Sam returned to the hospital, excited about his news. He was surprised to see the waiting room empty. He walked up to the nurse and asked which room Nikki was in. "I've been talking with her caseworker at CSD." He looked again around the room. "Where's my wife?" he asked.

"I don't know about your wife, sir, but unless you are a family member, you are not allowed to see Nicole Horns–"

Just then, Nikki came stumbling out of the double doors in her hospital gown. "Sam!" she yelled.

When Sam saw the condition of the small girl, his heart sank. Just before she collapsed, he caught her. "Nikki, what're you doing out here?"

The nurse picked up the phone. "We need help in the waiting area - STAT!"

"You have to go after her!" Nikki screamed.

"Who?" He saw the nurse coming towards them.

"Emma - she went to my house to find Walter!"

"I'll be back," he said, then placed Nikki gently into the nurse's arms. Before he left, he told the nurse, "Call the police and send them to Nikki's address, now!"

As he raced there, Sam could only think about that night he'd found Joe attacking Emma. He sped down the roadway, wondering if, once again, he could have murder in his heart.

****

Walter held Emma to the floor, hitting her and pulling at her clothes as she tried to fight him off. "You're all alike," he yelled, spitting into her face, "always asking for it!"

"Get off of me!" Emma screamed and tried to bring up her knee, but Walter blocked her. He reached back and slapped her hard enough to make stars shoot through her eyes.

Just then, Sam ran in and pulled Walter off, throwing him into one of the corners. He saw Maria cowered in a doorway - seemingly unable to do anything to stop Walter.

"Are you okay?" he asked Emma, trying to help her up and cover herself with her torn blouse. He checked to make sure Walter was still down, and then he looked at Emma again. Anger jolted in his gut as he thought of what could have happened if he hadn't arrived when he did. He was surprised to see Maria had disappeared.

Suddenly, he heard Walter stirring. When Sam turned, the man was about to attack him. A shot rang out. Walter crumbled to the floor, a pool of blood seeping out from under his body.

Stunned, Sam looked around the room and saw Maria standing in one of the doorways with a gun in her hand, her eyes glazed as she stared at her husband. "Enough is enough..." she said in a tired voice.

Slowly, Sam walked towards her, his body blocking Emma's. "Maria," he said softly. "Give me the gun."

By the time he reached her, the gun was pointing to the floor and they could hear sirens approaching. Sam grabbed the barrel of the gun and pulled it from Maria's hand. Then, he checked Walter for a pulse. There was none.

He ran to Emma and held her close, making sure she was all right.

"Oh, my God!" Emma said, still in shock. "I can't believe this."

Then, the police arrived. Officer Taylor was a guy Sam knew from a horse theft case they'd worked on together. "What the hell happened here, Sam?" the officer asked.

Sam gave him the gun and pointed to Maria. "That's Maria Mitchell. She shot her husband, Walter. When I got here, he was attacking my wife."

After the police processed the scene, Maria was arrested and finally admitted everything to the police. She told Emma that she regretted hurting her sister years ago and for allowing this to happen to Nikki. Emma was confused, but she let it go for now.

The ambulance arrived and the EMT's loaded Walter's body, while the police drove Maria away.

"What the hell were you thinking...coming here alone?" Sam finally said, relieved that it was all over. He took Emma into his arms, glad that she was safe.

"I don't know - I just got so angry after I saw Nikki." She looked up at Sam. "I'm sorry, I know now that was stupid."

Sam walked Emma out to their car. He gave her his jacket.

"What did Maria mean about her sister?" she asked.

"It's a long story...been going on for years. Maria is actually Divina's sister," he said. "And, Walter is Divina's ex-husband."

"Oh, my god, I can't believe it! Does Divina know all of this?"

"Not yet," Sam said.

Emma turned to get into the car and said, "I want to see Nikki."

****

At the hospital, they were met by a young woman with dark hair, who was standing by the nurse's station.

"Hello, Lynn," Sam said, shaking the woman's hand. "Thank you for coming. Em, this is Nikki's caseworker, Lynn Chamberlain."

" Hello, you must be Sam's wife," Lynn said to Emma. " I heard what happened. Are you okay?"

Emma nodded, pulled Sam's jacket closer around her, and said, "It's nice to meet you." She looked at the double doors that led to the patients' rooms. Through the long windows, she saw a policewoman standing outside of Nikki's room. "Can I see Nikki?" she asked.

"She is doing well," Lynn said. "But the hospital rules won't allow you to see her right now - only immediate relatives."

When Sam saw Lynn smile and nod, he knew.

"But, one of her foster parents is dead and the other has been arrested," Emma said, close to hysterics now. "She doesn't have any other family."

"It's okay, Em–" Sam began.

"I'm sorry," Lynn added, placing her hand on Emma's arm. "But, I will stay for a while, and I'm sure the staff here will look after her. You can see her tomorrow–"

"But, I must see her now!" Emma insisted, walking through the double doors, with Lynn and Sam following her.

The policewoman stepped towards her. "Ma'am, you can't go in there."

"Please...I need to make sure she's okay."

Sam could see the panic in Emma's face. Knowing she was probably still in shock from what had happened at the Mitchell's, he knew what she needed. He placed his arm around her. "Come on, honey," he said softly. "We have to go home. She's in good hands here."

"We can't do anything right now," Lynn said. She nodded again at Sam.

He smiled, understanding, then he said, "We'll come back tomorrow morning."

Suddenly feeling weak and tired, Emma allowed Sam to lead her from the hospital.

CHAPTER TWENTY-EIGHT

The next morning, Emma asked Sam, "Before we go to the hospital, will you take me to see our lamb?"

They stood together on their hilltop, a soft breeze rustling the oak leaves overhead as the sun began to rise in the east. The sideways light beamed on the white lamb, now lying on top of the gray stone with their daughter's name etched on the front.

"Sophia," Emma said, "you will always be loved - even if we didn't have the chance to know you. We will never forget the possibility of you..."

She knelt down and began to gather up the wilted flowers that had been given by their friends at the memorial. "I'll bring some fresh ones up later," she said, tears streaming down her cheeks.

Sam stood behind her, his own grief welling inside. He reached down and pulled Emma up to him, holding onto her. They sobbed in each other's arms, numb with the fact that after such a tragedy, life could go on.

"One thing I've learned from all of this," Sam began, "is that life is too damned short not live it to the fullest."

"I'm so sorry..." Emma began, wiping her eyes.

Sam pulled out his handkerchief and gently touched her face. "Shhh," he soothed. "It's not your fault. We don't know why these things happen."

Emma clung to him, her face against his chest. "But, we can never have children."

Sam raised her chin and looked into her eyes. "I have something I need to ask you..."

****

Later, Sam and Emma arrived at the hospital.

"Will they let me see her?" Emma asked nervously.

Sam smiled. Because of a phone call he'd made earlier, he said, "Yes, I'm sure they will."

He and Emma walked down the hall and into Nikki's room. The young girl was propped up with pillows, but she still looked so frail. She was eating some red Jell-O.

"How are you feeling, sweetie?" Emma asked, gently brushing some of her hair behind one ear.

"I've been better," she said, trying to smile. "I'm just glad you are okay."

They stood together on one side of the bed while Sam told Nikki about Maria and Walter.

"What's going to happen to me now?" Nikki cried. "I don't want another foster family!"

Emma hugged Nikki gently.

Sam looked at the two of them and smiled. "What if this moment never had to change?"

Emma smiled at her husband.

"What if..." he began, then cleared his throat. "What if Nikki stays with us?"

Nikki's eye that wasn't bandaged grew wide, and then she winced with pain. "You mean, you two would be my new foster parents?"

"Nah," Sam said, "I don't mean that."

The small girl looked sad and confused, but Emma grinned. "Just hear him out."

"Nikki, how would you feel if we adopted you - if you became our daughter?"

Looking from one to the other, Nikki asked, "Really? You really mean that? I'd never have to go anywhere else - ever again?"

Sam laughed. "Well, until you go to college or get married."

Nikki hugged them with her thin, bruised arms. "Take me home!"

KENTUCKY

It was several months later when everyone arrived at Essen Farms for George and Karen's wedding. The patio and gazebo were elaborately decked out in flowers and ribbons. Numerous guests sat in rows of white chairs on the beautiful Bluegrass lawn. George had been greeting everyone as they arrived, but now, his best man, pulled him to one side.

"We have some fortification waiting." Fred winked, then led the groom to the den, where Sam waited with glasses filled with George's favorite bourbon.

"Are you ready for this?" Fred asked.

George beamed and said, "Absolutely!"

"Karen's the right one for you," his friend said, offering George a glass.

The men talked about Koenig Spirit's fight. "You should see all the letters and gifts that horse has received from all over the world!" George said proudly. "He is more famous now than if he'd won the Triple Crown!"

Sam nodded. "He's touched so many hearts during his struggle to recover."

"I'm just glad he has an easy life ahead of him." George sighed, turned to Sam and said, "Now, we'll see what the future holds for us!"

Sam nodded and took a sip. "How's your new operation at Gallano Farm?"

"It is going slower than I expected," George said. "But, I'm going to need a new manager and trainer there. I wanted to wait until Divina left for the Philippines before making any changes." He looked into his glass and added, "She knows about her sister and ex-husband."

Sam said, "I always thought that Gordon Evers was the mastermind - both here and in Oregon. But, it was Walter all along."

"I don't believe it!" George said. "The moment I met Evers, I knew I didn't like him." He looked at Sam and said, "Remember how I knew the name Owen Busch?"

"Yes."

"That was the farm here in Louisville that Evers bought a few years ago."

36466016R00179

"What a strange coincidence," Sam said, but then, he didn't really believe in coincidences...

"Well, there's the last piece of the puzzle," Fred said, clinking his glass against his friend's in hopes of closing that discussion. "So, George, where are you two going on your honeymoon?"

"Karen wants to visit Italy," George said. "I've never been there...I'd like to go to Germany while on the continent. So, we will see."

Fred raised his glass. "To the future!" And, all drank to the toast.

****

"Oh, you look so beautiful!" Nikki said to Karen's reflection in the tall mirror. The two stood in a bedroom at Essen Farms.

Emma came in as her aunt turned one way, then another, making sure her wedding dress was lying perfectly on her body. It was a soft mauve chiffon fabric, with a full, calf-high skirt, that flowed when she moved. The top lay slightly off her shoulders, revealing her creamy skin.

"Here's something blue," Emma said, placing a gray, velvet box and envelope on the dresser. She opened the box and took out the shiny jeweled piece, then placed the teardrop Sapphire gem dangling from a gold chain around the bride's neck. "Uncle George has good taste, huh?"

Karen fingered the gemstone and smiled at her reflection. "Yes, I think he does."

"This is so exciting!" Nikki said, twirling in her teal dress made of the same fabric as Karen's. "My first time as a bridesmaid - I've never been to a fancy wedding before."

Emma hugged Nikki. "Sweetheart, someday we will be dressing up for your wedding!"

Nikki blushed and ran to put on her shiny, black patent-leather shoes, then stood and twirled again.

"I chose not to wear a veil," Karen said as Emma placed the ring of white roses in her hair. "I did that at my first wedding with Oliver."

"Who's Oliver?" Nikki asked, stopping her twirling.

"He was my first husband...and I thought my only love." Karen smiled at Emma. "I guess I was wrong."

Emma turned and picked up the envelope lying next to the box Karen's necklace had been in. "Oh, I forgot - this was lying on the entry table downstairs. It was sent to your New York address, but came here since you've forwarded your mail to the farm."

When Emma handed the letter to her aunt, she saw her face go pale as she looked down at the foreign stamps and postmark. "What is it?"

Karen stared at her niece for a moment.

"Look at those stamps!" Nikki said, joining them. "I've never seen anything like them."

Quickly, Karen seemed to collect herself. She placed the letter into her larger, wooden jewelry box, closed the lid and sighed. "It's probably from someone I met while I was traveling...I'll open it later."

She looked at herself again in the mirror, pinching her cheeks to return color to her face. Then, she turned, picked up her bouquet of white roses and said, "I think it's time."

****

After the ceremony, everyone was in the garden, which was also lavishly decorated with white bows and mauve roses. The cloth-covered tables and chairs were filled with guests, while a string trio played softly in the background.

Emma watched as her aunt and uncle, now happily married, danced their first dance to the French song, *L'amour*. She smiled and thought, *How appropriate! These two favorite people in my life have found love at this point in time.*

"I'm having so much fun!" Nikki sighed, her chin in her hand as she looked around her. "I had no idea that life could be this beautiful." She wiped away a tear, then took a bite of cake.

A faster song began. Sam reached over and hugged Nikki and said, "I'd like a dance with my daughter. Will you dance with me?"

Nikki looked at her new parents. "Is that okay? Can kids dance at these things?"

"Absolutely," Sam said as he stood and held out his hand. "I just hope I don't step on your feet."

Emma laughed. "He's only joking - Sam's a good dancer. I'll take the next song!"

She watched as her husband and child now danced together to a sixties song. Nikki was trying to show her new dad how to do the Twist. Emma thought for a moment, thankful that their adoption went so smoothly. Lynn Chamberlain had handled everything for them, allowing them to be Nikki's foster family, until the young girl's mother had waived her parental rights. That's when Emma had learned about the father's death.

She saw her uncle walking towards her, bringing her out of her reverie.

George was beaming as he sat next to her. "This is the happiest day of my life..." he started, and then he looked at his niece." Well, maybe the second happiest."

"When was the first?"

"When I met you for the first time."

They laughed together. She looked around and asked, "Where did Aunt Karen go?"

"She said she wanted to powder her nose." He stood and asked, "Will you dance with me?"

"Yes," Emma said proudly and stepped into her uncle's arms.

****

In the bedroom, Karen sat down at the dresser. She raised her hand to straighten and re-pin the ring of flowers in her hair. Then, she took out her makeup bag and reapplied a little blush to her cheeks.

"I'm procrastinating," she said to herself in the mirror. "You're stronger than this! It's what you thought you wanted."

She took a deep breath and slowly opened her jewelry box. She looked again at the return address on the letter and her hands began to shake. It was from the orphanage in Siena, Italy!

THE END

ABOUT THE AUTHOR

This is Linda Kuhlmann's third novel. It is the second sequel to *Koenig's Wonder*, a story of Thoroughbred racehorses running for the coveted Triple Crown. It all began with a family mystery that evolved into today's current fiction. She has also written *The Red Boots*, stage plays, screen plays, and a small non-fiction book for Kindle, called *Shameless Marketing*. Ms. Kuhlmann lives in Oregon.

Made in the USA
Middletown, DE
29 March 2021

36466016R00179